ONLY CHILD

ONLY CHILD

Rhiannon Navin

ALFRED A. KNOPF

NEW YORK

2018

THIS IS A BORZOI BOOK PUBLISHED BY ALFRED A. KNOPF

Copyright © 2018 by MOM OF 3 LLC

All rights reserved. Published in the United States by Alfred A. Knopf, a division of Penguin Random House LLC, New York, and distributed in Canada by Random House of Canada, a division of Penguin Random House Canada Limited, Toronto.

www.aaknopf.com

Knopf, Borzoi Books, and the colophon are registered trademarks of Penguin Random House LLC.

Library of Congress Cataloging-in-Publication Data
Names: Navin, Rhiannon, [date] author.
Title: Only child / by Rhiannon Navin.
Description: First edition. | New York : Alfred A. Knopf, 2018.
Identifiers: LCCN 2017006251 (print) | LCCN 2017021896 (ebook) |
ISBN 9781524733360 (ebook) | ISBN 9781524733353 (hardcover)
Subjects: LCSH: Loss (Psychology)—Fiction. | School shootings—
Fiction. | Grief—Fiction.
Classification: LCC PS3614.A932 (ebook) | LCC PS3614.A932 O55 2018 (print)
| DDC 813/.6—dc23
LC record available at https://lccn.loc.gov/2017006251

Jacket background texture: Beliavskii Igor/Shutterstock
Jacket design by Jenny Carrow

Manufactured in the United States of America
First Edition

For Brad, Samuel, Garrett, and Frankie

For Mama

I have to keep facing the darkness. If I stand tall and face the thing I fear, I have a chance to conquer it. If I just keep dodging and hiding, it will conquer me.

—Mary Pope Osborne, *My Secret War: The World War II Diary of Madeline Beck, Long Island, New York, 1941*

ONLY CHILD

[1]

The Day the Gunman Came

THE THING I LATER REMEMBERED the most about the day
the gunman came was my teacher Miss Russell's breath. It was
hot and smelled like coffee. The closet was dark except for a little
light that was coming in through the crack of the door that Miss Russell was holding shut from inside. There was no door handle on the
inside, only a loose metal piece, and she pulled it in with her thumb
and pointer finger.

"Be completely still, Zach," she whispered. "Don't move."

I didn't. Even though I was sitting on my left foot and it was giving
me pins and needles and it hurt a lot.

Miss Russell's coffee breath touched my cheek when she talked, and
it bothered me a little. Her fingers were shaking on the metal piece.
She had to talk to Evangeline and David and Emma a lot behind me
in the closet, because they were crying and were not being completely
still.

"I'm here with you guys," Miss Russell said. "I'm protecting you.
Shhhhhhh, please be quiet." We kept hearing the POP sounds outside. And screaming.

POP POP POP

It sounded a lot like the sounds from the *Star Wars* game I sometimes play on the Xbox.

POP POP POP

Always three pops and then quiet again. Quiet or screaming. Miss Russell did little jumps when the POP sounds came and her whispering got faster. "Don't make a sound!" Evangeline made hiccupping sounds.

POP Hick POP Hick POP Hick

I think someone peed in their underwear, because it smelled like that in the closet. Like Miss Russell's breath and pee, and like the jackets that were still wet from when it rained at recess. "Not too much to play outside," Mrs. Colaris said. "What, are we made of sugar?" The rain didn't bother us. We played soccer and cops and bad guys, and our hair and jackets got wet. I tried to turn and put my hand up and touch the jackets to see if they were still very wet.

"Don't move," Miss Russell whispered to me. She switched hands to hold the door closed, and her bracelets made jingling sounds. Miss Russell always wears a lot of bracelets on her right arm. Some have little things called charms hanging off them that remind her of special things, and when she goes on vacation she always gets a new charm to remember it. When we started first grade, she showed us all her charms and told us where she got them from. Her new one that she got on the summer break was a boat. It's like a tiny version of the boat she went on to go really close to a huge waterfall called Niagara Falls, and that's in Canada.

My left foot really started to hurt a lot, and I tried to pull it out only a little so Miss Russell wouldn't notice.

We just came in from recess and put our jackets in the closet, then math books out, when the POP sounds started. At first we didn't hear them loud—they were like all the way down the hallway in the front where Charlie's desk is. When parents come to pick you up before dismissal or at the nurse's office, they always stop at Charlie's desk and write down their name and show their driver's license and get a tag that says VISITOR on a red string, and they have to wear it around their neck.

Charlie is the security guy at McKinley, and he's been here for thirty years. When I was in kindergarten, last year, we had a big party in the auditorium to celebrate his thirty years. Even a lot of parents came because he was the security guy already when they were kids and went to McKinley, like Mommy. Charlie said he didn't need a party. "I already know everyone loves me," he said, and laughed his funny laugh. But he got a party anyway, and I thought he looked happy about it. He put up all the artwork we made for him for the party around his desk and took the rest home to hang it up. My picture for him was right in the middle at the front of his desk because I'm a really good artist.

Pop pop pop

Quiet pop sounds at first. Miss Russell was right in the middle of telling us about what pages in the math book were for classwork and what pages were for homework. The pop sounds made her stop talking, and she made wrinkles on her forehead. She walked over to the classroom door and looked out of the glass window. "What the . . . ," she said.

Pop pop pop

Then she took a big step back away from the door and said, "Fuck." She really did. The F-word, we all heard it and started laughing. "Fuck." Right after she said it, we heard sounds coming from the intercom on the wall, and then a voice said, "Lockdown, lockdown, lockdown!" It wasn't Mrs. Colaris's voice. When we practiced lockdown drill before, Mrs. Colaris said, "Lockdown!" through the intercom, once, but this voice said it a lot of times, fast.

Miss Russell's face got whitish and we stopped laughing because she looked so different and wasn't smiling at all. The way her face looked all of a sudden made me scared, and my breath got stuck in my throat.

Miss Russell did a couple circles by the door like she didn't know where she should walk. Then she stopped doing circles and locked the door and switched the lights off. No sun was coming in from the windows because of the rain, but Miss Russell went to the windows and pulled the shades down anyway. She started talking very fast and her voice sounded shaky and like squeaky. "Remember what we practiced for the lockdown drill," she said. I remembered that *lockdown* meant don't go outside like for the fire alarm, but stay inside and out of sight.

POP POP POP

Someone outside in the hallway screamed very loud. My legs started shaking around the knees.

"Boys and girls, everyone in the closet," Miss Russell said.

When we practiced lockdown drill before, it was fun. We pretended that we were the bad guys and only sat in the closet for like a minute until we heard how Charlie opened the classroom door from the outside with his special key that can open all the doors in the school, and we heard him say: "It's me, Charlie!" and that was the sign that the drill was over. Now I didn't want to go in the closet because almost everyone else was already in there, and it looked too smushed. But Miss Russell put her hand on my head and pushed me in.

"Hurry, guys, hurry," Miss Russell said. Evangeline especially and David and some other kids started to cry and said they wanted to go home. I felt tears coming in my eyes, too, but I didn't want to let them come out and all my friends were going to see. I did the squeeze-away trick I learned from Grandma: you have to squeeze your nose on the outside with your fingers, the part where it goes from hard to soft, and then your tears don't come out. Grandma taught me the squeeze-away trick at the playground one day when I was about to cry because someone pushed me off the swing and Grandma said, "Don't let them see you cry."

Miss Russell got everyone in the closet and pulled the door shut. The whole time we could hear the POP sounds. I tried to count them in my head.

POP—1   POP—2   POP—3

My throat felt very dry and scratchy. I really wanted a drink of water.

POP—4   POP—5   POP— 6

"Please, please, please," Miss Russell whispered. And then she talked to God and she called him "Dear Lord" and I couldn't understand the rest she said because she was whispering so quiet and fast and I think she wanted only God to hear.

POP—7   POP—8   POP—9

Always three POPs and then a break.

Miss Russell all of a sudden looked up and said, "Fuck," again. "My phone!" She opened the door a little and when there weren't any POP sounds for a while she opened it all the way and ran across the classroom to her desk with her head ducked down. Then she ran back to the closet. She pulled the door closed again and told me to hold the metal piece this time. I did, even though it hurt my fingers and the door was heavy to keep closed. I had to use both hands.

Miss Russell's hands were shaking so much they made the phone shake when she swiped and put her password in. She kept doing it wrong, and when you put the wrong password in all the numbers on the screen shake and you have to start over. "Come on, come on, come on," Miss Russell said, and finally she got the password right. I saw it: 1989.

POP—10   POP—11   POP—12

I watched how Miss Russell dialed 9-1-1. When I heard a voice in the phone, she said, "Yes, hi, I'm calling from McKinley Elementary. In Wake Gardens. Rogers Lane." She talked very fast, and in the light that came from her phone I could see that she spit on my leg a little bit. I had to leave the spit there because my hands were holding the door closed. I couldn't wipe it off, but I stared at the spit and it was there on my pants, a spit bubble, and it was gross. "There's a gunman at the school and he's . . . OK, I'll stay on the phone with you then." To us she whispered, "Someone already called." Gunman. That's what she said. And then all I could think about in my head was gunman.

POP—13   Gunman   POP—14   Gunman
POP—15   Gunman

I felt like it was hard to breathe now in the closet and very hot, like we used up all the air. I wanted to open the door a little to let some new air in, but I was too scared. I could feel my heart beating at super speed inside my chest and all the way up in my throat. Nicholas next to me had his eyes squeezed shut tight and was making fast breathing sounds. He was using up too much air.

Miss Russell had her eyes closed, too, but her breathing was slow. I could smell the coffee smell when she went "Huuuuuu" to let some long breaths out. Then she opened her eyes and whispered to us again. She said everyone's name: "Nicholas. Jack. Evangeline . . ." It felt good when she said, "Zach, it will be all right." To all of us she said, "The police are outside. They are coming to help. And I am right here." I was glad she was right there, and her talking helped me feel not so scared. The coffee breath didn't bother me so much anymore. I pretended it was Daddy's breath in the morning when he was home for breakfast on the weekends. I tried coffee before and didn't like it. It tastes too hot and old or something. Daddy laughed and said, "Good, stunts your growth anyway." I don't know what that means, but I really wished Daddy could be here right now. But he wasn't, only Miss Russell and my class and the POP sounds—

POP—16   POP—17   POP—18

—sounding really loud now and screams in the hallway and more crying in the closet. Miss Russell stopped talking to us and instead she talked into the phone: "Oh God, he's getting closer. Are you coming? Are you coming?" Twice. Nicholas opened his eyes and said, "Oh!" and then he threw up. All over his shirt, and some throw-up got in Emma's hair and on my shoes in the back. Emma did a loud shrieking sound and Miss Russell put her hands over Emma's mouth. She dropped the phone and it fell in the throw-up on the floor. Through the door I could hear sirens. I'm really good at telling different sirens apart, the ones from fire trucks, police cars, ambulances . . . but now I heard so many outside that I couldn't tell—they were all mixed together.

POP—19   POP—20   POP—21

Everything was hot and wet and smelled bad and I started to feel dizzy from it all and my stomach didn't feel good. Then all of a sudden it was quiet. I couldn't hear any more POPs. Just the crying and hiccupping in the closet.

And THEN there were a TON of POPs that sounded like they were right by us, a lot of them in a row, and loud sounds like stuff crashing and breaking. Miss Russell screamed and covered her ears, and we screamed and covered our ears. The closet door opened because I let go of the metal piece and light came into the closet and it hurt my eyes. I tried to keep counting the POPs, but there were too many. Then they stopped.

Everything was completely still, even us, and no one moved a muscle. It was like we weren't even breathing. We stayed like that for a very long time—still and quiet.

Then someone was at our classroom door. We could hear the door handle, and Miss Russell let out her breath in little puffs, like "huh, huh, huh." There was a knock on the door and a loud man voice said, "Hello, anyone in there?"

[2]

Battle Scars

I T'S ALL RIGHT. Police are here, it's over," the loud man voice said.

Miss Russell stood up and held on to the closet door for a minute, and then she walked a few steps to the classroom door, very slow like she forgot how to walk and maybe she was having pins and needles like me from sitting on her legs. I stood up, too, and behind me everyone came out of the closet very slow, like we all had to learn how to use our legs again.

Miss Russell unlocked the door, and lots of police came in. I saw more out in the hallway. One policewoman was hugging Miss Russell, who was making loud sounds like choking. I wanted to stay close to Miss Russell and I started to feel cold because now we were all spread out and not close and warm anymore. All the police were making me feel shy and scared, so I held on to Miss Russell's shirt.

"All right, guys, please come to the front of the room," one policeman said. "Can you line up over here?"

Outside our window, I could hear even more sirens now. I couldn't see anything because our windows are high up and we can't look outside except when we climb on a chair or table and we're not supposed to do that. Plus, Miss Russell pulled the shades down when the pop sounds started.

One policeman put his hand on my shoulder and pushed me into the line. He and the other police had on uniforms with vests, the kind where bullets can't go through, and some had helmets on like in a movie, and they had big guns, not the regular ones from their belts. They looked a little bit scary with the guns and the helmets, but they talked to us in a friendly way: "Hey there, champ, don't worry, it's all over now! You're safe now." And stuff like that.

I didn't know what was "over now," but I didn't want to leave our classroom and Miss Russell was not at the front of the line with the line leader. She was still off to the side with the policewoman, making choking sounds.

Usually when we have to line up to leave the classroom, everyone pushes and shoves and we get in trouble because we're not making a nice line. This time we all stood really still. Evangeline and Emma and some other kids were still crying and shivering and we all stared at Miss Russell and waited to see if she would stop choking.

There were a lot of sounds coming from outside our classroom and shouting from down the hallway. I thought it sounded like Charlie's voice shouting, "NO, NO, NO!" over and over again. I wondered why Charlie was shouting like that. Maybe he got hurt from the gunman? To be the security guy in a school when a gunman comes in is a very dangerous job.

There were other crying and calling sounds, all different kinds— "Ooh, ooooh, ooooh," "Head wound DRT!" "Femoral bleed. Get me a pressure dressing and a tourniquet!" The walkie-talkies on the police's belts were beeping and beeping, and a lot of talking was coming out of them that was fast, and it was hard to understand it.

The walkie-talkie from the policeman at the front of the line beeped and said, "Get ready to move!" and the policeman turned around and said, "Moving out!" The other police started to push the line from the back, and we all started walking, but very slow. No one wanted to go out in the hallway where all the crying and calling sounds were still happening. The policeman in the front was high-fiving the kids that walked past him, and it was like he was making a joke. I didn't give him a high five, and he kind of did a pat on my head instead.

We had to walk down the hallway to the back door where the cafeteria is. We saw the other first-grade classes and the second- and third-grade classes walking in lines like us, with police as the line leaders. Everyone looked cold and scared. "Don't turn around," the police were saying. "Don't look behind you." But I wanted to see if I was right and if it was Charlie shouting "NO, NO, NO!" earlier and if he was OK. I wanted to see who was screaming.

I couldn't see much because Ryder was right behind me, he's really tall, and more kids were walking behind Ryder. But in between the kids and the police walking I saw some things: people lying on the floor in the hallway with ambulance people and police around them and bending over them. And blood. At least I thought it was blood. It was very dark red or black puddles, like paint that spilled, all around on the floor of the hallway and some on the walls. And I saw the older kids from fourth and fifth grade walking behind Ryder, with very white faces like ghosts and some of them were crying and had blood on them. On their faces and clothes.

"Turn around!" a policeman said behind me, and this time it was not friendly. I turned around fast and my heart was beating hard because of all the blood. I saw real blood before, but just a little bit like when I fall down and my knee bleeds or something, never a lot like now.

More kids were turning around, and the police started shouting, "Look ahead! No turning around!" But the more they said it, the more everyone turned around, because other kids were doing it. People started screaming and walking faster and bumping into each other and shoving. When we got to the back door, someone bumped into me from the side and I bumped my shoulder into the door, which is metal, and it hurt a lot.

It was still raining outside, pretty hard now, and we didn't have our jackets. Everything was still in the school—our jackets and backpacks and book baggies and stuff—but we kept walking without anything over to the playground and through the back gate that's always closed when we have recess, so no one can run outside and strangers can't come in.

I was starting to feel better when I walked outside. My heart didn't beat so hard anymore, and the rain felt good on my face. It was cold, but I liked it. Everyone slowed down, and there wasn't so much screaming and crying and shoving anymore. It was like the rain calmed everyone down, like me.

We walked across the intersection that was full of ambulances and fire trucks and police cars. All their lights were flashing. I tried to step on the flashing lights in the puddles, making blue and red and white circles in the water, and some of the water went into my sneakers in the part that has little holes on the top and my socks got wet. Mommy was going to be mad that my sneakers were wet, but I kept splashing and making more circles anyway. The blue, red, and white lights together in the puddles looked like the American flag colors.

The roads were blocked by trucks and cars. Other cars were driving up behind them and I saw parents jumping out. I looked for Mommy, but I didn't see her. The police made a line on both sides of the intersection so that we could keep walking, and the parents had to stay behind the lines. They were calling out names like questions: "Eva? Jonas? Jimmy?" Some kids yelled back: "Mom! Mommy? Dad!"

I pretended like I was in a movie with all the lights and the police with their big guns and helmets. It gave me an excited feeling. I pretended like I was a soldier who was coming back from a battle and I was a hero now and people were here to see me. My shoulder hurt, but that's what happens when you fight in a battle. Battle scars. That's what Daddy always says when I get hurt at lacrosse or soccer or playing outside: "Battle scars. Every man has to have some. Shows you're not a wimp."

3

Jesus and Real-Life Dead People

OUR POLICE LINE LEADERS walked us into the little church on the road behind the school. When we went inside, I started to not feel like a tough hero anymore. All the exciting feelings stayed outside with the fire trucks and police cars. Inside the church it was dark and quiet and cold, especially because we were really wet now from the rain.

We don't go to churches a lot, only to a wedding one time, and last year we went to one for Uncle Chip's funeral. It wasn't this church, but a bigger one in New Jersey where Uncle Chip lived. That was really sad when Uncle Chip died because he wasn't even that old. He was Daddy's brother, and only a little bit older than him, but he still died because he had cancer. That's a sickness a lot of people get, and you can have it in different parts of your body. Sometimes it gets everywhere in your body, and that's what happened to Uncle Chip and the doctor couldn't make him feel better anymore, so he went to a special hospital where people go who don't get better anymore, and then they die there.

We went to visit him there. I thought he must be so scared because he probably knew he was going to die and he wouldn't be together with his family anymore. But when we saw him he didn't look scared, he was just sleeping the whole time. He didn't wake up anymore after we saw him. He went straight from sleeping to dead, so I didn't think he even noticed that he died. Sometimes at bedtime I think about that and I get scared to go to sleep, because what if I die when I'm sleeping and don't even notice?

I cried a lot at Uncle Chip's funeral, mostly because Uncle Chip was going to be gone forever and I wouldn't see him anymore. Also all the other people cried, especially Mommy and Grandma and Aunt Mary, Uncle Chip's wife. Well, not really his wife because they weren't married, but we still call her Aunt Mary because they were boyfriend and girlfriend for a really long time, since before I was born. And I cried because Uncle Chip was in the box called a casket in the front of the church. It must have been really tight in there and I never wanted to be in a box like that, ever. Only Daddy didn't cry.

When the police told us to sit down on the benches in the church, I thought about Uncle Chip and how sad it was at his funeral. We all had to fit on the benches, and the police shouted: "Slide all the way in. Make room for everyone. Keep sliding in," and we kept sliding in until we were all smushed together again like in the closet. There was a walkway in the middle in between the benches on the left and the benches on the right, and some police were lining up next to the benches.

My feet felt freezing cold. And I had to pee. I tried to ask the policeman next to the bench I was on if I could please go to the bathroom, but he said, "Everyone stays seated for now, champ," so I tried to hold it and not think about how badly I had to go. But when you try to not think about something, it turns into the only thing you think about the whole time.

Nicholas was sitting close to me on my right side and still smelled like throw-up. I saw Miss Russell was sitting with some other teachers on a bench in the back, and I wished that I could sit with her. The older kids with the blood on them were in the back, too, and a lot of them were still crying. I wondered why, because even the younger kids weren't crying anymore. Some teachers and police and the man from the church—I could tell he was from the church from the black shirt and white collar he was wearing—were talking to them and hugging them and wiping the blood off their faces with tissues.

In the front of the church was a big table and it's a special table, called an altar. Over it was a big cross with Jesus hanging on it, like in the church where Uncle Chip's funeral was. I tried not to look at Jesus, who had his eyes closed. I knew he was dead with nails in his hands and feet, because people actually did that to him a long time ago to kill him, even though he was a good guy and God's son. Mommy told me that story, but I don't remember why they did that to Jesus, and I wished he wasn't right there in the front. It made me think of the people in the hallway and all the blood and I was starting to think maybe they were dead, too, so that means I saw dead people in real life!

Mostly everyone was quiet, and in all that quietness the POP sounds were back in my ears, like an echo coming back around from the walls of the church. I shook my head to make them go away, but they kept coming back.

POP POP POP

I waited to see what was going to happen next. Nicholas's nose looked red and had a snot drop hanging off it, which was gross. He kept pulling up the snot with a sniff sound, and then it came back down. Nicholas was rubbing his hands on his legs, up and down, like he was trying to dry them off, but his pants were really wet. He didn't talk, and that was different because in school we sit across from each other at the blue table and talk all the time about stuff like Skylanders, and the FIFA soccer World Cup, and which sticker cards we want to trade at recess and on the bus later.

We started collecting the sticker cards even before the World Cup started in the summer. Our sticker books have all the players from all the teams that play in the World Cup, so we knew all about the teams by the time the games started, and it was more fun to watch like that. Nicholas only needed twenty-four more sticker cards for his book, and I needed thirty-two and we both have a super-high stack of doubles.

I whispered to Nicholas, "Did you see all the blood in the hallway? It looked real. Didn't it look like a lot?" Nicholas shook his head yes, but still he didn't say anything. It was like he forgot his voice at school with his jacket and his backpack. He's weird sometimes. Just pulling up the snot drop and wiping his hands on the wet pants, so I stopped trying to talk to him and I tried not to look at the snot drop. But when I looked away, my eyes went straight to Jesus, dead on the cross, and those were the only two things my eyes kept looking at, the snot drop and Jesus. Snot drop, Jesus, snot drop, Jesus. My sticker cards and FIFA book were in my backpack still at the school, and I started to worry someone would take them.

The big door in the back of the church kept opening and closing with loud swish-squeak, swish-squeak sounds, and people kept walking in and out, mostly police and some teachers. I didn't see Mrs. Colaris anywhere or Charlie, so they probably stayed at the school. Then parents started to come in the church, and it got busy and loud. The parents weren't quiet like us, they were calling out names like questions again. They cried and yelled when they found their kids and tried to get to them on the benches, which was hard to do because everyone was sitting so close together. Some kids tried to climb out and started crying again when they saw their mom or dad.

Every time I heard a swish-squeak sound, I turned my head to see if it was Mommy or Daddy. I was really hoping they would come to pick me up and take me home so I could put new clothes and socks on and feel warm again.

Nicholas's dad came. Nicholas climbed over me, and his dad lifted him over the other kids on our bench. Then he hugged him for a long time, even though that probably made the throw-up get on his shirt, too.

Finally, the door opened again with another swish-squeak and Mommy walked in. I stood up so she could see me, and then I got embarrassed because Mommy came running over and called me "my baby" in front of all the kids. I climbed over the other kids to get to her, and she grabbed me and rocked me and she was cold and wet from the rain outside.

Then Mommy started to look around and said, "Zach, where's your brother?"

4

Where's Your Brother?

Z ACH, WHERE'S ANDY? Where did he sit down?" Mommy
stood up and looked all around. I wanted her to keep hugging
me, and I wanted to tell her about the POP sounds and all the blood
and the people lying in the hallway like maybe real-life dead people.
I wanted to ask her why a gunman came and what happened to the
people back at the school. I wanted us to leave this cold church with
Jesus and the nails in his hands and feet.

I didn't see Andy today. I almost never see Andy at school after
we get off the bus until we get back on the bus when school is done
because we don't have lunch or recess at the same time, the older kids
always go out before us. When we see each other at school by accident, like in the hallway when my class goes this way and his class
goes that way, he ignores me and pretends like he doesn't know me
and I'm not even his brother.

When I started kindergarten, I was worried because a lot of my
friends from preschool were going to Jefferson and I didn't know
many kids at McKinley. I was happy Andy was already there, in fourth
grade. He could show me where everything was, and I wouldn't feel
scared with him there. Mommy said to Andy, "Make sure you keep an
eye on your little brother. Help him!" But he didn't.

"Stay away from me, little creep!" he yelled when I tried to talk to
him, and his friends laughed, so then I did that, stay away.

"Zach, where's your brother?" Mommy asked again, and she started walking up and down the middle walkway. I tried to walk with her and hold on to her hand, but there were people everywhere in the walkway now, calling names and getting in between us. I had to let go of Mommy's hand because it hurt my shoulder to keep holding on.

I didn't think about Andy all day since the bus, only when Mommy asked me about him. I didn't think about Andy when the POP sounds started, or when we were hiding in the closet, or when we walked through the hallway and out the back door. I tried to remember when I looked back and saw the older kids walking behind me if maybe Andy was one of the faces I saw, but I didn't know.

Mommy was turning all around now, faster, and her head was going left, right, left, right. I caught up with her in the front of the church by the altar table and tried to take her hand again, but at the same time she moved her arm up and put her hand on a policeman's arm. So I put my hands in my pockets to make them warmer and stood close to Mommy. "I can't find my son. Are all the kids in here?" she asked the policeman. Her voice sounded different, squeaky, and I looked up at her face to see why she sounded like that. Her face had red dots around her eyes, and her lips and chin were shaking, probably because she got all wet and cold from the rain, too.

"There will be an official announcement in a few minutes, ma'am," the policeman said to Mommy. "Please have a seat if you have a missing child, and wait for the announcement."

"A missing—?" Mommy said, and she touched the top of her head with her hand hard, like she hit herself. "Oh my God. Jesus!"

I looked up to where Jesus was on the cross after Mommy said his name. Right then Mommy's phone started to ring in her bag. She jumped and dropped the bag, and some things fell out on the floor. Mommy went down on her knees and looked in her bag for her phone. I started to pick up her things, some papers and the car keys and a lot of coins that went rolling in between people's feet. I tried to get them all before someone else could take them.

Mommy's hands were shaking like Miss Russell's earlier in the closet when she found her phone and answered it. "Hello?" Mommy said into the phone. "At the church on Lyncroft. It's where they took the kids. Andy's not here! Oh my God, Jim, he's not in the church! Yes, I have Zach." Mommy started to cry. She was on her knees right in front of the altar table, and it looked like she was praying, because that's what people do when they pray, kneel down like that. I stood in front of Mommy and touched her shoulder and rubbed it up and down to make her stop crying. My throat started to feel really tight.

Mommy said, "I know, OK, all right. I know, OK," into the phone and, "OK, see you in a few," and then she put the phone in her coat pocket and pulled me close to her and hugged me, too tight, and cried in my neck. Her breathing felt hot on my neck and it tickled, but it also felt good because it was warm, and I was feeling colder and colder.

I wanted to hold still when Mommy was hugging me and stay close to her, but I had to move side to side because I still had to pee badly. "I have to go to the bathroom, Mommy," I said. Mommy pushed away from me and stood up. "Baby, not now," she said. "Let's go sit down somewhere until Daddy gets here and until they make the announcement." But there was nowhere to sit down with all the kids on the benches, so we walked to the side of the church and Mommy leaned with her back up against the wall and squeezed my hand tight. I kept moving side to side and tried to balance on my tippy-toes because my dinky hurt so bad from having to pee. I was scared I was going to go pee in my pants. That would be really embarrassing in front of everyone.

Mommy's phone started ringing again in her pocket. Mommy took it out and she said to me, "It's Mimi," and then she answered the phone. "Hi, Mom!" Right when she said that she started crying again. "I'm here now, with Zach. . . . He's fine, he's OK. But Andy's not here, Mom. No, he's not here, I can't find him. . . . They're not telling us anything yet. . . . They said they're making an announcement soon." Mommy was pressing the phone to her ear hard. I could see the knuckles on her fingers were all white from squeezing the phone so hard. She listened to Mimi talking on the phone and she shook her head yes, and tears were running down her face. "OK, Mom, I'm freaking out. I don't know what to do. . . . He's coming, he's on his way. No, don't come yet. I think they're only letting parents in right now. OK, I will. I'll call you then. OK, love you, too."

I looked at all the benches and let my eyes do some searching left and right, like when you do a word-search puzzle and look for the first letter of a word, like when you look for the word *PINEAPPLE*, for example. You try to find all the *P*s, and then when you find one, you look if there's an *I* next to the *P* all around it, and that's how you find the whole word. So my eyes went left and right like that to see if Andy wasn't on one of the benches after all. Maybe we just didn't see him earlier and then we could go get him and leave and go home. My eyes were searching, searching, back and forth, but Andy really wasn't anywhere.

I started to feel tired, and I didn't want to stand up anymore. After a long while, the big door opened, swish-squeak, and Daddy came in. His hair was wet and sticking to his forehead, and rain was dripping from his clothes. It took him a while to squeeze past all the people and get to us. When he did, he gave us wet hugs and Mommy started to cry again.

"It will be OK, babe," Daddy said. "I'm sure they couldn't fit all the kids in here. Let's wait and see. They said they were getting ready to make an announcement when I walked in." Right when he said that, the policeman Mommy talked to earlier walked in front of the altar table and said, "Hey, listen up, folks! Everyone, quiet down, please!" Then he had to shout, "Quiet down, please!" a few more times because of all the crying and calling and shouting, and no one was noticing he was talking.

Finally, everyone got quiet and he started to do a speech: "Parents, all children who were unharmed were brought to this church. If you have found your child, please leave the church quickly so we can restore some order in here and incoming parents will have an easier time finding their children. If you are unable to locate your child here in the church, please be advised that wounded children are being taken to West-Medical Hospital for treatment. I regret to inform you that there have been an unknown number of fatalities in this incident, and these will remain at the crime scene while the investigation is under way."

When he said *fatalities*—I didn't know what that meant—a loud sound went through the whole church, like all the people said "Ohhhh" at the same time. The policeman kept talking: "We don't have a list of the wounded and fatalities yet, so if you cannot locate your child, please make your way over to West-Medical to check in with the staff there. They are currently in the process of compiling a list of patients who have been admitted. The shooter was killed in a confrontation with the Wake Gardens police force, and we believe he acted alone. There is no further threat to the Wake Gardens community. That is all for now. We are setting up a support hotline, and the information will be posted on the McKinley Elementary and Wake Gardens websites shortly."

It stayed quiet for a second after he was done talking, and then it was like a noise explosion with everyone calling out and asking questions. I wasn't sure what the policeman said, except that he said the shooter was killed, and I thought that was a good thing, so he couldn't shoot other people anymore. But when I looked at Mommy and Daddy, it didn't seem like a good thing, because their faces looked all wrinkled up, and Mommy was crying a lot. Daddy said, "All right, he must be at West-Medical then."

I went to West-Medical before when I was four and I got allergic to peanuts. I don't remember it, but Mommy said it was scary. I almost stopped breathing because my face and mouth and throat got swollen. At the hospital they had to give me medicine so I could breathe again. Now I can't eat anything with peanuts ever again, and I have to sit at the no-nuts table for lunch.

Mommy also had to take Andy to West-Medical, last summer, because he was riding his bike with no helmet—that's a big no-no—and he fell down on his head. His forehead was bleeding and he had to get stitches.

"Melissa, babe, we need to keep it together," Daddy said to Mommy. "Take Zach and go find Andy at the hospital. Call me when you're there. I'll call my mom and yours to let them know, and I'll stay here . . . in case . . ."

I waited to see in case what, but Mommy grabbed my hand tight and pulled me with her, and we walked out of the church. When we walked through the big door, there were people everywhere, on the sidewalk and on the street, and I saw vans that had big standing-up bowls on the roofs. Lights were flashing and blinking in my face.

"Let's get out of here," Mommy said, and we got out of there.

5

No-Rules Day

W E'RE GOING TO BE ALL RIGHT, Zach, do you hear me? Everything will be OK. We'll get to the hospital, and we will find Andy, and this whole nightmare will be over, OK, baby?"

Mommy kept saying the same things over and over again in the car, but I didn't think she was talking to me, because when I said, "I really have to go to the bathroom when we get there, Mommy," she didn't say anything back. She was leaning forward and staring out the front window because it was still raining hard. The wipers were on the highest speed, the one where you get dizzy when you try to follow them with your eyes, and it can make you carsick, so you have to try to look out the front but try to ignore the wipers. Even with the wipers going at dizzy speed, it was hard to see anything. When we got to the road where the hospital is, there was traffic everywhere.

"Shit, shit, shit," Mommy said.

Today was a bad-word day. Fuck, stupid, shit, Jesus. *Jesus* is not actually a bad word, it's a name, but sometimes people use it as a bad word. There was loud honking. People had their windows down even though it was raining, and the inside of their car was probably getting wet. They were yelling at each other to get the hell out of the way.

Last time we came to the hospital, when Andy fell off his bike, there was a valet, and that means you can get out of your car with it still on and you leave the keys in it, and the valet man parks it for you.

And when you come back, you have to give him the ticket, and he goes and gets your car from where he parked it. This time there was no valet and like a thousand cars in front of us. Mommy started crying again and did drums with her fingers on the steering wheel, and she said, "What do we do now? What do we do now?"

Mommy's phone started ringing, loud in the car. I knew it was Daddy because in Mommy's new GMC Acadia in the front where the radio is you can see who is calling and press on the Accept button and hear the voice in the whole car and that's cool. We didn't have that in our old car.

"Are you there?" Daddy's voice said into the car.

"I can't even get close to the hospital," Mommy said. "I don't know what do to. There are cars everywhere. It's going to take me forever to get to the garage, if there are even any spots left. Crap, Jim, I can't take this, I need to get in there!"

"OK, babe, forget finding a spot in the garage. I'm sure it's madness over there. Dammit, I should have come with you. I just thought . . . ," and then it was quiet in the car, and Mommy and Daddy didn't say anything. "Dump the car somewhere, Melissa," Daddy's voice said in the car. "It doesn't matter. Dump the car and walk."

I think a lot of people were doing that, dumping their cars, because when I looked out the window, I saw cars parked everywhere, even on the bike paths and sidewalks. That's against the law and your car will be towed with a tow truck.

Mommy drove up on the sidewalk and stopped the car. "Let's go," she said, and opened my door. I saw that the back of our car was kind of sticking out into the street and the cars behind us started honking, even though I thought they could definitely still get past. "Oh, shut up," Mommy yelled. Bad-word list getting longer.

"Mommy, won't a tow truck take our car?" I asked.

"Doesn't matter. Let's please walk quickly."

I was walking very fast because Mommy was pulling so hard on my hand. The walking made some pee come out. I couldn't help it, it just came out. Only a little at first and then all of it. It felt good, and it made my legs feel warm. I thought it probably didn't matter that the pee got in my pants if it didn't matter that a tow truck was going to take our car. Today was a day with different rules or no rules. We were getting soaking wet from the rain again, so most of the pee was probably coming off anyway.

We walked on the actual road, in between the stopped cars. All the honking hurt my ears. Then we walked through the slidey glass doors that said ER on them. Now we could find Andy and see what happened to him and if he needed stitches again like last time or what.

Inside was like outside except with people instead of cars. People were everywhere inside the waiting room, in front of a desk that had a sign that said CHECK IN. Everyone was talking at the same time to the two women behind the desk. A policeman was talking to a group of people across the room, and Mommy moved closer to him to hear what he was saying: "We can't let anyone back there yet. We are working on a list of patients. There are a lot of wounded people, and taking care of them has to be the top priority now." Some people tried to say something to the policeman, and he lifted up his hands like he was blocking their words.

"As soon as things calm down a bit, we will start informing the relatives of the wounded we could identify. And we will go from there. I urge you to be patient. Look, I know it's hard, but let's try and let the doctors and staff do their jobs here."

All around the waiting room, people started to sit down. When there were no more empty seats left, people sat down on the floor by the walls. We walked over to the wall that had a big TV. I saw Ricky's mom sitting on the floor under the TV. Ricky is in fifth grade, like Andy, and they live close to our house, so Ricky is on the same bus as us. Andy and Ricky used to be friends and play outside a lot, but then they had a fight in the summer and didn't use their words but their fists, and later Daddy took Andy to Ricky's house to say sorry.

Ricky's mom looked up and saw us and looked back down in her lap really fast. Maybe she was still mad about the fight. Mommy sat down next to Ricky's mom and said, "Hi, Nancy."

Ricky's mom looked at Mommy and said, "Oh, hi, Melissa," like she didn't see us before Mommy sat down. I knew she did, though. Then she looked down in her lap again, and then no one said anything.

I sat down next to Mommy and tried to see the TV, but it was right over our heads, so I had to turn my head too far around, and I still only saw some of the picture. The sound from the TV was off, but I could see it had the news on, and the picture showed McKinley with all the fire trucks and police cars and ambulances in front. There were words running in a line underneath the news pictures, but I couldn't read them from where I was sitting with my head turned too far and the words were running across the TV too fast. My neck started to hurt, so I stopped looking at the TV.

We sat there on the floor for a long time, so long that my clothes weren't even wet anymore from the rain, they were starting to dry off. My stomach did a growl. Lunch was a long time ago and I didn't even eat my sandwich, only the apple. Mommy gave me two dollars so I could get something from the vending machine over by the bathrooms. I could pick whatever I wanted, she said, so I put in the dollars and pressed the button for Cheetos. That's junk food, and most of the time it's a no to junk food, but today was a no-rules day, remember?

The door at the back of the waiting room that said NO ENTRY on it opened and two nurses with green shirts and pants on came out. Everyone in the waiting room got up at the same time. The nurses were holding papers and started calling names: "Family of Ella O'Neill, family of Julia Smith, family of Danny Romero . . ." Some people in the waiting room got up and walked over to the nurses and went in the NO ENTRY door with them.

The nurses didn't call "Family of Andy Taylor," and Mommy plopped back down on the floor and put her arms on her knees and her head on her arms like she was trying to hide her face. I sat down next to her again and rubbed her arm up and down, up and down. Mommy's arms felt like they were shaking, and her hands were making fists. She opened and closed them, opened and closed them.

"If they haven't called us by now, it must be bad," Ricky's mom said. "Otherwise we would have heard something by now."

Mommy didn't say anything, she just kept opening and closing her fists.

More waiting and more nurses coming out, calling names, and more people getting up and going behind the NO ENTRY door. Every time a nurse came out, Mommy put her head up and looked at them with her eyes really big, making lines on her forehead. When they called a name, but not Andy's, she let out her breath really fast and put her head back down on her arms, and I rubbed her arm some more.

Sometimes the slidey doors in the front opened and people walked in and out. I could see outside and it was getting dark, so we were at the hospital for a long time and it was probably dinnertime by now. Looked like I was going to get to stay up late on no-rules day.

Not very many people were left in the waiting room, only me and Mommy and Ricky's mom, and a few people on the chairs and by the vending machines. A couple of policemen were left, and they were talking together with their heads down. There were a lot of empty chairs now, but we didn't get up to sit on them, even though my butt hurt from the floor.

Then the slidey doors opened again and Daddy walked in. I was excited to see him. I started to get up to go to him, but then I sat right back down because I saw his face and it didn't look like Daddy's face at all. My stomach did a big flip like when I'm excited, but I wasn't excited, just really scared.

[6]

Werewolf Howling

DADDY'S FACE WAS LIKE a grayish color, and his mouth looked all funny, with his lower lip pulled down so I could see his teeth. He shook his head no when he saw how I started to get up. He stood there by the slidey doors and stared at us, me sitting next to Mommy and Mommy next to Ricky's mom. I didn't move. I was staring back at him because I didn't know why his face looked like that and why he wasn't coming over to us.

It was a long time before he started to walk, and then he walked very slow like he didn't want to get to us. He turned around a few times—maybe he wanted to check how far he walked from the doors. All of a sudden I had a feeling that I didn't want him to get to us, because everything was going to get worse then.

Ricky's mom saw Daddy next and made a sound like she was pulling in a lot of air through her mouth. That made Mommy pick up her head from her arms. She looked up and for a minute she just looked at Daddy's weird face, and he stopped walking. Then everything did get worse, I was right.

First Mommy's eyes got really big, and then her whole self started shaking and she started acting crazy. She yelled, "Jim? Oh my God, no no no no no no no no no!"

Each "no" got louder and I didn't know why she was yelling so loud all of a sudden. Maybe she was mad that Daddy left the church, because he was supposed to wait there, just in case. Everyone in the waiting room was looking at us.

Mommy tried to get up, but then she fell back down on her knees. She started to make a loud "Aaaauuuuuuuuuuu" sound and it wasn't a sound like it was coming from a person, but maybe an animal, like a werewolf when he sees the moon.

Daddy walked the last bit to us and got down on his knees, too, and tried to put his arms around Mommy. But she started to hit him and yell "No no no no no no no no" again, so she really was mad at him.

I could tell Daddy felt bad because he kept saying, "I'm sorry, babe, I'm so so sorry!" But Mommy kept hitting him, and he let her even though everyone had their eyes on them. I wanted Mommy to stop being mad at Daddy and stop hitting him. But instead she got even more crazy and started screaming. She screamed Andy's name over and over again and it was so loud, I put my hands over my ears. There were so many too-loud sounds for my ears today.

Mommy cried and screamed and made more "Aaaauuuuuuuuuuu" sounds. After a long while she let Daddy hug her and didn't hit him anymore, so maybe she wasn't mad at him anymore. All of a sudden she turned around to the wall and started throwing up. Right where all the people could see her. A lot of throw-up came out, and she was making really gross sounds. Daddy was on his knees next to her, rubbing her back, and he looked like he was scared and like he was going to throw up, too, probably from watching Mommy.

But Daddy didn't throw up. He put his hand out to me, and I took it and then we sat there, holding hands, and I tried not to look at Mommy. She stopped throwing up and she wasn't screaming anymore. She just lay down on the floor with her eyes closed and made a ball with her whole body, her arms holding her knees, and she cried and cried.

A nurse came, and I had to move over to the side so she could take care of Mommy. I sat back down by the wall under the TV. Daddy scooched over and sat next to me and leaned his back against the wall. He put his arm around me, and we watched the nurse take care of Mommy.

Another nurse came out from the NO ENTRY door and brought a bag of stuff. She put a needle in Mommy's arm, and that probably hurt, but Mommy didn't even move. The needle was on a plastic string attached to a bag with water in it that the one nurse was holding up over her head. Then a man brought a bed on wheels, and he put the bed all the way down to the floor. The two nurses put Mommy on the bed, made the bed go back up, and then they started pushing it to the NO ENTRY door. I got up to go with Mommy on the bed, but one of the nurses put up her hand and said, "You have to hang back for now, sweetie."

The door closed and Mommy disappeared. Daddy put his hand on my shoulder and said, "They have to take Mommy back there to help her. Make her feel better. She's very upset right now and needs help. OK?"

"Why did Mommy get so mad at you, Daddy?" I asked.

"Oh, bud, she's not mad at me. I . . . I need to tell you something, Zach. Let's go outside for a bit and get some fresh air. I have to tell you some news, and it's really bad. OK? Come with me."

7

Sky Tears

ANDY WAS DEAD. That was the news Daddy told me when we stood in front of the hospital. It was raining still. So much rain all day long. The raindrops reminded me of all the tears, and it was like the sky was crying together with Mommy inside the hospital, and all the other people I saw crying today.

"Your brother was killed in the shooting, Zach," Daddy said, and his voice sounded very scratchy. We were standing together under the crying sky, and in my head the same words went round and round in a circle: *Andy is dead. Killed in the shooting. Andy is dead. Killed in the shooting.*

Now I knew why Mommy acted crazy when Daddy came in—because she knew Andy was dead, only I didn't know. Now I knew, too, but I didn't start acting crazy, and I didn't cry and scream like Mommy. I just stood and waited, with the same words doing circles in my head, and it was like my whole body didn't feel normal, it felt really heavy.

Then Daddy said we should go back to check on Mommy. We went back inside slow, and my heavy legs made it hard to walk. The people in the waiting room stared at us, and their faces looked like they were feeling very sorry for us, so they knew Andy was dead, too.

We went to the CHECK IN desk. "I would like to get an update on Melissa Taylor," Daddy told one of the women behind the desk.

"Let me check for you," the woman said, and went in the NO ENTRY door. All of a sudden Ricky's mom was standing next to us.

"Jim?" she said to Daddy. She put her hand on Daddy's arm, and Daddy took a really quick step back like her hands were hot on his arm or something. Ricky's mom dropped her hand and stared at Daddy. "Jim, please. What about Ricky? Did you ask about Ricky?"

I remembered Ricky doesn't have a dad, or he had a dad, but he moved away when Ricky was a baby. So his dad couldn't wait at the church, just in case, and now Ricky's mom didn't know if Ricky was alive or dead or what.

"I'm sorry. I . . . I don't know," Daddy said, and he walked a couple more steps back and kept looking at the NO ENTRY door. Then the door opened and the woman from behind the desk held the door open and waved to us to come in. Daddy said to Ricky's mom, "I'll try to check when I'm inside, OK?" and we walked in.

We walked behind the woman down a long hallway and came to the big room that I remembered from when we came here with Andy, it has little rooms all around the side with no walls, only curtains in between. One little room had the curtain open and I saw a girl I knew from McKinley—she's in fourth grade, I don't know her name. She was sitting on a bed with wheels and her arm had a big white wrapper around it.

The woman brought us to a little room where Mommy was. She was lying on a bed with a white blanket over her, and her face was also white like the blanket. The bag with the water was hanging on a metal stand, and the plastic string was stuck on Mommy's arm with a big Band-Aid. Mommy's eyes were closed, and her head was turned away from us. She looked like she was a fake doll, not a real person, and I got a scared feeling. Daddy went over to Mommy's bed and touched her face. Mommy didn't move at all. She didn't move her head, and she didn't open her eyes.

There were two chairs next to the bed, and we sat down on them. The woman said the doctor was going to be with us soon, and she pulled a curtain in front of the door when she left. We waited, and

I watched the water drops dripping from the bag into the string and then down into Mommy's arm. They looked like raindrops or teardrops dripping down, and it was like the bag was giving Mommy all the teardrops back she cried out earlier. Now only the bag was crying.

Daddy's phone started to ring in his pocket, but he didn't take it out to answer it. Usually Daddy always answers his phone because it could be work. He let it ring until it stopped, and after a little while the ringing started again. Daddy stared at his hands and they were the only things moving on him. First his left hand pulled all the fingers on his right hand, and then the right hand pulled all the fingers on his left hand, and they kept taking turns. I started copying Daddy and pulled my fingers at the same time as him. I had to pay attention to do it at the same time, and that made me stop thinking about Mommy lying in the bed like a fake doll. Daddy was making a pattern, so I knew what came next, and that helped. I wanted to sit here with Daddy and pull fingers for a long time.

But then the curtain got pushed to the side and a doctor came in and started talking to Daddy, and we stopped our finger patterns. "My sincere condolences," the doctor said to Daddy. Daddy only blinked with his eyes a few times but didn't say anything back, so the doctor kept talking. "Your wife is in shock. We had to sedate her and will keep her overnight. As soon as things settle down in here, we will find her a room for the night. She's heavily sedated, and I doubt she will wake up at all tonight. I think the best thing would be to regroup in the morning and assess her situation. Why don't you go home and . . . try to get some rest?"

Daddy still didn't talk, he just looked at the doctor. Maybe he didn't understand what he said. Then he looked back down at his hands like he was surprised they were holding still now.

"Sir? Do you have someone who can take you home?" the doctor said, and that woke Daddy up and he said, "No. We . . . we will go. I don't need anyone to take us."

The curtain got pushed open again and Mimi was standing there like frozen, holding on to the curtain. She stared at Daddy for a long time with really big eyes, and then she moved her stare to me and then to Mommy lying on the bed like a fake doll. Mimi's face started to crumple up like a piece of paper. She opened her mouth like she was going to say something, but only a quiet "oh" sound came out. She took a step toward Daddy, and Daddy got up like in slow motion. Maybe his body felt too heavy, too.

Mimi and Daddy hugged each other tight, and Mimi was making loud crying sounds into Daddy's jacket. The doctor and the nurse were standing next to them, and both of them were staring at their shoes. They had on the hospital kind, like green Crocs.

After a while Mimi and Daddy got done hugging. Mimi was still crying, and she came over to me and put her arms around me. She pulled me close to her belly. It felt smushy and nice and warm, and my throat got a tight feeling inside. Mimi kissed the top of my head and whispered into my hair: "My sweet, sweet Zach. My poor, sweet little boy." Then she let go of me. I didn't want her to, I wanted to stay there hugging her and feel warm and smell her sweater that smelled like fresh laundry.

But Mimi turned away from me and toward Mommy. She pushed some hair from Mommy's face with her hand. "I will stay with her tonight, Jim," Mimi said in a quiet voice, and tears were just running, running down her face.

Daddy made a sound in his throat and then he said, "OK. Thank you, Roberta." He took my hand and said, "Let's get you home, Zach." But I didn't want to go. I didn't want to go home without Mommy. So I grabbed the side of Mommy's bed.

"No!" I said. My voice came out loud and it surprised me. "No, I want Mommy. I want to stay here with Mommy!" My voice sounded like a baby voice, but I didn't care.

"Please don't do this, Zach, please," Daddy said, sounding very tired. "Please, let's just go home. Mommy is OK, she just needs to sleep. Mimi will stay here and take care of her."

"I will, honey, I promise. I'll be here with Mommy," Mimi said.

"I want to stay here, too," I said with the loud voice again.

"We will come see her tomorrow. I promise. Please stop shout-ing," Daddy said.

"But she has to say good night to me! We have to sing our song!"

Every night at bedtime me and Mommy sing a song, and it's always the same. It's our tradition and it's the song that Mimi made up when Mommy was a baby, and then Mommy started singing it to me and Andy when we were babies. The song sounds like the "Brother John" song, but with our own words made up. You change the name in it for who you are singing it to. For me, Mommy sings it like this:

Zachary Taylor
Zachary Taylor
I love you
I love you
You're my handsome buddy
And I'll love you always
Yes, I do
Yes, I do

Sometimes Mommy changes up the words and sings it like this: "You're my smelly buddy, but I love you anyway . . . ," and it's really funny, but in the end, she always has to sing it the regular way so I can go to sleep.

Now she was going to stay here in the hospital and not be at home with me for bedtime.

"Just . . . OK, do you want to sing it now, then?" Daddy asked, and the way he said it sounded like that was going to be a stupid thing to do. I shook my head yes, but then I didn't want to sing with Daddy and Mimi and the doctor and the nurse all looking at me, so I only kept holding on to Mommy's bed until Daddy came over and forced me to let go.

Daddy picked me up and carried me back through the big room and the hallway, out the door to the waiting room, and back out through the slidey doors into the rain. He carried me all the way to his car that was a long way from the hospital, but parked in a real spot, so it didn't get towed. I wondered if Mommy's car got towed and how she was going to get home without her car.

Daddy opened the car door and at the same time we both saw Andy's sweater on the backseat. It was the sweater he had on at lacrosse practice last night, and he took it off after we got in the car. Daddy picked it up and sat down in the driver's seat. Then he put his face in Andy's sweater and for a long time he sat there like that. It looked like his whole body was shaking and crying and he made little rocking moves forward and backward, but no sounds.

I sat very still in my seat in the back and watched the raindrops on the sunroof, the sky crying on top of the car. After a while Daddy put the sweater down on his lap and wiped his face with his hand. Then he turned around to me. "We need to be strong now, Zach, you and me. We need to be strong for Mommy. OK?"

"OK," I said, and then we drove home through the sky tears, just me and Daddy.

8

The Last Normal Tuesday

DADDY WALKED AROUND the house with me right behind him, and my socks made wet footprints on the floor. Daddy turned on all the lights in all the rooms, and that was the opposite of what he does on other days, which is turn all the lights off all the time because lights use up electricity and electricity costs a lot of money.

"I'm hungry," I said, and Daddy said, "Right." We went in the kitchen, but then Daddy just stood there and looked around like he was in someone else's kitchen and he didn't know where stuff was. I heard his phone ringing again in his pocket, but he didn't take it out to answer it again. He opened up the fridge and looked inside for a while and then he took out the milk. "Cereal OK?"

"Sure," I said, because with Mommy I'm never allowed to have cereal for dinner.

We sat down on the barstools at the counter and ate Honey Bunches—that's my favorite cereal. I looked at the family calendar on the wall next to me. It's Mommy's big calendar, and everyone in the family has a row with their name on the left and all the things we have on the days of the week next to the names. So that way Mommy can look at it in the morning and remember everything we have that day.

My row on the calendar doesn't have a lot on it, only piano for today, Wednesday, and lacrosse for Saturday. I wondered if Mr.

Bernard still came to the house today at 4:30 for my lesson, but no one opened the door for him because we stayed at the hospital the whole day.

Andy's row has something almost every day. He gets to do a lot more things because he's older, and also it's better when he's busy with activities. For yesterday, Tuesday, it said lacrosse for Andy and that was only one day ago, but it felt like a long time ago, maybe a month.

Yesterday we did all the things we do every Tuesday, because we didn't know that today a gunman was going to come. Sometimes on Tuesdays Daddy comes home early so he can go to Andy's lacrosse practice. He works in New York City where we used to live when I was little, but then we moved to this house because there's more space here, and New York City is not a safe place for kids to live, Mommy says. And here we could have a whole house, not just an apartment.

Daddy's office is in the MetLife Building, and that's really cool because it's a building on top of a train station. He made partner at his firm last year, and we had a party to celebrate. But I don't think it's such a great thing for celebrating because now Daddy is always working until late, so on school days I don't even see him, only on weekends. He always leaves before I wake up in the morning, and I have to go to bed before he comes back home. Andy gets to stay up longer than me, because he's three and a half years older, so he sometimes gets to see Daddy before bed, and that's not fair.

In the summer I went with Daddy to his office one time because Mommy had to take Andy to the doctor. I was excited to go and I was going to be with Daddy all day, and that never happened before. And also Daddy told me about the cool new office he got that has all windows on two sides, and you can see the Empire State Building from it. I couldn't wait to see it, and I even brought my bird-watching binoculars to see all the way downtown with them.

But then I didn't get to be with Daddy very much inside his new office because he went to a lot of meetings where I couldn't come. I had to stay with Angela most of the time. Angela is Daddy's assistant, and she's nice. She took me to Grand Central for lunch—that's the name of the train station under Daddy's office—and there's a bunch of restaurants all the way in the basement. Angela let me have Shake Shack and I even got a chocolate milkshake, and that's not a healthy lunch. Milkshakes are my favorite drink. I always dip my French fries in them, Uncle Chip taught me to do that, and everyone thinks it's disgusting, but me and Uncle Chip love it. Now I still always do it, and it makes me think about Uncle Chip.

Andy has lacrosse practice on every Tuesday and Friday and then games on the weekends, and the whole family has to go to show our support. He's really good at lacrosse, like all the sports, and he scores a lot of goals at the games. Daddy says Andy's probably good enough to play in college, like him when he went to college. He talks about that a lot and he still has a record at his college for most goals in one game, and no one has broken it yet even though that was a long time ago that Daddy made that record. But Daddy says Andy isn't trying hard enough to get better, and he should be working on his stick skills more. Andy gets mad and says it's a stupid sport anyway, and maybe he's only going to play soccer next year and no lacrosse.

I started lacrosse this year, too—it starts in first grade. But I only had three clinics so far, and the whole family did not come to show their support, because Andy's games are at the same time, so Daddy takes him and Mommy takes me. I don't think I am going to be very good at lacrosse, it's hard to hold the stick and scoop up the ball. I don't even like it, the other boys bump into me too hard, and I hate putting the helmet over my head, it's too tight.

On the last normal Tuesday, Daddy came walking in and I was waiting for him by the front door, but he was still on a phone call, so I wasn't allowed to say hi to him yet. He put a finger up on his mouth to say "Shush," and he went upstairs to change from his suit to his game clothes. He always does that, I don't know why, because Andy was playing, not him.

I waited in the hallway for him to come back down because there was fighting in the kitchen. The fighting was between Mommy and

Andy, and it was about homework. Andy wasn't doing it again, and it all has to be finished before practice because we come home really late, at nine almost, one hour after my bedtime. I did my homework already right after I got off the bus.

When I was sitting next to Daddy on the barstool, eating my Honey Bunches, I thought about the fighting yesterday. How Mommy yelled at Andy, and how the fighting got worse because of Daddy, after he came downstairs from changing his clothes. And I thought about how we didn't know then that it was going to be the last normal day, or maybe we would have tried not to have all the same fighting that we always have.

I looked over to Daddy and wondered if he was thinking about the fighting, too. He was putting cereal in his mouth, one spoonful after the next, and he didn't even chew, only swallowed. He looked like a robot, one that was moving too slow because it was running out of batteries.

"Daddy?"

"Hm?" Daddy turned his slow robot head and looked at me.

"Daddy, where's Andy?"

Daddy looked at me funny and said, "Zach, Andy is dead. Remember?"

"No, I know he's dead, but where is he right now?"

"Oh, I'm not sure, bud. I wasn't allowed to . . . go see him." Daddy's voice got different when he said the last words. He looked down fast and stared at his Honey Bunches floating in the milk, and he didn't blink for a long time.

"Is he still at the school?" I asked, and I thought about the people lying in the hallway with blood around them, and that one of them was Andy. Was he dead then already, when I walked down the hallway to the back door? And when I was hiding in the closet with Miss Russell and my class, was he already dead?

I thought about how it must have hurt badly to get killed with bullets from a gun, and Andy was probably really scared when he saw that the gunman was about to shoot him.

"Where did the gunman shoot him?" I meant where on his body, but Daddy said, "In the auditorium, I think. His class was in the auditorium when . . . it happened."

"Oh yeah," I said. "Today the fourth and fifth graders got to see the snakes!"

"Huh? What snakes?"

I remembered that I never got to tell Daddy about the emerald tree boa yesterday. Last night I waited in the hallway for Daddy to come down from changing his clothes because I wanted to tell him that I touched a real live snake at school. I really did. It was long and bright green with white marks on it, called an emerald tree boa, and all the kids were scared of it except me.

We had an assembly and this guy came in with different kinds of snakes and birds and a ferret, and he told us snake facts. It was so cool. I love snakes. I wish I could have one in a terrarium like my friend Spencer. But Mommy hates them and she thinks they're dangerous. I told her not all of them are, and she said, "Well, you don't know that though until they bite you, do you? And then it could be too late."

So when the guy asked if someone wanted to touch the boa, I raised my hand fast, and he picked me to come to the front and pet it. It was wrapped around his arm, like it would be around a tree branch waiting for its prey, he told me. The boa's skin was dry and had hard scales, and it wasn't slimy like I thought. The guy told us lots of facts about the emerald tree boa: emerald is a green color, the color of the snake. The snake doesn't have any venom, but it wraps its body around its prey and squeezes it so tight that the prey can't breathe and dies.

But when Daddy came down and I tried to tell him, he heard Mommy and Andy's fighting and said, "Hold on, bud, let me handle that first. Tell me later," and he went in the kitchen, and of course right away the fighting got worse. That's how it always is—it always starts because of Andy acting bad, and he and Mommy have a fight. When Daddy is home and gets involved, he and Mommy get into a fight, too. "Jim, I was dealing with this," Mommy tells Daddy, and then everyone is mad at everyone, except me, because I'm not part of the fighting.

I followed Daddy in the kitchen and started getting napkins out and forks and knives—that's my job before dinner. Andy's job is to get plates and make our milk cups, but he wasn't doing that again tonight because he was still not done with his homework. I did it instead. Daddy sat down at the table and said he worked like a crazy person all day and could he never come home and have dinner in peace? And by the way, the back door was open so the neighbors could probably hear all the yelling. Mommy sat down, too, and she gave me a fake-like smile and said, "Thank you for setting the table, Zach. You're such a good helper."

"Yeah, Zach, little suck-up," Andy said.

Daddy slammed his hands on the table so that everything moved and the milk spilled out of the cups. It made me jump because it was so loud, and then Daddy yelled at Andy, and the neighbors were definitely going to hear that.

That was the last normal dinner on the last normal day, and now it was only one day later and I was eating cereal for dinner with just Daddy, and not Mommy and Andy. That was going to be the last fight because now Andy was gone, and so there wouldn't be any more fighting without him here.

I wondered if the snake guy got killed from the gunman, too, and what happened to the snakes. Maybe they were on the loose in the school now?

[9]

Yellow Eyeballs

DADDY'S PHONE STARTED ringing again and this time he pulled it out of his pocket and looked at it. "Jesus Christ," he said. "I have to go make some phone calls. I have to call Grandma back and Aunt Mary and . . . some other people. It's really late. Let's go upstairs and get ready for bed, OK?"

The clock on the microwave said 10:30, and that is very late. I only stayed up that late one time before, on July Fourth. We went to see the big fireworks at the beach club and that was the first time we went to the club for a big party because we only got into the club this year. I love going to the club because we're allowed to go wherever we want, on the beach and by the tennis courts and cabanas, because it's safe for us everywhere. We went there a lot of days in the summer. Mommy and Daddy sit with their friends on the terrace and drink wine, and Mommy doesn't care that it's getting dark and I'm still up. A lot of Daddy's work friends are at the club, and it's important that Daddy spends time with them, and he wants me and Andy to play with their kids, so we don't have to leave early for bedtime.

The fireworks on July Fourth weren't starting until it was dark, and in the summer it doesn't get dark until late. We stayed to watch all the fireworks, which was really cool because on the other side of the bay they had lots of different kinds, and we could see them all from the beach.

When they were over it was time to go. The rule was to come back to the terrace after the fireworks, but Andy didn't come, so everyone had to start looking for him. Finally, Daddy found him on the fishing dock, and Andy wasn't supposed to be there without a grown-up because that's the only not-safe place to be in the whole beach club. There was a big fight in the car on the way home, and Daddy said how could Andy embarrass him in front of his work friends like that? I didn't go to bed until 10:30, like today.

We went upstairs, and to get to my room we had to walk past Andy's room. Daddy walked by really fast, like he didn't want to look inside. "Can you please put your PJs on and get ready for bed?" Daddy said, and kept walking into his and Mommy's room. Then I could hear him talk on his phone, but I couldn't tell who he was talking to because he talked very quiet and closed the door behind him.

I went in my room and everything looked exactly like this morning. But it didn't feel the same. Everything felt different without Mommy and Andy here, and also it felt like a very long time ago since I was in my room.

I looked at my bed, all made nice, and I thought about how Mommy made it after we left for school this morning—she does that every day. I don't know why, because you get right back in it at night, but Mommy says that's the old type A account director in her. Today started out like a normal day, and so after we left for school on the bus, Mommy made the beds like always. Maybe it was right when the gunman was coming in the school, but Mommy was at home making the beds and didn't even know that that was happening.

I thought about how me and Andy waited in Mrs. Gray's driveway for the school bus this morning. It wasn't raining then yet, the rain started when we were at school, it was cold though, but Andy still had shorts on. Andy always wants to wear shorts. In the morning he and Mommy have fights about it because Mommy says it has to be at least 60 degrees outside, or it's a no to shorts, but Andy still puts shorts on even when it's not 60 degrees, like today—it was 57 degrees when we left the house, I checked on the iPad. I know he had shorts on, but now I couldn't remember what color they were. I just remembered he had on a blue Giants jersey, and it really bothered me that I couldn't remember what color the shorts were.

Mrs. Gray's driveway is really skinny and has rocks on the sides, so we sometimes play this game called "Don't get eaten" where we try to jump all the way from the rocks on the one side to the rocks on the other side. We pretend that the driveway in between is water with sharks in it, so we can't touch it or we get eaten from the sharks. I asked Andy if he wanted to play "Don't get eaten" today, but he said no, he wasn't playing that baby game anymore. Andy calls everything I want to play baby games now. He just stood there and didn't say anything else and kicked the driveway rocks with his shoe over and over again. "Don't get eaten" was going to be the last thing I talked to Andy about, only then I didn't know that.

Today started out like a normal day, but now it was all changed. And Andy wasn't going to get in his bed anymore, so it would stay made nice.

I have sheets with racecars on them and they match my bed, which is a red racecar with wheels. Mine and Andy's beds are different because Andy has a bunk bed. He only sleeps on the top bunk because that is far enough away from us people, he said. But the rest of our rooms are almost the same, except that we have different toys. We both have a window from where we can see the street and our driveway, and we both have a desk under the window, and on the other wall we have two white bookshelves and a reading chair. There's a bathroom in between our rooms. That's not good, because when Andy goes to the bathroom, he always locks the doors on the inside and then he doesn't unlock them after. I always have to walk around into his room to get to the bathroom, and he yells at me to get out of his room and throws pillows at me from the top bunk.

The really big difference between me and Andy about our rooms is that I really like my room, but Andy doesn't like his. He doesn't go in it very much, except for sleeping and when he needs to take a time-away. Andy needs to take time-aways a lot when he gets his bad temper, and then he's supposed to go in his room to calm down. It's not a punishment, it's so he can learn to handle his big feelings. That's what the doctor said, his name is Dr. Byrne, and Andy has to go talk to him every week even though he doesn't want to. He has to because of his ODD—that's the thing Andy has that makes him have the bad temper.

When Andy gets his bad temper, it's scary. I got pretty good at telling when he's about to get it, and then I try to get away from him. I don't even want to look at him then because of how it makes his face look. His whole face gets red and his eyes get big and he starts to yell really loud. It's hard to understand what he's even saying because it sounds like one long word with no breaks in between, and a lot of spit comes on his lips and chin.

Sometimes when Andy has to go to his room for a time-away, Mommy has to stand in front of his door because Andy tries to come out and he pulls the door from the inside and he does his loud yelling. Mommy has to pull the door from the outside to keep it closed, and it takes Andy a long time to calm down and stop pulling and yelling. Or Andy tricks Mommy and runs out through the bathroom and in my room. One time he did that, and I saw Mommy go in Andy's room. She sat down on his reading chair that's way too small for her and she put her head on her knees, and it looked like she was crying. I got mad at Andy because he made Mommy sad like that.

I'm in my room all the time because it's quiet, and sometimes I want my own peace. I come back out when the fighting is over, so it's like I skipped it. I like to play with my cars and firehouse and trucks. I have a ton of trucks, all different kinds of construction trucks, fire trucks, tow trucks. . . . Every night before I go to bed I line them up straight in front of the bookshelves and say good night to all of them. This morning I played with my trucks for a little bit before the bus, so now they were not in a straight line and that bothered me. I stared at them, all mixed up, and I thought about how they needed to be fixed, but I didn't do it.

I went over to my window instead and looked outside. It was very dark, and the streetlamp in front of our house was making a round light ball in the dark air. Inside the light ball I could see raindrops falling. All the houses on our road have a streetlamp in front of them, on the grass in between the road and the sidewalk, and they were making a long row of round light balls with raindrops falling inside. They kind of looked like yellow eyeballs with lots of tears in them, and I got a feeling like they were staring at me. Creepy.

I sat down on my bed. My whole self felt tired, and my feet were still very cold. I tried to take my socks off and they were still wet a little, so pulling them off was too hard. I started to miss Mommy a lot, and I wished she was home so she could help me take my socks off and get ready for bed. I felt like I was going to cry, but I tried not to because Daddy said we had to be strong now for Mommy.

I squeezed my nose hard and I picked up Clancy—that's my stuffed giraffe I got from the Bronx Zoo when I was two. He's my favorite stuffed animal, and I always need him for bedtime. I can't go to sleep if I don't have him.

After a while Daddy came in my room. "Let's get you to bed, bud. We have to try and get some sleep. It's the best thing we can do right now. The next few days are going to be really tough and we need our strength, OK?" Daddy pulled the racecar sheets up. I got in my bed with my clothes on instead of my PJs, and that's gross because earlier I peed in my underwear, but it was dried now. And I didn't even brush my teeth.

"Daddy?" I asked. "Can you tell me a story?"

Daddy rubbed his hands over his whole face and it made a scratching sound on his chin. He looked very tired. "Probably not tonight, bud," he said. "I . . . I don't think I can . . . think of stories, not tonight."

"Then I can you tell one tonight instead. It's going to be about the emerald tree boa I saw yesterday," I told Daddy.

"It's very late. So not tonight," Daddy said, and he leaned over to give me a hug. I thought about how that was the only part of today that was the same as yesterday—that I didn't get to tell Daddy about the snakes.

"I'll be down the hall, OK?" Daddy said, but then he didn't get up to go, he stayed with his arms around me tight for a long time. I felt like I wanted to sing mine and Mommy's good-night song for Daddy.

I started to sing in a very quiet voice, and it was hard to do because Daddy's one arm was on top of my chest and it was heavy. I could feel his breath going in and out fast right next to my ear and it tickled, but I didn't move. I sang the whole song all the way through to the end: *"And I'll love you always. Yes, I do. Yes, I do."*

10

Handshakes

THE NEXT MORNING I woke up and I was in Mommy and Daddy's bed, and I didn't know why I was in here. It was quiet and I could hear rain outside plopping against the window—plop, plop, plop—and then the plops started to sound like POPs, and it made me remember the gunman, and then everything from yesterday and from last night came back in my head. And then it made sense, because I never get to sleep in Mommy and Daddy's bed, only last night, because I got so scared.

Daddy left my room last night after I got done singing. He turned off the lights in the hallway, and Mommy always keeps the lights on because it can't be too dark in my room. It got too dark in my room. I tried to squeeze my eyes shut tight, but then it was even more dark. Right away pictures of people with blood came in my head and my heart started beating at super speed and my breathing went in and out fast.

I heard a sound in my room somewhere or in the bathroom like somebody was coming, and I started screaming very loud. I screamed and I got up and ran in the hallway, but I couldn't see anything and I didn't know where Daddy was and I could feel a person coming closer behind me, he was going to get me, and I tripped and fell down. I couldn't get up and I screamed and screamed.

Then the door to Mommy and Daddy's room opened and Daddy came running out. He turned on the hallway lights, and it was too bright in my eyes.

"Zach, Zach, ZACH!" Daddy picked me up under my armpits and yelled my name in my face over and over again. He shook me and I stopped screaming and he stopped yelling. It got quiet except for a loud whoosh, whoosh sound in my head. I looked behind me, but no one was there. I looked in my room and it looked like a dark black cave and I wasn't going to sleep in there ever again by myself, and so Daddy let me sleep with him in his bed for once.

Now Daddy wasn't in the bed with me anymore, so I got up to look for him. I walked down the hallway and past Andy's room, and my hands felt sweaty and my legs walked very slow. I pushed Andy's door open and walked in his room with very small steps. I didn't want to look up to his top bunk at first. I thought that maybe I had a bad dream and Andy would be there, in his bed. But if the top bunk was empty, then it really happened, that Andy died, because Andy never gets up first, never before me. It's really hard for him to wake up in the mornings. Mommy says it's because of the medicine he has to take for the bad temper.

Andy takes the temper medicine in the mornings so he behaves at school, but it only works for a little while, and then his bad temper comes back when he gets home from school. One time I heard Mommy and Daddy fighting about the temper medicine because Daddy said Andy should take some in the afternoons so he behaves better at home, too. But Mommy said no, she wasn't going to give him more, it wasn't good for him, only before parties or special occasions where he has to behave good.

After a while I looked up at the top bunk. No Andy.

I knew Andy wasn't there, but I said his name into his empty room anyway: "Andy." There was no one there to hear it. It was like Andy's room swallowed up his name and then it was gone, like him.

I went out of his room fast and downstairs. I could hear voices and sounds coming from the kitchen. Maybe Mommy was back from the hospital. But when I walked in the kitchen, Daddy was there and Grandma and Aunt Mary, not Mommy.

Daddy was sitting on the same barstool where he ate his cereal last night and he was still wearing his work clothes from yesterday, except for the suit jacket. Everything looked all wrinkly, and his beard was starting to grow. Daddy's beard grows really fast, so he has to shave every day or he starts to look like Uncle Chip when he was still alive. Uncle Chip always let his beard grow, and it tickled me when he gave me a hug and a kiss, and sometimes food got stuck in it, and that was gross, so I'm glad Daddy always shaves, just today he didn't.

His face looked all whitish where the beard wasn't growing, like Mommy's face yesterday at the hospital, and his eyes were dark all around. Maybe he didn't sleep last night, even though he said it would be the best thing for us. The clock on the microwave said 8:10, and that meant I missed the school bus because it comes at 7:55 every day. So Daddy was going to have to drive me to school then probably. When I thought about McKinley, I thought about the POP sounds again and the people lying in the hallway, and the big scared feeling from last night came right back. I didn't want to go back there. What if Andy was still there? Then I was going to see him dead with blood on him.

Grandma was sitting next to Daddy on a barstool, talking on the phone. She sat with her back very straight. She always sits like that and sometimes she sticks her finger into mine and Andy's backs so we will sit up more straight, too, and she even does it to Daddy sometimes. Grandma didn't look like her normal self and it was because she didn't have on her red lipstick. I don't like her lipstick, because when she gives me kisses it leaves red lip stamps on my face. I never saw her without it on before, it made her look different—like, older. She looked a little bit more like Mimi now, who is really old, she has white hair, and Grandma's hair is blond. Also Mimi never wears lipstick. When Mimi smiles or laughs, her whole face gets wrinkles on it, especially around her eyes and her mouth. Grandma doesn't have those, her face stays the same when she smiles.

Grandma's lips shivered in between saying words into the phone. Aunt Mary was standing next to her with her hand on top of Grandma's hand on the counter, and a lot of tears were running down her face.

"Daddy?" I said, and all at the same time, Daddy, Grandma, and

Aunt Mary lifted their heads up and looked at where I was standing by the door.

"Oh my goodness, let me call you back," Grandma said into the phone, and she put it down on the counter. Then she walked over to me, and I could see her lips were shivering even more now. "Oh, Zach," she said, and she leaned down to me and her breath smelled bad, like old. She gave me a hug, and it was a little too hard and too tight. I moved my head to the side so I didn't have to smell her breath anymore.

I saw Daddy and Aunt Mary were looking at me. Aunt Mary had her one hand over her mouth and she made her forehead all wrinkly and more tears were running down her face. When Grandma's tight hug was done, Aunt Mary opened her arms wide and I walked to her fast. Aunt Mary's hug was soft and warm. I could feel her whole body shaking from crying, and I could feel her warm breath on the top of my head. "Hey, monkey," she said into my hair. We just stayed like that for a long time until I felt Daddy's hand rubbing my back.

"Hey, Zach," Daddy said, and then Aunt Mary stopped hugging me. "I'm glad you got some sleep."

"Daddy? I'm late for school, right?" I said. "I don't want to go today. I'm . . . I don't want to go there today."

"Oh, no, you're not going to school today," Daddy answered, and he pulled me close to him and up on his lap. "Not for a while."

From where I was sitting on Daddy's lap, I could see the TV was on in the family room. It was the news about how the gunman came to McKinley, but I couldn't hear what they were saying because the sound was turned all the way down like at the hospital. I didn't know why people put the TV on with no sound.

After Grandma made me breakfast, people started coming in our house, and all day long more and more people came. They made a big pile of wet shoes and umbrellas in the hallway, and the alarm box in the kitchen kept saying "Front door!" in the lady robot voice so you can know someone was leaving or coming in even if you can't see the door. Everyone brought food, and Grandma and Aunt Mary tried to fit all the containers and bowls in the fridge in the kitchen and the one in the basement, and they put some food out for people to eat, but no one ate anything.

Grandma made Daddy go upstairs to clean up, and when he came back down, his hair was wet but he still didn't shave. Daddy walked around and talked to all the people, and it looked like we were having a party.

We have parties a lot at our house, and sometimes people from Daddy's work come, from his office and his clients sometimes. Daddy always wants me and Andy to stand by the door to say hi to the party guests and do handshakes. Handshakes are very important for when you're older. Your hand can't be too loose because that's wimpy, but you also can't squeeze too hard, the handshake has to be just in the middle, it's called firm, and you have to look the other person right in the eye and say, "Nice to meet you." Sometimes I practice by myself in my room before parties so I do it right.

I thought it was weird we were having a party today, because Andy died and Mommy was at the hospital because of the shock and that's not a good time for a party, but more people kept coming in, all standing and sitting down in the kitchen and family room and living room. There were no kids, except me, only grown-ups, and it was like I didn't even belong in the party.

I stayed close to Daddy the whole time. I wanted to talk to him and ask him when Mommy was coming home, and could we go see her at the hospital, but Daddy didn't have time because he had to talk to the other grown-ups and do handshakes.

"I'm so sorry for your loss," "Our deepest condolences," "I just can't believe something like this could happen in Wake Gardens," the people said. Daddy had a little smile on his face, not a happy smile, but one that looked like he put it on his face on purpose and then left it there and it never went away. Some of the people, some I knew and some I never saw before, gave me hugs or patted me on the head and I didn't want that, to get hugs like that from everyone.

In the afternoon, one of the people who came to the party was

Miss Russell. I was just coming out of the living room, still following Daddy, when I saw her walk in the front door. She looked smaller or something and like she was cold, she was giving herself a hug with her arms. She blinked her eyes fast a few times when she looked around in the hallway. Her face looked very white and she had dark all around her eyes. When she saw me standing behind Daddy, she stopped blinking her eyes and gave me a little smile.

She came over to us and said, "Hi, Zach," in a very quiet voice. Daddy looked at her and reached out his hand. "Hello . . . ," he said, and Miss Russell took his hand and shook it slowly.

"Nadia Russell," she said. "I'm Zach's teacher."

"Oh, right, I'm sorry, of course," Daddy said.

"I'm so very sorry . . . about Andy . . . ," Miss Russell said, and her voice sounded like it got stuck in her throat a couple of times.

"Thank you," Daddy said. "Oh, and . . . thank you . . . very much. For keeping Zach safe yesterday. I'm . . . I'm very grateful."

Miss Russell didn't say anything back, she just shook her head yes. Then she looked around Daddy, at me. "Hey, Zach." She did a little smile again. "I'm not staying long, but I wanted to give you this . . . You can keep it, OK? Maybe you'll like having it." Miss Russell took my hand and dropped something inside. It was one of her favorite charms from her charm bracelet, she showed it to us a lot of times. It was a silver angel wing with a heart on it. She told us that her grandma gave it to her, and it meant love and protection and it was very special to her because now her grandma wasn't alive anymore.

"Thank you," I said, and my words came out like a whisper.

After Miss Russell left I walked around with Daddy for a little while longer, but then I felt like I wanted to take a break from walking around, so I sat down on the yellow chair in the corner of the family room. The yellow chair is kind of behind the couch, and the people in the family room were all looking at the TV and talking in quiet voices, so no one knew I was there. The sound on the TV was still turned all the way down. First it was commercials, but then the news came back on and it was still about McKinley.

A lady with a microphone was standing in front of McKinley next to the sign that says MCKINLEY ELEMENTARY. I could see it said WEDNESDAY, OCTOBER 6TH on it, and that was yesterday, so Charlie forgot to put the date on today, which is his job first thing in the morning before school starts. Behind the news lady were some police cars, but no more fire trucks and ambulances. There were a lot of the vans with the standing-up bowls on the roofs, like I saw in front of the church.

I could tell the lady started to talk in the microphone because her lips were moving, but in the family room it was just lips moving with no sounds coming out in a very quiet room. I really wanted to hear what she was saying and if she was talking about the gunman, but I didn't want people to know I was behind them on the yellow chair, so I stayed quiet and watched the lady's lips move.

Pictures of people came on the TV, and over the pictures it said "19 Confirmed Dead" and then the pictures got big on the screen, one at a time, and stayed big for a little while, and then the picture went back to small. The next picture got big and then the next. I realized it was pictures of people who got killed from the gunman. I knew who all the people were in the pictures, some kids from fourth and fifth grade, and it looked like the pictures of them were from field day because they all had on McKinley field day T-shirts. And there were pictures of some grown-ups from school, too: Mrs. Colaris, our principal, Mrs. Vinessa, Andy's teacher, Mr. Wilson, our gym teacher, and Mr. Hernandez, the custodian.

I knew all the people in the pictures, and yesterday I saw some of them at school, and now they were dead. In the pictures they looked like they always look at school, and I thought that now they didn't look like that anymore. Now they were lying in the hallway with blood on them.

The next picture that got big was Ricky, so that meant he was dead, too. I wondered if Ricky's mom knew that Ricky was dead, or if she was still at the hospital, waiting in the waiting room, and then I remembered that Daddy told her we were going to check if Ricky was there when we went through the NO ENTRY door to see Mommy, but we never did that, and that wasn't very nice of us.

After Ricky came Andy. He looked sweaty and was bending his knees like he was getting ready to jump. His blond hair was sticking up in the front from the sweat, and he was making a silly face with his tongue out of the side of his mouth. Andy always makes silly faces in pictures, and Mommy gets mad because we don't have a single good picture of our family where everyone smiles and we can hang it up on the wall.

I stared at Andy's silly face. It looked like he was going to jump out of the TV right into the family room, and I held in my breath and wanted him to jump, but then his picture got small and disappeared. Another picture got big, and Andy's silly face was gone.

11

Secret Hideout

I TURNED AROUND IN THE YELLOW CHAIR and saw Daddy sitting in the kitchen. I went to him and tried to swallow the lump of breath in my throat. I swallowed and swallowed and my mouth got really dry, but the lump didn't move. I tried to get on Daddy's lap, but Daddy was looking at his phone, not me. He only let me sit on one leg, and it wasn't comfortable.

I tried to sit all the way on Daddy's lap, but he said, "Buddy, give me a second to breathe, OK?" and he pushed me off.

Grandma came over and the red lipstick was back on her lips. "Zach, Daddy's very tired. Let's give him a break," she said to me. Then Mrs. Gray our neighbor came in the kitchen and said, "Oh my God, Jim, I'm so sorry for your loss," and Daddy got up to talk to her, so his second to breathe must have been over.

I had to walk some steps backward because Daddy's barstool pushed into me. I started not to like how Daddy's face looked with the smile/not smile that was back on it, so I left the kitchen and went upstairs.

The party sounds followed me up the stairs like they were taking a piggyback ride on my back, and they were getting louder. It was all I could hear, even though I was walking away from the party. I walked faster down the hallway and shook my head to get the sounds out. I wanted to get to my room and leave the sounds outside. But when I passed Andy's room, I had to stop and look inside. It was like there was an invisible force pulling me in. Right away my eyes went up to Andy's empty top bunk.

I always want to be in Andy's room and see his things and hang out with him, but Andy never lets me. He would probably be really mad at me for being in here now. I pretended like I was a spy, scouting out the enemy, looking all around, touching the enemy's things, opening drawers and doors and looking for clues. I touched the robot arm on Andy's desk and pretended it was the enemy's weapon and I had to figure out how to use it.

Andy got the robot arm from Mimi for Christmas, and that wasn't fair because she gave me Hungry Hungry Hippos, and that's a baby game. I wanted something cool to build like Andy. It looks like a real robot arm and has a motor and batteries. You can make the arm move up and down, and the claw can pick things up—it's so cool. I asked Andy if I could try, but of course it was a no. Andy built it all by himself, no grown-up helped him, even though the box said "12 & up," and he was only nine then.

I heard Mimi talk about it to Mommy in the kitchen: "Andy's so incredibly smart, too smart for his own good." People say that all the time about Andy—"He's so smart," and "I've never met such a smart kid." And it's the truth, he really is smart, like more smart than other people, he did a test once that showed that. He just doesn't feel like doing his work, and he doesn't want to sit in one place for a long time. He went to a special class for smart kids when we still lived in the city where they did third-grade work in first grade, but at McKinley they don't have a special class like that, so Andy hates school now because it's boring for him.

Andy read all the Harry Potter books in first grade. Daddy always tells that to everyone, and I can tell he's really proud about that. I tried to read the first Harry Potter book, *Harry Potter and the Sorcerer's Stone*, because I'm also in first grade now and I wanted Daddy to tell proud stories about me, too, but the book had a scary picture on the front and a lot of hard words. Andy made fun of me because it took me like half an hour to read two pages, so I stopped.

I found the On switch on the robot arm and flipped it up. I tried to get the claw to pick up a pencil from Andy's desk, but it was hard, and the claw kept dropping the pencil. Then I thought I heard a sound on the stairs like someone was coming up, so I turned it off really fast. If Daddy was coming up, he would probably get mad at me because I was in Andy's room touching his stuff. I saw Andy's closet door was open, so I went inside and pulled the door closed, but not all the way.

I almost couldn't hear the party sounds in the closet. Andy's closet is really big, such a waste for a boy, Mommy says. Andy didn't put his clothes away. There was a big messy pile of clothes on the floor behind the hamper. I put the clothes in the hamper and walked all the way in, behind the handsome shirts and the jackets that were hanging up, and there was a whole space in the back. It was dark back here, but I could see Andy's sleeping bag rolled up in the corner of the closet, and I sat down on it. I sat really still and my heart was beating at super speed and I was waiting to see if Daddy was going to find me, but nothing happened.

I sat on the sleeping bag roll and then I thought about how yesterday I was in the closet in my classroom, so now it was two days in a row that I was sitting in a closet. I never sat in a closet before today and yesterday, because closets are not for hanging out, they're for putting stuff away.

And there's not a lot of space in closets, which I don't like. I get scared in smushy places. Sometimes Andy puts a blanket over my head only because he knows how much I hate that. He holds it tight and laughs when I start feeling scared and try to get him off me, but he's too strong. And on elevators Andy always makes jokes like "Hey, scaredy-cat, I know this one's going to get stuck! We will be stuck in here for like days with nothing to eat, and we'll have to go to the bathroom right in here!" He keeps talking like that until Mommy tells him to stop, and then he makes faces like he's dying behind her back.

Daddy got stuck on the elevator at his office once and he wasn't scared, but other people next to him were. Daddy said it was funny because they were only stuck for a few minutes, so what did they even get scared about? But I don't think that's funny. I would get scared, too. Andy calls me a scaredy-cat all the time, and he's actually a little right about that. I get scared a lot about different things, especially at bedtime or in the middle of the night. It's stupid that it's like that. Sometimes I wish I could be more brave like Andy and Daddy. They're never scared of anything.

When I started thinking about what happened yesterday when the gunman came, I wanted to get up and get out of the closet, because my body started to feel exactly the same as yesterday with my heart beating fast. I was breathing too fast and it made me dizzy. But I couldn't get up for some reason. It was like my body was all hard and frozen from being so scared. I wished Daddy would come and open the closet door and find me, and that was the same as yesterday, too, when I was wishing that Daddy would come.

But Daddy and nobody else came, and I kept sitting there with my frozen body, listening for sounds. But it stayed very quiet. I put my hand in the pocket of my pants and took out the angel wing charm Miss Russell gave me, and I rubbed it in between my fingers. "Love and protection," I thought in my head. I started to feel better. My heart started to slow down and my breathing calmed down.

"No one is coming," I whispered, and it was strange that I was talking to myself and no one was here to hear it, not even Clancy. But it also felt good, like one part of me was talking to another part of me, and it helped me calm down. So I kept whispering: "There's nothing even scary in here. It's just Andy's closet, and it's not really that tight in here."

I unrolled Andy's sleeping bag and spread it out and sat on it criss-cross applesauce. I looked around and it was hard to see in the dark. There were only a lot of dusty fluffy things in the corners and some of Andy's socks but nothing else. It was like a secret space in the house that no one knew about except me. "Secret hideout," I whispered into the closet. "This is going to be my top secret hideout." I started to like sitting in the quiet and listening to my breathing: in— air up my nose—out through my mouth with a puff, in, out, slow now, because I wasn't really that scared anymore.

When I let myself think about yesterday, the scared feeling came back, so I tried not to let those thoughts float around in my brain anymore. "Get out of my brain, bad thoughts!" I pretended like there was a safe in the back of my head like the one Daddy has in his office where he keeps important papers so no one can steal them, and I pushed the bad thoughts into my brain safe. "Zip it, lock it, put it in your pocket."

I liked that I was in here and no one in the party knew where I was. I could come in here all the time now because Andy wasn't here anymore and he couldn't yell at me anymore and tell me to get out.

I started to think about how it was going to be without Andy—it was going to be better at home. There wouldn't be any more fighting, and I was going to be the only child in the family, so Mommy and Daddy could do a lot more stuff with just me. Like they could both come to my piano recitals and they could both stay for the whole time. That never happened before—because of Andy. At the spring recital, Daddy couldn't come because Andy had lacrosse practice, and at the summer one, right before school started, the whole family did come, Mommy, Daddy, and Andy, but before it was even my turn to play my song, "Für Elise," Mommy had to get up and leave with Andy because he was behaving bad.

After a while I had to pee, so I came back out of the closet and I went in the bathroom. Next I went into my room because I wanted to look for stuff to bring in my new hideout.

"I was looking for you, Zach."

I jumped because I didn't see Grandma standing in the door of my room and she surprised me. I didn't want Grandma to know about the hideout, so I made up a lie: "I was looking for my dump truck in Andy's room."

"I made you some dinner, OK, darling? Can you come downstairs?"

"Is the party done?" I asked.

"The . . . party? It wasn't a . . . Everyone went home, yes," Grandma said, and she looked at me funny.

"Is Mommy coming home for dinner?" If it was dinnertime, then Mommy stayed at the hospital the whole night last night and today all day, and that's a long time just to sleep.

"No," Grandma said, "she's not coming home yet. Maybe tomorrow. But I'll eat with you, all right?"

It wasn't all right. Daddy promised me yesterday that today we were going to see Mommy at the hospital, but we didn't because of the party, so Daddy said a lie, too.

[12]

Do Souls Have Faces?

AFTER DINNER WAS DONE, Grandma made me take a shower. Then she tucked me in for bedtime, and I was allowed to sleep in Daddy's bed again. I asked her about school: "Am I the only one who's staying home from school, because of what happened to Andy?"

Grandma was sitting on the side of the bed with her straight back. She wiped the hair on my forehead to the side. "No, darling," she said. "All the children are staying home. A terrible, terrible thing happened at your school yesterday. I imagine it will be a while until the school reopens. People will need time to heal."

"Grandma?"

"Yes, darling?"

"Is Andy still there, at the school?" I kept thinking about how Andy was lying there in the school, all by himself except for the other dead people. I was trying not to think about it all day, but now it was bedtime, and at bedtime it's harder to stop thinking about stuff, maybe because all you do is lie there, so all you can do is think.

Grandma made a sound like a cough with her throat, like something was stuck in it and she was trying to get it out. "Andy is not at the school anymore," she said, and she made the coughing sound a few more times. "Andy is up in heaven now with God. God is going to take care of him for us now."

"But how did he get up to heaven from the school? Did he get like zoomed up there?"

Grandma did a little smile with her red lipstick lips. "No. His body doesn't go up to heaven, only his soul, remember?"

I remembered that Mommy told me about that when Uncle Chip died. The body is still here on earth, but that's not the real person anymore, so it's OK that the body gets put in a casket and buried in a grave, because the important part of the person that is called the soul goes up to heaven. It goes up there right after you die. I wondered if all the souls of the people who died from the gunman went flying up when I was still in the school, hiding in the closet, and if someone saw them, maybe the gunman.

I don't know what a soul looks like. Mommy said it's all your feelings and thoughts and memories, and I thought maybe it looks like a bird or something with wings, like the wing on the charm Miss Russell gave me. I wondered if your soul still has your face when it goes up to heaven, because otherwise how do the people who love you who are already in heaven know it's your soul and find you so you're not lonely and you can be together?

After Grandma said good night and left Mommy and Daddy's room, I tried to think about Andy's soul up in heaven together with Uncle Chip's soul, but my brain kept switching to Andy's body in the school and the blood in the hallway and on the walls, and I couldn't get the bad thoughts to go into the brain safe.

Maybe the brain safe only worked in the hideout. I took Clancy with me and went in my room. I took my Buzz Lightyear flashlight from my nightstand drawer and went through the bathroom in Andy's room, trying to walk very quiet, because our floors are old wood, so they squeak when you walk on them, and I didn't want Daddy and Grandma downstairs to know I got out of bed. I flashed Buzz up to Andy's top bunk. Empty.

Then I went in Andy's closet and sat down on his sleeping bag. The flashlight made a little light circle in the dark closet, and I made zigzag patterns with the circle on the walls and shirts and jackets. I lay down on the sleeping bag and put my legs up against the wall, and that was comfy. I put Buzz down next to me and Clancy on my chest, and I crossed my hands under my head for a pillow.

Right away I felt like I wanted to whisper again: "OK, bad thoughts, go in the safe!" I thought about the bad thoughts like they were little people in my brain marching to where the safe was in my brain. Slam the door. "That's it. And don't come back out!"

It worked! I laid there like that for a while and thought about Mommy and about if she was coming home tomorrow. Then I got sleepy and went back in Daddy's bed.

Then, in the middle of the night, the gunman came back.

POP POP POP

I sat up and it was too dark. I couldn't see anything, I only heard the POP sounds in my ears.

POP POP POP

POP POP POP

Over and over again. Were they far away or close? I pressed my hands on my ears as hard as I could, but I could still hear them.

POP POP POP

I could hear sounds coming out of my mouth, but I should have been quiet so the gunman couldn't find me and shoot me.

NO NO NO

Screaming sounds were coming out of my mouth and I couldn't stop them. A hand touched me, and I didn't know where it came from, but then I heard Daddy's voice: "Zach, it's OK, it's OK." A light went on and I still made screaming sounds. I couldn't help it because the gunman was back. How did he get in our house? Now he was going to shoot us and we would have blood everywhere and be dead like Andy. Daddy said, "It's not real. You're having a bad dream," a lot of times and I stopped screaming. But I was still scared and my breathing went in and out too fast, and the POP sounds were still in my ears like an echo.

"You're fine. You're OK," Daddy said.

The next time I woke up it was morning and I didn't remember when I went back to sleep after I heard the POP sounds or when Daddy got up, because he wasn't on his side of the bed anymore.

I found him downstairs, sitting in the kitchen again, and he was staring in his coffee cup. He still didn't shave and his beard was getting longer. I went to him and sat on his lap, and I watched what Grandma and Aunt Mary were doing. They had our photo albums out and were taking out pictures, mostly of Andy and some of all of the family. They talked in quiet voices and wiped some tears off their faces, but sometimes they laughed a little about all the silly faces Andy was making in the pictures.

"What are you doing?" I asked. I didn't think Mommy was going to like that they were taking pictures out of the albums, because photo albums are special and you should wash your hands before you touch them, and you should turn the pages carefully so you don't make any wrinkles in the thin paper in between the pages.

"Oh . . . we need to pick out some pictures for the . . . ," Grandma said, and Aunt Mary interrupted her and said, "We just have to borrow a few of these. We'll put them back after. Hey, look at this one." Aunt Mary turned the photo album around and pointed at a picture. "Do you remember where this was?"

"On the cruise," I said. The picture had all of us in it—me, Mommy, Daddy, Andy, and also Uncle Chip and Aunt Mary and Grandma. We all had on the big hats, called sombreros, that we bought in the gift shop on the cruise ship. In the summer before I started kindergarten, we all went on a big cruise ship together, when Grandma turned seventy and we did a special family trip to celebrate. It was a lot of fun on the ship, it had a big pool right on top of the ship with water slides. There were a ton of restaurants where they had all kinds of different foods and they were open all day long, so you could just eat, eat, eat all the time. The ship made a lot of stops on different days in Mexico.

I looked at the picture next to the one Aunt Mary pointed at. It was also from the cruise, but it was just of me, Mommy, Daddy, and Andy. All four of us are laughing really hard in the picture, and it made me smile to think about why, because it was when they had a special Mexican party on the boat and they had a contest to see what family could eat the most spicy things. At first the foods we had to eat weren't very spicy, but then they gave us spicier ones and we still tried to eat them, even though our mouths were on fire and we had tears coming out of our eyes. We tried to drink lots of water, but that didn't help at all. In the picture, Mommy is laughing and she has her eyes squeezed shut tight. Daddy is looking at her from the side, laughing also, and me and Andy are sitting in front of them, holding up long red peppers. We didn't end up eating those, they were way too spicy.

"That was a fun time, wasn't it?" Aunt Mary said, and her voice sounded different. When I looked up to see why her voice sounded like that, she was still smiling, but she was also crying again.

"We should probably get going with these," Grandma said, and held up a stack of pictures. She picked up her bag from the counter to put them inside. Aunt Mary closed the album with the cruise pictures and ripped off a piece of paper towel to wipe off the tears from her face. Then she followed Grandma toward the kitchen door.

I leaned back against Daddy on the barstool.

"Daddy?" I said.

"Yes?" Daddy said behind me.

"Did the gunman come in our house last night?"

Grandma and Aunt Mary both turned back around when I said that.

"No, bud, you had a nightmare," Daddy said. "The gunman is not coming to our house. OK?" The way he said it sounded like I asked a stupid question, like *duh*.

"But what if he does come and shoots us like Andy?"

Grandma walked back toward us and she took my hands and held them tight. "Zach, the gunman can't hurt you anymore, or anyone else, because he's dead," she said. "I think it's important that you know that. There's no need to be afraid anymore. The police killed him."

Then I remembered the policeman at the church said that, I just forgot.

"He was a bad guy, right?" I asked.

"Yes, he was. He did a very bad thing," Grandma answered.

"Did the gunman's soul fly up to heaven, too? Will it try to hurt Andy's soul there?"

"Oh goodness, Zach, no! Heaven is for the souls of good people. The souls of bad people go somewhere else."

[13]

You Can't Be Here

I WAS IN MY BATHROOM brushing my teeth after breakfast when I heard voices from downstairs in the hallway. Daddy's voice and another voice, and at first I thought it was Grandma or Aunt Mary, and maybe they came back from where they went with the pictures. I heard Daddy say, "You can't be here. You . . . I'm sorry. . . ." I heard the woman's voice making crying sounds, or choking. I walked over to the stairs and tried not to make the floors squeak, because I wanted to see who Daddy said can't be here.

The woman's voice was from Ricky's mom. She was in the hallway by the front door, leaning with her back against it, and Daddy was standing right in front of her. Ricky's mom had both of her hands up, and Daddy was holding her wrists. She was crying and it made her whole face wet and the front of her shirt, or maybe that was from the rain. She had only a T-shirt on, and her arms looked very white and skinny.

"Jim. Please. Don't do this to me," Ricky's mom said. "Jim, please." She said that over and over, and I didn't know what she was asking Daddy not to do. Maybe she didn't want him to hold her wrists like that. "I am . . . completely alone." She did a big choking sound when she said that, and a big thing of snot came flinging out of her nose and it went all the way down to her mouth, and that was really gross.

Daddy let go of her wrists, and she wiped her nose with her arm, like she was a little kid. Then she started to slide down the front door kind of in slow motion, like she got too tired to stand up, and she sat down right in front of the door. She cried and cried. I could only hear it, not see it, because Daddy was standing in front of her.

"Nancy," Daddy said in a quiet voice, "I'm sorry, I really am. I wish I could . . ." Daddy didn't finish his sentence, and Ricky's mom didn't say anything back. All she did was sit there in front of our door and cry.

"Nancy," Daddy said again. "Please." He leaned forward and touched her cheek, and then I could see her again. "We both agreed that we needed to end . . . this. We both agreed that it's better this way, didn't we?"

Ricky's mom grabbed Daddy's hand with her hands and she put her face on his hand and her tears and snot were probably getting all over his hand, but he didn't take his hand back.

"Nancy, Zach is upstairs. And my mother and Mary will be back . . . soon. I'm sorry. Please, you have to go," Daddy said.

"No," Ricky's mom said, and she looked up at Daddy. "No, I have to be with you. I need you. How am I supposed to . . . ?" And she started to cry harder and louder, but she kept staring at Daddy. "He's dead," she said, and she stretched out the word like *deeeeeeeead*. "Ricky, oh my God. Ricky, my . . . what am I going to do? What am I supposed to doooooooo?"

Ricky died from the gunman like Andy, but Ricky's mom wasn't in the hospital because of the shock like Mommy. She came here, in our house, and she said she had to be with Daddy and was holding on to his hand like it belonged to her. I didn't like that and I didn't know why he let her do that.

I wanted her to let go of Daddy's hand, so I started to go down the stairs. When Daddy heard my steps, he pulled his hand away and turned around to me fast. Ricky's mom tried to stand up and banged her head against the door handle.

"Zach!" Daddy said, and then he stared at me like he thought I was going to say something, but I didn't. "Nancy . . . Mrs. Brooks is here," Daddy said like I was blind or something, because she was standing right there.

I stared at Daddy and Ricky's mom. Ricky's mom's face was very white, like the skin on her arms except there was a lot of red around her eyes, and even inside her eyes it was red instead of the white. Her eyes were very blue, like the bluest eyes I've ever seen. Her long hair was wet and it was stuck to her face and her neck. Through her wet T-shirt I could see two pointy circles from her boobs, and I couldn't look away from them.

"I . . . I'm going," she said, and turned around and grabbed the door handle, but she couldn't open the door because she didn't know you have to press it all the way down hard.

"Here . . . I'll . . ." Daddy stretched his hand out to open the door for her, and his arm touched against her pointy boob circles. He tried to open the door, but Ricky's mom was standing right in front of it, so they both had to move backward and they bumped into each other. When Daddy got the door opened, Ricky's mom walked down the front steps from our porch. I walked closer to the door to stand next to Daddy. We watched how Ricky's mom took little steps like the walkway was slippery from the rain and it was hard for her to walk on it. Then she turned on the sidewalk and walked down our road toward where her house is, and she didn't turn around once.

14

Where Did You Go?

MOMMY GOT CHANGED into a different person at the hospital. She came home after three sleeps and she looked different and acted different, too. Mommy always looks pretty, even in the mornings when she first wakes up. She has long brown hair that's very straight and shiny, and it's the same color as mine. We also have the same eyes—hazel. That's like a few colors mixed together, like a brownish green, and I like that me and Mommy are the only ones in the family who have the same hair color and eyes. Mommy says I have the same temperament as her, too, that means when you act the same, and I think she's right about that. We both don't like when there's all the fighting. I know that because sometimes when Mommy has a fight with Andy or Daddy she cries, so I know it makes her sad. Mommy says we're both people pleasers—that's when you want other people around you to feel good.

With Andy, a lot of people say he's the perfect mix in between Mommy and Daddy, but I think he looks like Daddy. Same hair color—blond—and same tallness, they're both really good at sports, and I think they also have the same temperament, because Daddy can get the bad temper sometimes, too, and that's probably why Andy has it.

When Mommy came home from the hospital, her hair was all mixed up in the back and not straight and shiny. She walked in the house, and Mimi walked next to her. It looked like she had to hold Mommy up or she was going to fall down. Mommy walked very slow like she was very tired, even though Daddy said all she did was sleep at the hospital. So that's why we couldn't go see her, because she wouldn't be awake anyway.

Before Mimi brought Mommy in the house, Daddy said I had to give her some space and I wasn't allowed to bother her right away and I thought that that wasn't fair because I didn't see her for three sleeps and I really missed her. But when she came in and looked all changed, I felt shy around her, so I did what Daddy said—gave her space.

Mommy had the same clothes on from when we went to the hospital to find Andy, and they didn't look pretty. Usually Mommy has on pretty clothes, even when she's not doing anything special. The really fancy clothes from her old job she doesn't wear anymore, except when her and Daddy have date night. I like to help her pick out her outfit from the fancy clothes section in her closet, and Mommy says I have good taste. Her old job was in the city, like Daddy's, but in a different office where she made commercials for TV, but she stopped working there after she had me and Andy. Now her job is being a mom and doing laundry and cooking dinner and stuff.

Mimi helped Mommy sit down on the couch, and it looked like Mommy was a little kid who doesn't know how to do stuff on her own. It made me feel sad that Mommy was looking like that with her hair all mixed up and acting like a little kid, so I decided to go sit next to her, even though I still had my shy feeling, too. I didn't look at Daddy because he was probably going to get mad that I wasn't giving Mommy her space.

When I sat down, Mommy turned her head very slowly and looked at me, and maybe she didn't see me earlier, when she first came in, because now she looked surprised. She pulled me on her lap and put her face in my neck. Her chest moved like she was crying, and I could feel her hot, fast breaths on my neck. The breaths tickled, but I didn't move. I let Mommy hug me tight, even though she smelled different, like the hand sanitizer we have at school.

I saw a Band-Aid on the inside of Mommy's elbow where she had the see-through string going in at the hospital, and I wanted to ask her if it hurt. I said, "Mommy?" and Mommy took her face out of my neck and then I was mad at myself that I did that because now my neck felt cold. Mommy looked at me, but her eyes weren't looking at my eyes, but sort of over them, maybe at my forehead. "Mommy?" I said again, and this time I put both of my hands on her face and put my face close to hers. It was like she was still sleeping, but with her eyes opened, and I wanted to wake her up gently. But then Mommy put her arms around her belly all of a sudden and leaned backward on the couch and made a long sound like *Ooooohhhhh!*

I let go of her face and I scooched off her lap because the sound scared me and it was probably my fault she was making it, because I didn't give her her space.

"Honey, give Mommy some time, OK?" Mimi said with a very quiet voice, and she put her hand on my arm. "She needs to rest."

"Come on, bud, let's leave Mommy for a bit and let her settle in," Daddy said, and he came over to the couch to take my hand and pull me off the couch. I snatched my arm away and ran upstairs. I stood in my room for a while and I was breathing fast. I was listening if Daddy was coming up behind me, but he didn't come. It gave me a mad feeling that I was upstairs all by myself and all the grown-ups were downstairs and no one even cared about that. My eyes got the tingly feeling like right before tears come out. I didn't want to start crying, so I did the squeeze-away trick fast, and right away the tingling feeling went away and the tears got stopped from coming out.

I like having my own peace in my room, but now I didn't have a good feeling. It was a lonely feeling. Lonely is not the same thing as alone. Me and Mommy noticed that together at bedtime one day. I called her back in my room and told her I was feeling alone, but Mommy said I wasn't alone because she was right downstairs, so we realized my feeling was lonely, not alone. Lonely is when you want to be with someone instead, and it's a sad feeling. Alone doesn't have to be bad, because you can feel good when you're alone. We decided we both like that sometimes, to be alone. My room used to be for alone, not lonely.

I decided to go in the hideout, because there I was alone but not lonely for some reason. It was starting to get cozy inside the hideout. I had my Buzz flashlight, and I brought in some pillows from the closet in the hallway that has a bunch of extra blankets and pillows, and no one ever uses them, so no one was going to notice that I took them. And Miss Russell's charm, I left that in the corner of the hideout. Every time I came inside, I picked it up and rubbed the wing between my fingers a few times, and I thought it was really nice that Miss Russell gave me her favorite charm, because it made me feel good when I rubbed it. Of course, Clancy was there, too. I moved him in between the hideout and the bed for sleeping, back and forth. I picked him up and sat down on the sleeping bag with a pillow in my back against the wall and started chewing Clancy's ear, the right one, not the left, because I already chewed the left too much, and Mommy says it's going to fall off any day now.

Andy always tries to take Clancy from me to throw him in the garbage because he says he stinks so bad. I try to find different hiding places for Clancy so Andy can't take him from me, and then sometimes at bedtime I forget where I left him and we have to look all over for him so I can go to sleep. I thought about how now I don't have to hide Clancy anymore, and he is going to be safe now, safe from Andy.

I wondered how Grandma could know that Andy went to heaven, or his soul, because she said only good people go to heaven. Andy wasn't really a good person a lot of times. He was mostly trying to be mean to me and make Mommy upset. He did the same things over and over again that made her upset, so it must have been on purpose, because otherwise why didn't he just stop it?

Now Andy couldn't be mean to me anymore and he couldn't make Mommy upset anymore. Right now Mommy was sad and in shock because Andy died from the gunman. But after she started to feel better from that she wouldn't have to be upset all the time anymore.

Uncle Chip definitely went to heaven, I knew that, because he was always nice to everyone. But Andy? Grandma said the souls of bad people went somewhere else, and I didn't know where, but if Andy went there instead of heaven, then he would be with all the bad guys now, like the gunman, and that would probably be very scary. I closed my eyes and tried to find a picture of Andy in my brain. I could see his face for a short while, but it was hard to get it to hold still. "Did you go up to heaven, or where did you go?" my brain said to Andy's face. Andy's face disappeared. "Anyway, I hope you did."

15

Walking Blind

CAN I HAVE SCREEN TIME?" I put my cereal bowl in the sink. "Can I watch a show?"

"Hmmhmm . . ." Daddy didn't look up from his phone, and that sounded like it was a yes, at least not a no, so I went in the family room and turned on the TV. The news came on right away, and the sound was still all the way down. I was going to switch to on demand to see if there was a new *Phineas and Ferb*, but then a picture came on the news, and on top of the picture there were words that said "McKinley Killer." I was like frozen and couldn't move at all. I stared and stared because the picture was of Charlie's son.

I knew it was Charlie's son right away. I recognized him from Charlie's thirty-years party last year in school. Charlie's wife, her name is Mary like my aunt, and son, I didn't know his name, came to the party. His wife was really friendly and called us "Charlie's angels" and said we were so cute, and no wonder Charlie talked about us all the time. Charlie's son didn't say anything at the party. He just stood there next to Charlie and looked at us in a mean way, like he was mad. His face looked exactly the same as Charlie's, only not so old. They looked the same except that his son didn't smile and Charlie always smiles. Charlie's mouth went up on the sides and his son's mouth went down, they were the same and opposites.

Charlie's son didn't even smile when Mommy talked to him. She said she couldn't believe the size of him, and did he remember that she babysat him when she was done with college and he was three or four then? He didn't smile and he didn't say anything back. Charlie's wife answered instead and said of course he remembered, and that Mommy was his favorite babysitter, right?

I wanted to hear what the news was saying about Charlie's son, but I didn't want to turn up the sound because I didn't want Daddy to know I was watching the news and tell me to turn it off. So I kept looking at the news without the sound. The picture stayed up for a long time, and then instead of "McKinley Killer" it said "Charles Ranalez Jr.," so that must be his name, because Charlie's last name is Ranalez. That's what his name tag says: CHARLIE RANALEZ. Then the picture changed and a new one came on. It was a picture of Charlie, smiling, and it looked like the same picture that was on the big screen in the auditorium when we had his party.

I really wanted to hear what they were saying about Charlie, so I turned the volume up a tiny bit. The picture of Charlie went away, and a man from the news came on with a microphone. He was standing in front of my school and was talking to a woman I saw at pickup before, I think she's Enrique's grandma.

"What was your reaction when you found out that the shooter was Charles Ranalez Jr., son of McKinley's very own security guard, Charlie Ranalez?" the newsman said into the microphone, and then he pointed the microphone at Enrique's grandma's mouth.

"I just couldn't believe it. No one can believe it," Enrique's grandma said, and she looked very sad and kept shaking her head no. "I mean, Charlie really is the sweetest guy, you know, and we all love him to death. I mean, not to death . . . I shouldn't have said it like that. But he loved the kids, you know, like they were his own. He's seen generations grow up at this school. My son went here and now my grandson. . . . Charlie was always friendly and helpful. . . . I just can't believe his son could have done such a thing."

The newsman looked right at me through the TV and said, "Few can appreciate the irony that the school's very own security guard's son is responsible for killing fifteen children and four staff in cold blood, before being shot and killed himself by the police. Eyewitnesses tell us his father pleaded with his son to stop shooting, but to no avail. . . ."

"Oh!" It was like a tiny little mouse sound, and it made me get goose bumps, because all I did was stare at the TV, and then all of a sudden that sound was right behind me. I turned around and I found out the sound came from Mommy's mouth. Earlier she wasn't downstairs, but now she was standing behind the couch where I was sitting, and she was also staring at the TV.

Daddy came in from the kitchen and snatched the remote out of my hand and turned the TV off. "What the hell are you doing, Zach?" Daddy was looking at me like he was really mad.

"You said I could watch TV." My voice sounded like I was about to start crying.

Mommy didn't say anything, she just stared at the TV even though nothing was on anymore, but it looked like she didn't notice that.

"Daddy? Did you know Charlie's son was the gunman? In the news they said—"

"Not. Now. Zach."

I could feel Daddy's breath in my face because he got so close to me. He made his eyes very small and he yelled those words at me, but he didn't open his teeth when he yelled, so it wasn't loud yelling, but scary yelling, and I got all hot and my stomach felt bad.

In New York City I saw a blind person once, a man, and I didn't know he was blind at first, and he had a really cute dog. I asked Mommy if I could pet him, and Mommy said no, because it's a special helper dog and you're not allowed to pet helper dogs, they have to help blind or sick people, and if you pet them, then they can't do their job. And I thought it was really cool that the dog could tell the blind man where to go, and the man followed the dog everywhere, even across the street. The streets in New York City are really busy and dangerous, and I'm not allowed to cross without holding hands.

The way Mommy walked back to the kitchen with Daddy looked like how the blind man walked with the helper dog, like Daddy was the dog and Mommy couldn't see anything, so Daddy had to lead the way. I waited until tears were definitely not coming in my eyes anymore, and then I went in the kitchen after them. Only Daddy was there.

"Where's Mommy?" I asked.

"Upstairs. I had to give her medicine to calm her down. She was really upset. She's going to sleep now." I could tell Daddy was still mad at me, and that made new tears almost come out of my eyes.

"I'm sorry, Daddy. I was going to watch a show and then the news was on, and I—" I wasn't finished talking yet, but Daddy started talking anyway.

"You shouldn't be watching the news. It's not for you, you know that. And it's not helpful for Mommy to be seeing these things. She just came home from the hospital, and at this rate we will have to take her right back. You don't want that, do you?"

I didn't want that, but I couldn't say anything, so I just shook my head no. I didn't want Mommy to go back to the hospital. I wanted the shock to be over so she could be like her normal self, not walking like a blind person or only sleeping all the time. I kept shaking my head no, and I didn't stop shaking it until Daddy said, "OK, take it easy, Zach. This is hard for all of us, OK? Can you please find something to do for a while? Mimi will be back later, so then you guys can do something, OK?"

"OK. But, Daddy? Did Charlie get hurt from his son?"

"What? No, Charlie didn't get hurt at all." The way Daddy said that it sounded like he was mad about that.

I went upstairs and saw the door to Mommy and Daddy's room was open, so I went to the door to see if Mommy was OK. She was in her bed, but she wasn't sleeping, she was lying on her side with her eyes open. When she saw me, she took out her arms from under the covers and stretched them out to me and I went over to her and lay down next to her. Mommy held me tight. We lay there for a long time and we didn't talk. It felt good with just me and Mommy, and it was quiet. All I heard was Mommy's breathing.

I turned around a little bit to see her face and I wanted to say sorry

I made her upset, but her eyes were closed now. I watched her face for a little while. I could feel her chest go up and down, and I didn't move at all. Then I whispered, "I'm sorry, Mommy," and I got out of her tight hug and off her bed and tippy-toed back away from the bed and out of the room. The door made a little squeaky sound. I looked back at Mommy, but she kept sleeping.

Then all I could think about was getting to my hideout. I closed the closet door all the way and found the flashlight in the dark and turned it on. I picked up Clancy and chewed his ear, and I didn't stop chewing for a long time. Clancy got wet all over from my spit.

[16]

Red Juice Spill

I WAS SUPPOSED TO SLEEP in my bed because now Mommy was home, but I got scared again at bedtime, and then Mommy told Daddy to put my mattress next to their bed on the floor. She lay down in her bed, and I lay down on the mattress and Mommy held my hand, and that was good for me to go to sleep like that. We forgot to do our song, and when I remembered, it looked like Mommy was sleeping, and I didn't want to wake her up. So I sang it very quiet by myself again, for me and Clancy.

I woke up the next morning because I was shivering. I noticed my whole mattress was really cold and wet all over, and my PJ pants were wet and my PJ shirt on one side and I didn't get why everything was wet. But then I knew why: I peed when I was asleep! I peed in my bed like a baby!

I never ever peed in my bed before, except when I was three and I stopped wearing diapers at bedtime. Mommy said I only had a couple of accidents then. Mommy used to wake me up in the middle of the night and carry me to the bathroom. She told me I peed in the toilet when I was still asleep, and the next day I didn't even remember it. But now I always wake up and go to the bathroom by myself.

My cousin Jonas pees in the bed all the time, he's six, too, and he's not my real cousin—he's the son of Aunt Mary's sister, so he's kind of my cousin. One time he had a sleepover at our house, and he slept on an air mattress next to my bed. He peed all over the mattress, and

Andy made fun of him and said only babies pee in the bed. I made fun of him a little, too, but then I felt bad because Mommy said it wasn't his fault, and we shouldn't tease him about it. He probably peed in his bed because he was scared and missed his mom, and he was probably ashamed.

And now I peed in my bed like Jonas. When I was thinking about it my face got really hot, and I know that meant it was getting red from being embarrassed, and that happens to me a lot of times. In school it happens all the time, like when Miss Russell talks to me and I didn't know she was going to, so it's like a surprise moment, and everyone looks at me when I have to answer. When I know I'm going to say something and I have time to think about what I want to say first and I'm sure I know the right answer, then it's fine. But when it's a surprise, I turn red and I call it the red juice spill, because it's like a cup of red juice spills up my neck and then up my face. I try to hide my face when that happens and wait until it doesn't feel hot anymore, and then I know the red juice spilled back down my neck.

Red-hot juice. Sometimes it leaves red dots on my neck for a while after. It spills back down fast most of the time, but not if someone says something about it or makes fun of me. Like Andy knows I hate it when someone talks about how my face looks red, so of course he loves to say it really loud so everyone can hear it, and he thinks it's so funny. Then it takes forever for it to go away.

I thought about what to do because I didn't want anyone to know I peed in the bed. I peeked up at Mommy and Daddy's bed and I only saw Mommy's back, and she didn't move so she was still sleeping, and Daddy wasn't there in the bed. I got up really fast and went in my room and took my PJs off, and that was gross because I was touching my own pee. I didn't want to put the wet PJs in the hamper because the other clothes would get wet, too, so I put them in the bathtub behind the shower curtain instead. I thought about how the mattress was still really wet, but maybe it was going to dry during the day?

I got dressed and then I sat on my bed for a little while and waited for the hot juice feeling to go away. I noticed my trucks. They were still in front of my bookshelf and this whole time I didn't even play with them one time, and they were still all mixed up and not in a row. It was weird that I was just leaving them there like that.

I got up and checked in the bathroom mirror that no red dots were left on my neck. I went in Andy's room to look at his top bunk and then I went downstairs. No one was in the kitchen, and Daddy was in his office on the phone. His office has a glass door, and when he saw me through it, he did a tired smile and pointed at the phone. I went in the kitchen and I sat down on the barstool. I was hungry, but no one was going to make me breakfast.

I noticed the iPad on the counter and decided to play my fire truck parking game. That's my favorite game on the iPad. It's a parking simulator where you have to try to park a huge fire truck, and it's hard because you can't bump into other cars or the walls of the firehouse, but I'm really good at it. I swiped the iPad and Daddy's newspaper came on.

Daddy always reads the newspaper on the iPad now or on his phone. He used to get the real newspaper and it came rolled up in a blue bag and got left on our walkway. It was my job in the mornings to get it for him—only on the weekends, because on workdays he took it with him to work before I got up. But then he stopped getting the newspaper in the blue bag and started reading it on the iPad instead, and that always takes a long time. I wished he was still getting it delivered so I could play on the iPad.

Daddy's newspaper came on and right away I saw it was about the gunman, Charlie's son. I scrolled down and there was the same picture of him I saw on TV yesterday. I felt like I shouldn't be looking at it anymore, because Daddy would get mad at me again. But Daddy was on the phone in his office, and Mommy was still sleeping, and I didn't know where Mimi was, so no one would know. I started to read what the news said about Charlie's son. In big fat letters it said "Killer's Motive," and underneath in smaller but still fat letters it said, "The act of a madman or a troubled child's cry for his father's attention?" and then a lot of smaller, not-fat words under that.

It was hard to read, but I understood some things, like that Charlie's son brought four guns to McKinley to shoot people, and at his house, Charlie's house, the police found more guns, and they didn't know yet where he bought them, it said.

There were pictures of the guns when I scrolled down, and a few of them looked like regular guns, like the ones policemen have on their belts, and some looked big and long in the front, they looked like army guns. Under the pictures it said what the guns were called, and they had cool names. Under the regular-looking guns it said ".45 caliber Smith & Wesson M&P pistol" and "Glock 19 9mm semi-automatic handgun," and under the army-looking guns it said "semi-automatic Smith & Wesson M&P15" and "Remington 870 12-gauge shotgun." I whispered the names of the guns when I tried to read them, but they were hard to say.

I looked at the pictures for a long time, and my heart was beating fast because guns are dangerous, I know that, but they're a little exciting, too, except I had to think about how Charlie's son used these guns to kill Andy, and I wondered which gun it was that the bullet came out of that killed Andy. And I wondered how Charlie's son brought four guns to the school, and how do you even use four guns at the same time? It must have hurt really bad when the bullet went in Andy's body, and I still didn't know where on his body it went in, and then he died from it.

Under the pictures of the guns it said Charlie's son put a message on Facebook when he was on his way to McKinley. I know Facebook from Mommy's phone. She goes on it a lot to see what her friends are posting, and she shows me pictures and funny videos on it. She posts pictures, too, mostly of me and Andy at sports and stuff like that. Daddy doesn't like Facebook and doesn't go on it and once Mommy and Daddy had a fight about it because Daddy said Mommy shouldn't post pictures of us for the whole world to see, and Mommy said, "Well, that's just a little ironic considering how much you like to show off."

This was the message Charlie's son put on Facebook:

Charlie's angels, today is the day I'm coming for you. See you soon, Dad! Pray for me.

That's what Charlie's wife called us at the party, "Charlie's angels."

The alarm box behind me said "Front door!" in the robot lady voice, and I almost dropped the iPad. I pressed the button on the top fast to turn it off, and I put it away. My heart was beating at super speed and my face felt like it was having the red juice spill. Mimi came in with bags from the food store, and I thought she was going to notice right away, but she didn't.

"Good morning, sweetie" was all she said, and I couldn't say anything back, only make a "Mmmmm" sound.

Mimi unpacked the bags and I watched her take out milk and eggs and bananas, and maybe she forgot that no one in our family likes bananas except Andy. Andy loves bananas, but now he wasn't here to eat them, so who was going to eat all the bananas Mimi got from the store? The bananas sat there on the counter, and I couldn't stop looking at them. In my head I was saying in a really loud voice, "Who's going to eat all those stupid bananas?" I was like screaming it in my head: "Stupid, gross bananas, they're all mushy inside!" And I grabbed them and threw them in the garbage. It felt good to do that. I walked out of the kitchen and didn't even listen to Mimi, who was calling: "Zach, honey, what was that for?"

17

Feelings Pages

I NEVER KNEW YOU COULD FEEL MORE than one feeling inside of you at the same time.

Especially feelings that are opposites. I know you can feel excited, but when you do what made you excited, the excited feeling goes away and you feel happy because it was fun. Or sad because it's over already, like right after everyone leaves from your birthday party. But more than one feeling at the same time, right next to each other or on top of each other and all mixed up inside you? I never knew that could happen.

But now it happened to me, and it was hard because when you're happy, you know you want to laugh or smile at least, and when you're mad or sad, you want to yell or cry, but when you feel all of those together, then you don't know what you want to do. I walked around the house and kind of went this way and that way, upstairs and downstairs, and it was like the inside of me couldn't settle down, so the outside of me couldn't settle down either.

I walked past the family calendar in the kitchen, and it made me stop. It still had all the activities on it from last week. Daddy's row is at the top, then Mommy's, then Andy's, and my row is at the bottom, because it goes by age and I'm the youngest. The names were on the calendar in permanent marker, they don't get erased when Mommy erases everything on Sundays to write down the activities for the next week. So now Andy's row was going to be empty, there was going to be an empty row between mine and Mommy's, but his name would still be there, so he was still part of our family, except not really.

I stared at Andy's row and what he was supposed to do last week, and he only got to Tuesday (lacrosse) because he died on Wednesday. He didn't get to do soccer on Thursday. For Friday it said "lacrosse game, 7 p.m." in his row. I wondered if Andy's team still had the game without him there on Friday. Maybe they got one of the players who normally stands on the side of the field and he played instead of Andy, and it was like Andy wasn't even missing and nothing changed. I started to feel mad about that, that they had their game anyway. Although Andy plays really good and scores a lot of goals, so maybe they didn't win without Andy.

Today was Tuesday and on Tuesdays I have art at school. I love art and I'm a really good artist. I was this close to finishing my portrait of Frida Kahlo, and it was starting to look good, like it's one of her own portraits. Frida Kahlo was a famous artist from Mexico we learned about in school. She painted a lot of colorful pictures of herself, and in them she has really big eyebrows, they meet in the middle, so it's like one long eyebrow, and she has a mustache, but she's a woman. I like to use a lot of different colors, too, when I paint. I was sad I couldn't go to art today, but I was happy, too, that there was no school. Sad and happy. See? That's opposites in feelings.

Frida Kahlo died a long time ago, and she wasn't old when she died, but she was really sick. I didn't know what type of sick, maybe cancer like Uncle Chip. She painted all the time because of her sickness and because she was lonely in her life. Painting helped her with her feelings. Our art teacher, Mrs. R, told us that. She said art is always about expressing your feelings and it's a good way to deal with feelings. Thinking about what Mrs. R said made me decide to do that, too: make art to deal with my feelings.

I went upstairs and got out my big bag of paints. I got my painting paper, too, and laid it out in my room. Then I sat there for a while, and I didn't know how you make art to deal with your feelings. Maybe paint a picture of myself, like Frida Kahlo. I got a cup of water from the kitchen, and Mimi made me promise I wasn't going to make any messes painting, and I wondered if Frida Kahlo had to try not to make any messes when she was painting, too.

I dipped my paintbrush into red, which is my favorite color, and I moved the brush up and down on the paper, so it wasn't going to be a picture of myself, but something else my hand decided to make, and I didn't know yet what it was going to be. A line up and a line next to it down, and then up and down again, like a long zigzag snake. The red started out really red when I still had a lot of paint on the brush, and then it got like thinner when I used up all the paint, and in the end it looked like light pink. The way the snake-line looked on the paper made me think about the red juice spill on my face after I peed on the mattress.

So red looks like an embarrassed feeling. Maybe I could pick one color for all the opposite feelings that were inside me and paint a lot of pieces of paper with only one feeling-color, and then the feelings would be separate and not all mixed up together, and that would help.

Red—embarrassed. Put that paper over to the side.

I thought about what feeling was next. Sad. Sad was everywhere inside our house, especially where Mommy was. Mommy was so sad, and you could feel it when you got close to her. The closer you went to her, the more you could feel the sad feeling. Mommy cried and cried all the time, and mostly she lay in her bed, and she had big red circles around her eyes from all the crying. I looked at all my paint colors. Sad could be gray. Gray like the sky outside and like the rain clouds. I washed my paintbrush in my water glass, and no water splashed on the carpet, and I painted gray all over a new piece of paper.

Sad piece of paper, next to the embarrassed piece of paper.

Scared. I was having a lot of scared feelings now all the time. Definitely black. That's how everything looked in the closet at school, black, almost no light to see the other colors. And everything is black at night when I wake up and think the gunman is coming back, except it's always just a dream. I made a paper black, and all black really did look scary.

I had to find a color for mad, too. Mad/angry. That's a feeling you have to use your words for, Mommy says, not your hands, like for hitting. "I'm mad at the gunman," I said. I thought mad/angry had to be green. Green because of the Hulk. The Hulk starts out like a regular person with beige skin, but when he gets mad he turns green all over, even his face. When the Hulk gets mad, he gets really mad. And he gets bigger with muscles all over, and he gets super strong. And green all over for some reason. So the color green reminds me of mad/angry, and I made a green page and put it next to the other feelings pages.

OK, so far:

Red—Embarrassed
Gray—Sad
Black—Scared
Green—Mad/Angry

And what color is for lonely? I thought that lonely had to be like a see-through color, so no color at all, because when you're lonely it's like you're invisible from other people, but not invisible in a good way like a superhero, but in a sad way. But the piece of paper is white, so how do you make a see-through color on a white paper? Then I had an idea for that. I got out my scissors and cut out the middle of the paper, so there was like a picture frame around a rectangle of see-through nothingness in the middle. Lonely—see-through.

I thought I was also feeling happy. I felt happy that I didn't die from the gunman. And I was a little happy because Andy wasn't here anymore to be mean to me, and I could have my secret hideout in Andy's closet now, and he couldn't tell me to get out. In the hideout I felt good/happy. Now it was a little happy feeling, it was just starting out, but when Mommy was going to feel better from the shock and her sadness, and the bad feelings were going to go away—mad, scared, and lonely—then it was going to be a bigger happy feeling. Me and Mommy and Daddy could be together with no fighting and we could have fun.

What color is for happy? Yellow. Yellow like the sun in the sky. A warm yellow sun in a pretty blue sky in the summertime, not the gray-sad sky we had right now.

Red—Embarrassed
Gray—Sad
Black—Scared
Green—Mad/Angry
Lonely—See-Through
Yellow—Happy

I waited for my feelings pages to dry, and then I went and got tape from the kitchen and hung them up on the wall inside my hideout. That was a good spot for them. I could lie down on Andy's sleeping bag and look at the feelings. Now they were separated and that made it easier to think about them.

18

Real-Life Bad Dream

THE GUNMAN CAME and real life went away, and now it was like we were in a new fake life. I was there, Daddy was there and Mommy, and Mimi was staying with us in the guest room so she could take care of Mommy, and Grandma and Aunt Mary came over every day, and that's how you know it was different, because usually they're not all at our house all the time.

Outside of our house it looked like everything else stayed normal and the same. When I looked out of my window, I noticed that real life was still there on our street, and it looked like before. Mr. Johnson was still taking Otto for walks around the neighborhood, and the garbage truck still came, and the mailman still brought the mail in the afternoon at four, always at the exact same time almost. All the people outside our house did the things they always do, and I wondered if they even knew that inside our house everything was changed.

The only thing from the outside that matched the inside of our house was the rain. It rained and rained, and it was like it was never stopping, like Mommy cried and cried and she was never stopping.

All the same stuff was still on TV, and they were still talking about the same stuff in the commercials, like how awesome Froot Loops are, like everything was how it always was and it still mattered. I thought that maybe watching my normal shows would make it so that it didn't feel like this fake new life anymore, but now the jokes on *Phineas and*

Ferb didn't sound funny to me anymore, and even when there was a funny one, I didn't laugh. Because mostly everything inside me felt like the opposite of laughing.

I started to pretend like I was in a bad dream and that I was watching myself walk around and do stuff in the dream, because this was not how I wanted real life to be like. I didn't want Mommy to always lie in bed and cry. I didn't want to keep walking in Andy's room in the mornings to check the top bunk, just in case. Every morning I did that, I couldn't help it. Right before I looked up I thought, "What if he's in his bed and it all wasn't real? What if he was playing a stupid joke on us and he will sit in his bed and laugh at me because I thought he actually died?" Because it was like POW!—like someone put his fist in my stomach every time I saw his top bunk was empty.

I didn't want to keep peeing on the mattress. Last night was the second time it happened, and that's two nights in a row of peeing in my sleep. Mommy found out and had to get the wet PJs from the bathtub and the wet sheets off the mattress and wash them. She didn't say anything about it, but I got embarrassed anyway.

We didn't go outside. It was like the inside and the outside were different worlds and we had to keep them separate. Even Daddy didn't go to work, but instead he kept going inside his office and closing the glass door behind him. I didn't know why he went in there, because it didn't look like he was doing work. He just sat there and stared at the computer. Or he put his elbows on the desk and his face in his hands.

After breakfast today I looked at the outside world through my window and I wished I could be on that side, where real life was still there. At first I just saw the rain and I watched the circles the raindrops were making in the puddles on the sidewalk. But then I noticed someone was standing on the other side of the road, across from our house.

It was Ricky's mom. She was wearing only a T-shirt again, and she didn't even have an umbrella. She stood there in the rain like she didn't even feel it, but she looked wet all over, and she was staring right at our house. It was weird, she was staring and not moving and not walking across the road to come inside. Then all of a sudden I saw Daddy walking across the street, also no umbrella and getting wet from the rain. He grabbed Ricky's mom's arm and turned her and they walked away down the road.

After a little while Daddy came back, but without Ricky's mom. I went downstairs and asked him where he went, and he looked at me funny and said he had to go for a walk to clear his head.

In all the days after the gunman came—and that was one week ago, I checked on the calendar in the kitchen—more people came to visit and brought more and more food even though the fridge in the kitchen and the one in the basement were full with food already. Today, in the afternoon, Mr. Stanley from my school came. Mr. Stanley's really nice. He's only been at McKinley since when I started first grade. I like him better than Mr. Ceccarelli, who was the old assistant principal. He was mean sometimes, and he didn't give us a lot of stars, even when we were acting good and respectful, so we never got to have PJ day in kindergarten because of him. Mr. Stanley always makes jokes and pretends like he got lost in the hallway and doesn't know which way to go, because he's still new, and he gives us stars all the time.

First grade probably has enough stars for PJ day by now, because we need two thousand stars, and the week before the gunman came we had one thousand eight hundred, so by now maybe they have two thousand. Maybe they would have PJ day without me because I was still not going to school, and that wouldn't be fair, because I earned a ton of the stars for behaving and being respectful.

Mr. Stanley didn't make any jokes when he came today. But he smiled at me and he bent all the way down to me—Mr. Stanley is very tall, that's why a lot of kids at school call him Tall Stanley, instead of Flat Stanley—and gave me a hug. I liked it when he hugged me, and normally I don't like people hugging me. I wanted to ask Mr. Stanley about PJ day, but he went in the living room with Mommy and Daddy, and I wasn't allowed to go in with them.

Mimi said I should stay in the kitchen with her, but I really wanted to know what Mr. Stanley was talking about to Mommy and Daddy. So I asked Mimi if I could go upstairs, and she said yes, but then I didn't really go upstairs. I sat down on the stairs instead and I tried to spy on Mr. Stanley and Mommy and Daddy. It was hard to hear because they were talking so quiet and I wished I could go closer, but then I was going to get busted spying, so I tried to turn on my sonic hearing super sense.

". . . I wanted to let you know that is a resource readily available to all affected families." That was Mr. Stanley talking. "And not just affected families—I mean, everyone was affected obviously, all the children who were at the school and had to live through that . . . terrifying experience. But for Zach—he lived through it himself AND lost his brother . . . I can't imagine . . . he must be struggling."

Then Mommy said something, but I couldn't hear, and Mr. Stanley said, "Yes. Well, every child responds differently, of course. And the signs of any post-traumatic complications don't necessarily have to manifest themselves right away, I believe."

Mommy said something again, and it was too quiet again, so I moved down one step to hear if Mommy was saying something about me. "He is having nightmares, but that's probably normal. . . ." I felt the red juice spill starting to happen, because I didn't want Mommy to tell Mr. Stanley about how I wasn't sleeping in my own bed.

"Well, thank you for letting us know. We do also have a very good family therapist, Andy's . . . so that's always an option, too," Daddy said.

"That's great, very good," Mr. Stanley said, and then it sounded like they were going to be done talking soon and come out of the living room, so I went upstairs fast before they could see me.

After Mr. Stanley left, Mommy got really tired and lay down on her bed again. I lay down with her, Mommy wanted me to, and she held me really tight and said, "Zach, my little, sweet Zachie," and "What are we going to do?" And she cried and cried until the whole pillow was wet, and her hair and my hair, and more and more tears were coming. Lying that close to Mommy and her sadness put a big lump in my throat that hurt bad when I tried to swallow. It hurt my whole neck and all the way up to my ears. It didn't make me feel good to be so close to Mommy's sadness, but I still stayed because Mommy didn't want me to leave.

Daddy came and lay down on the other side of the bed, so I was in the middle, and he watched Mommy cry. He put his arm around us for a little while, and I wondered if that made him have a lump in his throat, too, to be so close to Mommy's sadness. After a while Daddy patted Mommy's head and mine and got back up and left.

19

Waking Up

I DIDN'T KNOW WHY IT'S CALLED a wake if it's for someone who isn't going to be awake ever again. I was five at Uncle Chip's wake and it was the first time I saw a real-life dead person, because at the wake Uncle Chip's casket was in the front of the wake room and the lid was open. Uncle Chip was lying inside there, and he looked like regular. He had his eyes closed and it was like he was sleeping. I didn't want to go close to the casket, but the whole time we were in the wake room, which was a long time because there were two wakes, on two days in a row, I kept looking at Uncle Chip.

I thought maybe he wasn't really dead, or maybe he was making a joke, because Uncle Chip always used to make jokes and I thought maybe he was waiting for the perfect moment to sit up in the casket and scare us. A lot of people went to his casket and sat in front of it on their knees and touched his hands, which were folded on his chest and I wondered if he died with his hands like that, and I wondered what his hands felt like and if they were cold or what. That would have been the perfect time to sit up, and it would have scared the poop out of the people sitting in front of the casket. But Uncle Chip never sat up and he never moved, and at the funeral at the church, the lid of the casket was closed.

After breakfast Daddy helped me put on my black suit. Well, it wasn't my suit, it was Andy's, the one he had on at Uncle Chip's wake and funeral. I thought it was kind of funny I was going to wear Andy's wake suit at Andy's wake. Not funny like you want to laugh, but strange funny. When Uncle Chip died, Mommy took me and Andy to the mall to buy us suits because we didn't have any, and you have to wear a suit when somebody dies, and it has to be black, because when you wear something black it shows you're sad. So black also is a color for sad, but I picked gray for sad on my feelings pages and black for scared. The black suit matched my scared feeling about going to the wake. Andy made a fuss when we went shopping for a suit because he didn't want to wear one, but I liked it. I looked like Daddy when he goes to work.

First I tried on my suit from when Uncle Chip died, but it was too small and I couldn't even button my pants. So Daddy got Andy's suit from his closet, and I got worried that he would see my hideout, but then it didn't look like he did because he didn't say anything about it when he came back with Andy's suit. He held up the jacket and I put it on. You couldn't see my hands because the sleeves were too long.

"Daddy, the sleeves are annoying me," I said, because my hands kept getting stuck in the sleeves, and I had to put my arms all the way in the air to get them out. Andy's a lot taller than me because he's three and a half years older, and also he's really tall for his age. I'm not. I'm regular tall.

"Sorry, bud, it's going to have to do," Daddy said, and that was a surprise, because Daddy always wants us to be dressed nice. "We're not going out looking like hoboes," that's what he says to us, and he makes us go change and put on more handsome clothes.

I didn't know why we couldn't go to the mall and buy a new suit for me. The long sleeves were really bothering me, and my stomach was starting to bother me, too.

"Can you roll up the sleeves?" My voice sounded whiney. I moved side to side a lot, because of my stomach.

"You don't roll up the sleeves of a suit. Just leave it, it's really not important, OK? Can you hold still for one second so I can put the tie on?" Daddy said in a mean voice, and then I could tell he felt bad about talking like that because he said, "You look handsome, buddy," and he put his hand through my hair.

"Listen. Today is going to be hard for all of us, understand?"

I shook my head yes.

"I need you to do me a favor and be a big boy today and help me with Mommy, all right? I need your help today."

I shook my head yes again, even though I wasn't sure I was going to be a good helper today, because of how I was feeling.

We drove to the wake in Mommy's car. It didn't get towed at the hospital. Grandma and Aunt Mary went to pick it up the day after Mommy parked it on the sidewalk. Mommy didn't drive, though. She sat in the passenger seat and stared out the window, although it wasn't even possible to see anything with all the rain splashing against the windows, and also the windows were getting fog on them from our breathing. Mimi sat next to me in the back and also stared out of the window. Daddy was driving really slow, and the more we got away from the house, the slower he was driving, even though there was no traffic.

It was really quiet in the car with no radio on. All I could hear was the rain on the sunroof and the squeaky *wish-wish* from the windshield wipers going at dizzy speed. I liked that it was quiet. At the wake there would be a lot of people and a lot of talking, and I wished we could keep driving, just us.

"Mommy?" I said into the quiet car, and it sounded too loud.

Mommy's shoulders went up a little, but she didn't turn around and she didn't give me an answer.

"Mommy?"

"What, bud?" Daddy said.

"Do we have to go to the wake?" I asked, and I knew it was a stupid question. Miss Russell always says there are no stupid questions, but that's not really true, because when you already know what the answer is going to be, it's kind of stupid to ask the question anyway. Mimi grabbed my hand and gave me a sad smile.

"Yes, Zach, we have to go to the wake," Daddy said. "We are

Andy's family, and people are coming to say good-bye to him and express their condolences to us."

I started to think about Uncle Chip's wake again, and it made my stomach go into overdrive. I tried to open the window to get some fresh air, but my window was locked. Daddy always locks the windows from the front so we can't open them in the back, even though I get carsick a lot and it helps when the windows are open, but Daddy says it hurts his ears, so it's a no to opening the windows. I mostly only get carsick when Daddy drives and never when Mommy drives.

I didn't want to see Andy dead in a casket. When we got to the place of the wake and Daddy parked the car, my heart was beating really fast. I felt like I had to throw up, and tears were coming in my eyes. I squeezed my nose so hard it hurt.

"Get out of the car, Zach, come on," Daddy said.

I wanted to stay in the car, but Daddy went around and opened my door. I saw Mommy standing next to the car, getting wet from the rain, and she looked really small and scared, too. She held out her hand, and her face gave me a look like she wanted me to go to her, and so I got out of the car and took her hand and we started walking together.

Inside were some men in suits, and they talked with quiet voices to Mommy and Daddy and Mimi, and no one else was there except us. I looked around, and it looked like the place where Uncle Chip's wake was, in New Jersey. It looked like a lobby in a fancy hotel, the one we go to sometimes when we stay overnight in the city. It had big comfy chairs with little tables in between and a big sparkly lamp hanging from the ceiling and a red carpet that was very soft under my shoes. Quiet piano music was playing from somewhere in the room.

The lobby room felt cozy. I wanted to go sit in one of the comfy chairs, but then Daddy told me it was time to go into the wake room and BAM! my stomach went right back to roller-coaster mode. Mommy was holding my hand. She squeezed it tighter and tighter, and it got too tight, but I didn't try to pull my hand away. Mommy needed to squeeze it, I thought.

Daddy had his hands on Mommy's back and on the top of my head, and he started to push us toward a door across the lobby room, and that was probably going to be the wake room behind it. Mimi walked behind us, and we all took tiny steps.

We got closer to the door, and I held my breath in and looked at my feet. Every time I took a step, my shoe sank into the soft red carpet. I looked behind me to see if I was leaving footprints. I was, but then the carpet went right back to normal after I picked my feet up. I kept my eyes on my feet the whole time, and it felt like behind the door something scary was waiting. Something really big and scary, and the doors should definitely stay closed.

20

Jumbo Twin Roll Tissue Dispenser

Somebody opened the door. The carpet changed from red to blue. The room was quiet and it smelled good, like a garden. Mommy made a sound like a lot of fast breaths. She let go of my hand and walked away from me, but I didn't know where because I still didn't look up, my eyes were stuck on my feet on the blue carpet.

Without Mommy holding my hand tight, I felt like I was in a strange place all by myself and I got lost or something. I stayed by the door, and because I didn't want to use my eyes, I tried to use my other senses to figure out what it was like around me. I used my touch sense and my fingers touched the wall, and it had patterns on it that were smooth. And I felt my feet touch the blue carpet that was soft like the red carpet in the lobby room. I couldn't use my taste sense because there was nothing in my mouth, but I had a bad feeling in my mouth from when I started to feel sick in the car. I used my smell sense, and it really did smell like a garden, like flowers, and it smelled really sweet. I liked that at first, but then it smelled too sweet or something. For my hearing sense, I thought maybe there would be bird or bee sounds, because you can hear those in a garden, but it was completely quiet. Even with the hearing super sense all I could hear was quietness.

But then came a crying sound that was quiet at first and it sounded far away from me, but then it got louder, and it came from Mommy somewhere in the room. Mommy's crying got louder and it went on for a long time and I thought that maybe I should go find her, but

I didn't move from my spot by the door, because I started to get to know this spot and I didn't want to get to know anything else in the room. All of a sudden I heard a loud crash, and it made me look up from my feet. Right away I saw everything I didn't want to see.

The casket, right in the front of the room, in the middle. It was a different color than Uncle Chip's—this one was light brown and Uncle Chip's was black—and this one was smaller. The lid was closed, not open like Uncle Chip's, and lots of flowers were on top of the lid. I started to feel all hot under the suit. Andy was inside of there, his body.

Daddy and Mimi were in front of the casket, and they were pulling Mommy up—she was on the floor, next to a big vase with purple flowers that was fallen over. Between my spot by the door and Andy's casket in the front were a lot of chairs all in a row with a walkway in between them, almost like how the benches were in the church after the gunman came. There were flowers along the walls and next to the casket. They were pretty and in lots of colors and now I knew why it smelled like a garden in here. I saw pictures everywhere, too, mostly of Andy and some of all our family, and the pictures were on boards and some in picture frames on skinny tables.

I heard sounds behind me, and people started to come in the wake room. Grandma and Aunt Mary, my cousin Jonas who pees in the bed, and his mom and dad, and some other people from our family. Mommy and Daddy and Mimi stood in the front. Mommy was holding on to Daddy's arm, and she looked like she was going to fall down again. She stared straight in front of her and didn't make any crying sounds anymore. Tears were running down her face and dripping on her black dress, but she didn't wipe them off, just let them drip, drip, drip.

More and more people came in, and everyone talked in quiet voices like whispering, like maybe they were afraid to wake Andy up in his casket. All the whispering together sounded loud in my ears.

"Let's go and stand with your mom and dad in the front," Grandma said. She pushed me with her hand, and her fingernails were digging in my back a little. We all made a line in the front, very close to the casket: me, Mommy, Daddy, Grandma and Mimi and Aunt Mary. I didn't want to be there, so close.

All the other people came in the front to talk to us. The sleeves of my suit started to bother me again, and my right hand got stuck every time I tried to put it up to do handshakes. At the top of the shirt by my throat where Daddy made a knot with the tie, it felt tight. I swallowed a lot of times, and every time I could feel the swallowing get stuck on my tie knot. More people came and said, "My condolences," more hugs, more handshakes with my hand getting stuck in the sleeve.

My stomach did a growl like I was hungry, but I didn't feel hungry. I tried to pull on the tie knot with my fingers to make it not so tight. It didn't move, and now it started to feel hard to breathe. I got hot all over and no air was going in when I tried to breathe, and my stomach started to feel worse.

I left our line in the front and I walked to the lobby room. I wanted to run because I felt like poop was going to come, but I didn't run, there were too many people and they were all looking at me, and the red juice spill was starting to happen. When I got to the lobby room I spotted the bathroom sign, and it was all the way at the other end of the room. I tried to get there fast, and I was sweating a lot and breathing a lot, but no air was coming in. I finally got in the bathroom. I could feel the poop coming, and I tried to open the pants from my suit, but it had a slidey button that was stuck and I couldn't get it open.

The poop came. It came and came, and I could feel it hot in my underwear. I think it was diarrhea, because I could also feel something hot on my left leg, running down all the way to my sock.

I tried to stand very still because everything felt wet and sticky and I didn't want to feel it. The smell was making me feel sick, it smelled really bad. I didn't know what to do. I was stuck in the bathroom with poop all in my pants, and outside the bathroom were all those people and everyone was going to know.

There was a sign on the toilet paper thing: JUMBO TWIN ROLL TISSUE DISPENSER. I read it over and over again.

JUMBO TWIN ROLL TISSUE DISPENSER.
JUMBO TWIN ROLL TISSUE DISPENSER.
JUMBO TWIN ROLL TISSUE DISPENSER.
I traced the words with my finger.
JUMBO TWIN ROLL TISSUE DISPENSER.

It helped me calm down a little bit to read it a lot of times. I knew which word was coming next, and when I was done, I started all over again.

I stood in the toilet stall for a long time and nothing changed. It smelled worse, so I had to do something about it, except I didn't know what and we didn't bring any extra pants. No one came in, and I didn't hear any voices from outside, so I tried to take my pants off again and this time the button opened right away, and that was really unfair that it opened now but not earlier when the poop was coming.

I slowly pulled the pants down. The smell got worse, and I felt like I had to dry-heave. Dry-heaving is when you feel like you have to throw up and your mouth moves like you are throwing up, but nothing comes out. When I get carsick when Daddy is driving and I throw up in a bag that Mommy holds for me, right away Daddy and Andy start dry-heaving and they act all dramatic. Then Daddy opens all the windows, and he should have opened them before I got carsick.

I dry-heaved and took off my shoes and socks, and there really was poop in my left sock and all the way down on my left leg. I took my pants and underwear all the way off and poop fell out and landed on the floor and it was so gross I started to cry.

All this time I didn't cry. When the gunman came and I had to hide in the closet with my class I didn't cry. When Daddy told me Andy was dead and Mommy acted crazy at the hospital and we had to leave her there I didn't cry, and all the times after that when tears were coming in my eyes, I never cried. But now I did. And now it was like all the tears that didn't come out before all came out together, and it was a lot. I didn't try to do the squeeze-away trick, I didn't even want to. I just let the tears come out, out, out, and it felt good.

I tried to get some toilet paper and wipe the poop off the floor, but

I made it get spread all around. I tried to clean off my leg and butt, and I used a lot of toilet paper from the Jumbo Twin Roll Tissue Dispenser. I cried and I wiped and I ripped off more toilet paper and then I tried to flush, but it didn't go down, probably from too much paper.

Then the door opened and a man walked in that I didn't know, and he saw me without my pants on because I never closed the door from my stall, so he saw me right away. He covered his mouth with his hand and went right back outside. I locked the door to the stall. A little while later someone came in again and I heard Daddy's voice.

"Zach? Jesus Christ. Oh my God. What's going on in here?"

I didn't answer him because I didn't want him to know.

"Open the door, Zach!"

So I opened the door and Daddy saw my whole mess, and he pulled his suit jacket over his nose, and I could tell he was trying really hard not to dry-heave.

I was supposed to be a big boy today, and now it was the exact opposite. I was being a baby. Mommy came in the bathroom, too, even though it was a bathroom for boys, and girls are not supposed to go in the boys' room, she could get into trouble for that. When she saw me, she made a loud "OH" sound, and she pushed Daddy out of the way and hugged me tight. She didn't even care that poop probably got on her dress. She hugged me tight and rocked me and cried and cried, and I cried and cried, and my head was starting to hurt from all the crying. Daddy stood there with his suit jacket over his nose and just stared at us.

21

Battle Cry

FINE, WHATEVER, YOU CAN STAY if you're not annoying," Andy called to me from the top of the rock, and I started to climb up to him before he changed his mind. The rock was very high and the side was smooth and I kept sliding down.

"Take your Crocs off, then it's easier," Liza said. She was climbing up behind me.

I kicked off my Crocs and they bounced down the rock and half-way down Liza's yard that was like a small hill down to her house. Liza put her hand on my back and pushed me up.

From up here, I could see right into Liza's bedroom—that's how high the hill and the rock are in her backyard. The rock was hot under my feet and it hurt a little, but I got used to it. The air was very hot, too, and the back of my T-shirt was wet from sweat. It was like you could see the hotness in the air, coming off the rock. It looked blurry, and the sun made little crystals in the rock very sparkly.

I could hear the hotness, too—it was making a "zzzzzzzz" sound. Crickets were all around us. I couldn't see them, but I could hear them: *zeep-zeep-zeep*, all singing together, but starting and stopping at different times.

First Andy said I wasn't allowed to play with him and Liza and the others, but then he said OK. Maybe because Aiden was there, too, and he was six, like me, he's James and June's cousin, and their mom said they had to play with him. And probably because of Liza: she is nice to me, and when she's there, Andy acts nicer, too. That's probably because Andy has a crush on Liza and wants her to have a crush on him. When she asks him to stop doing something, like calling me a loser or telling me to get lost, he does it and he doesn't get his bad temper.

"You can be on the tribe," Andy said to me when I sat down on the rock next to him. I watched him make a bow out of a stick with the pocketknife. It was Daddy's pocketknife, and Mommy didn't want Andy to use it because it's too dangerous and he could get hurt from it. But Daddy said, "I've had this knife since I was younger than Zach, for God's sake! Let the boy do regular boy things. Always being so overprotective, right?" and he slapped Aiden's dad on the back, and then Mommy didn't say anything else about it.

The game we were playing was Indian tribe. Andy was the chief and he was sitting in the middle of the rock, crisscross applesauce, like how Indian chiefs sit. Around his head was a blue headband with different-colored feathers glued on it. The headband pushed his hair up on the side so it looked messy.

"It's important that all the little branches get cut off on the sides and the stick is really smooth, see?" Andy said to me. I knew we were pretending, but it felt real, and I had an excited feeling in my belly.

"Can I try?" I asked.

"No, you can't use the knife, it's way too dangerous for you. That's only for me," Andy said.

I could feel the rock making my butt hot through my shorts.

"It's a good lookout up here," Aiden said.

"Yeah, and the wall behind us is good protection for our camp," Andy said.

Liza pointed at the left and right side of her house. "That way enemies can only come from there and there and we can see them coming." On the right side of her house was their patio, where Mommy and Daddy were hanging out with Liza's parents and the other grown-ups for the barbecue.

"We still need a name for our tribe," James said. He was working on making a long spear for hunting.

"Maybe Lost Boys like in *Peter Pan* when they start to be friends with the Indians," I said. "Well, Lost Boys and Girls," I said, because of Liza and June.

"OK, that's dumb," Andy said. "We'll use the names of all the tribe members, or maybe the first two letters of all the names." For a while we tried out how we could put the first two letters of everyone's names together. In the end, we decided on "JaZaJuLiAnAi." It sounded Indian, and we practiced saying it fast: "JaZaJuLiAnAi, JaZaJuLiAnAi, JaZaJuLiAnAi."

"That's also going to be our battle cry for when we go into battle with enemy tribes," Andy told us, and he hollered, "JAZAJULI-ANAI!"

"JaZaJuLiAnAi!" It came back to us like a little echo from Liza's house.

All our supplies were spread out on the rock: sticks and different-colored strings for making bows and arrows and spears, and feathers and beads. We also had two little bags with arrowheads inside, they were mine and Andy's and we got them when we went to a park with camp a couple weeks ago and we did mining. Mining is when you get a big bag and it looks like only sand is in it. You get a board that has a net in the middle with little holes, and then you go to the river. When you put the board with the net in the water and pour the sand in, all the sand gets washed away through the holes, and then you see fancy rocks that were hiding in the sand. And arrowheads if you got lucky. They were real arrowheads that the Indians made out of black shiny rocks, and they were very sharp on the sides and pointy at the top. Me and Andy both brought a whole bag home from mining, full of rocks and arrowheads.

The strings and feathers were from Liza and June, they had them at home in their art supplies. They kept remembering other supplies we could use for decorating the arrows and spears and ran off to get them.

"Zach, we need more perfect sticks for bows. Go look in our yard, too," Andy said, and I did. The sticks for the bows had to be long and thin, so you could bend them. Andy did a cut at the ends of the sticks, and we tied string on both ends. You had to tie it to one end first and then pull that end down with the string and tie it to the other end so it looked like a big *D*. The sticks for arrows had to be shorter and not so thin, and Andy did a cut on only one end. He made an X with two cuts so we could put feathers on that end, and then we tied the arrowheads to the other end with string. Spears were longer and thicker sticks. We didn't have enough arrowheads for those, and they weren't big enough anyway for spears, so we made fake arrowheads out of cardboard.

We worked on our weapons for a long time, and we talked about what the battles with the enemies were going to be like. We worked like a real tribe team. There was no fighting and I never played with Andy like this before. We laughed because our feet were really dirty and black, but that's how you know you're real Indians, Andy said. We had mosquito bites all over us, especially me because mosquitos love me, but we didn't care.

Finally, when all the weapons were done, it was time to go into battle. We split up into two teams. I thought we were all going to be in the same tribe, but Andy said he changed his mind about it and it wouldn't be so much fun to go into battle against an invisible enemy, so he changed it to two teams, and they were going to be enemy tribes. I wanted to be with Andy, but he picked Aiden first, not me, and he didn't want two six-year-olds on his team. So now we were going to be enemies again.

Andy's tribe disappeared around the left side of Liza's house, and I saw Andy, the chief, run ahead and June and Aiden follow him. Me and James and Liza spread out in the bushes to be on the lookout for them. We carried our bows and arrows and spears, and we ran behind the bushes and trees for cover, from Liza's backyard, around her house, across the street into our backyard, and into the yards of our other neighbors.

"Can you see them?" Liza whispered, and her voice sounded like she was scared, so then I started to get a scared feeling in my stomach. My heart was beating fast. It was like we were hunting for a real enemy. But then I thought about when Andy disappeared in the darkness he didn't look scared, he looked brave. I decided that I was going to do that, too, be brave.

"Take cover," I said with a loud whispering voice, and I ducked behind a tree. James and Liza ducked behind the tree next to me. "Don't make a sound," I said.

My breath was going in and out fast, and I tried to make it go slower. Then I heard a loud "JAZAJULIANAI!" coming from somewhere in front of us, and I couldn't see where it was coming from, but I jumped out from behind the tree and I yelled, "ATTACK!" It was like I was a real Indian who was brave and going into battle.

I heard another loud "JAZAJULIANAI!" that sounded like Andy's voice coming from somewhere in front of us. All of a sudden, James was next to me, and he threw his spear in the direction from where Andy's battle cry was coming. I got my bow and arrow ready.

"JAZAJULIANAI!" I heard again, and it sounded closer this time. I fired an arrow and it disappeared into the darkness. A second later I heard a loud scream: "Aaaaaahhhh!"

"You guys, stop. Andy got hurt," I heard June call.

I ran to where her voice came from, and then I saw Andy. He was lying on the road between our yard and Liza's house. My arrow was sticking out of his chest. He didn't move, his eyes were closed, and in the light from the streetlamp I saw the blood. There was blood on his T-shirt, and there was a puddle of blood around him on the road that was getting bigger and bigger, like all the blood from his whole body was running out of him onto the road.

I sat down next to Andy on the road and started screaming: "Andy! Andy! Wake up, Andy! Wake up, wake up, wake up! Andy! Mommy! Mommy! Mommy!" I screamed and screamed, and then someone touched my shoulders from behind and started shaking me. I kept screaming and screaming, and someone kept shaking me and shaking me.

"Zach! Zach! You have to wake up, Zach. You have to wake up!" I saw Daddy in the darkness, and he was the one who was shaking me.

"Daddy, I shot Andy with my arrow, Daddy. I think I killed Andy.

I think he's dead! I'm sorry, I'm sorry, I didn't mean to do that. We were playing, it was just pretend!"

"What? No, you were dreaming. You had a bad dream again. Look," Daddy said, and he put his hand up and pushed something to the side. Then it wasn't so dark anymore, and I could see we weren't on the road behind our yard. We were in my hideout.

I was blinking my eyes because of the light that was coming in the hideout now, and because of the tears, and I didn't know why I was in here all of a sudden and why Daddy was in here with me. "But . . . but . . . it happened. It really happened. I saw him with all the blood. From my arrow, I killed him."

"No, buddy, that didn't happen. You didn't kill Andy. My God, did you scare me just now," Daddy said. "Come here." He pulled me out of the closet and we sat on Andy's rug, me on Daddy's lap. I put my head on his chest, and I could hear his heart pounding loud.

"I heard you scream, but I didn't know where you were. I looked everywhere for you, but I couldn't figure out where the screaming was coming from. Took me forever to find you in there. What are you even doing in Andy's closet, bud?" Daddy petted my back when he was talking. I started to calm down a little, and the pounding in Daddy's chest got quieter, too.

"I guess I was sleeping maybe," I said.

"But why in Andy's closet?"

"It's my hideout now," I said, and Daddy answered, "I see."

"I was dreaming about when we played Indians on Liza's rock at the barbecue," I told Daddy, and it still felt like it happened like a minute ago.

"That was a great time you guys had, I remember that."

"It was like an actual adventure," I said.

"Sure was."

"But I didn't kill Andy."

"No, you didn't."

"But he's dead," I said, and it sounded like a question.

"Yes, buddy, he's dead."

22

Good-bye

WHEN YOU DIE and it's time for your funeral, that's when people say good-bye to you. At the wake you're kind of still with your family and friends, and they can look at you in the casket if the lid is open or at least in the pictures that get hung up everywhere. But at the funeral everyone says good-bye and it's forever. Final good-byes, that's what Mommy called it when it was time for Uncle Chip's funeral.

People start to forget about you after you die and they can't see you all the time anymore. It was already happening with Andy. I started to notice that at his funeral that was on the day after the wake. Everyone was talking about Andy, but they talked about him like they only remembered some parts of him, not all the parts.

"Oh, Andy was just such a darling, such a pleasure to have in class."

"He was hilarious, wasn't he? What a character!"

"He was so bright, incredibly smart."

It was like they weren't really talking about Andy or they were starting to forget about what he was like.

At the funeral I sat in between Mommy and Daddy on the first bench in the front of the church. It wasn't the church by McKinley or the one where we went to Uncle Chip's funeral, but a different one we never went to before. Inside it didn't really look like a church, more like a really big room with a lot of benches. It was freezing cold in the room. There was an altar table in the front, too, and Andy's casket was in front of it with flowers on top. There wasn't a Jesus hanging from a cross, only a cross and no Jesus, so that was good. I didn't want to sit there again and look at Jesus with the nails in his hands and feet like when I was at the church by McKinley.

The whole big room was full of people, and a lot of them couldn't even sit down and were standing in the back. I turned around and I saw a lot of the people from the wake yesterday. I didn't stay there for the whole time. I had to go home with Aunt Mary because of the poop. At the funeral it was our family and friends, our neighbors, and parents and kids from school and lacrosse and Daddy's work and a lot of people I didn't know, too. When I was just about to turn back around, I spotted Miss Russell on a bench in the back of the church, and she still looked very white with a lot of black around her eyes. When she saw me looking at her, she did a little smile and then she lifted up her arm. At first I thought she was waving at me, but then I realized she was shaking her charm bracelet. It made me think of the charm she gave me, and I thought about it laying in the corner of my hideout, and now I wished I brought it here with me. I smiled back at Miss Russell and turned back around.

I didn't like sitting all the way in the front. I could feel everyone's eyes on me from behind. Mommy had her arm around me and she was holding me very tight, her fingers were grabbing my arm and the grabbing made her fingers look white. The sadness I could feel coming off her made my chest feel tight. And it was like the other people coming in the church room brought more sadness with them, and the room was too full with people and their sadness, and it squeezed my chest tighter and tighter until I could only take small, fast breaths.

Andy's casket was right in front of where we were sitting. I wondered if Andy up in heaven or wherever his soul went knew that right now was his funeral and people were saying their final good-byes to him, and then his body in the casket was going in a grave in the graveyard. Could he see us sitting on the bench in this freezing cold room, and could he feel the people's sadness?

First the man from the church who was wearing like a black dress or something and had a cross necklace on said a speech on a microphone, and it was long, and I didn't understand everything he said, but some of it was about God. And he said things about Andy, and I didn't know how he knew all those things about him, because we never saw him before. He also sang songs in between his speech that I didn't know, and the people in the room sang the songs with him, except for Mommy and Daddy, they were very still and quiet. All three of us were sitting very close together, legs and arms touching.

After the man from the church was done with his speech and songs, Daddy got up. He walked to the microphone very slow, and I guessed he was going to say a speech, too, and I didn't know he was going to do that. My left side where Daddy was sitting close got cold.

Everyone was staring at Daddy, only Mommy wasn't. She was looking down at a tissue she was holding in her lap, and she was squeezing it with one hand and squeezing my arm with the other hand. It was very quiet in the church room, and Daddy didn't say anything for a long time. I started to think he was just going to stand there and then people were going to get bored, but then he made a coughing sound in his throat like he had to make room for his words.

Daddy took out a piece of paper from the pocket of his suit jacket and started to read what it said on it: "I want to thank everyone for coming today and helping us say good-bye to our son Andy." The paper in his hands was shaking so much, I didn't know how he was even reading it. His voice was shaking, too, like the paper. He made a long break, and maybe he was only saying thank you, but then he said more, the words coming out slowly and quietly: "A week ago my son's life was cut short in the most horrific way I can imagine." Break. "Never in a million years do you think something like this could ever happen to you . . . your family. Your child! And yet here we are. It's hard to believe this is our reality now and we are supposed to continue on living our lives somehow, without him. . . ." Daddy put the piece of paper down and made the sound again in his throat a few times.

"I'm . . . I'm sorry, I'll keep this short. There is now a big gaping hole in our lives where a week ago there was our smart, funny, outgoing boy with his big personality. Andy always made us laugh and he made us . . . so proud, every day. He was an amazing son and loving brother, the best we could have ever asked for. I can't even begin to wrap my mind around how to keep on living like this, without him, with that huge hole in our lives where my son is supposed to be. He was taken from us, . . . and I don't know how anything will ever make sense again without him."

Daddy looked down at the piece of paper like he was trying to find the spot where he stopped reading earlier. I could see his chin was shaking. He kept looking at the paper and said: "I want to ask all of you to please keep Andy and the memories you have of him close and carry him with you always."

Mommy started shaking next to me. She let go of my arm and crossed her arms in front of her belly and leaned forward, so her head almost touched her legs, and her shoulders went up and down from crying. All around us people cried, and the sadness was like a big heavy blanket all around us and on top of us.

I thought about Daddy's speech, and I watched Mommy and everyone else cry, and it all didn't feel like real life. Because Daddy did it, too: he didn't talk about Andy like how he actually was. And so it was like everyone was crying and being sad, but not about the actual Andy, just a version of him that wasn't the right one. It was like no one was saying good-bye properly to him. I felt like I wanted to stand up and yell at everyone to stop lying about my brother.

The sadness blanket didn't go away even after we left the church room, and it got more heavy when we went to the cemetery. We stood around Andy's grave with our shoes in the mud and we got wet from the rain. I tried not to look at the deep, dark hole in the ground that Andy's casket was going into, and I tried to keep my eyes on the big tree that was right next to his grave. It was full of yellow and orange leaves that were shiny from the rain. It looked like the whole tree was on fire. I thought it was the most beautiful tree I ever saw, and I was happy that it was going to be right there, next to Andy's grave.

After Andy's casket went in the hole, it was like the sadness blanket got too heavy for Mommy and she couldn't stand up anymore with it on top of her. Daddy and Mimi had to hold her up from the sides and put her in the car. And it stayed heavy on my shoulders, too, all the way home, and it made it hard for me to get up the stairs. I could only be upstairs for a little while, Grandma said, because people were coming over, and that was not good because all I wanted to do was be in my hideout.

I sat crisscross applesauce on Andy's sleeping bag and didn't move and didn't say anything. I just waited. I waited for the sadness blanket to come off my shoulders and for my chest to stop feeling so tight. I wanted to see if it was going to feel different now, if the funeral made it so that Andy would feel more gone than before.

I wondered again if Andy could see us from somewhere at his own funeral, and if he also noticed that people were talking about him like he was a different person—even Daddy didn't say the real truth about him. Andy probably thought it was funny and now all the bad stuff he did didn't matter anymore. But I thought that if it was me, I would be afraid that if people didn't remember me right, my actual self, then it would be like I was really gone from earth forever.

"Andy," I said in a quiet voice. "It's me, Zach." I waited like he was going to answer me back, but of course that wasn't going to happen. I was hoping that maybe I would know if he could hear me. "I'm in your closet. It's my hideout now. It's a secret, no one knows I'm in here. Well, Daddy knows now." I was telling him things that if he was seeing me right now, he would know already, but I said them anyway. "I bet you're mad I'm in your room and you can't do anything about it. You would try to kill me if you were here right now and not dead."

I thought that that was mean to say to a person who's dead, but it was saying the truth. Saying the truth to Andy felt good. "Anyway, you were really a jerk to me all the time." *Jerk*. That's a bad word. But Andy said it a lot, so now I was going to say it, too. I heard someone calling my name from downstairs, so I got up fast. Before I left the hideout I turned around and said, "I'm still mad at you about that."

23

Death Stare

I HEARD HE HAD PROBLEMS for a long time and the family didn't know how to deal with him." Mrs. Gray, our neighbor, and Miss Carolyn, that's Mrs. Gray's daughter, were standing by the sink, washing dishes. Mrs. Gray handed a wet plate to Miss Carolyn and she took it to dry it off and put it away in our kitchen cabinet. From the back they looked exactly the same—same body, same way of moving around, same long hair with curls—you could only tell Mrs. Gray is the mom because her curls are gray and Miss Carolyn's are brown.

"Yeah, he never graduated, so he's just been sitting in his parents' basement for the last couple years doing who knows what on the computer. How could they have not known how sick he was?" Miss Carolyn took another plate from Mrs. Gray, and they both shook their long brown and gray curls no.

"Right?" Mrs. Gray said, "It's bizarre. I mean, this is Charlie we're talking about! And Mary! They're such nice people. Charlie is so great with kids, but his own son . . . What a horrible thing to happen to a parent."

"Yes, but, Ma, he shouldn't have had access to guns. In his mental state? They didn't know he had all those guns in the house?"

I watched Mrs. Gray and Miss Carolyn clean the dishes, and I listened to them talk about Charlie and his son, the gunman, and they didn't know I could hear them from where I was sitting on the yellow chair in the family room. The yellow chair was starting to be like my spy chair. People never realized I was sitting there, and I could hear everything that was going on in the kitchen and in the family room.

After the funeral a lot of people came to our house, and they were staying for a long time. There was a lot of whispering and crying everywhere. I sat on the spy chair because I didn't want to talk to anyone, and Daddy said I wasn't allowed to go back upstairs.

"He bought guns on the Internet, too. Where the hell did he come up with the money for that? Makes you wonder, doesn't it?" Mrs. Gray said. "I can't get over the message he posted on Facebook. It gives me goose bumps every time I think about it."

Miss Carolyn said, "I heard that Mary found out about the message and tried to reach Charlie, but it was too late. Obviously."

I thought about how it was when Charlie let his son come in the school that day. He has a little TV by his desk, and when someone rings the bell at the front door, he can see who it is on the TV because there's a camera outside. So probably his son rang the bell and Charlie thought, "Oh, my son is coming to visit me," and he let him in, and so it was like it was his fault, too, what happened next.

"Let me check if anyone else is done with their plate," Miss Carolyn said, and she turned around to come in the family room. I didn't want her to notice me in the spy chair, so I got up fast, and right then I heard the doorbell. I went to open the door and my belly did a super big flip, because standing right there on our porch was Charlie and next to him his wife, and just a minute ago Mrs. Gray and Miss Carolyn were talking about them.

In all of kindergarten and on all the days I was in first grade so far, I saw Charlie every day and he always looked the same. Same glasses, same McKinley shirt with his CHARLIE RANALEZ name tag on it, and same face with the big smile. Charlie always talks a little bit loud and jokes around and right when you start kindergarten he learns all the names, and that's a lot of names to remember. Every time I walk past his desk by the front door, he yells out: "Hey, Zach, my best buddy!

How you doing today?" He calls the other kids "buddy" and "princess," but not "my best buddy"—that was only for me.

This Charlie standing in front of my house now wasn't the same jokey Charlie. Everything about him was changed. He looked really old, and I could see all the bones in his face, and his smile was gone. His wife stood next to him, still holding an umbrella over their heads even though they were under the roof from the porch and no rain was coming down on them.

For a long time I stared at Charlie and he stared at me. I didn't know if I should say hi to him or what, because his son killed Andy and maybe it was Charlie's fault, too, because he let him in the school.

After a while his wife said, "Sweetheart, are your parents available?" and right then Grandma came up behind me and she put her hand on my shoulder and pushed me out on the porch. With the other hand she pulled the door almost all the way closed behind us.

"What in God's name . . . ? How dare you . . . ?" Grandma started her sentences and didn't finish them, and her hand was holding my shoulder hard. Charlie and his wife looked like they were scared of Grandma, and they both went back a few steps on the porch, but they didn't leave.

Then Charlie talked, but in a voice that didn't sound like his own voice, it was low and very quiet: "Ma'am, we are sorry to intrude. . . ."

"You are sorry to intrude?" Grandma's voice went up and Charlie's voice went down. "Yes, very sorry. We came to express our condolences to Melissa and . . ."

"Oh, you came to express your condolences?"

I was starting to feel annoyed at Grandma. All she was doing was copying Charlie, and that's not a polite way of talking. Charlie's wife was holding on to Charlie's arm and trying to get him to leave, and I saw tears on her face.

Behind us the door opened again, and this time Mommy and Daddy stepped out on the porch, and Grandma moved over to the side away from the door to make room for them. Out of the corner of my eye I could see she was giving Charlie and his wife a death stare.

A death stare is when you look at someone like you want to kill them. Like your eyes are weapons, like invisible lasers or something. I know what a death stare looks like, because that's what Mommy called it when Andy used to look at her like that a lot of times. When Andy had his bad temper and all the fighting and yelling was over, but Andy was still mad, he sometimes gave Mommy that stare. "Wow, if looks could kill," Mommy said then, and tried to make a joke out of it.

I was standing on the porch in between Mommy and Daddy and Charlie and his wife, and I could feel Mommy and Daddy close behind me. I got a feeling in my stomach like something bad was going to happen. There were tears on Charlie's face, and he let them run down. He was looking at something over my head, Mommy maybe.

Mommy used to be Charlie's favorite student when she went to McKinley. Mommy told me that one time, when there was a father-daughter sack race at her field day, when she was in fifth grade, Charlie did it with her. Mommy's dad died when she was in third grade, he had a car accident, and so Mommy had no one to do the sack race with, except then Charlie did it, and Mommy was really happy about it. Now, when Mommy comes to school for something, Charlie always says to me, "Don't tell anyone, but your mother was always my favorite when she went here. And you are like a mini version of her." He always says that, and he gives Mommy a wink.

Charlie lifted up his hands and took a step forward, and then he was really close to me and it looked like he was trying to give Mommy behind me a hug. "Oh, Melissa!" It sounded like Charlie had to press out Mommy's name, and then right behind her name was like a volcano of sadness that started erupting, because Charlie started crying and not just in his face, but with his whole body. I've never seen anyone cry like that before. It looked like it was hard for him to keep standing up and his whole body was shaking and he cried really loud. It sounded like it came from somewhere all the way down inside of him.

His hands dropped back down to his sides, and his wife grabbed his arm again. For a long time everyone stood there and watched Charlie's whole body cry, and no one did anything about it. I could feel

Charlie's body shaking in front of me, and my throat hurt a lot. I wanted to take a step forward and hug Charlie's body and make it stop shaking.

When I was about to do that, Charlie's wife started to say something: "We are sorry to intrude like this." That's what Charlie said earlier. I heard Grandma make a sound like a snort, but she didn't interrupt or copy the words this time. "We . . . we wanted to come and see you in person to . . . We are so very sorry. . . ." And then it was like she forgot what she wanted to say and she was quiet again.

"Sorry?" That was Mommy's voice behind me, and she said it very quiet. The way she said it made the back of my neck feel like it was getting goose bumps, and the bad feeling in my stomach was right. "You're sorry? And you wanted to come here? To our house. Our home. To tell us that?" Mommy's voice was still very quiet, but her words were like they were pointy. She was shooting them out like flying icicles, and Charlie and his wife flinched like real icicles were hitting them.

"Your psycho son killed my Andy. My baby. And you wanted to come here and tell us you're sorry?" Mommy was talking louder now, and then she started shouting. I could feel more people coming in the hallway behind us. I turned around to see who it was and to look at Mommy.

Daddy grabbed Mommy's arm. "Melissa, let's not . . ."

"No, Jim, let's. Let's absolutely," Mommy said, and she pulled her arm away.

I heard Grandma say, "Good heavens."

Mommy walked around me toward Charlie and his wife like she was going to hit them. Charlie's wife took another step back and she probably forgot that there were steps behind her and she kind of tripped down to the first step and she almost fell down all of the porch stairs. She stayed behind Charlie like she was trying to hide.

"Don't tell me you're sorry. That's too little, too late, wouldn't you say? Don't tell me you didn't know. Everyone knew Charles was a fucking freaker—all you had to do was look at him! Why didn't you stop him? Why the hell didn't you stop him?" Mommy was screaming now, and it really was like she was hitting Charlie, just not with fists, but with words.

"Believe me, Melissa, if there was a way to go back and undo what happened . . . I would gladly give my life. . . ." Charlie put his hands up again toward Mommy, but she moved away from him like she was grossed out.

"Don't you Melissa me," she said, and she wasn't screaming anymore. She looked at Charlie in a very mean, death-stare-y way. "Get away from my house and my family. Or what's left of it." Then she grabbed my hand and pulled me inside the house. I didn't want to go with her, but she was holding my hand tight and was pulling it hard, so I had to. She shoved her way through the people in the hallway, and when I turned around to look at Charlie, there were too many people in the way and I couldn't see him anymore.

But I remembered the way Charlie looked at Mommy when she said those mean words to him. His eyes looked very big in his old-looking face with all the bones sticking out. It was the saddest face I've ever seen in my whole life.

I thought about how Daddy was wrong when he said Charlie didn't get hurt, because he did. His son died, too, so his feelings were hurting about that, like ours because Andy died, except it was worse for Charlie because his son killed his angels, and that was worse than just dead.

[24]

Poking a Snake with a Stick

THE TOWEL UNDER ME was wet when I woke up today. Last night Mimi put the towel on the mattress because when it was bedtime my sheets were still in the bathtub, wet from pee. Mommy forgot to wash them.

I took the wet towel off the mattress and the wet PJs off of me, got dressed, walked through Andy's room to check the top bunk, and then I went downstairs to find Mommy. She was in the kitchen, talking to Mimi.

"It says it right here, Mom. He had Asperger's," Mommy said, and showed Mimi something on the iPad. "I mean, officially diagnosed when he was in middle school. Apparently he had all sorts of issues in school and dropped out in tenth grade. No friends. No job. Just been hanging out in the basement ever since, basically. For two years!"

"Well, I don't think Asperger's makes people violent, though, does it?" Mimi said. "I guess that explains why we've seen so little of Charlie and Mary these last few years." Mimi looked up and saw me in the doorway. She put her hand on Mommy's arm, but Mommy didn't pay attention.

"Some neighbors thought he had other problems, too, that didn't seem Asperger's-related, and they even asked Charlie and Mary about it. Listen to this: 'A couple times I saw him acting odd around the neighborhood, walking up and down the street and gesturing, talking to himself. And he scared the hell out of old Louisa across the street last year when he yelled at her not to put up her Christmas decorations.' That's a quote from their next-door neighbor. I knew there was something wrong with him. I knew it when I saw him at Charlie's party. I always thought he was such a cute kid when I babysat him, but now that I think about it, he was a bit strange even when he was little. But at the party he was downright creepy. He was standing there, staring at the kids and—"

"Melissa, honey," Mimi interrupted Mommy and nodded her head at me.

Mommy saw me standing there and said, "He'll hear about this anyway."

"Mommy, I'm sorry, but I got the towel wet and the mattress," I said. I went over to Mommy and sat on her lap and she hugged me, but only with one arm, because the other arm was holding the iPad.

"Mommy?"

"Oh, sweetie, don't you worry," Mimi said. "Come on, let's go and get it all cleaned up for you." She took my hand and I got off Mommy's lap. Mommy was looking back down at the iPad. She had lines on her forehead and made clicking sounds with her teeth.

Do you know something that you should never ever do? Poke a snake with a stick. The snake guy who came to McKinley the day before the gunman came told us that. When you go for a walk or a hike and you see a snake—well, you wouldn't really see a snake where we live, because there aren't any here, or at least not any dangerous ones, but maybe when you go on vacation or somewhere else where they have dangerous snakes—and even if it looks tiny or like it's sleeping—don't poke it with a stick or touch it with your shoe. It's a bad idea. He even showed us why with one of the snakes he brought, not the emerald tree boa, but another one with red and black and yellow stripes. I forgot her name, but the snake guy said that some snakes with stripes are poisonous and some aren't. He taught us a poem so you can remember which are the dangerous ones:

"Red and black, friend of Jack. Red and yellow, kills a fellow."

The one the snake guy brought out had red next to yellow, so that means she was dangerous. At first she just lay there and didn't move, so it looked like she was sleeping. The snake guy got out a long stick and he poked her with it. She jumped up at the stick right away and then she didn't let go and was hanging from the stick with her teeth. It scared everyone, and some kids screamed, which was kind of dumb because we were sitting far away from the front where the snake was, so it wasn't even dangerous.

This snake fact popped into my head yesterday when I was sitting on a barstool in the kitchen and I was eating a sandwich Mimi made for lunch for me, and I was watching Mommy. She was standing on a ladder and cleaning on top of the kitchen cabinets. And she reminded me of the snake that got poked with the stick. When Charlie and his wife came to our house on the day of Andy's funeral, and that was three days ago, she jumped at them like the snake at the stick, but then they left—only Mommy's mad feeling didn't leave. She switched from sad to mad in a second and kept hanging on to the stick.

Mimi was watching Mommy clean the top of the cabinets, too, with a sad face that looked like it had even more wrinkles on it now. "Sweetie, why don't you let me do that? Is it really necessary to clean up there right now?"

"What? No . . . yes, Mom, it is!" Mommy took another step up on the ladder and scrubbed the cabinets really hard. "It's absolutely filthy up here!" Mommy thought everything in the house was absolutely filthy all of a sudden, and she cleaned and cleaned, even where I didn't see any dirt and it looked clean.

When Mommy first started with the cleaning, on the day after Charlie and his wife came over, I tried to be her helper so we could do the cleaning together. Mommy told me when to give her a new paper towel piece and when to hold the bag open so she could throw out the dirty ones. But a couple times I didn't open the bag fast enough and the dirty paper towels landed on the floor, and then Mommy got annoyed and said I should find something else to do. And she kept on cleaning without me.

After I helped Mimi wash off the mattress with a wet sponge and we put the towel and PJs in the washing machine in the basement, I went back in my room and looked at my books on my bookshelf. I have a lot of books, and my favorites right now are the Magic Tree House books. I have them all in a row on my shelf, from number 1 to number 53—that's how I like it. They used to be Andy's, and he read the whole series by himself a long time ago. He didn't want them anymore, and so Mommy moved them onto my bookshelf.

There was still no school this whole week. Daddy said next week the other kids were going back to school, but not to McKinley for now. They were getting split up and were going to the other schools in Wake Gardens. But not me. Daddy said I didn't have to go to school yet next week because we're one of the affected families. Maybe the week after, we would see. I was happy about that, that I didn't have to go back and that we would see when, maybe not for a while. Every time I thought about school, I got a bad feeling in my stomach, like I really didn't want to go back ever.

When I looked at my books and I thought about school, I remembered my book baggie that was still in my backpack at school. I wished I could have it, because on the day before the gunman came, Miss Russell let me pick out all new books, and I didn't even get to read them yet. I wondered if the backpacks were still in our cubbies or what, and if we were going to get them back, and I really hoped so, because my FIFA sticker book and cards were in there, too.

The Magic Tree House books are my favorite books because it's a brother and a sister going on a lot of adventures in different places and different times. Even if it happened in the past, they can still go there because of their tree house. They're really brave, especially the sister, even though she's the younger one. She's not scared of anything. When you read about how they're going on adventures, it feels like you go with them and you are brave, too.

By the way, the brother's name is Jack, and the sister's name is Annie. Jack and Annie—that sounds almost like Zach and Andy. We noticed that when we were taking turns reading at bedtime one night.

That's our tradition, mine and Mommy's—we take turns when we read a book. At first, when I couldn't read so good yet, I did one sentence and then Mommy did a few sentences and then me one sentence again. But now I can read a lot more than one sentence. I can read a whole page or even more, and then we switch.

When we noticed the thing about Jack/Zach and Annie/Andy, Mommy said, "Hey, we can pretend it's you and your brother going on adventures," and I said, "Yeah, except we don't do adventures together, so it's just the names that are like the same, but not the rest." And Mommy looked at me with a sad face when I said that.

I decided to pick one of the Magic Tree House books and see if Mommy wanted to take turns reading. Maybe she was done with the iPad and we could have time to do reading together. I went downstairs to look for Mommy but she wasn't in the kitchen anymore. I thought maybe she started with the cleaning again, but I saw her through the glass door in Daddy's office. I was about to go in, but then I heard Mommy and Daddy talking, and the way their voices sounded made me not open the door. Daddy was sitting in his big brown chair at his desk by the window, and Mommy was standing next to him, so I could only see their backs.

"No, I can't wait and see how things play out!" I could hear Mommy say, "You're a lawyer, for fuck's sake. Our son got mowed down by a madman and you're just sitting here. I'm tired of watching you sit here. We should be doing something about this!"

Daddy scooched backward like he was trying to get away from Mommy. "I'm not saying let's do nothing about it. I didn't say that. I—"

Mommy interrupted him. "You did, actually."

"I did NOT!" Daddy's voice sounded louder now. "All I said was it's been two weeks, Melissa, that's it. Not even."

"Exactly. Which is why now is the time to do something!" Now Mommy was yelling, and I could feel my chest starting to get tight.

"Can you please . . . ?" Daddy made his voice quiet and waved his hands like he was pushing the air down.

Mommy's voice got even louder. "Don't shush me! It's on them, Jim. It's on them. My son is dead because of them, and I'm not going to sit on my ass and let them get away with it." All of a sudden Mommy turned around, and I didn't have time to move away from the door. Mommy was going to get more mad now because I was listening to their fighting.

Mommy opened the door. "What, Zach?"

I held up the book and said, "I wanted to see if you wanted to take turns reading."

Mommy stared at me for a minute. I thought maybe she didn't hear me, but then she said, "I can't. Not right now, OK, Zach? Later, OK?" and then she walked out of Daddy's office and around me back to the kitchen, and I heard the TV go on in the family room. Daddy leaned forward in his chair and put his elbows on the desk and his face in his hands again.

I was wrong about how it was going to get better after Mommy stopped being sad and in shock. There was still fighting, even without Andy here. I went back upstairs and into my hideout. After I got comfy on Andy's sleeping bag, I switched on my Buzz flashlight and opened the book to the first chapter, and I read all the way through the whole book, no taking turns.

25

The Secrets of Happiness

"I feel like I'm seeing spring for the first time," said Jack.

"Me too," said Annie.

"Not just for the first time this year," said Jack. "But for the first time in my whole life."

"Me too," said Annie.

Jack felt happy, really *happy, as he and Annie headed for home in the sparkling morning light.*

I closed the book and put it on the stack of books in the corner of the hideout, all the books I read in the last few days, and I stood up to stretch my legs. They hurt from sitting crisscross applesauce the whole time, and my neck hurt from leaning over the book. My throat felt scratchy from reading out loud. At first, when I started reading the Magic Tree House books all by myself, I read them quiet in my head, but then I switched to reading out loud. Miss Russell says it's good to practice your reading out loud. You can read to a person or pretend, and your brain can record the sound of the words and learn faster.

So I started pretending like I was reading to someone.

And that someone was Andy.

I didn't even know why I started doing that, except that after the funeral, when I first talked to Andy in the hideout and I said the truth to him, that he was being a jerk to me, it felt good to say that. So I decided I wanted to keep saying stuff to Andy. I started out with whispering, I didn't know why. No one was going to hear me anyway, with Daddy staying in his office with the door closed all the time and Mommy reading on the iPad or cleaning invisible messes. And Mimi wasn't staying overnight anymore, so we could have space, she said, even though there was already all that space in between everyone in the house.

But I still only whispered at first: "Hi, I'm back in your closet," and it was like I could hear Andy say, "Duh," because "Hello, I can see you sitting in there!"

"You didn't always have to talk to me like that in your meany way," I told Andy, and then I said all the truth things, all the stuff that he did that was really mean, to me and to Mommy. And it was weird because it was like the most I ever talked to Andy in my whole life.

But then I started to feel bad about saying just the bad things to him and nothing nice, because he was dead, and who knows, maybe he was really sad about that and lonely where he was now, so I wanted to say other things to him, too, but then I didn't know what, so that's when I decided to start reading out loud to him instead. Not in a whispering voice because that hurts your mouth after a while.

I started on Magic Tree House #30—that was the one I picked out to read with Mommy—and I read all of that and then #31, 32, 33, 34, 35, and 36, and it took like one whole day to read one book, so I was reading out loud for a lot of days already. The book I finished today was #37, *Dragon of the Red Dawn,* 105 pages and not a lot of pictures.

I liked reading to Andy, even if it was only pretend. When I was in the middle of reading, it didn't feel like pretend. I had a feeling like he was right there, listening to me, and I went on adventures with Jack and Annie, and Andy went, too, all four of us.

After I was done stretching my legs, I sat back down and I looked at the wall with my feelings pages. A few days ago, I hung up something else on the wall, a picture of me and Andy. I found it on a whole pile of pictures on the dining room table, the ones that were hanging up at the wake, and I sneaked it upstairs.

When I took breaks from reading, I looked at the picture a lot. It was from when we went to Grandma's beach house in the summer, not this year, but last year. Uncle Chip was still alive, but he was really sick, and in the same year, in the fall, he died. Grandma wanted us all to wear matching clothes, white shirts and beige pants, and a photographer came and took a bunch of pictures of us on the beach. There was fighting, because Andy ran in the ocean and his pants got wet, and that wasn't going to look good in the pictures. Also he kept making his funny faces in almost every picture.

In this picture, we were sitting on the beach on the big sand hills in front of Grandma's beach house, and Andy wasn't making a funny face in it, but a serious face. I was sitting next to Andy with some space in between us, and I did a cheese for the camera, but Andy looked like he was staring at something next to the camera. His wet pants were rolled up to his knees, and he was sitting with his legs pulled up and his arms were hugging his knees.

He looked sad, and when I first noticed Andy's sad face, my throat started to hurt a lot. I moved the picture onto the sad feelings page, the gray one, and the whole picture didn't look like it belonged there, because it had a sunny blue sky, but it did, because of Andy's face and because of how it made me feel when I looked at it.

I never saw a sad face on Andy before when he was still alive, only the funny faces he made and the mad faces, always the mad faces. But maybe I never looked at his face for a long time, like now.

I liked the ending of *Dragon of the Red Dawn* and how Jack and Annie are feeling in the end. In this book, Jack and Annie go on a quest to find one of the secrets of happiness, the first one—there are four secrets in total—to help the magician Merlin. Merlin doesn't feel good and doesn't eat and sleep, and he's tired a lot. The secrets of happiness are going to make him feel better. Jack and Annie travel in the Magic Tree House to a place called Japan, and they meet a famous poet named Matsuo Basho. Matsuo Basho invented a type of short poem called haiku, and Jack and Annie learn how to make haikus, too.

And they learn what the first secret of happiness is: *"Paying attention to small things around you, like in nature."*

I said it a few times so I would remember it: "Paying attention to small things around you, like in nature." I didn't know that was something that you could do to get happy, but when Jack and Annie came back from their adventure, they were feeling very happy, so it must have worked.

"I really wish we could have done adventures, too, like Jack and Annie," I said to Andy in the picture. "Before you died. Like do more fun stuff."

I tried to look for small things around us in the beach picture. I couldn't see any, but I remembered some things that are at a beach: sand and rocks and seashells—those are all pretty. And the grass that grows on the sand hills that gets really tall and it's sharp, so you have to be careful when you try to rip a piece off because you can get a cut, but it still looks pretty.

Right next to where we were sitting, I noticed patterns in the sand, maybe from the wind or the ocean, and they looked cool. I didn't see those when we were at the beach to take pictures. So maybe then if we could have tried to notice those things around us, everyone would have felt happier, and then we would have had no fighting. Maybe then Andy's face wouldn't be sad in the picture.

I wanted to go try out the first secret of happiness with Mommy and Daddy. I could tell them about it and we could try it out together, and then maybe we could feel happier again. "I'll be back later," I said into the closet before I went out.

Every time when I first come out of the hideout, it hurts my eyes because it's dark in the closet with just the light from Buzz. When you first come back out, it's too bright and it takes a while to see things right.

I didn't hear any sounds anywhere, and our house was like the Magic Tree House after it spins and lands in a new place. It's always the same in every book: *"Then everything was still. Absolutely still."* When I went downstairs to look for Mommy and Daddy, I thought that our house did kind of spin and it landed in a new place after the gunman came, except we didn't land somewhere to start a fun adventure. We just landed somewhere and it was absolutely still. And everyone was sad or mad. And we weren't doing stuff together, like Jack and Annie when they go someplace new, but we all did separate things most of the time.

I walked past Daddy's office, but he wasn't in there, and I heard Mommy's voice in the kitchen: "I think this will be good, to start with this interview. . . . Yes, let people see my family and what this . . . what they did to us. I just want to start the conversation, . . . raise the questions, you know? Exactly . . . It can't just be like, oh, what a horrible thing that happened and everyone will be upset about this for a while and then people will move on and nothing changes. . . . I want to at least start the conversation about them, how they could let this happen. Put things in motion to . . . Exactly . . ." Then Mommy was quiet for a while and listened to someone talking on the phone.

"All right . . . that sounds good. . . . Exactly," she said in between listening, and then she said, "Oh, Zach?" I went to her because I thought she was talking to me. "Mommy?" I said. But Mommy was still talking on the phone, and when I said her name, she got up fast from where she was sitting and walked in the family room and stayed with her back to me like she didn't want me to hear her, but she wasn't even standing far away from me, so I still could.

"Oh, I'm not sure. I don't know if we should involve him . . ." Mommy turned back around and looked annoyed when she saw I was looking at her.

"Mommy?"

"I . . . I need to go. But OK, we can give it a try, see how it goes. Thank you, see you then." Mommy hung up the phone. "Zach, what's up? Didn't you see me talking on the phone? Why are you interrupting?"

"Where's Daddy?" I asked.

"At work. He . . . went to work."

"But he didn't say good-bye to me." I could feel tears coming into my eyes.

"Sorry, Zach. Why are you looking for him?" Mommy said.

"Do you remember in *Dragon of the Red Dawn,* the first secret of happiness?" I asked.

Mommy made wrinkles between her eyes. "What?"

"The first secret of happiness that Jack and Annie learn from the man in Japan, and it's to make Merlin feel better. It's that you have to pay attention to the small things around you in nature."

"OK, Zach, sweetie? I don't know what you're talking about right now, but I have a lot of things on my mind. Can we talk about this later?" Mommy said, and then she walked past me back into the kitchen, and it looked like she was going to make a new phone call.

I could feel a hot wave come up from my belly up to my head, a mad wave. "NO!" I said, and it was loud like yelling. It surprised me, and Mommy, too, because she turned around fast and looked at me. "I want me and you and Daddy to try out the first secret. We have to try it out so we can feel better again. Maybe in the backyard we could do it, and we have to pay attention to all the small things there, and then we can feel happier. If we do it later, it will be dark and then we can't see anything. I want to do it NOW. It has to be NOW."

I didn't know why my words were coming out so loud, but the hot mad wave came flying out of my mouth. I couldn't stop it, and I didn't want to stop it because it felt good to yell.

Mommy made her eyes really small and she stared at me and she made her voice very quiet: "Zach, Mommy needs you to stop yelling like that right now. I don't know what's gotten into you, but you can't talk to Mommy like that."

My heart was beating fast. I stared back at Mommy, and I could feel the tears starting to spill over from my eyes, so I tried not to blink.

"Front door!" the lady robot voice said on the alarm box, and we both jumped. Then Mimi came in the kitchen and put grocery bags on the counter and a ginormous pile of mail. She looked at us. "Everything all right?" she asked.

"Everyone's losing it in this house," Mommy said, and she looked at me again with small eyes. Then she went back in the family room with the phone.

I went out on the deck and slammed the door behind me, and that felt good, too. I walked down the steps to the backyard. I tried to stop feeling so mad, because you probably can't try out the secret of happiness when you're in a mad mood. I tried to pay attention to everything around me, but it was hard to see with more stupid tears coming in my eyes. And the stupid rain was making me wet and cold all over.

I put my hands inside my sleeves and looked all around. I saw leaves on the ground everywhere, brown and red and yellow, and some green ones still, too. I saw shells from some nuts that squirrels cracked open, they ate the insides but left the shells. There was the skin of the big tree that's in the middle of our yard, and it had patterns that looked a little bit like the patterns in the sand in the beach picture. I looked for all the small things, but the mad feeling didn't go away and I didn't start to feel happy.

"Sweetie, if you want to be out here, you need to put a coat on, OK? You're getting all wet," I heard Mimi calling, so I went back inside and slammed the door again on my way in. The first secret of happiness didn't work.

26

Making News

YESTERDAY DADDY TOLD ME that the news people were coming today. Yesterday was Tuesday, and it was day number two that Daddy drove me to school before he went to work. Not McKinley, because McKinley was going to stay closed longer, but the school where I was supposed to go for now, Warden Elementary.

On the first day when Daddy said we were driving to school, Monday, I got really upset because I didn't want to go. Everyone else already went back to school, except me. They were all going to have their eyes on me because I was coming back after them and also because of what happened to Andy.

"You don't have to," Daddy said, and he made me a promise that I didn't have to go in until I felt ready. "Let's just take a drive over there."

So we did, and when we pulled up in front of the school it looked like McKinley, except it was brown, not greenish beige like McKinley, and there was a playground on the right side of it that looked fun. The front door looked the same like at McKinley's, with little windows in it, and I thought about how the gunman came in through the door because Charlie let him in, and maybe a gunman, not Charlie's son because he was dead, but a different one, could come in through that door, too.

Daddy asked, "Do you want to go in?" and I said, "No."

"OK, maybe tomorrow," Daddy said, and we drove home again and Daddy dropped me off and went to work.

On our drive yesterday he told me we weren't going to drive to school today because the news people were coming to our house. They were coming to give us an interview. An interview is when the news lady, her name was Miss Wanda, asks you questions and you have to answer them. It was going to be about what happened to Andy, and they were going to make a video out of it and then show it on the news.

"So everyone is going to see us there, on the news?" I asked Daddy, and that was not good because I didn't want that, to be in the video so everyone could look at me on TV.

"Well, not everyone. Look, this is important to Mommy, so . . . but let's not get worked up about this right now, OK? I just wanted to give you the heads-up that that's what's happening tomorrow. We can talk about it later. Hey, maybe it will be exciting to see how they make the news!"

We got to the school and Daddy parked the car in front but didn't turn it off.

"OK, but, Daddy?"

"Uh-huh?"

"What are the things the news lady's going to ask us on the interview? About Andy?"

"Um, well, I think she's going to ask us to talk about your brother and how we feel after he got . . . after he died. I think Mommy is going to answer most of the questions and do most of the talking. And maybe Miss Wanda will ask you a question or two. Why don't we wait and see, OK?" Daddy turned sideways in his seat and looked at me. "Are you going in today?"

I shook my head no.

"Didn't think so," Daddy said, and pulled away from the school.

"On the interview, are we supposed to say the truth?" I asked.

"The truth? The truth about what?"

"About Andy."

Daddy looked at me quickly and then back at the road. "What do you mean?"

"I mean like at the funeral you said Andy made us laugh and that he made you proud every day, but that wasn't the truth."

Daddy stared straight ahead at the road and didn't say anything for a long time. We got to our house. "Go ahead and go inside, OK?" That was all he said, and his voice sounded like something was stuck in his throat.

Today after breakfast I went upstairs to put on a handsome shirt like Mommy said, and I was about to go in my room when I heard Daddy talking in his and Mommy's room. I went closer to the door because it was a little bit open. I saw Daddy standing by the window, talking on his phone: ". . . I know that. I don't think it's right either. I tried to talk her out of it, but there's no reasoning with her right now . . . No . . . Yes, I know that, Mom. Look, I already told you that I agree, Zach shouldn't be included in this interview. I'll see what I can do. Listen, I should go. They will probably be here soon."

I could tell Daddy was about to hang up, so I backed up from the door and went in my room with very quiet steps. I put on the shirt and then I sat by my window to be on the lookout for the news van. The sky was still gray and the rain was still pouring down, making rivers on the side of the road. In all the days since the gunman came, every time I looked out the window or went outside it rained.

I kept an eye out for the news van and watched the raindrops coming down, down, down and that made me think about a story I heard one time about when it rained for a really long time and it never stopped. The whole earth was going to get a big flood, and all the people and animals were going to drown. A man decided to build a big boat, and it fit only two of every type of animal on it, a boy and a girl, so they could have a new life with a new family after the flood and not be extinct. I looked at the rivers running down our road and I wondered how much more it had to rain before it got so much that maybe we were all going to drown. Or maybe we could build a boat and then start a new life after the flood.

The news van was supposed to come right after breakfast, but it didn't. I had to wait for a long time and I started to hope that maybe it wasn't going to come, but then it did. I could see it coming up our road, and I knew it was the news van right away because it had that big standing-up bowl on the roof. It stopped in front of our house and it said LOCAL 4 on the side of it in big red letters, and some other cars pulled up behind the van. I watched two doors on the side of the van pop open, and some people came out and walked to the house, and a second later the doorbell rang.

I wanted to stay upstairs and hide so I wouldn't have to be on the interview, but I also wanted to see how they make the news. Daddy said maybe it was going to be exciting. I had a curious feeling—that's when you want to find out more about things—and it was funny that I was having a curious feeling today, because I just read about that a couple of days ago. In Magic Tree House #38, *Monday with a Mad Genius,* at the end Jack and Annie find out that to be curious is the second secret of happiness for Merlin.

Earlier on the phone Daddy said that maybe I wouldn't get included in the interview and my curious feeling told me to go downstairs to see what the news people were going to do in our house. Downstairs, Daddy made me do handshakes with a woman with short, really red hair. Her name was Tina, and she had headphones around her neck like a big necklace. Daddy said Tina was the producer, and I didn't know what that meant, but she acted like the boss and told everyone where to put things. I stood by the living room door and watched.

"Dude, this shit's heavy." A man with all black clothes on and long black hair in a ponytail and a long skinny beard on his chin was trying to push our coffee table to the end of the living room. The table really is heavy, it has a big rectangle stone on the top. I can't even move it a tiny bit. Tina waved her hand over to me where I was standing by the door. "Dexter, could you . . . ?"

"Oh, sorry, man, sorry," the man gave me a wink and went back to pushing. "Son of a bitch!" I heard him say very quiet, and that made me smile.

Other news people were walking in and out of the house, to the news van and back, bringing in big black boxes that had little wheels at the bottom and tables that also had wheels and a bunch of stuff on them. They brought everything in our living room, and the wheels made wet lines on our floor. All our furniture had to get pushed to the side—that was Dexter's job.

"Hey, man, wanna come check this out?" After he got the coffee table moved, Dexter started putting up cameras in front of the couch that was still where it was supposed to be, and he waved me over. There were two cameras, and Dexter was putting them on stands that had three legs.

"Look, you put the camera on sideways like this and then turn until it clicks in. You try." He took the camera back off and handed it to me. It was a big camera, much bigger than our picture camera, and I'm not really allowed to hold our camera, only when the strap is around my neck. This camera had a long thing on the front and tons of buttons on the side. I tried to lift it up on the stand, but it was too heavy. I could feel it falling out of my hands, but Dexter grabbed it quickly. "Ooookay, let me help you!"

Dexter was nice. He said I was his setup assistant, and he told me what all the things were for. There were high stands with microphones, and the microphones looked like furry squirrels at the end. We put up lights, there were three different kinds, and Dexter said you had to put them in the right spots for the interview so the light looks perfect. There were a ton of cables everywhere. I was in charge of taping them to the floor so no one would trip over them. Dexter sat next to me on the floor and ripped off pieces of black tape and gave them to me.

"Hey, I'm sorry about your brother, man," Dexter said. He kept ripping off tape pieces, and I kept sticking them on the cables.

"Me too," I said.

"That really sucks, huh?" Dexter said.

"Yeah," I said.

Then we were done and stood up and looked at the living room. It looked totally different now.

"What do you think?" Dexter asked.

"Looks cool."

"Very cool," Dexter said, and he slapped his hand on my back.

Then Tina came in and Mommy and the lady from the news, Miss Wanda, and I knew it was her because I saw her on TV before and it was the first time I ever saw a person in real life that I saw on TV. Mommy was wearing one of her old fancy outfits, and she had on a lot of makeup and lipstick and usually she doesn't wear lipstick because she knows I don't like it when people have lipstick on, like Grandma. Mommy sat down on the couch.

Dexter changed the lights around a little bit, and some of the other people did stuff on the cameras and microphones that me and Dexter set up. Miss Wanda sat down on a chair in front of the couch, close by the one camera.

"OK, Melissa, I think we're ready to begin. Remember, please look at me and not directly at the camera, OK?"

Mommy squeezed her hands tight in her lap.

"Do me a favor and slide right into the very center of the couch. Then we can have Jim and Zach join you on either side later on, OK?" I wanted to tell Mommy that I didn't want to sit on the couch later, with the cameras pointing right at me and the lights, and I didn't want to be on the interview, and Daddy said maybe I didn't have to.

"Mommy?" I said.

Mommy looked up, but one of the lights got in her eyes and she couldn't see me.

"Mommy?" I said again. I felt a hand on my shoulder, and when I turned around, I saw Tina smiling at me.

"Hey, buddy, can you come with me and maybe you can hang out with your dad in the kitchen for a little while?"

Me and Daddy sat in the kitchen when Miss Wanda started giving Mommy the interview. We could hear a loud man's voice say, "Picture's up! Quiet, please!" and all the people in the house said "Ssshhhhh" together. Daddy sat up very straight on the barstool, like Grandma, and made a fake serious face at me and pretended to use a zipper to close his mouth.

27

Breaking News

ILIKED SITTING IN THE KITCHEN with Daddy. It was like we were in trouble together so we had to take a time-away in the kitchen. We had to sit and be quiet for a long time and weren't allowed to come out from our time-away. A couple times Daddy pretended like he was falling asleep from being bored, and it made me laugh. I put my face in my elbow on the counter really quick so I wouldn't make a sound.

Tina came back in the kitchen and ruined Daddy's and my fun. "All right, guys, you're up!" Daddy followed Tina into the living room, and I waited for him to tell her that I wasn't going to get included in the interview, but he didn't say anything.

In the living room, Mommy's face had red dots on it like she cried, but she wasn't crying now.

"Let's have Jim sit right here, and Zach, can you sit next to your mom right there?" Tina pointed on the couch next to Mommy.

Daddy sat down and I sat down. I could feel the eyes of everyone in the living room on me, and the cameras were like extra-big eyes staring at me.

"Zach, honey, can you please not look at the cameras? Can you please look at me?" Miss Wanda said to me. I looked at her and I noticed her curly black hair was very shiny in the lights like it was wet, and then my eyes went back to the cameras. "Can you . . . can he please not look at the cameras?" she said to Mommy, and it didn't sound friendly, and her face didn't look friendly.

"Zach, can you please just . . ." Mommy's voice didn't sound friendly either. I tried to get my eyes to stop looking at the cameras, but they kept doing the opposite. "Zach, stop it!" Mommy squeezed my leg hard. It was like a hard pinch, and tears came in my eyes.

"Melissa . . . ," Daddy started to say.

"Hey, man!" All of a sudden Dexter was behind Miss Wanda and he looked short because he was on his knees, and it looked funny. He gave me a wink and a smile. "Can you try to look at me? I'll stay here if you want. Keep your eyes right on me for the next few minutes?" I shook my head yes, and the tears went away.

"OK, great. Here we go then. Let's get started," Miss Wanda said, and a man next to the camera said in a loud voice again, "Picture's up! Quiet, please!" and everyone else answered with the "Ssshhhhh" again. Then it was quiet for a little while before Miss Wanda started to talk.

"Jim, you learned about Andy's death while waiting at St. Paul's Church for news about your son. Can you tell me about that?"

It took Daddy a while until he said his answer. "Yeah. OK. I . . . stayed behind at the church where the children and families gathered after the shooting to wait for updates from the police regarding the . . . missing children. Melissa took Zach to West-Medical to try and see if Andy had been taken there. Um . . ." Daddy coughed and then he was quiet.

"Can you describe to us the situation at the church?" Miss Wanda said.

"OK," Daddy said. "It had emptied out quite a bit. It was chaotic at first when parents were coming in looking for their children, but over time most families left the church and there were only a few of us left. I hadn't heard from Melissa at the hospital yet, and waiting for news was . . . it was hard. We were told there had been fatalities, and not being able to locate Andy . . . It wasn't a good sign. We waited for a long time."

"How did you finally learn that Andy was indeed one of the casualties?" Miss Wanda asked.

"Eventually some clergymen entered the church. A priest and a rabbi . . . and they came with Mr. Stanley, the assistant principal. I knew when I saw them. I knew right away."

I didn't move and I kept staring at Dexter. Dexter looked right at me, and I could see his long beard on his chin was shaking.

"And you had to break the awful news to your wife and son," Miss Wanda said. It was weird she said "break the news"—I know it's called "make the news."

Daddy coughed again. "Yes. I drove to West-Medical and I found them in the waiting room. Me showing up there . . . Melissa knew what it meant." I thought about when Daddy came to the hospital and what his face looked like, and how Mommy started howling and hitting him and throwing up. My throat started to hurt a lot.

"Zach, do you remember what it was like—when your dad came to the hospital to tell you about your brother?" All of a sudden Miss Wanda was talking to me, and I didn't know it was going to be my turn on the interview and right away I got hot all over. I forgot what she asked me.

"Zach?" she said again. "Do you remember what it was like when your dad told you about your brother?" Now she was talking to me in a nice voice, not like earlier.

"Yes," I said very quietly. My throat still hurt too much to talk. I could feel the red juice starting to spill up my neck into my face, and I started to feel hot. Everyone in the room was going to see, and on the video on TV they were going to see, too. Dexter said something to me with his lips, no sound, and it looked like he said "OK," but I wasn't sure.

"What was it like, Zach?" Miss Wanda asked the same question again. I looked down at my lap because I wanted to hide my red face. I wanted to wait for the red juice spill to go back down.

"I don't want to say," I said, and it came out like a whisper.

"What was that, honey?"

I kept my eyes on my lap, but I started to feel a mad feeling starting up in my belly. I wanted her to stop asking me the same stupid question. I didn't want to talk.

Mommy bumped her arm into my side. "Zach?" she said.

And then I didn't know what happened. The mad feeling got big. Like the Hulk. "I don't want to say! I don't want to say!" I yelled a lot of times.

"OK, then you don't have to. . . ." I heard Mommy's voice next to me, and she tried to put her arm around me, but I pushed her away and it was too late, because when the Hulk gets mad, he stays mad. Everyone in the room stared at me, even Dexter, and stupid tears came back in my eyes.

"Stop looking at me!" I yelled, and the yelling felt good. I looked around, but everyone was still looking at me, and then I saw the cameras. Now I was going to be on TV like this, mad and yelling. So I went over to the camera that was next to Miss Wanda and I kicked it. It fell over, and the man with the loud voice tried to catch it, but he was too slow and the camera landed on the ground with a loud crash. Pieces fell off it, so it was broken.

All of a sudden I felt someone picking me up and holding me tight. I couldn't move, and I saw it was Daddy and I yelled, "Let go of me! Let go of me!" But Daddy didn't let go of me. He carried me out of the living room and up the stairs, and the whole time I yelled and tried to kick Daddy with my feet.

Daddy put me down on the mattress, but his arms stayed around me tight. I stopped yelling and kicking and I started crying, and then the crying made my mad feeling wash away.

28

Trick or Treat

TRICK OR TREAT, smell my feet, give me something good to eat!"

I sat on the stairs in the dark and I heard laughing and shouting outside. Halloween is my favorite holiday—well, maybe Christmas is the number one favorite, but Halloween is definitely number two. I love going trick-or-treating and we get new costumes every year, and all year long I think about what I should be on the next Halloween, but Mommy doesn't buy the costumes until right before because I change my mind too many times.

This year we were skipping Halloween. No new costume and no trick-or-treating. Daddy said we could go for a little while, but I didn't want to go as Iron Man again, two years in a row, plus there was a big rip in the pants. I was going to go as Luke Skywalker this year. That was going to be my final decision.

A few times already kids came to our front door and rang the doorbell even though our porch light was turned off and they should know that's a sign that we weren't giving out candy. And our house wasn't even decorated for Halloween this time, so that's another sign.

I had a bowl of Halloween candy on the step next to me that Mimi brought over earlier. At first, when the trick-or-treating started, I sat on the stairs with Daddy, and when the doorbell rang for the first time, we went to open the door.

"Happy Halloweeeen!" Some little kids stood right in front of me and yelled too loud, and their moms smiled big smiles behind them. The mad feeling came back in my belly because it wasn't a "Happy Halloweeeen," and I didn't want to look at how excited they all were.

"Here, only take one," I said to the little kids in kind of a mean way, and I shoved the candy bowl at them. Their moms' big smiles went away, and when they left Daddy said, "We don't have to do this, you know," so we decided to turn off all the lights inside the house, too. Daddy sat on the stairs with me for a little while longer and then went back in his office.

"Trick or treat!" someone yelled right outside our door. I went upstairs and into the hideout. I sat down on the sleeping bag and pointed Buzz's light circle on the picture of me and Andy.

"Happy stupid Halloween," I said to Andy.

Last year, at the end of Halloween, there was fighting. Daddy didn't come trick-or-treating because he had to stay at work late, so Mommy went with me and Andy before it started to get dark. Mommy had the same purple witch hat on that she always wears on Halloween, and Andy went as a zombie with a scary mask.

After the second house we bumped into James and some other kids from school. They were by themselves with no grown-ups, and they were going to go all the way down Erickson Road to go trick-or-treating there. Andy begged Mommy to let him go with them. Ricky and his mom bumped into us, too, and then Ricky wanted to go with the boys like Andy. Mommy said no, we should all go as a family, but then Ricky's mom said yes to Ricky, and that they were probably too old to go with their moms, so Mommy let Andy go, too. Mommy looked very mad after that.

Andy didn't come home until after it was really dark outside and me and Mommy were about to go back out to look for him. "Wait 'til you see all the stuff I got!" he said when he came running in, and he didn't notice that Mommy was mad and she just turned around and went in the kitchen to make dinner.

We poured out our bags on the living room carpet to see all the things we got. "Keep your pile on that side of the rug so we don't mix up our stashes," Andy said, and he pushed his pile of candy farther away from mine. His pile was huge, like double mine, because he was out a lot longer than me, and also because he always takes more than one candy, and you're not supposed to do that.

"Awesome, I got a bunch of big M&M's packs! One, two, three . . . like ten of them and a ton of small ones!" Andy said. M&M's are his favorite candy. I'm not allowed to have them because they could have peanuts. Andy started to make smaller piles around himself with all the different types of candy he got—M&M's, Tootsie Rolls, Skittles, Kit Kats . . . He kept eating the small candy bars, the ones that say "fun size," and they're so little you can eat them with two bites. He put the wrappers in his pocket so that Mommy wouldn't notice.

I started piling up my candy, too. "Can I have this one?" I held up a round ball that had an eyeball on it, but it didn't say what type of candy was inside. Andy came over and took it from me. "I don't know what this one is. So don't eat it," he said, and he threw the eyeball over on his pile. "This you definitely can't have. And that one and this one . . ." Andy started grabbing different candies from my stash.

"Hey, stop!" I yelled. "Those are mine. Don't take all of mine!"

"ANDY!" a voice yelled behind us. It was Daddy and he scared us because we didn't hear him come home from work. "Let go of his goddamn candy!" Daddy came over and grabbed Andy's arm and pulled him up hard. Andy dropped the candies he was holding.

"What the hell are you doing? Look at your massive pile and look at your brother's. Why are you stealing his?"

"I wasn't stealing his—," Andy started to say back, but Daddy got more mad because Andy was back-talking. He told Andy to stop lying, and he started to drag him out of the room by his arm.

Right then Mommy came in the living room. "Jim, let go of him. What are you doing?" she said to Daddy, and she grabbed Andy's other arm and now they were both standing there with Andy in the middle, and it looked like they were going to pull him from both sides.

"I'm throwing him in his room. This kid is overdue for a grounding!"

"That's not how we're supposed to be handling these types of situations," Mommy said, and her and Daddy stared at each other in a mad way over Andy's head.

"OK, why don't you tell me how I'm allowed to handle it then, Melissa, because your way is working so damn well," Daddy said, and he let go of Andy's arm. "So glad I tried to rush home to be with my family on Halloween!" And then he went in the hallway and slammed the front door. A minute later I heard his Audi turn on and drive out of the driveway.

"That's what I get for helping you, you little snitch," Andy said, and gave me a push.

Mommy said, "OK, that will do, Andy," and she took him upstairs for a time-away.

I bent down to pick up the candies Andy dropped. It was all Reese's and Butterfingers, all candies with peanuts in them.

I thought about last Halloween and the fighting, and I looked at Andy's sad face in the picture. I wanted to say something to him, that I was sorry that he got in trouble, because he was actually trying to help me with the peanut candies. But I didn't say it out loud, the words stayed in my head only.

29

Snow and Milkshakes

THE DAY AFTER HALLOWEEN, in the morning, it started to snow and that was a surprise—to see snow and not rain. The sky looked white and the air looked white from the snowflakes twirling around, and all the gray from the rain was gone. First it was rain, rain, rain for all the days and weeks since when the gunman came, and now, just like that, it stopped and there was snow instead even though it wasn't even winter yet. It was the first day of November.

Mommy wasn't in the bed again. It was like she was too mad to lie down and sleep now, and she went from sleeping all the time to no sleeping at all. Daddy was in the bed, and I tried to tell him about the snow, but he rolled over the other way. "Let me sleep for a bit, bud," he said with a sleepy voice, so I went to find Mommy downstairs. She was in the living room, making all the decoration pillows on the couch all straight in a line.

"Mommy, it's snowing!"

I went to the living room window to watch the snowflakes fall down and land on the piles of leaves on the ground.

"I saw," she said. "Finally, a break from the rain. Don't get too excited, though. It's not going to stick."

"OK, but if some of it sticks, can we go sledding?"

"It's not going to. Don't get your hopes up. I'm going to be very busy today anyway," Mommy said, and left the living room. "Hey,

Zach," she called from the kitchen. "Let's get you some breakfast and then I want you to get dressed. There are some people coming over to the house in a bit, so I want everything squared away by then."

"What people?" I asked.

"People I need to talk to."

The doorbell rang right when I came down from getting dressed. I opened the door and Ricky's mom stood outside, and this time she wore a coat, but she still looked cold and her face looked very white. I noticed a lot of reddish-brown spots on her nose and cheeks, and some snowflakes were on her hair, it was reddish-brown, too, except at the top it looked like it was coming out of her head in a different color, gray. The last time she was at our house, Daddy told her she couldn't be at our house anymore, but now she came back. I wondered if Daddy was going to get mad at her.

Mommy came from behind me and walked out on the porch to give Ricky's mom a hug. It was a long hug, and I watched how their hair was touching, the reddish-brown from Ricky's mom and the shiny brown from Mommy. I looked up the stairs. Before I came down, Daddy was in the shower and maybe he wouldn't come down yet and see Ricky's mom.

"Nancy. Come in, please. Let's head into the living room," Mommy said, and they both sat down on the couch, very close together.

I sat down on the chair across from them, and like two seconds later I heard Daddy's voice in the hallway: "Hey, Zach, do you want to come to the . . . ?" He walked in the living room and then he saw Ricky's mom sitting on the couch with Mommy. He stopped walking and finished his sentence very slow: ". . . store with me?" But he didn't look at me, he stared at Ricky's mom like she was a ghost or something. Ricky's mom stared back at him, and I saw her chin was moving up and down fast.

"What is this?" Daddy asked.

"Geez, Jim, that's polite. You remember Nancy Brooks, right?" Mommy said, and just when she said it the doorbell rang again. "Here come the others." Mommy got up and walked out of the living room to open the door.

Daddy walked a couple steps toward Ricky's mom and then stopped and looked over at me. "What's going on here?" he asked Ricky's mom in a quiet voice.

"Melissa, um, called me," Ricky's mom said. Her voice sounded like she was out of breath, like she just ran really fast. "She asked me over, and a few other parents of the . . . victims. For a meeting."

I could hear people talking in the hallway.

"A meeting?" Daddy said. "A meeting about what? And you said yes? To come here?"

I thought that Ricky's mom would probably start to get mad about how Daddy was talking to her. She answered Daddy, and her voice didn't sound so out of breath anymore. "Yes, Jim, I said yes. She wants to talk about . . . our options. If we can do something about Charles's family to . . . hold them accountable. And I think she's right about that. It has nothing to do with . . ."

"All right, guys, please come in, have a seat." Mommy walked back in the living room, and Daddy took a couple steps back. Three women and one man came in behind Mommy and sat down on the couch and chairs. "Do you all know each other?"

Some said yes and some said no, so Mommy said the names of everyone: "Nancy Brooks, Ricky's mom; Janice and Dave Eaton, Juliette's parents; Farrah Sanchez, Nico's mom; and Laura LaConte, Jessica's mom." Juliette, Nico, Jessica—they're all kids from Andy's class that got shot from the gunman, too. I saw their pictures on the news on TV.

"And that's my husband, Jim, and Zach, my other son." Mommy pointed at me and Daddy. Daddy didn't say anything, and he didn't do handshakes.

"Can I get you anything? To drink?" Mommy asked, and then she went in the kitchen because some of the people said water, please. The room got very quiet after she left. I saw Ricky's mom staring at Daddy. Her face looked very sad. Mommy came back with a tray with glasses of water on it, and she put it down on the coffee table. "All right, I think we can get started," she said. "Jim, could you . . . ?" and she pointed at me with her head.

Daddy stared at Mommy for a second and then he said, "Come on, Zach, let's go."

I wanted to stay to hear what Mommy and the other people were going to talk about in their meeting, but Daddy said, "Come on. Please, Zach," in the voice that he does when you better listen. I got up and walked out of the living room behind Daddy. "Let me grab you a sweater from upstairs. It got cold out," Daddy said, and walked upstairs. "Put your shoes on."

I sat down right outside the living room to put my shoes on so I could still hear the talking inside.

". . . We could go over the information we do have . . . and also what we don't have. More importantly maybe," I heard Mommy say, "I wanted to confirm we're all on the same page. Everyone in this room does want to pursue this . . . take action, right?"

"Yes," and "I think so, yes," the other people said.

"OK, good. I thought it would be good to get together and compare notes and figure out how we will proceed against them, the Ranalezes. I think it begins with us speaking out publicly, giving more interviews like the one I did with Wanda Jackson. And we should start looking into ways to take action against them, legally. . . ."

"Zach, that's not for you in there!" Daddy stood next to me all of a sudden and busted me spying.

Daddy drove out of the driveway fast, and the Audi made a loud sound when Daddy started speeding up our road. After we turned the corner, he drove slower and looked at me in the mirror. "Two stops: the dry cleaner's and the liquor store right next to it," he said to me. "It's almost lunchtime. What do you say we go to the diner after?"

When we got to the parking lot at the diner, there were still some snowflakes in the air. I tried to catch them on my hand, but they melted right when they touched my skin. Inside the diner we sat down in a booth, and that's my favorite spot because you can watch the gas station across the street. It's a gas station where they also fix cars, and you can watch how they lift the cars up so they can fix them from underneath.

Marcus, the boss of the diner, came over to our table, and he knows us because we come here a lot of times for breakfast on the weekends, but not for a long time now.

"Hi, Jim!" Marcus said to Daddy (it sounds like "Jeeem" when he says Daddy's name, and that sounds funny). To me he said, "Hi, Bob." He knows that's not really my name, but he says it as the same joke every time, and then he laughs loud about his own joke. But this time he just did a little smile, a sad smile.

"Jeeem, I'm very sorry about your son. Very, very sorry. All of us here," and he waved his hand around the whole diner, and a lot of people were looking at us now. "Lunch is on me today, OK, Jeeem?" Marcus said, and did a pat on Daddy's back.

"OK . . . that's . . . thank you, that's kind of you," Daddy said, and he looked embarrassed a little and I was feeling embarrassed, too, with everyone looking at us.

We ordered the same thing: cheeseburgers and French fries and chocolate milkshakes. We can't get that when Mommy is with us, but Daddy said, "Well, she's not with us, is she? Milkshakes on the first day of snow are a must."

We waited for the food and watched the workers at the gas station and the snowflakes flying all around. We didn't talk a lot, and I liked sitting there like that. The food came, and the first thing I did was take a French fry and dip it in my milkshake. Daddy smiled.

"Daddy?"

"Yes?"

"Why is Mommy having a meeting at our house? To talk about Charlie?"

Daddy was holding his cheeseburger and was about to take a bite, but then he put it back down on his plate and cleaned off his hands with a napkin. "It's . . . Well, your mother is very sad about Andy, right? Everyone is. Her, me, you . . ."

"Yes," I said.

"Well, Mommy is . . . She thinks that if things had been . . . different for Charles, for the . . . shooter, Charlie's son, then maybe he wouldn't have done what he did."

"Different how?" I asked.

"Um, it's complicated, Zach," Daddy said.

I looked at Daddy and waited so he would say more about it.

"OK, so the shooter, Charles, was sick. He had . . . behavioral . . . problems. You know?" Daddy said.

"What kind of sickness did he have? Like what Andy had?"

"Oh, God no. One that made him very depressed, . . . sad, all the time. And I think he didn't know what was reality, what was real. And what was right or wrong. I'm not sure exactly."

"So that's why he shot Andy and everyone else? Because he didn't know it was wrong?" I asked.

"I don't know, buddy. Some people think that his family should have known that he was . . . dangerous to other people, that he could hurt someone. And that they should have made sure he was getting proper care. Maybe that could have stopped it from happening," Daddy said.

"Do you think Charlie knew that? That his son was going to do that?" I picked up the ketchup bottle and squirted more ketchup on mine and Daddy's plates.

"Thanks," Daddy said, and dipped in a fry. "No. I don't think he knew Charles was going to do what he did. But I do think he and his wife didn't take care of him the way he needed to be taken care of. I think they were probably in denial. Know what I mean?"

"I don't know what that means, denial," I said.

"It means that they . . . they probably knew there was something very wrong with their son, but they didn't want to admit it. Or didn't know how to deal with it," Daddy explained.

"So that wasn't good that they did that."

"No, that wasn't good."

"So Mommy is mad at them, right?"

"Yes."

"And she wants them to get in trouble about it? Are the police going to put Charlie in jail?" I asked.

"No, that's . . . I don't think so, buddy," Daddy said.

"Good, because that wouldn't really be fair, I don't think," I told Daddy.

"No?"

"No," I said. "I have the winner, by the way." I held up my longest French fry from my plate. That's a game me and Andy always play when we go somewhere where we eat something with French fries—who has the longest one.

"What? No way! OK, that one is very long," Daddy said, and he started looking around his whole plate. "This one beats yours, though." He held one up, but I saw right away he was cheating and he was holding two together with his hand to make one really long one. That used to be Andy's trick. We laughed about that, and when I looked up I saw a lot of people in the diner were looking at us, and then laughing didn't feel like a good thing to do anymore.

[30]

The Hulk

THE THING ABOUT THE HULK is that he hates getting mad. I have a book about the Avengers, and the Hulk is part of the Avengers. I love the Avengers, they're my favorite superheroes. They fight bad guys and save people. The Hulk's real name is Bruce Banner, when he's the real human person. He's a scientist, and he made a bomb and the bomb went off by accident and he got caught in the blast, and that's why he turned into the Hulk.

So then he's like two people in one that are opposites, because when he's the human scientist he's quiet and a good person, but when he gets mad he turns into the big, loud Hulk—and he doesn't want to, but he can't control it. Then he yells, "HULK SMASH!" and goes crazy.

That's like how it is for me now. One minute I'm the normal Zach Taylor and I'm acting good, and then something happens and I turn into a different version of Zach Taylor, the mad, mean version. I got mad before, like when I didn't get to do stuff or when I was mad at Andy for being a jerk to me, but now it's a whole other mad feeling.

It's a surprise when it starts, like it sneaks up on me and then it jumps on me, and I don't notice it until it already lands on me, and then it's too late, because it changes my whole self. The first thing that happens is tears come out of my eyes, but not normal tears—they're hot. Hot, mad tears. And then all of me gets hot and like tight, and the hot and tight feeling makes me yell and act bad.

Today the Zach Taylor Hulk came out two times so far. The first time was when I went downstairs in the morning and I was looking for Daddy to do our school drive, and Mommy said he had to leave early, so no school drive today. Mommy said, "What's the difference, you don't go in anyway," and that was true, but I still got mad about it. I yelled at Mommy, and I lay on the floor and kicked. Mommy stood there and looked at me. She looked surprised and then she looked sad.

I acted bad and crazy for a long time, and my head started to hurt from all the crying and yelling. Mommy tried a couple times to talk to me, but I couldn't hear what she was saying because of all of my yelling. I didn't even want to hear it. Mommy tried to pick me up, but I didn't let her. So then Mommy sat down on the stairs and she put her arms on her knees and her head on her arms. I thought she was crying because of how I acted, like she did a lot of times when Andy had his bad temper.

That was the first time, and the second time happened later when Mimi came in the house and said, "Hey, honey, look what I picked up for you," and she was holding up my backpack from school. "You've been wanting to read your books in your book baggie, haven't you? Well, here they are! And Miss Russell gave me some work for us to do at home. Do you want to sit down and get started with me?" Mimi gave me a big smile, and I got mad at her. I didn't even want to read the books from my book baggie anymore, only the Magic Tree House books.

"No!" I yelled at her. "I don't want to do stupid homework!" Mad tears that were hot and the tight feeling in my whole body, and BAM! Zach Taylor Hulk was back. I kicked the backpack after Mimi put it down in the hallway and one of my slippers came flying off and hit Mimi on the leg, and Mimi made a face like it hurt. I didn't say sorry, I just ran upstairs.

I slammed my bedroom door hard and I wanted it to be loud, but it wasn't, and it popped back open and that made me even more mad, so I slammed it again, and this time it stayed closed. But my poster over my bed from school when I was class president for the day fell down on one side from the loud BANG! the door made. It was a stupid poster anyway, so I ripped it all the way off the wall and crumpled it up and threw it across the room.

All my trucks were standing there all mixed up, and that really started to bother me all of a sudden, so I jumped off the bed and kicked them all. Kicking stuff made the tight feeling get better, so I kept kicking and kicking.

"Zach, honey, can I come in?" Mimi said from outside my door.

I stood right in the middle of my room and looked at all the mess with the trucks everywhere. "No!" I called through the door.

"All right," said Mimi's voice. "Just . . . honey? Don't break anything in there, OK? Mimi doesn't want you to get hurt."

I didn't say anything back, and I heard Mimi walk away, back down the stairs.

I walked through the bathroom, in Andy's room, and in the hideout. I switched on Buzz, and his light wasn't very bright anymore. Next time I had to remember to bring new batteries in for him, because the old ones were almost empty. At first I thought I wanted to read, but my hands were still shaking too much from the mad feeling. I moved Buzz's light circle over the wall with the feelings pages instead, and I thought about how all the pages were the same size, and that wasn't really right, because not all the feelings were the same size.

Right now, mad was huge. Much bigger than the other feelings. It should be on a huge piece of paper, maybe even the whole wall, one whole wall of green. And the other feelings should be on a different wall.

Except sad should still be on the same wall as mad.

"I think now I know why you are making a sad face in the picture," I said to Andy. "I think it's because when the mad feeling goes away, a sad feeling always starts, right? It's like a pattern. Mad, sad, mad, sad."

I put Buzz down on the sleeping bag, and that made the closet almost all the way dark. I took all the feelings pages down and put them on the other wall next to me, except mad and sad, and I put those next to each other in the middle of the wall, green and gray, under the picture of me and Andy. Then I picked Buzz back up and stared at the two feelings and at the picture.

"I acted bad today and made Mommy upset. And Mimi," I told Andy.

I noticed the three words I was thinking about: *mad, sad, bad.* Those rhyme. I pointed the light circle at the green page and said, "Mad." Then I pointed it at the gray page and said, "Sad." I said, "Bad," and first I looked at Andy in the picture, but then also at me. "Bad."

"I didn't see that, that you were making a sad face on the beach. I didn't notice it." My throat got a lump in it when I said that to Andy and when I thought about his face. Maybe then he was feeling like me now, sad, but nobody knew that. And now he wasn't alive anymore, but when he was alive, everyone only noticed the mad feelings and not the sad feelings.

Buzz's light started to go on and off by itself, and that means the batteries were almost all the way dead, so I grabbed Buzz and came out of the hideout to get new batteries from downstairs. When I got to the bottom of the stairs, I heard Mommy and Mimi talking. Mommy sounded upset, so I sat down on the stairs to listen.

"He just needs so much right now," Mommy said. "The bed-wetting and this acting out . . . He gets so upset, and I can't figure out how to get him back down from it. It's like Andy all over again." That was me she was talking about, how I was acting bad. Like Andy. I was starting to be like him. Or like me and him together.

"I just can't . . . deal with him. I just can't do it, Mom. I wish I could, but I don't know how right now. How can I be there for him when I can't even . . . deal?" Mommy's words came out together with big cries, "I don't know how."

"I think all you can do is try your best. I'm a bit relieved, to be honest. That he's finally showing some emotion. The way he was before . . . the way he didn't cry at all after . . . Andy . . . That scared me," Mimi said.

"But that's just it. I'm tired of doing my best. You know, I want to get to act out like Zach. I want to kick and scream. I want to get to be mad at the world. But I have to keep it together. It's all on me, as always. Jim gets to leave. He gets to disappear, business as usual. He's not interested in dealing with the Ranalezes. And the one thing I asked him to figure out, the one thing, to get Zach to go back to school, not even that . . ." Mommy was talking very loud now.

"I know, honey, this is so impossibly hard for all of us," Mimi said. "You know, I think you should consider the counseling option Mr. Stanley mentioned. Or call Dr. Byrne. It's important for Zach to get the help and have someone to turn to, an outsider, so to speak. This is too much to handle on your own. You can't expect so much of yourself all the time. And you should really consider getting help yourself. There's no shame in admitting—"

Mommy interrupted Mimi's sentence and her voice sounded very mad. "I don't need help. What I really need is to get the hell out of here, OK? I can't be here anymore. It's like I can't breathe in this house. I'm trying to get justice for our family, for my SON, and everyone is telling me what I can and cannot do. You shouldn't be doing this, you really need to do this. . . . I'm sick and tired of it." I heard the squeak sound of one of the barstools getting pushed back on the floor.

"Can you stay here with him for a while?" Mommy asked. "If I don't get out of here, I'm literally going to go crazy."

"OK," Mimi said. "But do you think that's a good idea—in your state? Can you at least tell me where you will be? So I know?"

"I don't know yet, Mom." Mommy came walking out of the kitchen fast, and she stopped when she saw me sitting on the steps. Her face was all red from crying.

"I'll be . . . I'll come back in a little while, OK, Zach?" she said to me, and then she grabbed the car keys from the table and started to walk backward, away from me. She opened the door to the garage and disappeared through it. I heard the garage door open, and Mommy's car started and drove out of the garage. The garage door closed again and Mommy was gone. It was quiet, and it was like Mommy ran away from home.

31

Sharing Space

I PUT THE NEW BATTERIES in Buzz and flipped the switch on. Buzz made a bright light circle again. I looked through my book pile for Magic Tree House #39, *Dark Day in the Deep Sea*. On the back it said Jack and Annie were going to find the third secret of happiness to save Merlin, but then the Magic Tree House lands on a tiny island in the ocean. I wanted to know what was going to happen to them on the island, and how they were going to get off it, and also what the third secret of happiness was, so I started to read.

I was on page thirty when the door to the hideout opened a little from the outside and let some light in. I jumped because I didn't expect it.

"Zach?" It was Daddy, and that was a surprise because I didn't know Daddy came home. I didn't think it was even dinnertime yet. "Would it be OK for me to come in there with you for a bit?"

I flashed the Buzz light circle all around the hideout. Daddy was going to see all of this—the feelings pages and the picture of me and Andy and everything else. Maybe he saw it before when he found me when I had my bad dream about shooting Andy with my arrow, but I didn't think so. Also we didn't talk about the hideout again after he found me in it, so I thought maybe he forgot all about it.

I thought that it was going to make me embarrassed to show him my hideout. But maybe it was going to be good, too, if it wasn't a secret anymore.

"OK," I told Daddy, and the door opened all the way and Daddy came in and closed the door behind him. He couldn't walk in like me because he was too tall, so he crawled in on his hands and knees all the way to the back to where I was.

"Boy, this is tight," he said when he sat down on the sleeping bag. Then he started to look around and his eyes stopped on the picture of me and Andy, and he pushed a big breath out of his mouth. He leaned forward to look at the picture, and I pointed Buzz on it so he could see it better. He stared at the picture for a while and then he looked under the picture and pointed at the feelings pages. "What are those?" he asked.

"Feelings pages," I said, and I looked at Daddy's face to see if he was going to laugh, but he didn't. He was making a serious face, like he was thinking about it.

"Feelings pages," he said. "What are feelings pages?"

"They're for the feelings inside of me. I can make the feelings separated on the papers so it's easier and they're not all mixed up anymore," I told him.

"Huh. So your feelings are all mixed up?"

"Yes," I said. "It was too complicated like that."

"Yeah, I get that," Daddy said. "How did you figure out what colors they're supposed to be?"

"I don't know. I could just feel them. The colors come attached to the feelings."

"They do? I didn't know that." Daddy pointed at green and gray. "So what are those for?"

"Mad and sad."

Daddy shook his head yes. Then he pointed at the feelings pages on the other wall. "So all of those are feelings, too? What is red for?"

"Embarrassed."

"Embarrassed? Why embarrassed?"

"Because of the peeing," I said, and my face started to feel hot.

"Black?"

"Scared."

"Yellow?" It was like Daddy was giving me a quiz.

"Happy," I said, and I looked at Daddy again to see if he thought it was bad that I made a page for happy even though Andy died and I thought that actually, now, I didn't even want that page up there anymore.

"What's the one with the hole in the middle for?" Daddy asked.

"For lonely," I explained. "Lonely is see-through, so I made a hole because there's no see-through color."

"Lonely? Because of Andy?" Daddy made a sound in his throat.

"Well, inside my hideout I don't feel lonely," I said.

"No? Why not?" Daddy asked.

I didn't know if I should tell Daddy that in here I talked to Andy and read books to him. He would probably think that was weird. "I . . . it's because I pretend Andy can hear me in here," I said, and I pointed the light circle in a corner of the closet because I didn't want me and Daddy to see each other.

"You talk to him?" Daddy said in a quiet voice.

"Yeah," I said back. "And I read out loud."

Daddy wanted to find out everything at once about my hideout, and I didn't know that was going to happen. "I mean, I know it's not real life, because Andy is dead, and dead people can't hear you," I said. "So it's stupid anyway."

Daddy took my hand that was holding Buzz, and he put it in between us and then we weren't talking in the dark anymore, and that made it harder, because he could see my red face.

"I don't think it's stupid," Daddy said.

"It makes me feel good when I say stuff to him, that's all." I put my shoulders up and down.

"So why did you include lonely on your feelings pages?" Daddy asked.

"That's for the lonely feeling outside of my hideout."

"Outside of your hideout you feel lonely?"

I put my shoulders up and down again. "Sometimes."

For a little while we didn't talk about anything else. We just sat in the hideout and were quiet together, and I liked that.

"Daddy?" I said after a while.

"Yes, bud?"

"I think I should add one for sorry."

"Add one what?"

"A feelings page."

"For sorry? Why?"

"Because I acted bad and I made Mommy upset. And it's my fault that she ran away from home. I'm sorry that I did that. I want her to come home so I can tell her sorry." Tears came in my eyes.

Daddy looked at me, and then he put his hands on both of my arms and squeezed them in a gentle way. "Zach, listen to me, bud," he said. His voice sounded like something was stuck in his throat. "It's not your fault Mommy is upset. Do you hear me?"

Tears started to spill over on my face.

"She didn't run away from home. She . . . had to get away for a little while. She'll be home later, OK?" Daddy said, and then he put his forehead against my forehead and he pushed out a big breath. I could feel it on my face, but it didn't bother me. "None of this is your fault."

"OK, but, Daddy?"

"Yes?"

"I still have a sorry feeling sometimes, and it's about Andy. I feel like I want to say sorry to Andy."

"Why do you want to say sorry to Andy, bud?" Daddy pulled his forehead away from mine to look at me. Now more tears were coming out of my eyes, and I wiped them off with my hands, and that made the Buzz light circle bounce all around the hideout.

"When the gunman was at the school, I didn't even think about him," I told Daddy. "When we were hiding in the closet and we could hear the POP sounds, and then the police came and we walked in the hallway and I could see some of the hallway with the blood, and then we went to the church . . . the whole time I didn't even think about Andy." Big crying sounds were coming from my throat now and it was hard to talk, but I wanted to tell this to Daddy. "I only thought about him when Mommy came and asked me where he was."

"Oh my God, Zach," Daddy said. He grabbed me under my armpits and pulled me over on his lap. "You do not have to feel sorry about that. You were scared. You're only a child, you're only six!"

"I'm not finished yet about why I'm sorry about Andy," I said. "And the other thing is really bad."

"Tell me," Daddy said into the hair on the top of my head.

"After Andy got killed from the gunman, at first I was feeling happy sometimes. I mean not like super happy, but I remembered all the bad things he always did, and I thought it was going to be better without him here. I thought the fighting would be gone, and Andy couldn't be mean to me anymore. That's what I thought, and that's why I was kind of happy that he wasn't here anymore."

I waited for Daddy to say something, but he was quiet. I could feel his chest going up and down, and when his breath came out it made my head warm.

"That's bad, right?" I asked Daddy.

"No. It's not bad," Daddy said in a quiet voice. "Do you still feel happy about that?"

"No. Because it's not what happened. It didn't get better. And—he didn't only do bad things. Now I have good memories, too. I don't want Andy to be gone forever."

After a while Daddy started to shift around and said, "Gets hot in here, huh?"

"Yeah," I said. "But it's cozy. I like it in here."

"Me too," Daddy said. "I know it's your special, secret space. But maybe I could come visit you sometimes?"

"OK," I said.

32

Wild Rampage

W̲HEN I WENT TO BED, Mommy didn't come home yet, and I lay on the mattress and told this to myself: "I'm not going to get mad tomorrow. I'm going to behave tomorrow." I said it a lot of times so I wouldn't forget about it when I was asleep, and so I would still remember it the next day when I woke up.

And I did remember the next day. I did good until dinnertime, but then I forgot. I forgot because Mommy told me she was leaving again tomorrow, and she just got back from running away. Right away the mad feeling jumped on me. Mommy told me she was going to New York City to do more interviews and they were going to start really early in the morning, so she had to leave tomorrow before I was even waking up. She was going to sleep at a hotel in the city, because all day long she was doing the interviews, and the next morning early, too.

We were sitting at the counter in the kitchen, like we always do now for dinner. No more dinner at the table, like before Andy died, and no more setting the table before dinner. Mommy only puts down the plates and forks and knives on the counter and that's it. We were having meatloaf that Aunt Mary brought yesterday, and it was yummy, except only I was eating it. Not Mommy, her plate was still full.

"Why do you have to do more stupid interviews?" I asked when Mommy told me that she was going to New York City. I pushed my plate away hard and it bumped into my milk and it spilled a little.

"I . . . it's important that people hear our story," Mommy talked extra slow and quiet like she was talking to a stupid person. I could tell, and that made my mad feeling get worse.

"Why?" I asked in a loud voice, almost like yelling.

"Why? Because something terrible happened to your brother. And to us. And it wasn't our fault, it was . . . someone else's fault. It's important that we talk about that. Do you understand?"

I could feel hot tears on my face, and I didn't feel like answering. "It was Charlie's son's fault," I said after a while, and I felt mad all over about Charlie's son.

"Yes, but he was a kid, too. It . . . it's complicated, OK?" Mommy looked over at the clock on the microwave and stood up and took her plate that was still full to the sink.

"Why did he even do that to Andy and the other people? Why did he kill them?" I asked.

"He was not . . . normal. In the head," she said. "So it wasn't just his fault. It was . . . he wasn't taken care of properly."

"So when Charlie and his wife came here, that's why you got mad and talked mean to them," I said.

"I didn't talk—," Mommy started to say, but then she put her shoulders up and down and turned back around to wash the dishes.

"But I want you to stay here!" I told Mommy, and more hot tears spilled out. "Who's going to take care of me when you're in the city and Daddy's at work?"

"Zach, I'll only be gone for two sleeps, OK? And Mimi will be here with you. You guys can do some of the homework together that she picked up for you. And you can play and . . . read. Mimi can read with you. Doesn't that sound like fun?"

"No, I don't want you to be gone at bedtime. I want you to tuck me in, and you have to sing me our song. This whole time you're not even singing our song anymore, and it's not good for me to go to sleep like that," I said.

"Mimi can sing the song. Or you know what? You guys can call me at bedtime and we can sing it on the phone. How's that?" Mommy asked.

"Not good! I want you to stay here!" I yelled. I got up from the barstool fast and it fell over with a loud BANG!

All of a sudden Mommy was next to me, and it surprised me. She grabbed my arm and pulled it up hard. Her fingernails were digging into my skin, and it hurt a lot. Mommy put her face close to my face and talked right in my ear with her teeth together, sounding very mad. "Listen, Zach, I'm not doing this with you right now. I explained to you why it's important that I go, and that's the end of it. Do you understand?" She pulled my arm up more when she talked, and I got a hot feeling in my belly from how Mommy talked to me and she never talked to me like this before.

"Yes," I said, and my voice came out squeaky.

"Good," Mommy said, and she threw my arm down. "OK, look. I have to go pack. The car is picking me up very early tomorrow." She didn't say the words with her teeth together anymore, but she still sounded mad. "Here, let's turn the TV on for you. And your father should be home from work soon."

I followed Mommy into the family room and she turned on the TV. She gave me the remote and looked at me like she was going to say something else, but then she turned around and I heard her go upstairs. I sat down on the couch and looked at my arm, and I could see red and purple lines from where Mommy put her fingernails in my skin. Four lines on the back of my arm and one line in the front from the thumb. It still hurt a lot. I got back up and went in the kitchen to get my Iron Man ice pack from the freezer. The whole time more tears were coming on my face, and I wiped them off with the other arm that wasn't hurting.

I noticed the barstool was still lying on the floor, so I went to pick it up and pushed it back in to the counter. Then I put my plate in the sink, and it was still full, but I didn't want to eat anymore. I cleaned up my milk spill from the counter. The hot feeling in my belly started to go away. And the tears stopped, too. In the family room, I picked out *PAW Patrol* on demand. It's a baby show, but I started to like it again.

After a while, after the first *PAW Patrol* was almost over, Daddy came in the family room and said, "Hey, bud," and gave me a kiss on the top of my head. "Where's Mommy?"

"Upstairs packing," I said.

"What happened there?" Daddy pointed at my arm.

I didn't want Daddy to know I made Mommy upset again, so I said, "I just got a scratch."

Daddy made lines on his forehead.

"Can I watch another one?"

"OK, yeah, sure. I'm going to find Mommy upstairs, OK?"

"OK," I said. "But, Daddy?"

Daddy stopped in the doorway to the kitchen. "Yes, buddy?"

"Do you sometimes wish that I died? I mean, instead of Andy? That Andy could still be here and not me?" I started to feel tears come back in my eyes.

Daddy stared at me for a second and he opened his mouth a couple times, but no words came out, like he had to do a couple tries first before he could start talking. He walked back to me slowly and pulled me up so I was standing on the couch and we had almost the same tallness.

"No, Zach," he said, and his voice sounded like something was stuck in his throat. "No," he said again. "Why . . . why would you say such a thing? I would never . . . wish that you died."

"Does Mommy, do you think?" I asked, and tears started to spill over on my face when I thought about how she talked to me earlier in the kitchen.

"No, Mommy wouldn't ever wish that either," Daddy said. He lifted up my chin and wiped the tears off my face. "Did you hear me? Did you hear what I said?"

I shook my head yes.

"OK," Daddy said, and he gave me a hug. Then I sat back down on the couch, and Daddy stayed standing behind me for a while. He put his hand through my hair a few times and then he left to go upstairs.

I turned on *PAW Patrol*, "The New Pup," and I like this one because Ryder surprises the pups with the snow patroller, and that's a cool lookout truck on wheels. They also meet a new pup, her name is Everest, and she becomes part of the PAW Patrol. I watched that whole show, and I was about to start another one, but I saw on the cable box clock that it was 8:30 and that was late. I wanted to go see what Mommy and Daddy were doing and why they weren't getting me for bedtime.

When I walked up the stairs, I heard their voices, Mommy's and Daddy's, and I knew right away there was fighting again. The door to their room was closed, but I could hear the fighting through the door. I walked over to the door very quiet so there was no squeaking in the floor. I sat down in front of the door and leaned my back against the wall.

"All I'm saying is that this is our family's private issue, and we shouldn't constantly display it for the whole world to see! Can't we give it some time?" I heard Daddy say.

Mommy did a laugh, but like a mean laugh. "No, WE can't give it some time. That's the point—I don't want to keep it private. We shouldn't keep it private. And I honestly don't give a rat's ass if your mother agrees or not."

"It's not about my mother," Daddy said. "She was only bringing to my attention what people are saying."

"People. What people? No one's going to care about this anymore in a few weeks, Jim! Life's going to go on, and we'll be left here, with our lives in shambles, and people are not even going to care anymore then. Don't you get that? And then it will be too late to try to talk about it!" Mommy's words were coming out very fast. "I know you're worried about what it looks like," Mommy said, and she changed her voice when she said, "looks like," sort of made it deeper. "Me going in front of the cameras and letting it all hang out, right? But frankly, I don't give a shit about that anymore, Jim. I honestly don't give a shit."

"Please don't be ridiculous. It has nothing to do with that," Daddy said.

"It has everything to do with that! I'm tired of putting on a show! I'm so goddamn tired of it. And none of it matters anymore. Can't you see that?"

"Jesus Christ, Melissa, we're all hanging on by the skin of our teeth. We need to think about Zach. You saw how Zach reacted at the interview. It wasn't right to have him there, to do it in the first place. I told you that." Daddy talked more quietly now, but Mommy did not.

"That must have been embarrassing for you, right? To have him act out that way in front of people? Andy 2.0. And in front of cameras? Well, they ended up not showing that part, so what are you worried about?"

"That's really not fair," Daddy said. "That's not what I'm worried about at all. He is so upset. I've never seen him act like this before. And the nightmares and bed-wetting . . ."

"He lost his brother, for crying out loud," Mommy yelled. "Of course you've never seen him act like this! We're all trying to deal with our feelings here, the best we can."

"I know that. But do you know what he just asked me downstairs? If you wished that he had died instead of Andy," Daddy said. I got tears in my eyes again when I heard that.

Mommy was quiet for a while. Then she said, "I . . . we had a bad moment downstairs earlier. He gets so angry all the time, and it's a lot for me to handle on my own. I'm suffering, too. Everyone seems to like to forget that."

"I know you are, Melissa. And I wish you would accept some help. But when you just disappeared yesterday . . . Zach thought it was his fault, that he did something wrong."

"When. I. just. disappeared?" Mommy said every word with a space in between, and she sounded very mad. The way her voice sounded gave me goose bumps on the back of my neck. "Are you serious right now? When I just disappeared? That's really great, that's great. YOU are the one who ran back to work the first chance you got. You're as absent as ever. I'm not disappearing. I am here. I am always here. I dealt with all of it, all the hard stuff. With Andy . . .

that was all on me. So don't you dare talk to me about disappearing!" Mommy yelled the last part very loud.

"You made it that way! And you chose to be here," Daddy yelled back. "There was no place for me in any of it!"

"That's bullshit and we both know it. You wanted him conveniently medicated so we wouldn't have to deal."

"I never said that. I never fucking said that. That wasn't my idea. It's what the doctor said, the doctor that YOU wanted him to see so badly. You wanted him to see this doctor. He tells us what to do, and then you don't want to do what he says. It was all up to you. It was all your decision. You called the shots, and I had no chance to participate whatsoever!"

Mommy made a snorting sound. "The sad part is that you actually believe that. You wanted to participate, but I didn't let you? I suppose it's my fault that you went out and fucked around, too?" Daddy started to say something, but Mommy interrupted. "Please, I'm not stupid, Jim. I know something's been going on. You can stop lying now."

It was quiet in the bedroom for a while after Mommy said that.

Then Mommy started talking again. "You didn't want to deal with . . . this. You didn't want to deal with Andy's shit. A son with ODD wasn't part of the plan. You left me completely alone with it. How was not being here ever an option for me? And now . . . now . . . I'm still alone with all of it—Zach . . . I know he is struggling. Do you think I don't know that? I'm trying—" Mommy stopped talking, and I could tell she had started to cry. I heard her crying sounds.

"Melissa, can I please . . . ?" Daddy said very quietly.

"No! Don't. Just . . . don't." Mommy squeezed out her words in between crying sounds. "I don't know how to live like this, OK, Jim? How do I live like this? I need to do this thing, I need justice."

"How can we get justice?" Daddy asked. It sounded a little bit like when he talked to me in the closet and he was petting my back after I had the bad dream about Andy and it made me calm down.

But Mommy didn't calm down. Her voice got louder again, and

her crying sounds got louder, too. "For Andy. I can't just do nothing, let them get away with it. If I don't do this, then I don't know how to live anymore."

"Going on a wild rampage for revenge isn't going to bring him back—" Daddy started to say, and Mommy interrupted him.

"Wild rampage for revenge? Wild rampage for revenge? What the fuck?" she screamed.

I tried to cover my ears—they were hurting from all the screaming and all the bad words. My whole head hurt.

"I'm sorry, I didn't mean it like that," Daddy said.

"Yes, you did!" Mommy screamed. "You! So composed all the time, right? Don't show your emotions, or better yet, don't have any, right? How do you do that? I don't see you cry. How is that possible? How are you not crying? It's not normal!"

Mommy's sadness I could hear so loud, and I could feel it like it was coming right at me from under the door. But I could hear Daddy's sadness, too. It wasn't loud like Mommy's, it was quiet. Just maybe Mommy couldn't hear it, because she was being so loud. And Mommy didn't see Daddy in his car when I saw him after we left her at the hospital, when it looked like the sadness was hurting his whole body and he cried with no sounds.

"You know what, Jim?" Mommy said. "You want a chance to participate? Well, why don't you take a stab at it for once? I can't . . . deal with Zach right now. I don't have the capacity. I don't know how. I can't . . . give anymore. I just can't." Mommy wasn't screaming now. She sounded tired. After a while she said, "I need to finish packing."

I heard footsteps come close to the door, so I got up quickly and ran back downstairs. In my head I remembered what Mommy said at the end of the fight: "I can't deal with Zach right now," and when I got back in the kitchen I gave the barstool a hard kick.

33

An Impossible Life to Live

IN THE MORNING, Mommy's side of the bed was still made, and Daddy wasn't in the bed either. I went in my room and looked out the window. Daddy's Audi wasn't in the driveway, so he already went to work.

There was no more snow after the one day when Daddy and I had milkshakes at the diner, but also no more rain. It just stayed really cold. I could see the white from the coldness on top of the grass and the cars. I touched the window with my hand, and the cold glass made me do a shiver with my whole body.

When I went downstairs, I heard the TV was on in the family room and I saw Mimi sitting on the couch. "Is Mommy on the TV?" I asked, and Mimi turned around to me fast because I surprised her.

"Not yet, sweetie. Good morning," Mimi said, and she picked up the remote and turned off the TV.

"Can I watch with you?" I sat down on the couch next to Mimi.

"Oh, um, I don't think so, sweetie. I'm not sure . . ." Mimi was still looking at the turned-off TV.

"But I want to see Mommy," I said, and I felt the mad feeling starting out in my stomach. Then I yelled at Mimi: "I want to see Mommy on the TV!"

"Zach, honey, please don't get upset. I . . . I don't know if Mommy would want you to watch—" Mimi said.

I interrupted her and I said a lie to her: "Mommy promised me that I could watch it, so you can't break her promise."

"She did? I didn't talk to her about it, so . . . OK, well, I think she's about to . . ." Mimi picked up the remote again and turned the TV back on.

A man with very shiny black hair was sitting in the middle of a long red couch in between two women. He said, "Just over a month has passed since the horrific McKinley shooting. While we and our nation as a whole are still trying to come to grips with a tragedy of this magnitude, we continue to remember the nineteen families that are dealing with a loss that is impossible to imagine." The two women on the couch made sad faces. "Fifteen families in particular, trying to deal with the loss of a young child who was taken away from them in such a violent way."

The man turned to the side and talked to the one woman on the couch. "Jennifer, few of the families have come forward to speak about their loss, but you spoke to a handful of them in the last couple of weeks. Earlier this morning you had the chance to sit down and speak to one of the mothers, Melissa Taylor, who lost her ten-year-old son Andy in the McKinley shooting."

"Yes, Rupert," the woman Jennifer answered. "It's really heart-wrenching to see firsthand what these families are going through. They are trying to find ways to cope with their loss, day in and day out, and they hope to find comfort in the memories they have of their children. Especially now, with the holidays right around the corner, you know, they are often just trying to go through the motions for . . . the other kids in the family sometimes, the siblings."

The man Rupert and the other woman shook their heads yes.

"The Taylors are one of the families, like you said, Rupert. They lost their son Andy on that tragic day in Wake Gardens. Andy was in fifth grade—ten years old—and he was in the auditorium for an assembly when the shooter entered the school. As you probably know, the school's auditorium was the first place where the shooter opened fire and where most of the victims lost their lives. Andy's mother,

Melissa Taylor, kindly agreed to speak with me this morning. She gave me a very moving and, as you can imagine, emotional insight into her and her family's ordeal. Take a look with me."

Then the TV switched away from the man and the women on the couch and all of a sudden there was Mommy. She looked different. Her hair didn't look normal, it was bigger on the top of her head, and she had on a lot of makeup that made her face different. She was wearing a red jacket and skirt that I never saw before, and she sat in a big brown chair that made her look smaller. She looked like she was the girl from "The Three Bears" and she was sitting in the wrong chair, the Daddy or the Mommy Bear's chair, because it was too big for her. It was strange to see Mommy on the TV. I was here, in our house, on our couch, and Mommy was inside the TV like she was not a real person in the real world.

The woman Jennifer sat in a big brown chair, too, a little bit away from Mommy, and there was a table in between them with tissues on it and two cups.

"Mrs. Taylor, your son Andy was one of the fifteen children whose lives were taken on that terrible day in Wake Gardens. Thank you for being here today and agreeing to share your family's story and your memories of Andy with us."

On the TV, the picture switched from Mommy and Jennifer to a picture of Andy, the one from the field day where he has his silly face and it looks like he's about to jump off the screen. But I could still hear Mommy's voice: "Andy was a force of nature. He was incredibly smart and he had all this energy. He was this big ball of energy, you know?" It sounded like Mommy was crying.

"He turned ten, a few weeks before . . . he died. I wanted to have a party at our house like we always did, but he didn't want a party. He said he was getting too old. . . ." Mommy's voice went up very high, it sounded squeaky, and the TV switched back to her, and her face was big on the screen. I could see the tears coming out of her eyes, and some black from the makeup was on her cheeks.

Mommy wiped her eyes with a tissue, and then she talked again.

"Andy said he was getting too old for parties now. Now that he was 'double digits,' he loved saying that. So he wanted to invite a few friends to do something special. And we did, we went to this go-kart racing track and he had a blast. But I wish . . . I wish we had had a big party for him for . . . one last time. . . ."

I heard a sound next to me. It was Mimi crying. She was staring at the TV, and her whole face looked crumpled up with wrinkles.

"How are you and your family coping with your loss? You and your husband? And I know you have another son, Zach, who is six," the woman Jennifer said. My face started to feel hot when she said my name.

"I think all you can do is try to take it one day at a time," Mommy said, and she moved forward in the big chair and held on to the tissue with both of her hands. "Because . . . you have to, you've got no choice but to." More tears were running down her face, but she didn't use the tissue to wipe them off. She just let them drip down.

"I mean, every morning you think, I don't think I can do this. I don't think I can make it through this day, but then you do somehow because you have another child who needs you. And you do it again the next day and the next. Every day that passes is one day more that I haven't held my son, that I haven't seen my son, that I haven't seen his beautiful face and his smile. The gap between when I was last with him and now keeps getting bigger, and I can't stop it from happening. I want to pause time, stay as close to him as I can. Because this . . . this . . ." Mommy made a pause and her hands in her lap were shaking a lot. "This is the closest I'm ever going to be to my son again. I can't bear waking up in the morning and feeling that the gap has gotten even bigger. That my son has slipped away from me even further."

Mommy picked up her tissue and blew her nose. "My life without my son is an impossible life to live, but I have to live it and keep living it every day." Mommy's last words came out like big choking sounds, and the woman Jennifer leaned over from her big brown chair and she gave another tissue to Mommy, and then she petted Mommy's hand.

Mimi made an "Oh" sound and covered her face with her hands.

The TV switched to a picture of Mommy, but farther away, and she wasn't crying anymore, weird, like you blinked and she just stopped.

The woman Jennifer said, "Mrs. Taylor, you and a few of the other victims' families have come together and you are beginning to come forward to voice your anger about this tragic event that you believe might have been avoidable. Could you tell me more about that?"

"Yes, that's right," Mommy said. "I . . . we . . . don't believe that we can move on without . . . if the people we think are responsible are not being held accountable." Mommy talked fast, and I watched her hands mushing the tissue like it was a ball of Play-Doh.

"When you say 'the people we think are responsible,' you mean . . . ," Jennifer said.

"The shooter's family. His parents," Mommy said. Now she said the thing about Charlie and his wife, and she said it on the TV. Everyone was going to hear it, and probably even Charlie was seeing it on his TV right now.

"So you feel that Charles Ranalez's parents should be held accountable for what their son did? Do you think they are partially to blame?" Jennifer asked.

"Oh, I think they're more than partially to blame," Mommy said. Her voice sounded loud all of a sudden. Mimi closed her eyes and let out her breath long and slow. I felt like I wanted to close my eyes, too. I didn't know why, but I didn't like how Mommy was talking, and I kind of wanted to stop watching.

"Their son had been ill for years and years. And it appears there were all kinds of warning signs that he was on the path to . . . to something bad. Yet as far as we know there was no medical supervision or intervention in the past several years. Someone doesn't just snap like that out of nowhere. This was a long time coming. And my son . . . my son might still be here if . . . if things had been dealt with differently."

Mimi stood up and pointed the remote at the TV and turned the volume all the way down. "OK, Zach, I think that's enough," she said.

I was still looking at the TV, and I saw Mommy talking for a little while longer, and the woman Jennifer said something a couple more times, and then the picture went back to the man and the woman Jennifer and the other woman on the couch. They were all talking, I could tell by their lips moving, and they shook their heads a lot, yes and no.

"Let's get you some breakfast, sweetie, OK?" Mimi said, and she turned off the TV. I followed her into the kitchen and watched her make me eggs. The whole time I had a hurting feeling in my belly, a bad feeling, and then I realized it was an embarrassed feeling. But it wasn't embarrassed about me. It was embarrassed about Mommy.

[34]

Sympathy

THE DOOR OPENED and I knew it was going to be Daddy. When I peeked through the handsome shirts and jackets, I saw a hand swinging a bag of cookies through the crack in the door. Then the bag started talking to me: "Hello, I wanted to see if you might be interested in eating me, young man." It was really Daddy making a funny high voice, and I answered in a funny voice, "Yes, I would be very interested in eating you, thank you!" I leaned forward and snatched the bag out of Daddy's hand.

The closet door opened all the way and Daddy smiled at me and asked, "In the mood for sharing? Cookies and space?" and I told him yes, so he came crawling in.

"Next time you have to bring your own sleeping bag or like a blanket or something. This one is too small for two people," I told Daddy.

"Yes, sir," Daddy said, and he put his hand to his forehead like a soldier. He sat down crisscross applesauce like me and ripped open the bag of cookies and put it in between us. We both took a cookie. "What are you doing?" Daddy asked.

"Reading."

"To Andy?" Daddy asked, and he looked at the picture on the wall.

"Yeah."

"Can I listen, too? What are you reading?"

I showed him the cover of *Dark Day in the Deep Sea*. "I'm on page seventy-eight already, so you're not going to know what it's about," I told Daddy.

"Can't you tell me what happened so far?"

"OK. So Jack and Annie land on a tiny island with the Magic Tree House, and a ship called the HMS *Challenger* comes, and it has explorers and scientists on it. Jack and Annie are allowed to go on the ship with them, and the crew tells them they are looking for a sea monster that looks like a floating nest of snakes."

"Yikes," Daddy said.

"Yeah," I said. "And then a big storm comes and Jack and Annie get washed off the ship from the big waves, but they get rescued by a giant octopus. The giant octopus is the sea monster the crew is looking for, but he's not a monster, and he saves them from drowning in the ocean. But the crew doesn't know that, so they try to catch the octopus and kill him. And now Jack and Annie are trying to figure out how they can save the octopus. That's where I am, and there's only two chapters left."

"Sounds very suspenseful. Go ahead!" Daddy grabbed another cookie and leaned his back against the wall and closed his eyes. I took one more cookie, too, and then I started to read out loud again.

Jack and Annie end up using their magic wand. It makes the octopus talk, and the crew understands that the octopus is not a monster and they let him go. In the end Jack and Annie discover that the third secret of happiness for Merlin is to have compassion for all living creatures. I didn't know what compassion meant, but Jack explains it to Annie: *"That means feeling sympathy and love for them."*

"What does 'sympathy' mean?" I asked Daddy, and that was a hard word to read and say, *sympathy*.

Daddy opened his eyes. "Well, it means you care about how they feel. And you try to understand their feelings and share them. It's hard to explain."

"So you're like supposed to feel their feelings with them?"

"Yeah, I believe that's what it says here, right?" Daddy said.

"But then how is that going to make you happy? At first I thought maybe we could try out the secrets of happiness that Jack and Annie find out, but this is about living creatures, and that's like nature and animals and stuff, so I don't think we can use it to get happy."

"Hm. If this is the third secret of happiness, then what were the first two? And what are they for, by the way?" Daddy wanted to know.

"Jack and Annie are trying to find the four secrets of happiness to help Merlin. He's a magician, and he doesn't feel well. He's very sad and he needs the secrets to feel better. The first one was to pay attention to the small things around you in nature, and to feel curious was the second one. But I tried those out and they didn't work."

Daddy thought about it for a while before he gave me an answer: "Well, people are living creatures, too. I do think it makes sense what they're saying. It could make you feel good not to only think about yourself, but to think about others and care about them. When you try to be sympathetic, to have sympathy, maybe it helps you see why people behave in certain ways. So you don't just see their behavior, but you understand where it's coming from. What do you think?"

I thought about what Daddy said. Daddy and I both grabbed another cookie, and there were only a couple left in the bag. "I think I should have done that with Andy," I said.

"What do you mean?"

"I only noticed how Andy acted bad all the time. That he was being mean to me. A lot of times I didn't like him because of that, and I didn't try to feel the sympathy with him," I said. "Maybe Andy wouldn't have acted bad a lot of times if he could have noticed that we were feeling the sympathy with him. I don't know," I said, and I put my shoulders up and down.

Daddy put down his cookie and looked at me. He opened his mouth like he was going to say something, but no words came out.

"Why do you think he was doing that?" I asked.

"Doing what?" Daddy's voice sounded different.

"Acting like that all the time," I said. "Bad."

Daddy made a coughing sound. He looked down at his hands and started picking the skin around his fingernails. "I'm not sure, bud."

"I think maybe it was because of the Hulk," I said.

"The Hulk?" Daddy looked up from his nails and looked at me. He made lines on his forehead.

"Yeah, the Hulk gets really mad and then he goes crazy, even though on the inside he doesn't want to, but he can't help it, and after, when he turns back to normal, when he's Bruce Banner again, he feels bad about what he did. I think that's probably what happened to Andy, and now that happens to me a lot, too."

"Why do you think that is?" Daddy asked.

"I don't know. The mad feeling kind of sneaks up on me really fast, and then I can't do anything about it."

"But when does it sneak up on you like that? What happens before then?" Daddy asked.

I thought about it for a minute. "The first time it was at the interview, and I didn't want to talk."

"Yeah, you got very upset then."

"Yeah. And now I want to be with you and Mommy all the time, but I don't get to, and then the mad feeling happens," I said.

"I . . . that makes sense," Daddy said. And then we were quiet for a long while.

"Daddy?"

"Yes, bud?"

"Did you and Mommy feel the sympathy with Andy when he was still alive?" I asked, and I looked at Andy's sad face in the picture and I thought that it would be really sad if no one in his family tried to feel his feelings with him and now he was dead.

"Well," Daddy made another coughing sound, "I think we did. I think we . . . tried to. But . . . it wasn't easy, and I think we . . . probably could have done a better job at it. Or I should say I. I could have done a better job. Should have." Daddy's face looked very sad when he said that, and I could feel a lump coming in my throat.

"Do you think it's too late to think about it, because Andy's dead and he's not going to know about it now? Or do you think he can feel it or something? Now?" I asked.

"I don't think it's too late. I think it's . . . amazing you're thinking about it at all. You're a very special kid, Zach," Daddy said.

"I should make a page for sympathy, I think," I said.

"That's a good idea," Daddy answered.

"What color do you think it should be?"

"Oh, that's a tough one," Daddy said. "It's a good feeling, right? So I'm thinking a light color . . . How about white? White is . . ."

"Like clean or something?"

"Yes, clean. Pure. It's a pure feeling," Daddy said.

"What's pure?" I asked.

"Well . . . clean . . . honest. Not selfish, maybe?"

"OK, white. That's easy, all I need is the piece of paper. I'll go get it." I ducked out of the hideout and got a piece of paper from my room and went back inside. I found the tape and put up the sympathy page. We leaned our backs against the wall and looked at the new page on the wall with the other feelings pages.

"That's a lot of feelings," I said.

"Yeah. But you were right. It does help to look at them separated. That was smart of you," Daddy said, and I smiled because it made me feel good when he said it and I thought that the third secret of happiness was working, and I felt a little bit happy now.

35

Back to School

Mommy came back from New York City, but like a new version of her. The version she started to change into when she got mad when Charlie and his wife came to our house and it was like she got poked with a stick like the snake at school. But now she was like all of that new version, and nothing was left from her old self. She walked in our house with high heels, she never took them off, and she talked on the phone all the time. She was doing more interviews on the phone, and she talked to other people she called "survivors." Every time she put down the phone for a second it started to ring again.

At first I tried to spy on her and listen when she talked on the phone. It wasn't real spying because she wasn't trying to keep her talking a secret. She was talking loud on the phone, right in the kitchen or wherever in the house. She saw I was listening and she didn't say I couldn't. So it wasn't technically spying, except it didn't feel like a good thing to listen, but then it turned into that I didn't want to listen anymore. All Mommy talked about was Charlie and his wife, and that it was their fault what happened. She said all the same things over and over again. It got boring to listen to, and it was starting to give me a mad feeling, too.

The next morning, when I was waiting in the hallway for Daddy to come down and then we were going to do our school drive, I heard

Mommy getting done with a phone call in the kitchen. Then she came in the hallway and she said, "OK, that was the last one for this morning," and she smiled at me, but I didn't smile back.

"You're not having very good sympathy," I said to Mommy.

Mommy's smile went away, and she looked at me with a hard face, making her eyes small. Daddy came down the stairs behind me. "What the hell is that supposed to mean?" Mommy said, and her voice matched the hardness of her face.

"It means that you are not trying to feel the sympathy for Charlie and his wife. You are not trying to feel their feelings with them," I explained to her.

"Damn right I'm not," Mommy said.

"Come on, Melissa," Daddy said.

"No, I'm not going to COME ON," Mommy said, and she looked at us in a mad way. "Aren't you two a great little team now? What feelings am I not feeling with them, Zach?" Mommy asked like she was making fun of me.

I didn't look at Mommy, and I didn't give her an answer. I pretended like I had to tie my shoes again, even though they were tied good already.

"Well, you're right about one thing, Zach. I don't give a damn about their feelings," Mommy said, and then she went back in the kitchen. I kept looking at my shoes, but they looked all blurry from the tears that came in my eyes from how Mommy talked to me. Like she didn't even love me anymore.

"Let's just go," Daddy said, and we went.

In the car on the way to school, we didn't talk. But when Daddy pulled up in front of the school and kept the car running, I said, "That was a bad idea that I told Mommy about sympathy. I wanted to help her feel better and get happy again, but it made Mommy feel the opposite—mad. All of the stupid secrets are not working."

I looked out the window. There were kids walking in the front door of the school, and I could hear their voices coming through my window—yelling, laughing, and loud calling, and they were just going to have a regular day at school, and it was easy for them to walk inside.

"Are you going in?" Daddy said, of course.

"Not today," I said, of course.

"Got it," Daddy said, and he drove away from the school. For a while it was quiet in the car, and then Daddy said, "You know, I think people have to be ready to let the secrets of happiness work. The time has to be right."

"And it's not the right time for Mommy right now?" I asked.

"I don't think so, no," Daddy answered.

"Daddy?"

"Yes, bud?"

"I miss Mommy. The regular version of Mommy."

"Me too," Daddy said, just as we got to our house again.

Daddy walked me in the house, and right away Mommy was in the hallway and she still looked mad.

"Oh, no!" she said in a loud voice. "Enough of this, Zach. You need to go to school. You've missed almost six weeks. Get in the car, I'm taking you this time."

I grabbed Daddy's arm. "Daddy said I don't have to go if I'm not ready."

"You're ready," Mommy said. "We need a little bit of separation here. Get in the car."

"Melissa, can I talk to you in the kitchen, please?" Daddy said. I could tell by his voice that he was starting to feel mad, too, but Mommy didn't care.

"No, I'm done talking. Let's go, Zach," Mommy said, and she grabbed my arm and started pulling me hard toward the door to the garage. I turned around to look at Daddy, but he just stood there and he wasn't helping me.

Mommy drove fast on the way back to the school, and she used the brakes hard. I started to feel carsick, and I never got carsick before with Mommy driving. I had mad tears on my face. Daddy should have helped me. He promised me I didn't have to go if I wasn't ready, but now Mommy was taking me anyway, and Daddy was breaking his promise.

Mommy pulled up in front of the school, in the same spot where I was with Daddy a little while ago, in his car. She got out and opened my door. "Get out, come on, Zach," she said.

"I don't want to go," I said.

"I understand that," Mommy said. Her voice sounded like she was trying to make it more polite. "But it's time. I'll walk you inside."

"You're trying to get rid of me!" I yelled at Mommy. "All you want to do is be on your stupid phone. You don't even care about me anymore."

Some people in front of the school stopped and looked at us, and I turned my head so they couldn't see my face. Mommy said very quiet, "Get out of the car, Zach, for the last time," and I realized she wasn't going to give up. She was going to make me go inside anyway. I got out of the car, and I was still feeling sick from the car ride. I noticed the people were still looking at me, so I put my head down and looked at my shoes. Mommy started to walk in front of me, and I followed her.

When we got to the front door, there was a security guard waiting outside the door. It was a woman security guard and her name tag said MARIANA NELSON. She was pretty short, but like wide. She looked like a square almost, and her face was round like a ball.

"Hi, can I help you?" she asked Mommy.

"Yes, this is Zach Taylor. Today is his first day here. His first day after . . . um, McKinley," Mommy told her.

"I see," the security guard said. "Welcome, Zach. Who's your teacher, honey?"

I didn't say anything because I didn't know and I didn't want to talk.

"Miss Russell, his teacher from McKinley," Mommy said, and I looked up at her because I didn't know Miss Russell was going to be my teacher here and at least that was good.

"All right, my colleague Dave is inside. He can take you to the main office to sign you in and then show you to Miss Russell's room," the security guard said, and smiled at me.

I grabbed Mommy's arm. "You said you're coming inside with me," I said.

"Could I please . . . he's still . . . he's nervous still. Could I go inside with him?" Mommy asked.

"I'm afraid not. No parents are allowed inside the school during drop-off and pickup times," the security guard said. "One of the new rules since . . . you know."

"You promised me!" I said to Mommy, and I held on to her arm tighter.

"Don't worry," the security guard said. "We'll take good care of you here." She pressed the bell next to the door and the door buzzed open. "Dave?" she yelled inside.

"Yeah?" A man security guard came, and he was like the opposite of the woman security guard, very tall and skinny.

"Dave, can you help this young man Zach sign in and find Miss Russell's room? Today is his first day," the woman security guard told him.

"Sure thing. Come on, champ," the security guard Dave said to me, but I didn't move.

"Go ahead, Zach," Mommy said. "Listen, I need you to be brave now. I'll be here to pick you up, OK? OK, buddy?"

I didn't answer. I just shook my head no over and over again. Mommy gave me a hug, but I didn't hug her back.

"Sometimes it's best to just rip off the Band-Aid, so to speak," the woman security guard said to Mommy. "Two minutes later they're happy as can be."

"Yeah . . . ," Mommy said, and then the woman security guard gave me a little push inside and the door closed behind me, and her and Mommy were outside and I was inside with Dave. I felt like I wanted to turn around and push the door back open and yell for Mommy, but then I saw lots of kids looking at me in the hallway, so I didn't.

"Come this way, champ," the security guard Dave said, and started walking down the hallway, and I noticed that the hallway looked almost the same as at McKinley and it smelled the same, too. The security guard Dave walked into the main office on the right side of the hallway that also looked the same as at McKinley. "Claudia," he said to an old lady with gray hair who looked up and gave us a smile. The security guy Dave put his hand on my shoulder and said, "This here is Zach—what's your last name, champ?" he asked me.

"Taylor," I said in a very quiet voice.

"Zach Taylor for Miss Russell's class."

The old lady walked over to a cabinet and pulled out a red folder and looked at some papers inside. "Ah, yes," she said, "Zach Taylor, I see. We've been waiting for you, Zach," and she smiled at me again.

"All right then, let's get you to class," Dave the security man said, and he walked back out in the hallway and turned right and he talked to me the whole time we walked down the hallway, but I didn't say anything back. I had this scary feeling that something was behind me, behind my back in the hallway, and the feeling got bigger and bigger.

I was afraid to turn around to see what it was, and all of a sudden I thought there were going to be dead people on the floor behind me and blood everywhere. I walked faster, and my whole body started to feel hot all over. I saw a door at the end of the hallway, and I wanted to start running to the door, and the scary feeling got bigger still. Then the security guard Dave stopped walking and I bumped into him. He said, "Whoa, slow down, champ. Here we are. This is Miss Russell's classroom."

36

Thunderstorm

ZACH! HI! I DIDN'T EXPECT to see you today," Miss Russell said when the security guard Dave opened the door. She came from the back of the room, and she looked very happy to see me. She bent down and gave me a hug. All of my friends from my old class were there, and they said "Hi" to me and said they were happy I was back and stuff like that. I didn't like all the eyes on me, but Miss Russell showed me my seat, and I was at the same table with Nicholas again. It was like we were still at McKinley and nothing was changed.

"All right, class, let's get back to work," Miss Russell said. Everyone had workbooks out, and they picked up their pencils and did some quiet work. "Zach, why don't you come sit with me for a bit?" Miss Russell said to me, and I sat next to her by her desk.

"Do you still have the charm I gave you?" Miss Russell said to me in a quiet voice so that I was the only one who could hear her.

"Yes," I said. "It's in my . . . I put it in a safe spot and I look at it a lot."

Miss Russell smiled and said, "Good. It always helped me when I . . . was sad about something. It helped me to imagine that my grandma was out there somewhere looking over me, you know?" I shook my head yes. "I really do believe that with all my heart," Miss Russell said. "Your brother, too. He's not gone, he's looking over you, too." Miss Russell put her hand up and touched my cheek, and I started to feel a big lump in my throat from that.

"Have you been doing some of your schoolwork? Should we go over it together?" Miss Russell asked, and then she stopped touching my cheek. She got out a folder from her desk and she showed me the work the class did when I didn't come to school and it was the work Mimi brought home for me to do, and I did some of it, but not all of it.

I liked sitting there with Miss Russell. The room was really quiet, and everyone was doing their own work. But then all of a sudden somebody, I think Evangeline, did something and I didn't see what it was, but Miss Russell called over to her to stop. When she talked, her warm breath went right in my mouth. It smelled like coffee. And just like that the big scary feeling from earlier in the hallway was back, and I remembered Miss Russell's breath from in the closet. My heart started beating fast again, and I was starting to feel sick like when Mommy drove me here in the car.

I did big, heavy breaths because I knew I was going to throw up, and I hate throwing up so much.

"Are you all right, honey?" Miss Russell asked, and her voice sounded really far away, even though she was sitting right next to me. When she asked me that, I could smell her coffee breath again, and the throw-up came out in a big giant Whoosh! all over Miss Russell's desk and the front of my shirt. I started to stand up and another giant Whoosh! of throw-up came out and it landed all over my shoes.

"Ewwwwwwwww!" "Grooooooooooss!" all my friends in my class were saying.

"All right, honey, all right. Don't worry about it, it happens," Miss Russell said to me, but she also had an "Ew" look on her face.

A few more throw-up Whooshes came out—mostly on the floor— and then I was done.

"Are you feeling better?" Miss Russell petted my back.

I couldn't talk. There was throw-up still in my throat and up my nose. It felt burny, and I felt like I wanted to cry.

"Nicholas, take Zach to the nurse's office, please," Miss Russell said. "I'll clean this up. Zach, don't worry about it."

Nicholas looked at me like I looked really gross, but he walked to the nurse with me anyway. The nurse helped me wipe everything off and she called Mommy. I wasn't happy that I threw up everywhere and everyone watched me, but I was happy that Mommy was coming to pick me up. Nicholas went back to class, and I sat on the nurse's bed and waited for Mommy. I could smell the throw-up on my clothes, and it was starting to make me feel sick again.

A fifth grader that I knew from McKinley walked in, and when he saw me, he threw his arm over his mouth. "Oh my God, it smells so bad in here," he said very loud.

"All right, Michael, pipe down," the nurse told him. "Why are you here?"

But the boy Michael didn't give an answer to the nurse. He was still talking to me in a loud voice: "Ew, is that puke on your shirt?" A few other boys came into the nurse's office to see why he was talking so loud, and they all stared at me and covered their noses with their arms.

"Hey, aren't you Andy's brother?" another fifth-grade boy said to me.

I didn't say anything back.

"All right, boys, if you're not here for the nurse, get out of the office." The security guard Dave came up behind the boys, and a few of them started to leave. But Michael and a couple other boys stayed.

"Hey, isn't Andy's mom the one who's on TV all the time now?" Michael said to the boy next to him.

"Yeah. My mom said it's not right how she's talking about Charlie," the other boy said, and I started to feel the mad feeling in my stomach. I wanted to tell Michael and the other boy to stop talking about Mommy, but I couldn't open my mouth to talk. I was being stupid scared again.

"She's trying to get famous or something," Michael said, and then he looked at me and put his hands up. "No offense, kid."

That's when the mad feeling made my whole body get tight. Michael and the other boy were still talking to me about Mommy, but I couldn't hear what they were saying anymore, because my heart was pounding loud in my ears and it was all I could hear. Mad tears were on my face, and Michael was making a face at me like "Ohhhhh, he's crying," and that's when I went crazy.

I don't even remember what happened exactly, only that I heard myself yell, "Stop talking about my mom!" and then I was on top of Michael, and then somebody pulled me off of him. When I looked down, Michael was on the floor and he was holding his mouth, and I could see blood on his fingers.

Somebody was holding me tight from behind, and I was still trying to kick my legs to reach Michael. I wanted to beat him up, and he was a lot bigger than me, but the mad feeling gave me super strength. Just the person holding me was stronger. I turned around and it was a man I didn't know. He was talking to me, but my ears were still full with my loud heart pounding.

Then I saw Daddy come in the nurse's office and say something to the man who was holding me tight, and he gave me to Daddy and Daddy sat down on the floor and put me on his lap.

"OK, all right. That's good, settle down." Daddy was talking in my ear, and I was starting to hear what he was saying.

"Let go of me," I yelled at Daddy. "Let go of me, let go of me!"

"OK, I will let go, but you have to stop hitting and kicking, OK?"

The nurse was next to Michael. She helped him get up and made him sit on the bed. Michael was crying and holding his lip, and more blood was on his hands.

Daddy got up to talk to the man who was holding me earlier.

"I apologize, Mr. . . . ," Daddy said, and the man reached out his hand and they did handshakes.

"Martinez. Lukas Martinez. I'm the assistant principal here at Warden."

"Jim Taylor," Daddy said. "I apologize for my son's behavior. . . ."

I got up from the floor and walked out of the nurse's office and to the front door. I opened the door and walked outside.

"Zach!" I heard Daddy calling behind me. "Wait, Zach!" But I kept walking. I saw Daddy's car was parked in front of the school, and I walked in that direction. Daddy came up from behind me and opened the door and helped me get in. I was cold because my clothes were still all wet from the throw-up and from when the nurse tried to clean it off with a wet towel. I started shaking a lot from the coldness. Daddy got in the front seat and he sat there for a while.

"Wow, what a clusterfuck," he said, and started the car.

When we walked in the house, Mommy and Mimi were waiting for me, and they made a big fuss when they saw me and Mommy took me upstairs for a shower. I was still shaking when I was standing under the hot shower water. I was still mad. Mad at Michael and the other boy, and mad at Mommy and Daddy. I stayed in the shower for a long time, and after a while the shaking stopped and the mad feeling went away. I pretended like the shower water was washing it off and I was watching it disappear in the drain.

In the afternoon, Mr. Stanley came over to our house, and it was about how I acted at the new school. He talked to Mommy and Daddy about me, and it was like I wasn't there, even though I was sitting in the room also.

"I would suggest that we give him some more time," Mr. Stanley said.

"Definitely," Daddy said.

"He's been keeping up with his work quite well. And it's almost Thanksgiving. I don't see a reason why we can't push it until . . . say, after the Christmas break," Mr. Stanley said.

"That's quite a lot of school he would be missing," Mommy said. "I don't think it is in his best interest to—"

Daddy interrupted Mommy's sentence. "It's first grade, for heaven's sake. He's not prepping for the SATs. He'll be fine!"

Mommy looked at Daddy in a very mad way. Mr. Stanley looked a few times from Mommy to Daddy and he looked like he didn't know what to say. "OK, well, I wanted to let you know there is no rush from our point of view. If he keeps working and doesn't fall behind, there will be no need to think about repeating the grade or anything like that. But I do want to mention the importance of counseling in this kind of scenario. I . . . that really is important. That's . . . that's really all," Mr. Stanley said, and he started to get up.

"Thank you, Mr. Stanley," Mommy said. "We will discuss it and get back to you," and she walked Mr. Stanley to the door. Then she came back in the living room and she didn't sit back down, but she walked over to the window next to the chair I was sitting on and she stared out of it. She put her hand through my hair a lot of times, and I heard her take deep breaths in and out.

"Please let me call Dr. Byrne for Zach now," Daddy said in a quiet voice.

Mommy shook her head yes slowly. "I . . . yes, I think that would be for the best," Mommy said, and she stopped putting her hand through my hair, but she left her hand on top of my head.

Dr. Byrne is Andy's doctor, the one he went to for his ODD, and he made Andy do time-aways and so now Daddy and Mommy wanted me to go there, too, because I acted bad at school.

"I don't want to go to Dr. Byrne," I said, and my voice came out whiney. "I'm sorry how I acted bad in school today. I'm sorry, Mommy. I won't do it again, I promise." I could feel tears come in my eyes, and I started to feel hot all over. I grabbed Mommy's hand so that she would look at me instead of out the window. "I'm sorry, Mommy, OK?"

"Oh, sweetie," Mommy said, and she touched my cheek with her hand. "Don't get upset again. We're not deciding anything right now, don't worry."

"No, we are deciding this now, buddy. This is not a punishment. This is to help you feel better. Do you understand?" Daddy said.

"Well, we'll talk more about it," Mommy said, and she looked at Daddy. They didn't say anything for a while. They both just stared at each other in a mad way.

"Zach, do me a favor and go upstairs," Daddy said, and he didn't look at me, he was still looking at Mommy and I knew why he said that. It felt like when you know there's going to be a big storm: it's like extra quiet right before, but you can see the dark clouds in the sky and they're coming closer, and you can start to hear some thunder sounds far away. Then you wait for the thunder and lightning to come right above you.

I didn't wait for this storm to come in over me. I ran out of the living room and upstairs and into my hideout and closed the door before the thunder and lightning started.

[37]

Thankful

MOMMY AND DADDY made the world's longest thunderstorm. It went on for days. The storm wasn't happening all the time, but mostly when Mommy and Daddy were together it happened. It only took breaks when Daddy was at work. Daddy started to stay at work a lot again, and it went back to how it always was before when he was at work all the time, so he didn't come in the hideout anymore.

When Mommy and Daddy were in the same room, right away I could feel the storm clouds starting to grow, like they were getting all dark and heavy at the ceiling. I know a thunderstorm happens when warm air goes up and cold air comes down and they crash together and make big clouds, and the clouds make rain and lightning and thunder. Well, in our house it was like Mommy was the cold air and Daddy the warm air, and when they crashed together, they made a storm of words and yelling and crying.

I got pretty good at noticing when it was about to happen, and I tried to get out of there just in time. Upstairs, in the hideout, shut the door! Sometimes the storm got so loud, I could even hear it all the way in the hideout, but most of the time the closet door kept it outside.

The week before Thanksgiving, Mimi came over with dinner and her, me, and Mommy sat at the counter and ate. It was sausage and peppers, and that's one of my favorites. Daddy was still at work, so no storm.

"Have you thought about Thanksgiving at all?" Mimi asked Mommy. "It's only one week away, and if you want to do something, we should probably start planning."

Mommy looked down at her plate and moved her food around with her fork. She put her fork in a piece of sausage and moved it around the sauce and the rice like it was a car driving through an obstacle course. "I . . . I really wish the holidays weren't right now," Mommy said with a quiet voice, and she sounded like a little girl.

"I know, honey, I know," Mimi said. "And you don't have to do anything. I just thought maybe for Zach . . ."

"I know," Mommy said, and she looked up at me, and her eyes had tears in them.

We always have Thanksgiving at our house, and it's a big party with our family and friends. Mommy gets really excited about it, and she tapes a lot of lists on the kitchen cabinets, like what the menu is going to be and shopping lists and stuff, and she makes a special table with special place mats and decorations. We put an extra table next to the table in the dining room, so it's one really long table, and we need three tablecloths to cover it and Daddy has to get out all the extra chairs from the basement so there will be enough for all the guests.

Last year I got to help with the decorations, and we made the name cards for the table together. Me and Mommy went for a walk around the lake by our house and collected pinecones, and it took us a long time because there were going to be eighteen people for dinner and the pinecones couldn't be too big or too small. We had a whole bag of them when we came home from the lake. Mommy cut out leaves from brown and red and orange paper, and I wrote everyone's names on them. Mommy tried to get Andy to help, too, but Andy said arts and crafts are for girls. He said that with my bad handwriting no one was going to know where they were supposed to sit, and that wasn't fair because I used my best writing and Mommy said it looked very good.

Andy only made one name tag, the one for himself, so at least he was going to know where to sit, and then he went and played on the Xbox again. So I made the rest without him. We tied the leaves to the pinecones, and Mommy gave me a chart where everyone was going to sit, and I put the name-tag pinecones on top of the plates.

Last year on Thanksgiving, Mommy got up early because she had to put the stuffing inside the turkey and tie the legs together, and then it had to go in the oven, because it takes a long time to cook a turkey. Then we watched the Macy's parade on TV for a little while, and it was quiet with just the two of us, because Daddy and Andy were still sleeping.

At dinnertime we sat down around the table that looked beautiful with mine and Mommy's decorations, and everyone said how much they liked my name tags, so I gave Andy a "so there" look, and he gave me a "yeah, right" look back.

It was a little sad at the beginning of the dinner, because it was our first Thanksgiving without Uncle Chip, and Grandma and Aunt Mary cried when we went around the table and everyone had to say what they were thankful for.

That's the only part I don't like about Thanksgiving, because I don't like saying what I'm thankful for, and everyone has their eyes on me. At least I know it's coming and I can be ready, and that way the red juice spill isn't so bad. "I am thankful for Mommy and Daddy," I said, because everyone was saying the people they were thankful for, so I picked Mommy and Daddy. "Oh, thanks a lot, Dumbo," Andy yelled across the table, and Daddy got mad at him and that wasn't such a good moment at dinner, but I didn't feel thankful for Andy, so I didn't say his name.

"I'm thankful for my Xbox" was what Andy said when it was his turn, and that was a stupid thing to be thankful for on Thanksgiving.

I thought about last Thanksgiving, and I didn't think it was going to be nice this year and anyway, I wasn't sure what I should say I'm thankful for this time. My hideout, that was the only thing, and I wasn't going to say that in front of everyone because it was a secret.

"Front door!" the alarm box robot lady said, and then Daddy walked in the kitchen and Mommy looked back down at her plate. Another sausage car started to drive on the obstacle course.

"Hello," Daddy said, and he gave me a little smile.

Mommy didn't say anything, and Mimi said, "Hello, Jim," and her voice sounded changed from when she was talking to Mommy. It sounded like stiff and not Mimi-like.

"Roberta?" Daddy said Mimi's name like a question.

Mimi got up and made Daddy a plate, and Daddy took his plate and went in the dining room. I felt bad that he was sitting there all by himself, so I slid down from the barstool and carried my plate over and sat down next to Daddy. I noticed Mommy looked up from her plate and her eyes were following me. She made them very small.

Then Mommy turned back to Mimi and said, "I was thinking I could invite some of the survivors. I . . . that's the only way I think it makes sense for me this year . . . if we have to do anything at all."

"Oh . . . yeah, that might be a good idea," Mimi said.

"Invite them for what?" Daddy asked, and Mimi and Mommy looked over at him like he was interrupting their private conversation.

"Thanksgiving," Mommy said.

Daddy was about to put a fork with food in his mouth, but then his hand stopped and stayed there, in front of his mouth. "You want to invite . . . strangers? To Thanksgiving?" Daddy put the fork with the food back down on his plate.

"They are not strangers," Mommy said, and there they were, the storm clouds, starting to grow big by the ceiling again. "These are people who are . . . going through what we're going through. We're in the same boat. We all need the support to get through these holidays," Mommy said.

"What about family?" Daddy asked. "My mother, Mary . . . don't you think the support from our own family is what we need . . . ?"

Mommy's face looked frozen and had a little smile that didn't look like a smile. It looked like she was pressing her teeth together and pulling the sides of her mouth up. "I don't think I'll be entertaining this year," she said.

"I can see how it might be helpful to be surrounded by other people in similar situations . . . ," Mimi said.

"Thank you, Roberta," Daddy said. He was still looking at Mommy. "I think I'll work this out with my wife if you don't mind."

Mommy pulled in a big breath and looked at Mimi. "Unbelievable," she said, and she stood up and Mimi got up, too, and they both walked out of the kitchen.

Their plates were still sitting on the counter and I didn't know why they got up and left like that, right in the middle of dinner. It was quiet for a few minutes, and Daddy and I started eating again. Then the alarm box said "Front door" again.

Mommy came back into the kitchen. Her face looked so mad, it made me get a hot bad feeling in my stomach. "If you ever talk to my mother like that again, I swear to God, Jim . . . ," she said in a very quiet voice.

Daddy closed his eyes for a minute, and I could see he was breathing in and out slow. The storm clouds were about to explode, and my heart was beating very fast. I didn't want to be right in the middle of the storm, but it was like it was too late to get out of there.

"It is not how we will be celebrating Thanksgiving," Daddy said in a very quiet voice. He opened his eyes and stared at Mommy and Boom!—here came the thunder and lightning.

"Celebrating? I'm not going to be celebrating anything!" Mommy yelled.

I put my chin down on my chest and covered my ears with my hands.

"I'm not celebrating. I'm not entertaining," she said. "I'm going to invite some people who will help me get through the day, and maybe I can help them get through the day. Because that's all it's going to be about! But you go celebrate, Jim. You go hang out with your family and you guys celebrate together!"

Daddy yelled back at Mommy and his voice sounded like thunder. "But it's not all about you, is it? And about how you get through the day. How about helping us get through the day instead?" He moved his pointer finger between me and him.

Mommy stared at Daddy, and then she turned around and walked out of the kitchen again.

"I'm sorry, bud," Daddy said, and he leaned over and took my hands off my ears. "I'm sorry . . . it's . . . Let's finish dinner, OK?" But then we both just sat there and we didn't eat anything.

I wished that I said Andy's name last year at the table. Because that was going to be his last Thanksgiving ever, and now I didn't have the chance to say it anymore.

[38]

Keeping It Small

THANKSGIVING CAME, and there were no decorations and no extra table and chairs.

"We're keeping it small this time, OK, Zach?" Mommy said, and she didn't even have to put the turkey in the oven until after the parade was over because it was so little and it wasn't going to need a long time to cook.

Mimi came and Grandma and Aunt Mary and that was it. Daddy watched football in the family room, and I watched with him for a little while, even though watching football is mostly boring, but I just wanted to be with him.

The phone rang in the kitchen and I heard Mommy say "Hello?" and then after a little while I heard her make a very loud "Oooohh!" sound.

Daddy and I looked at each other, and Daddy put his eyebrows up high. I got up and went in the kitchen to see why Mommy made that sound. Mommy was leaning against the counter. One hand was over her mouth and the other hand was holding the phone to her ear.

"Thank you, I appreciate it," Mommy said, and then she put the hand that was holding the phone down very slow, but she left the other hand on her mouth.

Mimi and Grandma and Aunt Mary all looked like they were frozen with different things in their hands—hand towels, a potato, and the brush for scrubbing the potatoes—and they all stared at Mommy.

"Nancy Brooks is dead," Mommy said through her fingers. Tears started to come out of her eyes, and she kept her hand over her mouth like she wanted to keep the crying inside.

Daddy came in the kitchen and looked at Mommy. "What happened, what's going on?" he asked.

"Nancy is dead," Mommy said again.

Daddy stared at her like he didn't understand what she said.

"She committed suicide last night," Mommy said.

Daddy took a few steps back like he was falling backward, and then he grabbed the side of the counter and held on to it.

"Ricky's mom died?" I asked.

No one answered me.

"How do you . . . ?" Daddy said, his words came out squeaky.

"Mrs. Gray called me. She was out walking this morning. When she walked past Nancy's house, she noticed a . . . smell coming from her garage, and she called the police. It was from her car. She kept it running . . . in there," Mommy said.

"Good heavens," Mimi said, and she walked over to Mommy and hugged her.

Daddy stared at Mommy and Mimi and he didn't say anything. I saw his fingers were white from holding on to the counter so hard. He swallowed a lot of times like he had a bunch of extra spit in his mouth. Then he turned around very slow and let go of the counter carefully like he was going to maybe fall down. He started to take some slow steps toward the hallway.

When he got to the kitchen door, Mommy said, "It's because she was going to be all alone today," and she let out some more crying sounds. "She had no one. After Ricky died . . . it was just her. We should have had her here today. . . ."

"Oh, honey, it's not your fault," Mimi said, and rubbed Mommy's back.

"I know," Mommy said, and she stopped hugging Mimi and took a step to the side and looked at Daddy. He was standing by the door, but he didn't turn around. Mommy pointed at Daddy's back. "It's his."

Grandma and Aunt Mary looked at each other, and Grandma pulled her eyebrows all the way up like how Daddy did earlier when Mommy made the loud "Oooohh!" sound. Daddy started to turn around. His face was white all over, and his bottom lip was shaking.

"I should have invited her. I shouldn't have listened to you," Mommy said. She kept talking like she didn't notice Daddy's face or she didn't care. "She was facing this day all by herself, and it was too much for her," Mommy cried, but her voice sounded mad. "And because you didn't want to invite . . . strangers . . ."

Daddy stared at Mommy for a long time with his white face and his shaking lip. Mommy stared back like they were having a staring contest, but then Mommy looked down and lost the contest. Daddy turned around and walked in the hallway and left through the front door. He never even said anything the whole time. Everyone in the kitchen looked at the place where Daddy was standing a minute ago. It was like the air was all heavy, like it was sitting on top of me, my shoulders, my head, my whole body.

"Excuse me," Mommy said in a quiet voice, and she didn't look at anyone. She also left the kitchen and then went upstairs.

No one said anything for a while, but then Aunt Mary started talking: "Monkey, want to help me make those Brussels sprouts?" And she helped me pull a chair up to the sink and I had to pull all the leaves off from the outside of the Brussels sprouts, and there were a lot of them and I was glad we had a job to do.

Me and Mimi and Grandma and Aunt Mary got all the dinner ready and we set the table in the dining room. Mimi and Grandma didn't say anything, so Aunt Mary did all the talking, and she talked a lot, probably because when she wasn't talking, it was too quiet and it made the air heavy again.

"Zach, we need one, two, three, four, five big forks and one little fork for you. Five knives. Which napkins do you think we should use? Yes, I like those. Let's fold these up like this. . . ." Aunt Mary talked to me about all the things we had to do in kind of a happy voice. I think she was trying to cheer me up, because Mommy and Daddy had another fight and Daddy left, even though it was Thanksgiving, and now it wasn't going to be nice at all.

"I'm calling him," Grandma said after a while and picked up our kitchen phone and called Daddy. It rang for a long time, and then Grandma pressed the "off" button. "No answer."

"Well, the turkey has been done for a long time. It's probably all dried out by now," Mimi said. "I'm going upstairs to get Melissa. We should eat." After a while Mimi came back with Mommy and we all sat down at the table.

We didn't go around the table to say what we were thankful for. We started to eat, and mostly you could just hear the clinking sound from the forks and knives on the plates. It was like clink, clink. "The turkey isn't as dry as I thought." Clink-clink. "The Brussels sprouts turned out tasty, Mary." "That's because of the bacon. That's my secret weapon." Clink-clink.

I looked at Daddy's empty seat, and I could feel tears coming in my eyes. The doorbell rang, and for a second I thought Daddy was home, but he had a key, so why would he ring the doorbell? Mommy got up to open the door and I followed her.

A policeman was standing outside. "Mrs. Taylor?" he asked.

"Yes?" Mommy said.

"May I come in for a minute?"

Mommy opened the door all the way, and the policeman came inside.

"Hey, buddy," the policeman said, and put out his hand for a high five. I high-fived him.

Mimi and Grandma and Aunt Mary all came out of the dining room. Grandma made a sound like she was pulling in a lot of air through her mouth. "Is this about my son? Jim Taylor? Did something happen to him?" Grandma asked, and my stomach started to hurt a lot.

"Well, I was hoping to speak with Mr. Taylor. Is he not home?" the policeman asked.

"No . . . no, he's not here," Mommy said.

"Why do you think something happened to him?" the policeman asked.

"No, he just . . . left . . . a while ago, and when you came to the door, that was my first thought," Grandma said.

"As far as I know, nothing happened to him," the policeman said. "I had a few questions regarding . . ." He looked over at me and stopped talking. "Is there a place we can talk privately?" he asked Mommy, and she said sure, in the living room, and they went there together, and Grandma and Aunt Mary went, too. I wasn't allowed to go and listen. Mimi took me back in the dining room.

The policeman wasn't there for long. In the hallway I could hear him say to Mommy, "Please have your husband give me a call when he returns. I'm sorry to have interrupted your dinner. Good day. Happy Thanksgiving."

"Good day," Mommy said back in a quiet voice, and then she came in the dining room. She was moving in slow motion when she sat down on her chair. Her face was white like Daddy's face was earlier.

"Is Daddy OK, Mommy?" I asked, and I could feel the hurting in my stomach get worse.

Mommy didn't answer me, but she looked at Mimi and said to her, "She left a note for him. It was her, Mom. It was Nancy, the woman that he . . . ," and she stopped in the middle of her sentence and started laughing and that was a surprise. She started out laughing a little bit, and then her laughing got louder and louder and I didn't know what was funny. In the middle of her laughing, Mommy said, "I'm such an idiot!"

Special Surprise

THE NIGHT OF THANKSGIVING I went to Aunt Mary's house for a sleepover. Daddy didn't come back home before we left. Aunt Mary moved from their house in New Jersey to an apartment after Uncle Chip died. It was close to our house, and I went there before a couple times. The apartment was small with only a tiny kitchen that was right when you walked in, and a counter with three barstools like ours and no other table. Just a living room and Aunt Mary's bedroom and one other bedroom, but that was full of boxes and there was no bed in it. Everything smelled funny.

"Oh, gross, what stinks?" Andy said when we went there for a visit.

Aunt Mary said in a jokey voice, "I take it you are not a connoisseur of curry then, Andy? They love that stuff downstairs. Curry for breakfast, curry for lunch, and curry for dinner. Anyway, you get used to it." I could still smell the curry smell when we walked in this time, but it didn't bother me that much.

"How about we watch a movie and make popcorn . . . Oh wait, I don't know if I have popcorn," Aunt Mary said, and she started looking in her cabinets in the tiny kitchen. "Yeah, sorry, bud, no popcorn. But I have pretzels. You like those, right?"

I didn't say anything because I had a big lump in my throat and I thought that if I talked I was probably going to start crying. I missed Mommy and Daddy.

I walked through the apartment and looked around. Aunt Mary had a lot of things everywhere that her and Uncle Chip brought home from when they did trips all over the world—funny-looking masks and paintings and cups and vases and stuff like that. In their old house, Uncle Chip always showed these to me and told me stories about where they were from and why they were special.

On a table next to the couch were a lot of different picture frames with pictures of Aunt Mary and Uncle Chip on their trips, and also from our family and Aunt Mary's. One picture frame that had all kinds of different sunglasses painted on the sides had the same picture in it that Aunt Mary showed me in our photo album when her and Grandma were taking out pictures from them—the one of all of us on the cruise ship with the sombreros on. In the back behind some other picture frames I spotted a picture of Mommy and Daddy. I reached over to pick it up, and I had to be careful so I didn't knock over the other ones in front.

I saw this picture a lot of times before. We have it in a frame also in Mommy and Daddy's room. It's from their wedding, and they're both in a pool—with their wedding clothes on. Mommy looks beautiful. Her white dress is floating in the water all around her, and Daddy has his head to the side close to Mommy's face, like he's about to give her a kiss.

All of a sudden Aunt Mary put her hand on my shoulder and I jumped a little because I didn't hear her come up behind me.

"I love this picture of them," Aunt Mary said, and she took the frame from me and looked at the picture from closer up and laughed. "I still can't believe they really jumped in. That beautiful dress!"

"They jumped in because of Grandpa, right?" I asked.

"Well, it was a really long day for them and all of us because—you know, Grandpa got sick earlier that day," Aunt Mary said.

"Yeah, he got his heart attack," I said.

"Yes. It was just . . . everyone was very emotional, and it was really hot, and we spent most of the day at the hospital. . . . By the time we knew Grandpa was going to be OK and your mom and dad decided to have the wedding after all . . . boy, we really had to scramble to get ready," Aunt Mary said. "I looked a serious hot mess, I can tell you that much. But your mom somehow managed to look breathtaking. Don't ask me how she pulled that one off."

"Did you jump in the pool, too?" I asked.

"I did! Almost all of the guests did. It was an amazing ending to an amazing wedding. It is still the most beautiful wedding I've ever been to. Maybe because of all the drama earlier in the day. But they were also such a gorgeous couple, your parents, so in love," Aunt Mary said. She smiled at me, and then she put the picture frame back.

"And did you see that one here?" Aunt Mary asked. She picked up a picture frame from way in the back and it was of Mommy and Daddy again, and they were lying down together in a hospital bed with a baby in between them. They both were kissing the baby's head at the same time.

"Is that me or Andy?" I asked.

"That is you. Can't you tell from all that hair?" Aunt Mary laughed. "That's why I always call you monkey, because you were hairy like a little monkey when you were born."

"Where was Andy?" I asked.

"He was with us, your uncle and me. We took care of him for a few days so your mom and dad could be just with you," Aunt Mary said.

"Were they happy they got me?"

"Are you kidding? They were over the moon. You were their special surprise," Aunt Mary said.

"Because they thought they were only going to have Andy," I said. Mommy told me that story a lot of times, that they had Andy as their first baby, and then the doctor told them that probably he was going to be their only baby because something happened in Mommy's body. But then they had me and it was a big surprise.

"You made the family complete," Aunt Mary said, and she gave me a kiss on top of my head.

We watched *Night at the Museum 3*, and that's one of my favorite movies. Aunt Mary didn't see it yet, and she was laughing really loud.

It was funny to watch her, and it helped with the lump in my throat. Aunt Mary took a bunch of pretzels and put them in her mouth, and when something was funny, like when the bad guy's nose starts melting and it dangles off his face and he doesn't even notice, she started laughing and pretzel bits came flying out of her mouth and her long earrings jumped up and down.

After the movie, Aunt Mary started to take the pillows off the couch to make a bed for me.

"Aunt Mary?" I said.

"Yes, bud?"

"I think I'm going to be scared here on the couch by myself."

Aunt Mary stopped taking the pillows off and looked at me. "Oh. Right."

"I think I want to go home now," I said.

Aunt Mary came over and got down on her knees in front of me and gave me a hug. She smelled good, like cookies or something. "I know, monkey. But . . . not tonight, OK? Tonight it would be better if you stayed with me, all right? How can we make you not scared?"

"Maybe I could sleep in your bed?"

"Well, why not! I've been sleeping alone for way too long now as it is," Aunt Mary said, and she got me my own pillow and blanket and put them on her bed next to hers. Her bed wasn't big like Mommy and Daddy's, it was small, but it looked comfy.

"Aunt Mary?"

"Yes?"

"I . . . I sometimes . . . in the middle of the night I get bad dreams. About the gunman and stuff. And . . . sometimes I have accidents." I could feel my whole face starting to get hot when I told her.

"Oh," Aunt Mary said. "Well, that happens to the best of us, doesn't it? Here, I have an idea. Don't you worry now." She got a big towel out of her closet and put it under the sheet on her bed. "There. No big deal."

I changed into my PJs, and when I took my pants off, Miss Russell's angel wing charm fell out of my pocket. When I was getting ready for my sleepover, earlier, after the policeman left and Mommy didn't stop laughing for a long time, I went in my hideout fast and got out Clancy and the charm because I wanted to bring them with me to Aunt Mary's house. Now I picked up the charm from the floor and I put it on the little table next to Aunt Mary's bed.

"What you got there?" Aunt Mary asked.

"It's a charm that Miss Russell gave me, my teacher," I told her.

"Can I see it?" Aunt Mary asked, so I gave it to her to look at.

"It's beautiful," Aunt Mary said.

"It means love and protection," I explained. "She got it from her grandma, and it helped her when she got sad, because she remembered that her grandma was still looking out for her even though she's dead now."

"And she gave it to you after Andy died?" Aunt Mary asked, and I shook my head yes. "Well, that was very thoughtful of her. I really love it," Aunt Mary said, and she handed the charm back to me.

Aunt Mary went to bed at the same time as me and at first it was weird that I was lying down so close to her in the small bed, but then I liked it. Lights from the street were coming in so it wasn't too dark, and Aunt Mary told me some funny stories about Uncle Chip, and we both had to laugh a lot.

"Your uncle was a nut," Aunt Mary said.

"Do you miss him a lot?" I asked.

"Oh, Zach, I can't even tell you how much I miss that crazy man. Every day. But I know he's up there cracking his jokes and mixing things up." Her voice sounded sad, but like she was smiling, too.

"And taking care of Andy," I said.

"And taking care of Andy."

"Do you know our good-night song?" I asked.

"The one Mimi made up?" Aunt Mary asked.

"Yes," I answered.

"Of course, I love that song! How does your mom sing it again?"

I told her, and then we sang it together a few times, with my name and hers in it.

[40]

Moving Away

AFTER TWO SLEEPS at Aunt Mary's house, Daddy came over. He sat down on Aunt Mary's couch, and he was like a different person. His whole self looked very tired. His clothes looked messy, and his hair, and he didn't shave again.

He looked so different, it made me feel shy around him. I stood by the coffee table and looked at my feet, because I didn't want to look at Daddy's new self.

"Come sit by me," Daddy said, and his voice sounded scratchy. He patted his hand on the couch next to him. I went over and I sat down and I noticed that Daddy smelled a little bad. I left a space in between us. Daddy looked at the space and then he looked at my face.

"Are you having a good time at Aunt Mary's?" Daddy asked.

I looked at Aunt Mary. She was standing in the tiny kitchen, and she gave me a little smile.

"Yes," I said.

"I'm going to give you two some time," Aunt Mary said, and went in her bedroom. I didn't want her to do that. I wanted her to stay.

"Buddy, I . . . I have to talk to you about something," Daddy said, and his knee from the right leg went up and down fast a million times.

I could tell it wasn't something good he was going to talk about. It was going to be bad. My stomach started to hurt.

"It's . . . when you come back home, when your sleepover with Aunt Mary is finished, tomorrow maybe, so when you come home,

I'm not going to be there." Daddy talked fast, and the words were coming out stumbly.

"Where are you going to be, at work?" I asked, and I didn't know why he came to tell me that, because he always goes to work.

"No. I mean, yes, during the day I will be at work, but I'm not coming home after work either. I'm not going to be . . . at the house for a while." Daddy's knee was going up and down very fast. It made me dizzy to watch it and it bothered me, and I wanted to tell him to stop moving his leg like that.

"Why not?" I asked.

"Your mother . . . Mommy and I decided that it would be better if . . . if I don't live with you for the time being," Daddy said. The whole time he didn't look at me, but he stared at his own jiggly leg. I wondered if he wanted it to stop moving, too, but maybe he couldn't figure out how to make it stop.

"You're not going to live with us anymore?" I asked. The hurting in my stomach got so bad that it made tears get into my eyes.

"No. At least not for now," Daddy said.

"Ouch." I grabbed my belly with both of my hands and tried to squeeze the hurting with them.

"I'm so sorry, buddy. I know that must be confusing for you," Daddy said. He looked at me holding my belly, and he scooched closer and put his arm around me.

"No!" I said, kind of loud. I felt the mad feeling pounce on me, and it made me jump off the couch. "Why are you not going to live at home with me and Mommy anymore? Why would it be better? That is not better!"

Daddy tried to hold my hand, but I pulled it away hard. My whole body was shaking from the mad feeling, and I was hot and tight all over.

"I know you're upset . . . ," Daddy started to say.

"It's because of the thunderstorms, isn't it?" I yelled.

"Thunderstorms? I'm not sure I . . . What do you mean?" Daddy asked.

"All the fighting between you and Mommy, all the thunderstorms you're making all the time."

Daddy stared at me, and he said in a quiet voice, "Yes. Yes, that is why."

"Then why do you have to fight all the time? Why don't you just stop it?" I yelled. Hot, mad tears were all over my face now.

"It's not . . . that easy," Daddy said.

"It's because Mommy got poked with a stick like the snake," I said. "And now she's doing all the stupid interviews, and she's not even nice anymore. I hate her! I hate her and I hate you!" I said that I hated Mommy and Daddy a lot of times. I yelled it out loud, and it made me feel better a little. Daddy's face looked very sad, and that made me feel better, too.

I never said "I hate you" to anyone before. Andy used to say it to Mommy all the time, and Daddy sometimes, and I could see it hurt their feelings a lot, especially Mommy. I got mad at Andy for doing that, and now I did it and now I know why Andy used to do it. It felt good.

Daddy tried to hold my hand again and he tried to pull me closer to him. He was still sitting on the couch and I was standing up, so we had almost the same tallness. Daddy used both of his hands to wipe the tears off my face. New ones came out, and he wiped them off. New ones came out again, and he wiped them off again. We did that for a while.

"It's not only the interviews and all that," Daddy said. "It's . . . Mommy and I have to figure some things out, and we can't do that while we live together. I'm not going to be far. You're still going to see me all the time, I promise."

My mad feeling started to go away a little, and then of course the sad feeling came, like always. "I want to go with you. I don't want to stay home with just Mommy. I want you!"

Daddy let out a long breath and it touched my face and it didn't smell good. His breath smelled old. I took a step back and moved my head to the side to get some fresh air.

"That's not going to work, buddy," Daddy said.

"Why not?" I asked.

"I still have to go to work and . . . Mommy . . . we decided this would be the best for everyone right now." Daddy's words were stumbly again.

"You don't want me. I shared my space with you, in my hideout. I let you come in there with me, and now you're leaving. You don't even want to stay with me!" I shouted.

"That's not true," Daddy said. "I love you very much. I'm . . . so so sorry." Daddy tried to hug me, and his beard hurt my face.

I tried to get out of the hug, but Daddy was holding me tight and it hurt my back. I said in a loud voice, "Let go of me!"

"For Christ's sake, I said I was sorry!" Daddy yelled, and he pushed me away. I had to sit down hard on the coffee table. Daddy stood up and now I was sitting and he was standing and we did not have the same tallness anymore.

Aunt Mary came out of the bedroom and looked at Daddy in a mad way. "All right, I think that's quite enough," she said, and I never heard Aunt Mary say something in a mad way before. Her and Daddy stared at each other, and then Daddy took a step back and sat back down on the couch.

"I have to go, Zach," he said, and his voice wasn't loud anymore. It sounded tired and slow. "Can you look at me?" But I didn't. "I'm very sorry you're so . . . upset. I'm going to see you very soon. OK?" I didn't say anything back and it was quiet for a little while.

"OK, I'm going then. . . ." Daddy got up and walked to the door. My eyes wanted to follow him, but I didn't let them. I heard the door open. "Bye, Zach," Daddy said, and I still didn't say anything and I still didn't look over, and that was really hard to do. Then I heard the click from when the door closed. I sat still for a little while longer, but then all of a sudden I didn't want Daddy to leave after all. I jumped up and I ran to the door and yelled, "Wait, Daddy, wait!" But the hallway was empty and Daddy was gone.

41

Stupid Soup

Aunt Mary took me back home in her car, and when she parked in front of our house, I had a feeling like I didn't want to go home again. I didn't want to be home with only Mommy there, and Daddy wasn't going to come home after work.

"I want to stay at your house and have more sleepovers with you," I told Aunt Mary when she started to get out of the car.

Aunt Mary kept her car door opened, but she turned around and looked at me. "I know, monkey, and you definitely can, soon. But not today, OK? Your mom's inside waiting for you, so let's get you inside, all right?" I still didn't want to go in, but Aunt Mary got out of the car and went around to open my car door. She held her hand out and I took it. She didn't let go of my hand all the way to the front door.

Before we even pressed the doorbell button, the door opened up and Mommy came out. She looked very tired, like how Daddy looked when he came to Aunt Mary's apartment yesterday. She did a sad smile when she looked at me, and she opened her arms for a hug, so I went one step to her and Mommy hugged me, but I was still holding on to Aunt Mary's hand. I didn't want to let go of her hand.

"Thank you, Mary," Mommy said, and then Aunt Mary let go of my hand.

"All right. You're welcome," Aunt Mary said, and she started to walk down the porch steps and to the walkway to go back to her car, but then she turned back around. "Hey, Zach, you can call me, OK? Give me a call if . . . when you feel like it, all right?" Then she got in her car and left. My throat started to hurt and tears came in my eyes.

"OK, sweetie, I'm glad you're home. I was lonely without you," Mommy said. "I made you dinner. Turkey soup with noodles, from the leftovers. You liked that last year, remember?" I didn't say anything because of my throat. "Let's go inside. It's freezing out here," Mommy said.

We sat down in the kitchen with our bowls, and the soup smelled yummy, but I didn't eat it. Mommy rubbed my back with her hand. "Come on, Zach, eat your soup. It's really good."

I picked up my spoon and I moved the turkey bits around with it, but I still didn't take a bite.

"I know this is all confusing for you, buddy. It's all . . . complicated now. Right?" Mommy asked, and she kept rubbing my back. It felt good and tears came back in my eyes. "Hey, listen, I want to talk to you about something. Remember when we talked about Dr. Byrne and that it might be a good idea for you to talk to him?" Mommy said.

I sat up straight when she said that. "But you said we don't have to decide it right now. I said sorry," I said, and my voice came out squeaky, probably from my throat hurting so badly.

"Sweetie, please try not to get so worked up about this. You've had a lot . . . you've been through a lot. I think that . . . Dr. Byrne could really help you, talking about your feelings. . . . That's a good thing," Mommy said.

"NO!" I said, and now my voice came out louder and not so squeaky anymore. "I don't want to go there. I want to . . . When is Daddy coming home?"

"He's not . . . coming home for now. He explained that to you, right?" Mommy asked, and she smiled at me, but it looked like a fake smile a little. Her voice sounded different from her regular voice, too, like it was fake friendly.

"Yes," I said.

"Good. OK. You will still see him. He will come . . . pick you up on Friday, so you can do something fun . . . or something. OK?"

But it wasn't OK, and I didn't want to wait until Friday to see Daddy and that was going to be five more days. I didn't want to be home for five days with just Mommy.

"I want to go stay with Daddy," I told Mommy, and her fake smile went away. "I want to stay with Daddy and then you can pick me up on Friday."

Mommy looked at me and her eyes got small. "Zach, I know you're upset right now. I'm upset, too, and this is not my . . . It's not how I want things to be either. But I'm trying to help you here, I'm trying to . . . I'm taking you to see Dr. Byrne, and that's only to help you. OK? Can you eat your soup, please? It's good, and it was a lot of work for Mommy to make it for you. So can you eat it, please?"

"I don't want to eat stupid soup!" I yelled.

Mommy got up fast and grabbed my bowl and hers, and she threw them in the sink. It made a loud crashing sound like the bowls got broken. Mommy turned around and leaned against the sink and closed her eyes. I looked at her. I didn't know why she was standing there with her eyes closed like that, but then she opened them back up and looked at me.

"Fine. That's fine. No soup, then," she said with a quiet voice. "Listen, Zach. I'm sorry you're so upset, I really am. But we have to try to make this work here, you and me. I can't have you get so mad at me all the time, do you understand that? And I've made an appointment with Dr. Byrne for you for tomorrow. He's very nice, you'll see. You'll like him, OK?"

"Can I go upstairs?" I asked. Mommy didn't say anything. She only put her shoulders up and down and her face looked very tired. So I went upstairs and right in my hideout, and I switched Buzz on. Then I remembered that I left Miss Russell's charm and Clancy downstairs in the bag I had at Aunt Mary's, but I didn't want to go back down to get them and see Mommy again. So I started chewing on the corner of Andy's sleeping bag instead of Clancy's ear. I did hard bites and my teeth made clicking sounds. I did it so hard because I didn't want to start crying again.

42

Alone at Last

There were four in the bed
And the little one said,
"Roll over! Roll over!"
So they all rolled over and one fell out.

There were three in the bed
And the little one said,
"Roll over! Roll over!"
So they all rolled over and one fell out.

There were two in the bed
And the little one said,
"Roll over! Roll over!"
So they all rolled over and one fell out.

There was one in the bed
And the little one said,
"Alone at last!"

"Ten in the Bed" is a song I learned in Mrs. C's class in preschool, and it popped in my head when I was sitting in the kitchen the next morning. I was looking at the calendar in the kitchen again, and then the song played over and over in my head and it got really annoying. The calendar was still hanging there on the wall and I thought about how we started out with four people in our family—four people on the calendar. The calendar was still the same with the four rows, and no one changed it.

Then it was minus one person because Andy died, and then it was another minus one when Daddy left me here with just Mommy. I got out the marker from the drawer and I made lines to cross out Andy's row and Daddy's row. Then mine and Mommy's rows were the only ones left. I was going to put the marker back in the drawer, but then I went back to the calendar and crossed out Mommy's row, too. Because Mommy was also like a minus one. She was a minus one because she started acting mean, and it was like she disappeared from the family, too.

My friend Nicholas has a dog. His name is Terminator, but they call him Nate for short. His name is funny, because you think he's this giant, dangerous dog with that name, Terminator, but he's really small and has a squeaky bark that is not scary, only funny. Anyway, in their yard they have an invisible fence, and Terminator has a special collar. Every time he gets too close to the fence he gets an electrical shock so he won't run away. Nicholas said that most dogs only get shocked one or two times and then they learn and don't go close to the fence anymore, but Terminator wasn't so smart maybe, because he still got shocked all the time. Sometimes we just watched him, and that wasn't really a nice thing to do, but it was funny to watch how he got shocked and then he did his squeaky bark and ran away from the fence.

I thought about Terminator and the invisible fence, because it felt like now there was the same kind of fence in between me and Mommy. When I got close to Mommy it was like I got shocked from her meanness, and I still tried a few times, but then I got smarter than Terminator and I didn't go close anymore. I didn't actually want to be on Mommy's side of the fence anymore anyway.

So that's why Mommy was a minus one, too, and so I was the only one who was left from the four. My row was the only one on the calendar that wasn't crossed out, but I didn't need it because I didn't have to remember anything on the days of the week. I wasn't even doing anything, except staying home, and on Mondays now I had to go to Dr. Byrne. This morning Mommy took me for the first time. She didn't come inside his office with me. She stayed in a chair outside in the waiting room. It was weird. They had a machine on in the waiting room that was making a loud sound like rain.

I didn't want to go in Dr. Byrne's office by myself at first, but he was actually nice, and his office didn't look like a doctor's office. It looked like a playroom. He had a bunch of toys everywhere and different-colored big pillows to sit on on the floor. He sat down on a big orange pillow and asked if I wanted to do Legos. They were the big baby kind, not the kind I use. But I did it with him anyway, and all we did was build Lego towers and see which one would crash down first. Then Dr. Byrne—he said I didn't have to say Dr. Byrne to him, I could say Paul—said it was time to go, and did I want to come back next week, and so I said, "Sure."

So that was going to be OK, going to Paul on Mondays if all he wanted to do was play Legos and I didn't know how that was supposed to help me with my feelings. And I didn't think I was going to need the calendar to remember to go there, so I took the marker and did scribble scrabble over the whole calendar.

That was me, the little one in the song, because I was the youngest in the family and I was the only one left in the bed. Except in the song, the little one wanted that to happen, to be alone. That's why at the end of the song it says, "Alone at last!" I didn't want that to happen to me, but it happened anyway. And so now I was like in this giant bed that was too big and too empty, and there was a ton of space all around me with nothing in it.

The next bad thing that happened was that the hideout stopped helping. After I did scribble scrabble all over the calendar, I went in the hideout. I thought that I probably liked it in there because there was only a little space inside and it got all filled up with me in it and my feelings pages and the picture of me and Andy and my books and Miss Russell's charm and Clancy and Buzz. And Andy. Because Andy was pretend in there with me, so it was like there were still two in the bed when I was in the hideout.

I went in the hideout and closed the door behind me, like I always did. I switched on Buzz and sat on Andy's sleeping bag, like I always did. I did everything I always did, and everything looked like it always did. But I didn't start to feel better like I always did. The scared feeling and the lonely feeling from outside the hideout followed me in and didn't go away. I closed my eyes and tried to think about the brain safe and how I had to push the bad feelings inside. It didn't work. I opened my eyes again and all of a sudden I realized what was changed.

Andy wasn't there anymore. He was gone. I couldn't feel him anymore.

"Andy?" I said, but I knew he wasn't there. I started to make loud crying sounds. "Please come back, Andy, please please please." I picked up the angel wing charm and rubbed it in between my fingers. I waited and I asked Andy to come back a thousand times, but nothing changed.

So then I put the charm in the pocket of my pants and I took the picture of me and Andy off the wall and I hugged it against my chest and I got up and went out of the closet and closed the door behind me.

43

Balloons to Remember

Today was DECEMBER 6, and that meant it was only three weeks, not even, until Christmas, and also it was exactly two months ago that the gunman came and killed Andy. They were making a special memory ceremony at McKinley today. Me and Mommy and Daddy were going there together and it was going to be the first time for us to be together since Daddy left.

Daddy came in the morning to pick us up, and when he came in the house it felt like he was visiting. Mommy told him he was late, and then there was no talking in the car on the way to McKinley. Daddy had to park the car far away from the school because there were cars parked everywhere.

"We should have been here a half hour ago," Mommy said, and started walking to the school with fast, big steps. She held on to her hat with one hand, and her breath was making the air white around her. Me and Daddy walked behind her, and I had to walk/run because Mommy was going so fast. We walked around the corner with the big water tower and the basketball blacktop and there was McKinley. It looked normal, but it didn't feel normal. It felt like a place I never went to before.

When I saw McKinley I stopped walk/running and I got really slow. Mommy didn't notice. She kept walking fast, and the space between me and her got bigger and bigger, but Daddy turned around.

"You coming, Zach?" he asked.

I stopped and looked at McKinley, and all of a sudden all the windows looked like eyes or something. It looked like they were all staring at me. It was really creepy. "I don't want to go in there," I said.

"Guys, can you pick up the pace? We're so late already," Mommy called to us. Daddy put up one hand to Mommy like he was saying "stop." Mommy made a mad face and turned around and kept walking.

Daddy walked back to me where I stopped, and he put his arm around my shoulder. "I don't think we're going inside," he said. "The ceremony is going to be outside, and it won't be long, OK?" We followed behind Mommy, and I tried not to look at McKinley with the creepy window eyes.

There were people everywhere in front of the school. Some people were on the grass and the round driveway, and a lot of people were on the blacktop next to the kindergarten playground. I saw some people were holding huge floating plastic bags with tons of white balloons in them. They looked like big white clouds. On the other side of the street were a bunch of news vans, and in front of them I saw news people with microphones, and some were giving interviews to people. I spotted Miss Wanda. She was leaning against her van that said LOCAL 4 on the side, but she wasn't doing an interview, she was reading something. I was happy she wasn't looking up and seeing me because of what happened at our house. I tried to look for Dexter, but I couldn't see him anywhere.

Mommy was on the blacktop now and she was hugging people and talking to them. I spotted Grandma and Aunt Mary standing on the side of the blacktop. Aunt Mary smiled and waved. Me and Daddy walked over to them, and Aunt Mary gave me a hug. "Hey, monkey," she whispered in my ear. Then we stood there and watched Mommy, and no one said anything. I looked around to see if maybe I could spot Miss Russell, but I didn't see her anywhere.

"Hey, Zach, sweetheart," a voice said next to me. I turned around and it was Mrs. Stella, the lady from the main office, and she smiled at me, a sad smile. "How are you? This must be Dad?" Mrs. Stella said, and Daddy said, "Yes." Mrs. Stella said, "My condolences, Mr. Taylor," and her and Daddy did handshakes.

I didn't know why people were still saying that to us. That happened two months ago that Andy died, but people were still saying "I'm sorry" and "My condolences" to us. It was like at New Year's. Sometimes when you didn't see people at New Year's, but then you see them a while later or even a long time later, people still say "Happy New Year!" even though the new year started like a long time ago.

"Thank you," Daddy said. "This is my mother. And my sister-in-law."

Grandma and Aunt Mary also did handshakes with Mrs. Stella.

"Here, did you get a hope and support pin yet?" Mrs. Stella said, and she gave us each a white pin that was shiny and looked like a ribbon, but it was metal. Daddy helped me put mine on my jacket. I touched the ribbon with my fingers—it was cold and smooth.

"Make sure you get a balloon at the end of the ceremony. We are going to release them all together to remember . . . your brother and the others. Won't that be lovely?" Mrs. Stella said to me.

Aunt Mary gave me a look like "Uh, no?" and it made me smile, so I looked down at my feet fast.

I looked around to see where Mommy was. I spotted her on the other side of the blacktop talking to Juliette's mom from the survivors' group. Behind them was the fence from the playground, and on it were big pictures. I noticed it was pictures of all the people who got killed from the gunman. In front of the pictures were white flowers, and in the middle was a stand with a microphone. I tried to look around all the people to find Andy's picture, but someone was probably standing in front of it. I couldn't see it. But I saw Ricky's picture. It was right next to the microphone. And next to Ricky's was a smaller picture of Ricky's mom, because she was dead now, too.

Mr. Stanley walked behind the microphone. "Good morning, everyone," he said, and the microphone made a loud squeaky sound that hurt my ears. Mr. Stanley turned some round switches on a speaker next to the microphone. "Is that better?" he asked, and it was better.

"We're about ready to begin. May I ask everyone to come on up closer to join us?" He waved to the people who were still standing on the grass and the driveway. People came walking over and the news people came closer, too. Everyone pushed closer to the front and it got too crowded. And I couldn't see Mr. Stanley and Mommy anymore because the grown-ups in front of me were too tall.

"As you all know, today marks the two-month anniversary of the terrible tragedy here at McKinley that took nineteen lives, the lives of our family members, friends, and colleagues," I heard Mr. Stanley's voice say over the microphone. "I would like to begin our memorial service with a minute of silence to remember each and every one of them." Then it was quiet and I saw everyone around me had their heads down and their eyes closed. I didn't know what they were doing. I looked at Daddy and he gave me a little wink.

Then Mr. Stanley did a speech, and he talked about all the people who died from the gunman, and he said the names. When he said Andy's name, Daddy squeezed my hand inside my glove. My feet were starting to feel cold inside my shoes. After he said everyone's names, Mr. Stanley said he was now going to turn over the microphone to Mayor Rudy Murray who was going to say a few words also. A different voice that was very low started talking. The mayor is the boss of the city and I wanted to see what he looked like.

"Can you pick me up, Daddy?" Daddy picked me up under my armpits and held me up. The mayor had on a black suit and a red tie, and he didn't have a lot of hair on his head, only around the back. He was very tall, even taller than Mr. Stanley, so he was bending down to talk into the microphone. That way you could see that the top of his head was shiny and he looked like a regular person, not like the boss of a whole city.

I looked over to where Mommy was standing, and I saw Mimi was standing next to her now. Mommy wasn't looking at the mayor doing his speech, but she was looking the other way, behind us. When I turned my head to see what she was looking at, I saw Charlie's wife was standing on the grass, a little bit away from everyone else. Just then Daddy put me back down on the ground.

I pulled Daddy's sleeve, so he would bring his head down to me, and I whispered in his ear, "Charlie's wife came, too."

Daddy stood back up and looked behind us, and then he looked over to where Mommy was standing. He closed his eyes and said, "Crap!"

The mayor kept doing his speech in the microphone, but then I noticed that a lot of people started turning their heads and started whispering, and some people moved to the side, and that made us even more smushed.

Then I heard Mommy's voice. "Mary!" she said very loud. There were more people moving around, and when I heard Mommy's voice again, it wasn't coming from the front where she was standing earlier, but it was moving to the back to where Charlie's wife was.

"Mary!" Mommy yelled again. "How dare you show up here!"

"Good heavens," I heard Grandma say behind me.

The mayor was still talking, but his voice got quieter and then he stopped. Everyone was now turned around looking behind us. I still couldn't see anything, so I tried to push through the people to get to the back where I heard Mommy's voice.

I saw Mommy and Charlie's wife standing on the grass with some space between them, and they were staring at each other, and it looked like they were going to have a fight right in the middle of the grass, where everyone was going to see.

Some of the news people were turning around, too, and that's when I saw Dexter. He was standing on the side of the grass, and he was holding a camera and pointing it at Mommy and Charlie's wife. It gave me a mad feeling that he was doing that. Miss Wanda was standing next to him and making an excited face. Happy excited.

"How dare you come here today!" Mommy shouted at Charlie's wife, and it looked like Mommy was about to jump on her.

"Stop!" Charlie's wife said. She didn't shout like Mommy, but she said it loud so everyone could hear. "You have to stop," she said. She took a step toward Mommy and she was holding her hands out. "Please, why are you doing this to us?"

"Why am I doing this to YOU?" Mommy laughed a loud laugh. I didn't like the way it sounded. It sounded kind of like a witch laugh. Mommy turned around and looked at everyone on the blacktop. She yelled over to us, "She wants ME to stop what I'm doing to them!"

"Jesus Christ," Daddy said behind me in a quiet voice. I turned around and next to Daddy I saw Mimi. She covered her mouth with her hands and tears were spilling out of her eyes. Someone next to me said, "That's awful."

I didn't want Mommy to talk like that and laugh the witch laugh. The cameras were all pointing at her, so people watching TV would see how she was acting, too.

"I'm asking you to please leave us alone. We are . . . our family is suffering, too. You have to leave us be," Charlie's wife said. She was holding her hands together in front of her chest like she was doing a prayer.

"That's great! That's just great!" Mommy yelled. "They're suffering, too. Everyone, did you hear that? They're suffering, too. And it's because of what I'm doing to them." Mommy laughed her witch laugh again, and her voice didn't even sound like her own.

"See this?" she said to Charlie's wife, and she waved at all the people. "All of this is because of you. Because of what YOU did to US! Because of the . . . monster that you raised and because you didn't stop him!"

A lot of people around us said, "Oh" and "Oh my," and that's when Charlie's wife fell down. She landed on her knees and she covered her face with her hands.

"You need to leave!" Mommy yelled at her.

Daddy squeezed my shoulder with his hand and then he started walking to Mommy. He had his head down, like he was hoping maybe no one would see him like that. He got to Mommy and he talked to her in a quiet voice and tried to touch her arms.

"NO!" Mommy yelled very loud, and she gave Daddy a push. "You don't tell me to calm down!" Daddy tried to grab Mommy's arm, and he looked at her in a mad way, but she snatched her arm away. Her eyes were really big and her whole body was shivering.

A woman walked over to Charlie's wife and helped her stand up, and they walked away to the cars. Daddy went closer to Mommy and talked to her again, and then Mommy turned around and walked away from him. Daddy waved at me to come, and I did and my whole face and neck and whole entire body was like on fire from the red juice spill when I walked across the grass. I could feel all the eyes on me.

I looked over at Dexter and his camera was still pointing at us, me and Daddy, walking after Mommy to the car.

We sat in the car for a long time and no one said anything and I didn't know why we weren't driving away. I stared out my window and all of a sudden I saw a big white cloud go up in the sky from behind the water tower. It was the balloons to remember. I watched them go really high up in the sky, and it looked like they were going to fly all the way up to heaven.

44

A Minute in the Spotlight

O N THE DAY AFTER the memory ceremony, some news trucks came in the morning and they parked in front of our house, like when the LOCAL 4 news van came and parked in front of our house for the interview. I watched them from my window for a while, but nothing was happening and no one came out of the vans. They just stayed parked there. I was glad about that because I was definitely not going on an interview again. I was only wondering what they were doing there, and then it got boring to keep watching them.

I went downstairs to find Mommy and to ask her why the vans were there in front of our house. She was in the family room, watching TV. I sat down next to her on the couch. It was like Mommy got famous or something, because on the TV she was watching herself. It was the news, and it was about the memory ceremony and the fight between Mommy and Charlie's wife on the grass. I didn't like that I was seeing it all again—how Mommy yelled, "Everyone, did you hear that? They're suffering, too," and then she did the witch laugh. And then she said the thing about how Charlie's wife raised a monster, and Charlie's wife fell down on the grass.

Then the news showed me—I was right there on TV—I was walking behind Daddy on the grass. The TV like zoomed in and showed my face, and it was red all over. That was from Dexter's camera when he was pointing it right at me, and he made it so that it got all the way close to my face like that. My face got burning hot when I watched my red face on the news. Tears came in my eyes. I really hated Dexter a lot because he did that to me.

The news switched away from my face and it showed Miss Wanda. She was holding a microphone and she was talking to a woman and I noticed it was the woman who went over to Charlie's wife yesterday and helped her get up from the ground.

"I just think she's taking it too far, that's all," the woman said to Miss Wanda. Right then, after she said that, the balloons to remember started to go up in the sky behind them, so that was when we were sitting in the car after we left the memory ceremony. On TV the woman and Miss Wanda turned around to look at the balloons. They made sad smiles, and then the woman kept talking: "I mean, I can't imagine the pain she's going through, and her family, losing her little boy like that. But I don't see how this is going to help anybody, that's all. It's not going to bring her son back. And you have to feel bad for them, too, you know? I can see both sides, that's all I'm saying." Miss Wanda shook her head yes, and she was making a serious face.

Mimi walked in the family room. I didn't even know she was here. "Honey, why are you still watching this? They're just going to show the same thing over and over." Mommy kept staring at the TV and said: "Can you believe this, Mom? Fucking Michelle, anything for a minute in the spotlight, huh?" Mimi looked over at me, probably because of the F-word Mommy said.

Mimi let out a long breath. "Maybe it would do you some good to take a step back, give it a little time? You're so exhausted, honey." Mommy looked down in her lap and didn't say anything for a while, and I could see tears dripped from her eyes in her lap.

"How can I give it time, though?" Mommy said. She wiped away her tears, but more kept dripping in her lap. "I AM exhausted, I really am. But what am I supposed to do—move on? Accept that their son did this to us?" Mommy made choking sounds like she was trying to hold in her crying, but it came out anyway. Her whole face got red dots on it.

"I don't know, honey," Mimi said. Her voice came out shaky. "But

I hate to see you wearing yourself down like this. It's all so . . . hard already."

"It's . . . it's almost like they're painting them as the victims now," Mommy said, and pointed at the TV. "Look, they're sensationalizing this one thing, this one particular situation. Like Mary is the victim here. Her son did this! I know it's not bringing Andy back . . . what I'm doing. I know that! I don't know what to do . . . ," Mommy said, and got up and walked in the kitchen fast. Mimi looked at me with a sad face and put her hand through my hair. Then she went in the kitchen after Mommy.

I stayed on the couch and kept looking at the TV and it was commercials, but then the news came back on. It wasn't about Mommy and Charlie's wife anymore. It showed a cemetery at nighttime—it was dark and hard to see, but it looked like the cemetery where we went for Andy's funeral. I recognized the road inside the cemetery where all the people parked who came for Andy's funeral and where Daddy and Mimi had to hold up Mommy on the sides and put her in our car because she couldn't stand up anymore from the heavy sadness blanket.

Now only one car was parked there on the road, and a man was walking to it. The TV zoomed in and I could see the man was Charlie and Charlie took keys from his pocket and tried to open the car door, but then he dropped the keys on the ground.

"Charlie, can we talk to you for a second? Charlie?" I heard a voice say, or maybe it was two voices, the second "Charlie" sounded like from a different voice. A man walked up next to where Charlie was bending down to pick up his keys and he was holding a microphone, so he was from the news. A light was shining on him and it made the darkness around him get lighted up. When Charlie stood back up, the man from the news pointed the microphone at him. Charlie blinked his eyes because the light was pointing right in his face. He looked even more old than when I saw him when he came to our house and Mommy talked to him in a mean way. All the bones in his face were sticking out and his eyes had dark all around them.

"Charlie, would you like to comment on the allegations that are being made against you and your wife? By some of the victims' families?" the man from the news asked. Charlie didn't say anything. He just turned his head very slow away from the light and looked at the man like he was trying to figure out who was talking to him. Then he turned around and opened his car door and he didn't drop the keys this time. He sat down in the car and closed the door.

Charlie's car started to drive away very slow, and the man from the news talked in the microphone: "Every evening, Charlie Ranalez, the father of Charles Ranalez Jr., the McKinley shooter, can be seen visiting his son's grave. Not a day has gone by that he hasn't—"

"Zach?" Mimi called from the kitchen. I didn't answer her. I wanted to hear what the man from the news was saying about Charlie. But then Mimi came in the family room and she picked up the remote from where Mommy left it on the couch and she turned off the TV, right in the middle of what I wanted to listen to.

"Your dad is here to pick you up for breakfast. Let's get you ready to go, OK?" Mimi said. I forgot that it was breakfast-at-the-diner day with Daddy today. Every Sunday now he picks me up and we go to the diner and have breakfast. It was like a new/old tradition and it used to be me and Andy and Mommy and Daddy, all of us going, but now it was down to me and Daddy.

"Front door!" I heard the lady robot voice say in the kitchen, and then the front door got slammed loud. "Goodness," Mimi said, and we went in the kitchen. Daddy came walking in from the hallway. He had a mad look on his face.

"Did they hound you, too, when you came in?" Mimi asked Daddy.

"It's ridiculous, the whole damn thing," Daddy said. "Totally getting blown out of proportion."

Then Daddy made his voice quiet and said to Mimi, "Has he been out there yet?"

"Not yet," Mimi said.

"Jeez. OK," Daddy said.

He came over to me and said, "You know what, Zach? I think maybe it's best if we skip the diner today, OK?"

I didn't know why Daddy didn't want to go get breakfast all of a sudden. I didn't get to see him this whole week except for at the memory ceremony. Why did he even come to the house if he didn't want to go with me? I could feel the mad feeling starting out in my belly and tears came in my eyes.

"Here, let me show you something," Daddy said, and he went to the front window and moved the curtain to the side a little. I saw the news vans that were still parked there in front of our house, and now some people were there, too, one with a camera and one with a microphone. They were standing next to one of the vans and were looking at our house. I recognized the man with the microphone, it was the man that I saw on the news, the one that was talking to Charlie at the cemetery.

Daddy let go of the curtain and turned around to me. "See those guys out there?" he asked. "They're trying to get us to talk to them and they're being a little pushy about it. That's why I thought you should probably stay here today. Do you understand?" Daddy asked.

"OK," I said, and I thought about how Charlie was blinking his eyes in the light that got pointed at him at the cemetery and how his face looked—old and sad and scared.

45

Do Something

AFTER DADDY LEFT, I went upstairs, and when I walked down the hallway I heard sounds coming from inside Andy's room, crying sounds, but they sounded like they were far away or like underwater. I stopped walking and listened to the sounds and I didn't know what they were. "Uhuu, uhuhuhu," like ghost sounds, they gave me goose bumps.

Then it was quiet for a while and I went closer to the door of Andy's room and peeked inside. No one was there. I thought maybe it was just my imagination that I heard the sounds, but right when I was thinking that, they started again. My eyes followed where they were coming from. It was Andy's top bunk.

I could see the back of Mommy's head—her hair was spread out all over Andy's pillow. I tiptoed inside the room and closer to the bed to see what Mommy was doing up there, but I couldn't really see her, she was up too high, so I climbed up the first couple steps of the ladder very quiet.

Mommy was lying under Andy's blanket, and her whole self was shaking a lot. She was holding Andy's pillow with her hands and pressing it against her face. She was making crying sounds inside the pillow—that's why they sounded far away before. I watched Mommy, how she was lying there crying, and it made a big lump come in my throat.

Then I climbed all the way up the ladder and onto Andy's bed and

I lay down next to Mommy. Mommy let go of the pillow and she looked at me. Her face was red and wet all over, and the insides of her eyes were red, too. I put my hand out and touched her face. It was very hot and sweaty. Her hair was wet and sticking to her face from sweat, or from tears, I didn't know which.

"Are you OK, Mommy?" I said, and my words came out like a whisper.

A lot of wrinkles came on Mommy's face. She lifted up Andy's blanket and I lay down under it next to her. Mommy put her arm around me and pulled me close, and we put our foreheads together.

It was very hot under the blanket because I could feel all the hotness coming off of Mommy's body. She had her eyes shut tight and was breathing in and out fast. Her breath came right in my face, but I didn't move away. Tears kept running down Mommy's face, and she just let them run over her nose and drip into Andy's pillow.

"Mommy?" I whispered.

"Yes?" Mommy said, but she kept her eyes closed.

"Are you crying because of the news?" I asked. "Because of how Miss Wanda and the other lady were talking about you?"

Mommy opened her eyes and did a little sad smile. "No, sweetie, that doesn't matter. I'm . . . I miss your brother so much, you know? I miss him so so much." She hugged me tighter and we didn't say anything. I listened to Mommy making quiet crying sounds and I thought about Charlie on the news again.

"Are you still going to be mad about Charlie?" I asked.

Mommy let a breath come long and slow out her nose. "Ugh, Zach," she said, and her voice didn't sound mad, just very tired. "I don't want to be . . . but it's his fault that Andy isn't here with us anymore."

"But I think he feels really bad about that," I told Mommy.

"Maybe, "Mommy said.

"He does. I know that. And he feels sad, too, like us."

"Yeah?" Mommy said. She moved her head back on the pillow a little bit and then our foreheads weren't touching anymore. "How?"

"He's my friend. I'm his best buddy. And you're his friend, too, aren't you? He did the sack race with you," I said.

"That was a long, long time ago," Mommy said.

"We are his favorites at school," I said.

"Oh, Zach, he says that to everybody," Mommy said, and she closed her eyes again and I thought that that wasn't true. He didn't say that to everybody, just us.

Mommy's breathing went in and out slow, and I could tell she was falling asleep. I kept lying very still next to her. I liked lying here with Mommy and we didn't do that in a long time, not after Mommy got poked with the stick.

After a while it got too hot under the blanket and I got up slow to not wake up Mommy and I climbed back down the ladder. I went downstairs and Mimi was making dinner in the kitchen. It was going to be spaghetti with red sauce, and Mimi let me help make the salad—spin the lettuce in the salad spinner and cut the cucumbers. When we were almost done making dinner, Mommy came downstairs again, too, and her hair was messy on the one side and her eyes looked red and puffy all around. She sat down on a barstool and put her chin on her hands on the counter and watched me and Mimi make dinner, making a sad smile.

We sat down at the table in the dining room and started eating dinner, but nobody talked. Mommy didn't eat anything again, all she did was move her fork around in the spaghetti. The phone rang in the kitchen and Mommy got up to answer it. After a few minutes, she came back in the dining room.

"OK, the Eatons are still coming tomorrow with the lawyer," Mommy said when she sat back down at the table.

Mimi made her lips in a thin line and then she said, "Honey, I'm wondering . . . have you thought more about what we talked about . . . to maybe start thinking about this in a different way? Instead of focusing on Charlie and Mary? This group I mentioned to you—MOMS DEMAND ACTION—they're really doing some important things. Use your voice, get involved to try and prevent—"

"I know . . . I mean, I want to," Mommy said. "But not now. I don't want to think about that now."

"Who's coming?" I asked.

"Oh," Mommy said. "Um, the Eatons, remember? Juliette's parents?"

"Yeah?" I said.

Mommy looked over at Mimi and Mimi pulled up her eyebrows high.

"Why are they coming with a lawyer?" I asked.

"Well, sweetie, it's . . . we planned to talk to him about the next steps with . . . the Ranalezes, Charlie and his wife, to schedule a court date," Mommy said.

"You're going to go in court with Charlie?" I asked, and my stomach started to feel bad and I knew what that meant from Daddy's work, going in court. It means that there's going to be a judge and he decides who's right, and the other person gets punished and has to go in jail. So Mommy was trying to do that—put Charlie in jail. When me and Daddy went to the diner and we had milkshakes on the first day of snow, Daddy said that Charlie didn't have to go in jail, so he didn't say the truth about that.

I started to feel hot all over and I got up fast from my chair. My knees were shaking a lot. "But you said you don't want to be mad at Charlie anymore," I said, and my voice came out loud, but it was shaking, too. "Earlier you said that, when we were lying down in Andy's bed. That's what you said!"

"Zach, honey, calm down. I did not—" Mommy started to say.

"Yes, you DID!" I yelled at Mommy, and then we stared at each other. I was feeling very mad at her. When we lay in Andy's bed together it was nice, but I was wrong—it wasn't going to get better. It was going to get worse now. Now Mommy was going to try to make Charlie go in jail, and that was making everything even worse.

"Zach, can you please come here? We're just . . . this is just to talk about possible steps," Mommy said, and she tried to take my hand, but I ripped it away from her.

"Leave me alone!" I yelled, and I ran out of the dining room and upstairs. I really wished I could go in my hideout and talk to Andy about it, but I wasn't going in there anymore.

I didn't know why I stopped feeling like Andy was in the hideout. A few times after I noticed that the feeling stopped, I went in Andy's room and I looked at the empty top bunk and I thought I was going to check the hideout again, but then I didn't because I knew it was changed inside, and I didn't want to feel again that Andy was gone from there because it was like someone put a fist in my stomach.

So I went in my room instead and closed the door. I sat down on my chair and my breathing was going in and out fast and my stomach hurt a lot. Everything was getting worse and worse all the time, and it was giving me a big scared feeling. I felt like maybe I had to throw up, so I went in the bathroom fast and sat down in front of the toilet. The floor was really cold under my legs and my stomach felt bad, but nothing was coming out, only tears, tears, and more tears.

I heard a knock on my bedroom door, and I got up fast to lock my bathroom door and Andy's.

"Zach?" I heard Mommy call in my bedroom. Then she knocked on the bathroom door. "Zach, are you in there? Can I come in?" Mommy said.

I didn't feel like talking to Mommy, so I said through the door, "I'm going to the bathroom."

"OK, honey. I just wanted to . . . make sure you're OK," Mommy said.

"Mhmm" was all I said back, and then I heard Mommy go back out of my room and close the door.

After a while I got up and washed my face with cold water and then I looked in the mirror. My eyes were red all around. I stared at them in the mirror, and when you look at yourself in the mirror when you feel like crying, then you cry even more.

"Stop crying," I said out loud to myself.

"Stop crying, I said!" I said, and it was like one part of me was talking to a different part of me. "Stop, stop, STOP."

I washed my face again and went back in my room, and then I stood there in the middle of my room and thought about what I should do.

"You have to do something," I said to my other part. "Everything is getting worse."

"OK, but what can I do about it?" the other part of me answered, but not out loud, just in my head. I thought about it for a long time, and I didn't move and I didn't sit down. I just kept standing there in the middle of my room, thinking about it.

Urgent Mission

Is it time to go on another mission?" said Annie.

"Indeed," said Kathleen.

"And it is quite urgent now," said Teddy.

"Merlin is failing quickly," said Kathleen. She blinked back tears.

"Oh, no!" said Annie.

"Morgan wants you to find the final secret of happiness today," said Teddy.

Today was the day when Jack and Annie are going to look for the fourth secret of happiness for Merlin. Their two friends, Kathleen and Teddy, they are sorcerers, show up in the Magic Tree House and give them their mission from Morgan, who is like their teacher—the Magic Tree House belongs to her.

And today was the day when I was going on my mission, too. All morning my stomach was doing the roller-coaster thing like crazy, and my legs were so twitchy I had to move them all the time. I tried to sit still on my bed with Clancy on my lap, and I tried to read Magic Tree House #40, *Eve of the Emperor Penguin,* so I could think about Jack and Annie's adventure and not mine.

Every time I thought about my mission I started to feel scared, and then I had to do the thing again where the one part of me talks to the other part: "Stop being scared. Time for the mission. Time to be brave. Remember?"

It wasn't time for my mission yet, but almost. I tried to read, but I kept thinking about other stuff. All the time I had to go back to the top of the page and read it all over, and then I still didn't remember what I just got done reading.

My plan was ready, my supplies were ready, but it wasn't time to go yet. The perfect time was going to be later after lunch, when Mommy was having her lawyer meeting, because then Mommy wasn't going to notice and I could get a head start.

My mission was to go to the cemetery where Andy's grave was. And Charlie's son's grave. The man from the news said that every day in the evening Charlie goes there to visit his son's grave. So I was going to the cemetery, too, and I was going to wait there for Charlie to come. I had to go to the cemetery, because I didn't know where his house is or what his phone number is.

I wanted to talk to him to say sorry about how Mommy was talking about him. I wanted to ask him to come back to my house with me so we could talk to Mommy together and then all the fighting could be over and then maybe Daddy could come back home.

Getting ready to go on a mission was a lot of work—I was working on it this whole morning and I kept thinking about other things I had to bring with me. For Jack and Annie, it's easy. All they have to do is point to a book and say, *"I wish we could go there!"* and BAM! they end up exactly where they were supposed to go. Also they don't have to worry about packing for their trip because they're already magically wearing what they will need. In *Eve of the Emperor Penguin,* they end up in Antarctica and they are wearing snow pants and gloves and goggles. And Jack's backpack changes into a hiker's backpack.

I wished I could find a book about the cemetery and say "I wish I could go there," and then just show up there with all the supplies I was going to need. But that wasn't happening. I had to make the plan on my own and pack my stuff on my own and then go there all by myself.

That was the part that was making my stomach do all the flips and making my legs all twitchy, when I thought about how I had to sneak out so Mommy wasn't going to notice, and then get to the cemetery all by myself. I knew the way because it was right by my old pre-school and I went that way a thousand times. But I never walked there even though it's close, only like five minutes in the car, and Mommy always said we should really walk there instead of drive, but then we never did because we're always in a rush in the mornings.

I decided to put Magic Tree House #40, *Eve of the Emperor Pen-guin,* in my backpack, because sitting still and reading wasn't working out anyway, and I only read like three chapters this whole time, but I wanted to bring it for later. I pulled out the backpack from under the bed and it was very heavy because earlier I tied Andy's sleeping bag to it at the bottom with a suitcase strap. The book was the last thing that was going to fit in the backpack because it was so full.

I thought about my plan again in my head, and that's when I remembered the thing about the alarm box. Last night, when I was thinking about sneaking out, I thought about the alarm box and that when I was leaving the house, when Mommy had her meeting, the robot lady voice was going to say "Front door!" and then Mommy was going to know that I opened the front door. And by the way, I couldn't go out the front door anyway because the news vans and the news people were going to see me. So I came up with a cool plan, and I almost forgot to do the most important part.

I checked and Mommy was in her room with the door closed, so I grabbed a pencil from my desk real quick and went downstairs. I opened the door to the garage a tiny bit and from the kitchen I heard "Garage door!" I put the pencil on the floor in between the door so it stayed open, but only a tiny bit so Mommy wasn't going to notice. Then I ran back upstairs fast.

Right after that the doorbell rang a few times and I heard Mommy go downstairs. Voices came up from downstairs, and I stood in my room with my heart pounding, pounding, pounding. It was almost time to go. I waited for all the voices to move from the hallway, and everyone was probably sitting down in the living room.

I went to the bathroom one more time. I put on my shoes and my jacket that were hiding under my bed next to my backpack. I was about to put the backpack on, and that's when my eyes got stuck on the trucks. They were still lying all over the place from when I got mad and kicked them. I didn't want to leave them like that, so I went over and put them in a straight line. That was better, and now it was the right time to go.

I waited at the top of the stairs and I listened to the voices. This was going to be the hardest part. Get downstairs and outside. I went downstairs on my tippy-toes and I tried not to make the stairs squeak—and you have to try to walk all the way on the side of the steps, that's where they don't squeak. The thing was that you can see the bottom of the stairs from the living room, so that was going to be tricky. I paused a few steps up and my heart was pounding so loud that everyone in the living room was probably hearing it. Then I went down the last couple of steps very fast and around the banister and over to the door to the garage. I waited to hear Mommy's voice saying, "Zach, where are you going?" but it never came. The people in the living room kept on talking, and no one even noticed that I came down the steps.

The pencil was still in the door, and the door was still open a tiny bit. I opened it more and squeezed through and closed it behind me. I walked through the garage and unlocked the side door that always has a key sticking in it on the inside because it got bent and you can't take it out, but it still works to open the door. I walked in our backyard and I stood there for a minute, and the coldness outside made my nose get tingly. I put my hand in the pocket of my pants and felt the angel wing charm with my fingers. Then I checked the time on Andy's Lego watch that I took from his desk, and it said 2:13.

Scooby-Doo in a White Van

IN THE FRONT POCKET of my backpack was a map that I made last night of the way from my house to my old preschool and the cemetery across from it. It reminded me of what Dora always says in the beginning of all the shows—before her and Boots go somewhere: "Who do we ask when we don't know which way to go? The map!" And then the map comes jumping out of Dora's backpack and sings, "I'm the map, I'm the map, I'm the map, I'm the maaaaap!" in a voice that's really annoying. The map tells Dora and Boots which way to go, and they have to cross like three obstacles every time—a creepy forest, a windy desert, the crocodile pond, and stuff like that. I don't watch Dora anymore, that's really a baby show, but I watched it all the time when I still went to preschool, so that's funny that I was thinking about that when I was getting ready to go find the preschool.

In my head, I pretend-walked the way a lot of times last night, but I made the map anyway, just in case. The way to my old preschool is like this: Cut through our backyard and then go to the corner where the school bus stops for the middle school kids. It's not a yellow school bus that comes, but a regular bus that gets used as a school bus because there aren't enough yellow school buses. After fifth grade, that's what Andy was going to do, get on the regular bus to go to the middle school, and he was excited about that.

So you go past the middle school bus corner and then up the hill to where the big green field is and the college behind it, and then after that you get to the road with the firehouse on the corner. Walk around the firehouse and then it's another hill up. The preschool comes on the right, where the church is, it's in the basement of the church. And the cemetery where Andy's grave is is across the street from the preschool.

That was going to be my mission, to find the way, and no one could see me walking there all by myself or they would think, "Why is a kid walking there all by himself?" and then they would ask me about it and my whole mission was going to be blown.

After the map tells Dora and Boots which way to go, they say the three stops like the creepy forest and the windy desert and the crocodile pond a lot of times before they go, and they make check marks when they pass the stops. When I crossed the road in between our backyard and Liza's house, I stopped and stared at the place where Andy was lying in my dream, with the arrow sticking out of his chest and the blood everywhere.

After I got around the middle school bus corner, I stopped and pulled out the map. And I got out a pencil from the front pocket and made a check mark next to "middle school bus corner." Then I put the map in the pocket of my jacket and started walking up the hill to the big green field that was the next stop on the map.

Walking up the hill was hard. My legs started to feel tired, mostly because the backpack was really heavy from all the supplies I packed and it was starting to hurt my neck, and Andy's sleeping bag was swinging against my legs. I decided to take a little break and take off the backpack. Then I realized I stopped right in front of Ricky's house. There was a whole pile of newspapers rolled up in blue plastic bags on the walkway. No one lived in Ricky's house anymore because Ricky was dead from the gunman and now his mom was dead, too. I looked at the garage door. Mommy said that in there she made herself dead, and I was wondering if she was still in there or what, and that gave me a scared feeling, so I put the backpack on again and started walking fast.

"Time to be brave," I said to myself in my head.

Maybe Ricky and his mom had graves at the cemetery, too, like Andy and Charlie's son. I was going to check when I got there.

At the top of the hill came the big green field. Behind the field I could see the college, and no college kids were outside of it, so that was good. I made a check mark next to "college" on the map.

Everything was fine until I got to the road. It was quiet at first and I didn't see anyone, but just when I got ready to walk around the firehouse, cars came from the left and the right, and people were going to see me from the cars. I noticed a doorway next to the firehouse and I stepped inside it and turned around in it. I pretended like I was opening the door. The cars drove by me and didn't stop. I peeked my head out of the doorway to see if more cars were coming, but I didn't see any.

I walked around the firehouse fast, and around the corner from it, before the street goes up the next hill, there was a parking lot with benches, so I decided to sit down for a minute. I made a check mark on the map next to "firehouse" and looked at Andy's watch: 2:34. I decided to get out one of the snacks I packed. Snacks and my water bottle were in the middle pocket of my backpack. I pulled out a granola bar and I was trying to get it open when all of a sudden I saw a white van coming down the hill and it was going very slow.

My heart started beating at super speed. I dropped my granola bar on the ground and my map and I grabbed my backpack and looked around fast. I spotted the clothes bin that Mommy and I went to a few times to drop old clothes in that we didn't need anymore but poor people were going to use them, and I ran and scooched in behind it.

It was very tight because the clothes bin had a fence right behind it, and it smelled bad like throw-up or something. My breath was going in and out fast, and my heart was still beating very fast. "Please don't let the bad guy find me. Please don't let the bad guy find me," I said in my head and I hugged my backpack tight.

There was a white van with a bad guy in it in Wake Gardens, and in the summertime the bad guy was driving around with a big Scooby-

Doo stuffed animal in the van, and he tried to get kids to come to the van to look at the Scooby-Doo, because he wanted to steal them. Andy told me that, and it made me really scared, and I didn't want to go outside to play anymore. Mommy said it was true. There really was a bad guy in a white van. She read it on Facebook. She told me it would be better if I stayed close to the house, and it was definitely a no to going up to strangers' cars. "So much for being safer in the burbs," Mommy said.

Now I wasn't close to our house. I was all by myself, and now the bad guy was going to steal me and put me in the white van. I tried not to move and not to make any sounds. Maybe the bad guy didn't see me when I was sitting on the bench. But then it looked like he did, because I heard the white van drive up in the parking lot. My whole body was shaking, and I started to cry a lot. I put my face in the backpack so no sounds were coming out of my mouth. I really wished I didn't go on my mission. If I was still at home in my room, the bad guy wouldn't be coming for me right now.

I heard a car door slam and then another car door, and I didn't let any breaths go in and out of my mouth. Then I heard voices, but it was woman voices, and they were talking about the crazy long line to see Santa at Macy's. I knew what they were talking about because we always went to see Santa at Macy's in the city before Christmas, and the line always took super long, like an hour, except this year we didn't go.

The woman voices sounded like they were moving away from me. My heart wasn't beating so super fast anymore, and the crying got better, but I still tried not to move in case the white van was still there somewhere. I checked Andy's watch and it said 2:39. I stared at the watch and nothing else happened, so at 2:45 I decided to look around the clothes bin. There was no white van anywhere.

I really wanted to go back home because I still had a bad scared feeling and I wasn't feeling brave at all anymore. But then I thought about my mission and about how I didn't want Charlie to go in jail, so I decided to do Dicky Dicky Diamond between going back home or keep going to the cemetery: "Dicky Dicky Diamond, step right in. Dicky Dicky Diamond, step right out." Home was out.

I got out from behind the clothes bin and looked up the hill where my old preschool and the cemetery were going to be. I put on my backpack and started walking up the hill fast.

There were buildings on the left side of me, and some teenagers were hanging out there. One called over to me, "Hey, kid, are you going camping? That backpack is bigger than you!" and all the other teenagers laughed, and some made whistling sounds. I tried not to look at them. I kept my eyes on the sidewalk, square and rectangular stones, and I tried to get all the way up the hill without touching any rectangular ones.

[48]

Whispering Winds

I WALKED UP THE HILL to where my old preschool was on the right, but I walked on the other side of the street where the cemetery was going to be. It took me a long time to walk up there, and then the watch said 3:10, so it was one hour minus three minutes from when I left my house. I saw the preschool up on the right side, and lots of cars were driving in and out and that made sense, because 3:00 is pickup time.

I walked the rest of the way fast and turned left and went through the big black gate in the cemetery, because I didn't want someone from the school to spot me. The big gate had two like towers made out of rocks on the sides, and half a circle made out of black metal went from one tower to the other one, and a sign said HOLY SEPUL-CHRE CEMETERY. On the two ends of the half-circle were lamps that looked like big candles. I didn't see the gate when we came here for Andy's funeral because we drove here from the church and parked our car on the other side of the cemetery on the little road inside. Through the gate I could see the cemetery, and this part looked different from the part where they put Andy's grave. Maybe this was the old part or something.

I walked in the cemetery and everything got very quiet after I passed the gate. Behind me were the cars from the preschool and all the traffic sounds, and in front of me was nothing but quietness—the gate like blocked out the sounds.

Here the cemetery didn't have any walkways like in the part where Andy's grave was, but grass growing everywhere and gravestones sticking out. The gravestones looked all beat-up and creepy, and some were not standing up straight and all around them it looked like a garden with bushes and big trees everywhere. I tried to read some names on the old gravestones, but I couldn't see the whole names, they were mostly disappeared. A lot of the gravestones had cool designs at the top, all different kinds of crosses.

I tried to walk with careful steps because I didn't want to step on the graves with the dead people in them. It was creepy to walk and to think about that there were actual dead people under the ground. But these graves were really old, so there were probably only bones left and no other parts of the bodies, because everything but the bones turns back into earth.

The wind was making the bushes and trees move around, and they made a scary sound like someone was whispering and making shushing sounds. I thought about the old dead people under me and I listened to the whispering and shushing, and it was giving me a bad feeling in my stomach, so I started to walk faster and I looked for the way over to the other part of the cemetery, where they put the new dead people. When we were there for Andy's funeral, it was a little pretty, even though it rained the whole time. There were lots of flowers everywhere on the other graves, and the wet leaves from the trees made the ground look colorful and shiny, and everything smelled good from the rain.

I walked up a little hill, and on the other side was where the other, prettier part started. It looked much bigger than how I remembered it from the funeral. Also I didn't look at it from this side before, so now I wasn't sure anymore where Andy's grave was. The wind was blowing harder, and it made my forehead hurt, and my eyes got tears in them from the coldness. I got out my hat and gloves from the big pocket in my backpack and put them on, and I pulled the hat all the way down to my eyes to get my forehead warmer. Then I started to walk around to look for Andy and his grave.

There was no one in the whole entire cemetery, so that was good, because if someone came they were probably going to think it wasn't right that a boy was at the cemetery alone, and then they were going to ask me about it and find out that I came here all by myself.

I stopped a lot of times to look at the gravestones, and I actually didn't know what Andy's looked like because it wasn't there yet at his funeral. It takes a long time to make gravestones, and so they're not ready for the funeral and get set up later.

I saw the road at the end of the cemetery where we parked our car at Andy's funeral. I went down there and turned around and then I recognized the cemetery better and I knew Andy's grave was going to be all the way on the right side and not very far in.

There were a lot of walkways around all the graves, and the gravestones were new-looking and shiny, and I could read all the names on them and the numbers. The first number is the birth year from the people in the graves, and the second number is the year they died, and that way you can tell how old they were when they died. Mommy told me that when we went to the cemetery in New Jersey where Uncle Chip's grave was and we brought flowers to put on his grave, it was exactly one year ago that he died, and that was only like a couple weeks before Andy got killed from the gunman.

I looked at the gravestones to find Andy's name.

HERMAN MEYER

1937–2010

ROBERT DAVID LULDON

1946–2006

SHEILA GOODWIN

1991–2003

I counted from 1991 to 2003 and that was only twelve, so Sheila was twelve when she died. That was just two years older than when Andy died, and I wondered why Sheila died when she was only twelve. I walked and I walked and I read the names, and sometimes I stopped and checked to see how old the people were when they died. I started to get tired, and the backpack was starting to feel really heavy on my back. Maybe it wasn't on the right side where Andy's grave was, but on the left? Now I wasn't sure anymore.

Then I remembered the big tree next to Andy's grave from when we were there for the funeral, the one that looked like it was on fire from all the orange and yellow leaves. Now there weren't any leaves left on the trees because it was going to be the first day of winter next weekend. But I looked around for tall trees, and there was one close to me, so I walked over. And then I saw it, right next to the tree: Andy's grave. Andy's gravestone was blackish grayish and very shiny, and at the top it was the shape of a heart. The letters and numbers on it were white, and my throat started to hurt when I read them. I whispered even though there was no one there to hear me: "Andrew James Taylor 2006–2016."

The wind was swooshing around me like it was picking up my words and whispering them back to me and carrying them up and all around. I liked the sound now. It wasn't giving me a bad feeling anymore. It kind of made it feel like Andy's name was all around me. Now I thought it was good that I came, and maybe now I was going to feel Andy again and talk to him like in the hideout—when he was still in there.

I checked Andy's watch and it said 3:45. The man from the news said that Charlie was always coming in the evenings, and it wasn't evening yet, so I still had to wait for him to come. My belly started to feel hungry again, and I remembered I never ate the granola bar because I got scared about the bad guy in the white van and I dropped it in the parking lot. So I decided to take out all the things I brought and eat something. It wasn't dinnertime yet, that was going to be around six or seven, so only a snack for now.

I untied the suitcase strap and rolled out Andy's sleeping bag next to Andy's gravestone and I sat on it crisscross applesauce like when

I was in the hideout. I got out everything from the backpack and laid it out next to me: the Buzz flashlight for when it got dark, my book, my water bottle that I filled up all the way, four granola bars, three bags of Goldfish, two string cheeses, a ham and cheese sandwich that I made after lunch today and that was going to be for dinner later, and an apple. Everything was laid out, and it looked like I was having a picnic.

The last thing I took out from the backpack was the picture of me and Andy, and I put it in between two pages of the book. I opened a bag of Goldfish, and for that I had to take my gloves off. Right away my fingers started to feel cold from the wind.

After the Goldfish were all finished, I picked up the book again and put the picture in my lap and found the page where I stopped reading at home.

"Hey, Andy," I said. "Want me to read you some more?" I looked at the picture and I looked at the gravestone with Andy's whole name on it, and I waited to see if it was going to feel like Andy was listening to me. "OK, I'm going to tell you what I read so far so you know what you missed, and then I'll keep reading. OK, Andy?"

49

Friendly Ghost

So, IN THIS ONE Jack and Annie go to Antarctica to try and find the fourth secret of happiness for Merlin, and they find a research station where researchers from all kinds of different countries work. Jack and Annie hide behind their goggles and masks and go on a trip in a helicopter to a volcano with some of the researchers. So I'm guessing someone's going to find out they're kids and they will probably get in huge trouble, don't you think?"

I waited for something to happen. For something to change and make it feel like Andy was listening to me again. Nothing happened.

I read two more chapters out loud, but it was getting hard to turn the pages because my fingers were so cold. When I looked up from the book, it was like a surprise, because I was only thinking about what I was reading and I forgot about where I was and I didn't notice that it was getting a little dark all around me.

I checked Andy's watch: 4:58. I looked all around, but I didn't see Charlie anywhere, so maybe it was still too early. I put my gloves back on and blew my warm breath inside the gloves, like Mommy always does to help me with cold hands. I started to feel sad a little when I thought about Mommy, so I tried to keep reading to stop thinking about her, but it's not even possible to turn book pages with gloves on.

My whole entire body was feeling very cold, so I opened the sleeping bag and put my legs in, and that helped my legs but the rest of me was still cold.

When I was planning for my mission, I didn't think about the darkness. I packed Buzz, but I didn't think about how that was going to be when it got dark outside and I was at the cemetery all by myself. I only thought about how I was going to be here with Charlie and then we were going to go to my house together.

That's not how it actually was now. It wasn't all the way dark yet, I could still see all the gravestones around me, but in between the trees it looked dark and spooky. And all of a sudden I thought about what if Charlie wasn't coming today? I could feel my heartbeat all the way up in my throat, and I moved closer to Andy's gravestone and leaned against it. I pulled my backpack close and looked for Clancy.

Clancy was not in the big pocket. I checked the middle pocket and the little pocket and no Clancy anywhere. I looked all around me, because maybe he fell out earlier when I took out my other supplies, but he was nowhere. I forgot him or I lost him, I didn't know which. No Clancy, no Charlie, no Mommy, no Daddy. Just me.

I felt like crying, and I thought I wanted to go back home, but I was too scared to get up or do any moving. I started thinking about the dead people in the graves and I couldn't stop it. I thought about their bones in the caskets and also maybe that the dead people turn into ghosts after it gets dark. I thought about the bad guy in the white van and the scared feeling got bigger and bigger.

From the book, I pulled out the picture of me and Andy, and I could still see it a little bit in the darkness. "Andy," I whispered. My chin was moving up and down fast and it made my teeth click together. "Andy, are you there? Can you please please be there? I really need you." Nothing happened again. Then I remembered the angel wing charm in my pants pocket. I took one glove off and tried to stick my hand inside my pocket, but it was hard because I couldn't even move my hand anymore, it was like stiff from the coldness. Finally, I got my hand in and I rubbed and rubbed the angel wing. "Your brother is not gone. He's looking over you, too"—that's what Miss Russell told me—and I tried to say this to myself over and over again in my head: "Andy's not gone. He's looking over me. Andy's not gone. He's looking over me."

I was holding the picture of me and Andy in my other hand and all of a sudden a big wind blew against me, and I wasn't holding the picture tight enough, and the wind ripped it out of my hand and blew it on the ground. It rolled on the ground and flew up against a gravestone and got stuck there.

"No!" I shouted and I jumped out of Andy's sleeping bag and ran over to the gravestone to grab the picture, but the wind snatched it from me again and made it fly farther away. I tried to keep my eyes on it so it couldn't get lost in the darkness. I ran after it and then I bumped into someone.

It was a big surprise because I didn't see anyone before. Maybe it was a ghost. The ghost held on to both of my arms, and I started kicking and screaming: "NO! Let go of me!"

"Zach, is that you?"

I looked up, because it was another big surprise that the ghost said my name and it wasn't a ghost. It was Charlie. Charlie's face looked very surprised.

"Zach?" Charlie said. "What . . . what are you doing here?" He looked up and behind me. "Why are you running like this? What's wrong?"

It was hard for me to talk because my breath was going in and out fast from the running and kicking and screaming. I tried to tell Charlie about the picture: "It blew away . . . from the wind. My picture . . ."

"A picture blew away? Where?" Charlie asked.

I pointed to where it flew over in between the trees, where it was really dark and scary now.

"OK, let's check," Charlie said. He held on to my shoulder, and my scared feeling started to get better with him there. We looked all around for the picture and then there it was, stuck in a bush.

"Can I see it?" Charlie asked, so I showed him the picture. Charlie looked at it for a little while and did a little sad smile, and then he gave it back to me. My hand was shaking a lot from the cold when I took it from him.

"Zach?" Charlie asked. "What are you doing here? Are you here to visit your brother?"

"Yes," I said. "But mostly I came because of you."

"Me? Because of me? How did you know I would be here?" Charlie asked.

"They said it on the news," I told Charlie. "They said you come here every day when it's evening."

"I see," Charlie said. He pointed at a gravestone and we walked over to it. In the almost-dark I could see:

CHARLES RANALEZ JR.

1997–2016

"I come to say good night to him in the evenings," Charlie said. "My boy." His voice sounded like the saddest voice I ever heard.

50

Going Home

WE STOOD IN FRONT of Charlie's son's gravestone, and I looked up at Charlie's face.

"Charlie?" I asked.

"Yes?"

"Why did he do that? Why did he come in the school and kill Andy and all the other people?" I asked.

Charlie put his hand over his mouth and then he wiped his forehead with his hand, up and down, up and down. He made a long breath go in his mouth and looked up at the sky. I looked up, too, and I saw the moon right over us. It looked like a full moon, except maybe on the left side there was a piece missing. Then Charlie let his breath come out long and slow.

"I don't know," he said, and it was hard to hear because his voice came out so quiet. He was still looking up at the sky and put his shoulders up and down. Then he started talking again, and his voice sounded like something was stuck in his throat. "I don't know, Zach. I honestly don't know. I'm asking myself that same question every single day."

"Daddy said it's because he didn't know it was wrong. It's because he had a sickness," I said.

Charlie shook his head yes and wiped his hand over his eyes a couple times.

We were quiet for a while and then Charlie said, "Why did you come here to see me, Zach?"

Now was the part where I was going to tell Charlie about my mission. "I wanted to talk to you," I told him. "I don't know where your house is, so I came here."

"It's almost dark. Do your parents know where you are?" Charlie asked.

"I didn't tell anybody," I said.

"What did you want to talk to me about?" Charlie asked.

"I want you to come with me, to my house. I want us to talk to Mommy together and then all the fighting can be over." I was talking really fast because Charlie had a sad smile on his face, and it looked like a no smile and not a yes smile.

"So can you come? Please?" I asked.

"Oh, Zach! I wish I could. I wish that . . . but I can't. It's . . . I can't do that," Charlie said, and he started to put his arm around my shoulders, but I didn't let him.

All of a sudden I didn't feel cold anymore. My whole body got really hot.

"Why?" I yelled, and tears started coming in my eyes. "Why can't you? Everything . . . everything's bad there. We have to talk to Mommy or she's going to take you to court, and then you have to go in jail," I told Charlie. I was making big crying sounds and my teeth were clicking together from the coldness.

Charlie didn't say anything. He put his arm around my shoulders again and pulled me close to him, and I let him this time. It felt good that Charlie was hugging me tight. It made me not so cold anymore. We stayed like that for a long time, me with my head against Charlie's belly and crying, crying the whole time, and Charlie petting my head. After a while my crying got better and my whole head hurt from the crying and my whole self was very tired.

Charlie took his arm off my shoulders, and right away I started to feel colder again. Charlie went down on his knees and took out a tissue from his coat pocket, not the paper kind, but the kind that's like a little napkin like Uncle Chip had with his letters on it, c.t., and Charlie wiped all the tears off my face. Then he put his tissue back in his pocket and said in a quiet voice, "Zach. My best buddy. I think it's time to get you home. Your parents must be worried."

He helped me pack up my things. I put the picture back in the book and put the book back in the backpack. We walked to his car that was parked down on the cemetery road. Charlie opened the back door for me. He turned up the heat in the car, and my teeth stopped clicking together. Charlie drove very slow the same way I took when I walked here, and it still only took a little more than five minutes to get to my road. I checked on Andy's watch, and it took me one whole hour when I walked that same way earlier. We didn't say anything in the car. Then Charlie stopped by the middle school bus corner and he turned around to me.

"I think it's better if I drop you off here," Charlie said.

"Can't you please come in my house with me?" I asked. "Please? That was my mission—that you were supposed to go in the house with me and talk to Mommy. Then maybe she's not going to be so mad at you anymore. OK?"

"I'm sorry, Zach. I can't do that. It wouldn't be . . . it's not appropriate, me showing up there with you," Charlie said.

I could feel tears coming back in my eyes, and I didn't want to start crying again, so I put my arms in front of my belly and looked out of the window. I tried to not blink my eyes, so the tears weren't going to spill over.

"Zach?" Charlie said, but I didn't say anything back because there was a big lump in my throat. "Please, Zach? Please don't be mad at me. I know you are trying to help and it's . . . you are such a good boy, do you know that? Listen to me, Zach," Charlie said. "Can you please look at me?"

I moved my eyes from outside the window to Charlie, and I could see he had tears in his eyes, too, but he let them spill over on his face.

"Please don't worry about me. It's not . . . you don't have to worry about me. It will be all right. OK?" Charlie said.

I looked back out the window.

"Please? My best buddy?" Charlie said, and he sounded like he was a kid asking me that question.

"OK," I said. I looked back at Charlie and we both let our tears spill over.

"Charlie?"

"Yes?"

"I'm sorry about . . . how Mommy is talking about you like that," I told him.

"Your mom . . . she is in a lot of pain right now," Charlie said. The car was warm, and I wanted to stay here, with Charlie.

"Charlie?"

"Yes?"

"Can you still feel your son? Do you . . . is it still like he's with you or something?" I asked.

"Sometimes. Sometimes it feels like he's right here, close to me. And sometimes . . . it feels like he's been gone a long, long time," Charlie said.

Then he said, "Go now. Time to go home. Listen, I'll watch you from here, OK? I'll watch you walk up to your house and until you go inside, all right?"

I grabbed my backpack and opened the back door, and before I got out I said, "Bye, Charlie."

"Bye, Zach. My best buddy," Charlie answered.

When I walked up our road, I could see two police cars in front of our house and the news vans were still there, too. I thought that I was probably going to get in huge trouble. When I walked to our house, I started to feel cold again, and I walked with slow, tiny steps. I turned back around and I saw the lights from Charlie's car behind me. I pressed the button on Andy's watch that makes it light up: 6:10.

When I got close to our house I saw a man was leaning against one of the news vans. I realized it was Dexter, and then he saw me, too, and started walking to me fast.

"Oh man, Zach, there you are, man! Everyone's been looking for you," he said, but I didn't say anything back. I gave him a death stare and walked past him and to our front door. My heart was beating super fast when I pushed the doorbell button.

This Crying Thing

AFTER THE DOOR OPENED, nothing went how I thought it was going to. I didn't get in huge trouble, not even in a little bit of trouble. Mommy opened the door and she was hugging Clancy, so that's where he was—I forgot him at home. When she saw me, she yelled, "Oh my God, he's here!" Then she went down on her knees and hugged me and like rocked from the left side to the right side over and over again.

"My baby, my baby, my baby," she said a lot of times. Behind her I saw Mimi and Grandma and Aunt Mary and two policemen coming out of the living room. But no Daddy.

Mommy stopped hugging me and held me a little away from her and looked at me all over. "Are you all right, Zach?" she asked.

"Daddy isn't here," I said in a quiet voice.

"Oh, jeez," Aunt Mary said, and she pulled out her phone and pushed a button. Into the phone she said, "Jim, he's home. He came back home!"

"He's out looking for you, honey," Mommy said. "He'll be here soon, OK?"

My body did a shiver and my teeth started clicking together again.

"Oh, Zach, you are freezing," Mommy said, and then everyone made a big fuss: "Here, let's take your shoes off. And the backpack. Let me feel your hands. Oh my God, they're ice-cold. You must be starving. Let's make you something to eat."

The policemen said they would have to ask me some questions, but Mimi said, "Let's get him settled first. Here, let's have another cup of coffee," and so everyone sat down in the kitchen, even the policemen.

The alarm box lady said "Front door!" and right after that Daddy came in the kitchen. He stood in the door for a second and he didn't say anything, just stared at me. Then he walked across the whole kitchen with giant fast steps to where I was sitting. He pulled me off the barstool and lifted me up and hugged me so tight, it was hard for me to breathe, and then I heard the sound. And I could feel the sound.

It was like it came from all the way inside Daddy's belly, and then it moved up his throat and came out through his mouth next to my ear. It was like a very low choking sound. Daddy's chest went up and down fast, and that's when I realized he was crying. That's what it sounds like when Daddy cries.

Now he cried with the low, loud choking sound, and he held me tight like that for a long time. I pulled back, because I wanted to see what it looked like when Daddy cried. His face looked younger, like from a boy and not like a man, with his face wet all over from tears and his chin was shivering up and down.

"Zach," he said, and my name came out like a big breath from his mouth. "I thought I lost you, too."

"I'm OK, Daddy," I told him, and I wanted his chin to stop shivering and it was my fault that he was so sad, and I felt bad about that. I put my hands on Daddy's cheeks and they got wet from all his tears, and I rubbed my hands over his beard.

"I'm sorry," I said, and Daddy did a little laugh.

"You sweet, sweet boy," Daddy said, and he hugged me tight again. "You have nothing to be sorry about."

He put me back down and I saw that everyone else in the kitchen was crying, too. Mommy was crying and Mimi and Grandma and Aunt Mary. They looked at me and at Daddy and cried, and maybe it was the first time they saw Daddy cry, too, I didn't know, probably, though.

After everybody got done crying, one of the policemen got up and said, "We don't want to intrude any longer than necessary. Just a few things we need to ask this young man. We can always circle back around tomorrow for the details." And he asked me some questions about where I was the whole time, and I told him that I went to the cemetery and how I got there and all that stuff.

The policeman had a little notebook and he wrote down some things. "Is there anything else you feel like you need to tell me?" the policeman asked, and I shook my head no. I could feel the red juice spill starting to happen because I didn't tell him that I went there because I wanted to talk to Charlie. The other policeman got up, too. "All right, we'll check back in tomorrow and get all the necessary paperwork done. Everything looks like it's in order for tonight."

The policemen left, and then Mimi said the three of us could probably use some time—and that meant me and Mommy and Daddy, and so her and Grandma and Aunt Mary left, too.

When everyone was gone, it felt weird to be home with just us three and it was like we didn't know how to act anymore when we were together. It gave me a shy feeling.

"You didn't eat anything yet, honey," Mommy said. "What would you like?"

"Cereal, please," I said, and all three of us ate cereal, and we sat at the counter, me in the middle in between Mommy and Daddy and for a little while it was only the crunch, crunch from our chewing.

Then Mommy asked in a quiet voice, "So you went to the cemetery?"

"Yeah," I said.

"Why?"

I thought about my mission and how Charlie didn't come home with me, so my mission didn't work out. I put my head down because I didn't want Mommy and Daddy to see that tears were coming back in my eyes.

"Why did you go there, Zach?" Mommy asked again, and she pushed my chin up with her hand and looked at me. "Because of Andy?"

"Yes," I said, and that was not lying because I also wanted to go to

Andy's grave when I went there. But it wasn't telling the truth either, because I didn't tell her that I went there to find Charlie.

"I wanted to visit Andy and . . . be with him again. Like before in . . . here at home," I said.

"In Andy's closet?" Mommy asked, and I looked at Daddy, because he told my secret.

"I had to tell Mommy, Zach. It's the first place I looked when we couldn't find you. OK?"

"OK," I told him, and it didn't matter anymore, because the hide-out wasn't special anymore anyway.

"You wanted to be with Andy again?" Mommy asked.

"Yes," I said. "I used to feel him in the hideout. It's hard to explain. I could talk to him and stuff and it made me not lonely. Daddy noticed that, too, right, Daddy?"

Daddy said, "It felt like it, yes. It was nice . . . to imagine that."

"I didn't only imagine it," I said. "That's really how it was. But then it stopped working. I couldn't feel him anymore in there, and then it was just me, alone in the bed. . . ."

"Alone in the bed?" Daddy asked, and he looked like he was crying again. He wiped his eyes with his napkin. "Man. This crying thing. I could get used to this."

"Alone in the bed like in the song, you know? 'Ten in the Bed'?" I said, and Daddy looked like he didn't get it. "Never mind," I said.

Mommy pushed her cereal bowl away and took my hand. "Zach, I'm . . . so sorry. I'm sorry that you . . . felt so lonely." Mommy's voice came out with a lot of breaks in between. "If something bad had happened to you . . . ," and then it was like she couldn't keep talking.

"It's OK, Mommy," I said.

"No. It's not OK, honey. You were feeling so alone that you ran away to be with your brother at the cemetery. And I didn't realize you were gone for . . . quite some time. That was not OK."

"It's because you're feeling a lot of pain. Charlie told me that today," I said.

"Wait," Mommy said.

"What?" Daddy said. They both stared at me, and right away I was sorry I said that, because now I got worried that I would get Charlie in more trouble.

Mommy sat up straight. "What does that mean, Zach: Charlie told you that today? How?" I could tell she was getting mad.

Daddy leaned over and covered Mommy's hand with his hand and he said, "Zach, it's important that you tell us what you meant by that. OK?"

"But is he going to be in more trouble? He didn't do anything wrong. He helped me," I said, and my words were coming out fast.

"How did Charlie help you?" Mommy asked.

"He told me it was time to go home because you were probably worried about me. And he took me home in his car."

Mommy looked at Daddy, and she let out a long breath very slowly. "You were in Charlie's car?" she asked.

"Mhmm."

"You have to give us the full story, buddy," Daddy said.

"OK. I went to the cemetery because I wanted to find Charlie. I mean, I wanted to visit Andy, too, but mostly I went because of Charlie. I wanted him to come here with me and we could talk to Mommy and make it so that all the fighting could be over. And so that Charlie doesn't have to go in jail. And Daddy could come back home," I said.

"You went to the cemetery to find Charlie?" Mommy asked.

"Yes. He goes there every day," I explained. "He says good night to his son every night there."

Daddy pressed his lips together and shook his head up and down slowly. "How did you know that?" he asked.

"From the news," I said. "But he didn't want to come here." I started to cry because I did that whole thing, and I tried to be brave and not scared for once, so that I could make everything better, and it didn't even work. "My mission didn't work like how I planned it. I wanted you and him to talk, and then you could see that he's really sorry and he feels bad about what his son did," I said to Mommy. "And so then you could stop being so mad at him."

Mommy stared at me for a minute.

"He took you home in his car?" Mommy asked.

"Yes," I said. "He said I should go home, and I told him I didn't want to go back home, but then we went anyway. He dropped me off at the middle school bus corner, and I walked the rest of the way. I think he didn't want to come, because of . . . because of how mad you are at him."

"You didn't want to come back home?" Mommy said. Her words came out quiet, and her nose sounded very stuffy from all the crying. For a while no one said anything, and then Mommy asked, "Do you think you could show me your hideout? I'd really like to see it."

52

The Last Secret

STILL SMELLS LIKE BOY in here," Mommy said when me and her crawled in the hideout. "Wow, I always forget how big this closet is."

"Can I join you, too?" Daddy asked from outside the closet, and Mommy said, "OK."

We all sat down in the back, and it was very smushed with three people, but I didn't mind it. I liked being in here with Mommy and Daddy. I sat in front of Mommy and leaned back against her, and she put her arms around me. Daddy sat across from us and leaned his back and head against the wall.

"What are those?" Mommy asked, and pointed at the feelings pages.

"Feelings pages," I said, and I explained to her what they were and why I made them, like I explained it to Daddy when he first came in the hideout.

"Let me see if I still remember which is which," Daddy said, and we played a game where I quizzed him.

"Black?" I asked.

"Scared."

"Red?"

"Embarrassed."

We went through all the colors, and Daddy remembered them all.

"You were feeling a lot of feelings, huh?" Mommy asked.

"Yeah," I answered.

"So the white one is for sympathy? Why did you make one for sympathy? That's a feeling you have?" Mommy wanted to know.

"Me and Daddy came up with that one. Sympathy is the third secret of happiness."

"The third secret of happiness . . . ?" Mommy asked.

"Yes, remember from the Magic Tree House Merlin missions?" I said.

"Um," Mommy said.

"Remember I was going to try out the first secret of happiness with you? Pay attention to the small things around you in nature? But then you didn't have time because you were on the phone."

"I . . . I don't remember that," Mommy said.

"Zach has been reading about the secrets of happiness, and he wanted to try them out because he felt like we could use them around here," Daddy said.

"We're like Merlin," I told Mommy. "He's sick from all the sadness, and that's why Jack and Annie try to find the four secrets of happiness for him, so he can get better. And we're like sick from sadness, too, because of Andy, so it's the same, kind of."

"Huh," Mommy said, and she put her head down on my head. "So sympathy is one of the secrets?" she asked.

"Yeah," I said. "I don't think I did that with Andy when he was still alive and he was acting mean, but then after I got it and I started to feel the sympathy for him."

Daddy made his eyebrows go up. He looked at Mommy and shook his head a little.

"Mommy?" I said.

"Yes, baby?"

"I think you have to try to feel the sympathy with Charlie, too. Please don't make him go in jail. I could feel his feelings with him today, at the cemetery, and he is sick from sadness like us and Merlin."

Mommy was quiet for a long time after that. I thought maybe she got mad at me again, like the last time I told her that she should have sympathy with Charlie, before she made me go to school.

But then she asked, "What are the other two secrets?" and she didn't sound mad.

"One is to be curious about things. And the fourth one I don't know yet. I tried to finish the book at the cemetery to find out, but it got too cold and too dark," I said.

"Should we finish it now?" Mommy asked. "Or are you too tired? We can always do it tomorrow."

I didn't feel tired, and I didn't want us to leave the hideout, so I jumped up and said, "I'll go get the book. It's in my backpack." I zipped downstairs and grabbed the book and also Buzz, so we would have enough light to read, and then I zipped back upstairs.

Right when I was about to go back in the closet, I heard Mommy and Daddy's voices and I stopped to hear what they were saying.

". . . we both played our part in this," I heard Mommy say. "You can't put this all on me."

"I know, I know," Daddy answered. His voice was very quiet. "Please let's not argue, OK? Not tonight. I'm so damn relieved we have him back safe and sound."

Then they didn't say anything else for a while, so I went back in the closet.

Mommy had her head down on her knees, and Daddy had his head against the wall. Their heads popped up when they heard me come back in.

I told Mommy and Daddy what happened so far, how Jack and Annie got to Antarctica and how they go on a helicopter trip to a volcano with the researchers. And of course the researchers find out Jack and Annie are kids—I knew they were going to—but they don't really get in trouble. They're supposed to wait at the house until someone comes and brings them back down from the mountain. But they leave the house instead and they fall into a ravine.

That's how far I got at the cemetery. When I was telling Mommy and Daddy about it, I was starting to feel a little tired, so I gave the book to Daddy so he could read the rest. Daddy opened it and the picture of me and Andy fell out. Daddy looked at it for a while and then gave it to me. I found the tape in the corner of the hideout and taped the picture back on the wall where it was before. Then I snuggled my back against Mommy and listened to Daddy's reading. Mommy's body made my body warm, and Daddy was reading in a quiet voice. My eyes started to feel heavy, and it was hard to keep them open.

53

Club Andy

THAT WAS THE LAST THING I remembered, and then I woke up and I was in Mommy and Daddy's bed and it was light outside. I didn't remember how I got out of the hideout and in the bed, and I didn't remember what happened in the book and if Jack and Annie found out the fourth secret of happiness.

Mommy was asleep in the bed next to me, and I shook her shoulder a little bit.

"Mommy?" I said. Mommy rolled over and opened her eyes. When she saw me, she smiled and put her hand on my cheek.

"Mommy, did Daddy leave again?" I asked.

"No, sweetie. He's sleeping on the couch downstairs." Mommy rolled over and looked at the clock on her nightstand. It said 8:27. "Wow, we slept late. You can go wake up Daddy if you want."

I went downstairs, and Daddy wasn't sleeping anymore. He was in the kitchen, reading the newspaper on his iPad.

"Hey, sleepyhead," Daddy said when he saw me. He picked me up and squeezed me tight, and I could smell his breath—it smelled like coffee. "Hey, I want to tell you something, Zach. I am incredibly proud of you, I really am." I got a warm feeling in my stomach when Daddy said this to me.

"That was a brave thing you did yesterday, do you know that?" Daddy asked.

"I wanted to be brave for once like you and Andy. But it didn't work. My mission didn't work," I said.

"Oh, I wouldn't be too sure about that," Daddy said, and he grabbed my chin with his hand and looked at me with a serious face. "And I think you're brave all the time."

"Not at Andy's wake. I acted like a baby then. And when Mommy took me to school I wasn't brave," I said.

"Oh, Zach, that had nothing to do with you not being brave. That was . . . it wasn't the right time to ask you to go back to school," Daddy said.

"OK, but, Daddy?" I asked.

"Yes, bud?"

"I think after Christmas I could go back. To school."

"Yeah? Cool," Daddy said. "Is Mommy still in bed? Do you want to bring her a cup of coffee?"

"OK," I said, and Daddy let me put the sugar in Mommy's coffee and the half-and-half and stir everything up. I tried to carry the cup, but it was very full with coffee and hot, so Daddy took it and we went upstairs together. Mommy did a little smile when Daddy gave her the cup.

"Did you finish the book?" I asked.

"No way. You passed out pretty much right after I started reading. We want to finish it together, right?" Daddy said.

"Can we finish it now?"

"Sure, if it's OK with Mommy," he said, and Mommy said, "Well, we need to find out what that last secret is, don't we? Back to the hideout?"

I put my shoulders up and down. "We can stay in the bed, too. The hideout isn't working anymore," I said.

"Oh, but I liked it in there yesterday," Mommy said. "I would like to finish the book there if you don't mind."

So we crawled back in the hideout and sat the same way like yesterday, me leaning against Mommy, and Daddy against the wall. Daddy picked up the book. "What's the last part you heard?"

"I don't remember. Just how they were in the ravine," I said.

"OK, let me see. . . ." Daddy went through the pages. "Chapter seven then, I think." He started and he read the book all the way to the end. Jack and Annie meet some dancing penguins. There's a little orphan penguin that Jack names Penny, and Jack and Annie take Penny with them to Camelot, where Merlin lives. They tell the first three secrets of happiness to Merlin and give him Penny. Merlin takes care of Penny and he gets happy again.

Jack and Annie realize that the fourth secret of happiness is to take care of someone who needs you. And Jack thinks it maybe works the other way around, too: *"I think sometimes you can make other people happy by letting* them *take care of* you.*"

After Daddy got done reading he closed the book and he looked at me and Mommy, and his eyes looked very shiny. No one said anything for a while.

Then Mommy said in a quiet voice, "This is a good one, this secret. What do you think?"

"Yes," I said. "We could try this one maybe. Me, you, and Daddy. Take care of each other. Right?"

"Yes," Mommy said.

"Is it going to make us happy again?" I asked.

"Well, I think it could help us feel better," Daddy said. I saw him look at Mommy behind me and he gave her a little sad smile.

"I think that the way we've been trying to deal with . . . everything, the death of your brother, all separately, instead of together—that wasn't the right way," Mommy said.

I leaned forward and looked at the picture on the wall. "I really miss Andy," I said. "It's like it hurts my whole insides sometimes."

"Me too, buddy," Daddy said.

"I wish I could still feel him in here, but I can't. Now I'm scared he went away forever." A big lump came in my throat when I thought about that.

Daddy leaned over and hugged me for a long time. He said with a quiet voice, "Missing Andy—that's a form of feeling him, though, isn't it? Don't you think? Maybe one day it won't hurt our whole insides anymore, I don't know. I think we will miss him and we will be thinking about him all the time, our whole lives. That's always going to be part of . . . who we are. And that way he's never gone, he's always going to be with us and inside us."

"He's looking over us from heaven?" I asked.

"Yes, sweetie, he is," Mommy said.

I touched Andy's face in the picture with my hand. "And then we will see him in heaven after we die?" I asked.

"I hope so," Daddy said, and tears ran from his eyes into his beard.

"I think Daddy's right," Mommy said. "You've been doing the right thing all along, talking to him and about him, keeping him close to you."

Daddy stretched out his back and wiped the tears off of his face. "We don't have to hang out in this closet forever though, do we? Because it's killing my back right now. And I stopped feeling my left butt cheek a while ago." He poked his finger in the left side of his butt a few times.

"It could be our meeting spot in here," I said. "Like our clubhouse or something."

"I like that idea," Mommy said. "What should we call our club?"

I thought about that for a minute. "Club Andy?" I said.

"Club Andy it is," Daddy said. "Now let's go get some breakfast."

54

Keep On Living

R EADY, MOMMY?" I asked, and Mommy stared at the handle of
the front door for a little while like she was waiting for the door
to open by itself. I looked up at Mommy's face, and she had her lips
pressed together. I grabbed her hand and squeezed it tight. Mommy
squeezed my hand back, and then she let go of it and opened the door.

A big cold wind came in the house, and Mommy took the two
sides of her sweater and pulled it closed in front of her belly.
She walked down the porch steps, and the wind blew her hair all
around. I walked down the porch steps behind her, and Daddy was
behind me. Mommy turned around and looked at us, and her chest
went up like she took a big breath in. Then she turned back and went
straight to the news van that was still parked in front of our house.

Mommy looked in the front seat of the van, but no one was there,
so she knocked on the side of the van. The side door popped open and
I could see Dexter and another man coming out of the van. Dexter
was holding a plastic container with food in it—rice and chicken, it
looked like—in his one hand and a fork in the other hand.

"Oh hey, guys, um . . ." Dexter looked at the food container in
his hand, and then he put it inside the van and wiped his hands on his
pants. "Hey, what's going on?" Dexter asked. He looked at Mommy
and then over at me and Daddy. I looked down at my feet because I
didn't want to look at Dexter.

"I would like to give a brief statement," Mommy said.

"Right now?" the man who came out of the van with Dexter asked.

"Yes," Mommy said.

"Oh OK, cool. That's cool," Dexter said. "Can you give us just a minute? We didn't expect . . . sorry, we were just eating lunch."

"That's fine," Mommy said, and another big wind came blowing up against us and made her hair fly all around again. I could feel the wind go all the way through my clothes and I did a shiver. Daddy put his arm around my shoulders and pulled me close to him.

Dexter and the other man went back inside the van, and Dexter came back out with a camera. It looked like the ones me and him put up in our living room, only smaller, and Dexter pushed some buttons on the side of the camera, and then he put it on his shoulder and looked through the one end of it at Mommy.

"Where do you want to be?" he asked Mommy.

"Oh, I don't care. Right there is OK," Mommy said.

"Sure, great," Dexter said, and then the other man came back out of the van with a microphone in his hand.

"OK, if you're ready, we can begin," he said, and he pointed the microphone at Mommy. Mommy looked at Daddy, and Daddy gave her a little smile and shook his head yes. Mommy looked back at the camera.

"This is just a recording, so don't worry. We can do this a few times if you want," the man with the microphone said.

"OK," Mommy said. "Um, so I wanted to say, just briefly, that I have decided to no longer pursue the Ranalezes about . . . in regards to the shooting. I've spoken to the parents of the other victims and we . . . we agree." Mommy's lower lip went up and down like her teeth were clicking together from being cold. She put her sleeves over her hands, and she crossed her arms and tucked her sleeve-hands into her armpits.

"I know I've been very outspoken since the shooting committed by their son, and I've placed the blame . . . I blamed them for his actions and for the death of my son Andy." Mommy did a pause and then she took another big breath and kept talking in the microphone: "I've come to realize that further pursuing them, the Ranalezes, is not . . . it's not going to bring my son back. It's not going to undo the terrible thing that happened to me, our family, and the families of the other victims." Tears started rolling down Mommy's face.

"What my family is going through—I don't wish that on anybody. And I . . . I can now see that the Ranalezes themselves are also faced with loss. They are grieving, like us. They are going through hell, like us." Mommy looked over at me and did a little smile. I smiled back. I was feeling very proud of Mommy that she was saying these things.

"My very wise son Zach was the one who made me see that. We . . . our family is going to focus on taking care of each other now and try-ing to heal, together, and figure out how to keep on living without Andy in our lives. Find some peace. We would like to, in the future, try to figure out ways how we can contribute to . . . how we can help prevent something like this from happening again, to other families. To help keep guns from ending up in the wrong hands and to help protect our children and loved ones. That's it . . . that's really all I wanted to say." More tears were running down Mommy's face, and she wiped them away with her sleeve-hands.

"Thank you," the man with the microphone said. "I think, I mean that was good the way it was, right? We can keep it like that unless you want to do it again or something?"

"No," Mommy said, and her voice came out very quiet.

Dexter took the camera off his shoulder and stared at Mommy. "Wow," he said. "That was big . . . of you," he said.

"OK," Mommy said, and then she turned around and walked over to me and Daddy.

Daddy touched Mommy's arm and rubbed it up and down. "You all right?" he asked.

"I'm OK," Mommy said. "Freezing. I just want to go back inside with you guys and close that door behind me. What do you think?"

"I think yes," I said, and I ran ahead and sprinted up the porch stairs.

55

Still Here with You

DADDY PARKED OUR CAR, but he didn't turn it off right away. We just sat there, me, Daddy, and Mommy, and no one said anything. My heart was pounding loud in my chest and my ears. I looked out the window and in the almost-dark I saw all the rows of gravestones, and further in the back, on the right side, I saw someone standing.

"Shall we?" Daddy asked, and turned off the car, and I said, "We shall." Mommy didn't say anything, but she opened her door and started to get out of the car. I picked up the flowers from the seat next to me, and Daddy opened my car door. When I got out of the car, I saw Charlie's car parked right in front of ours.

I started to walk up the walkway. The ground was all hard and frozen underneath my shoes, and my breath was making white clouds in the air around me. Daddy and Mommy walked behind me and they were going very slow. I was holding the flowers pressed against my chest, and when I got to Andy's grave, I put them down on it gently.

Daddy and Mommy got to Andy's grave, too. Mommy went down on her knees and touched the flowers that I laid down for Andy. Then she took one of her gloves off and put her hand up and her fingers touched Andy's name on the gravestone.

"Hi, sweet boy," Mommy whispered. Tears ran down her face, and she let them drip down.

Then she touched the ground on Andy's grave. "It's so cold and hard," she said, and then she put her arms around her belly and made loud crying sounds. Daddy was standing behind Mommy. He put his hands on her shoulders, and I leaned my head against Daddy's arm. We stayed like that for a long time with Mommy on her knees, crying, and Daddy holding on to her shoulders and me leaning against Daddy.

After a while I looked over to where Charlie's son's grave was and I saw Charlie was staring over at us. He didn't move, he just stood there with his arms hanging down on his sides. From how far away I was from him, he looked like a very old and skinny man.

"Can I go over now?" I asked.

"Go ahead," Daddy said.

I started to walk to where Charlie was standing when I heard Mommy's voice behind me: "Wait, Zach."

I turned back around and Mommy was looking down at the flowers that I laid down on Andy's grave. They were all white—some with big petals and some with tiny petals that looked like a bunch of snowflakes. All the petals were hanging down and they looked sad. Mommy picked up a few of them and held them in front of her belly for a minute like she was giving them a hug.

"Here, take these . . . with you. OK?" Mommy said, and she gave me the flowers.

I turned back around and walked over to Charlie. I looked behind me a couple times and Mommy and Daddy were standing next to each other, watching me. When I got closer to Charlie, I could see his chin was shaking a lot.

"Hi, Charlie," I said.

"Hi, Zach," Charlie said.

"We came to say good night to Andy. Like you."

Charlie shook his head yes very slow.

"Mommy told the people from the news yesterday that she doesn't want to do any more fighting," I told Charlie. Then I remembered I was still holding the flowers, and I gave them to Charlie.

Charlie did a little cough and his chin was still shaking a lot. "I saw," he said.

"I wanted to come tell that to you, and Mommy and Daddy said OK."

"Thank you, Zach," Charlie said.

"Mommy doesn't want to talk to you still, though."

"I understand," Charlie said, and he looked behind me to where Daddy and Mommy were standing. His face looked very sad. He pressed his lips together tight and held up the flowers a little bit to where Mommy and Daddy were standing.

I took my glove off and put my hand in my pants pocket. I pulled out the angel wing charm and rubbed it a couple of times in between my fingers. Then I held it out on my hand to Charlie.

"This is for you," I told him. Charlie took the charm and looked at it.

"What is it?" he asked.

"It means love and protection," I said. "It means your son is still here with you."

Charlie stared at the charm in his hand for a long time and his chin kept shaking and shaking. Then he whispered, "Thank you," and it came out so quiet, I almost didn't hear it.

I stayed there for a little while with Charlie and I didn't know what else I should say, so I said, "Merry Christmas," and Charlie said, "Merry Christmas," and then I went back to Daddy and Mommy and it was time to say good night to Andy.

"Can we sing our song?" I asked.

Mommy did a little smile. "Oh, Zach, I don't think I can sing right now. Maybe we could say the words?" and so we did that. We said the words of our song, taking turns.

Andrew Taylor
Andrew Taylor
We love you
We love you

You're our handsome buddy
And we'll love you always
Yes, we do
Yes, we do

Our breath made white clouds in front of our faces.

I could feel the coldness from the ground come through my shoes, and I stomped my feet a little to make them warmer. My fingers felt cold, too, so I blew air in my gloves.

"Here, let me," Mommy said. She went down on her knees in front of me and blew her warm breath in my gloves, and my fingers started to feel warmer.

I looked at Mommy's face and she looked cold, too. Her nose was red and she had goose bumps on her cheeks. Her face looked really tired and sad. I put my arms around her and gave her a hug, and we stayed like that for a while on top of Andy's grave, hugging, with Mommy on her knees.

"Should we say good night now?" Daddy asked in a quiet voice.

Me and Mommy stopped hugging. Mommy looked at Andy's gravestone and started crying again.

"Good night, sweet boy," Mommy whispered.

"Good night, Andy," I said.

"Good night," Daddy said.

Mommy stood up and we looked at Andy's grave for a minute longer and then we turned around and walked back down the walkway to our car with me in the middle. Me, Daddy, and Mommy.

Acknowledgments

Everyone in my camp, on my team—I am so grateful you came along on this crazy, new journey with me.

Thank you to the extended Carr and Navin families for believing in me and supporting me, most notably:

My mother, Ursula Carr, for passing down her fierce love of books and for pushing me to "finally use one of the many talents you have!"

Brad, my husband and best friend, who encourages me in every endeavor and whose idea it was in the first place.

Thank you to my children, Samuel, Garrett, and Frankie, the loves of my life, for being my focus group and for sharing me with Zach all those months.

I want to thank my friends and first readers for reading and rereading drafts, making suggestions, and cheering me on, especially Swati Jagetia and Jackie Comp.

Allison K Williams—where do I begin with you? I am eternally grateful to you for teaching me the ropes and for being by my side every step of the way. I'm so lucky that I found you and I hope I get to meet you in person one day! Let's do this again soon!

Thank you to my amazing team at Folio Literary Management. Jeff Kleinman, you are a rock star! Thank you, Jamie Chambliss and Melissa Sarver.

Acknowledgments

Huge thanks to my editor, Carole Baron. I couldn't have asked for a kinder, more knowledgeable, and patient editor—what an honor to get to work with you! Thank you, Sonny Mehta, for your support. Genevieve Nierman, my fellow crazy cat lady, thank you for taking care of all the details, big and small. Kristen Bearse, I'm in love with your beautiful design of the book, and many thanks to the talented Jenny Carrow for designing a phenomenal book jacket. Ellen Feldman, I am grateful that you kept us honest in the process of bookmaking. Thank you, Danielle Plafsky, Gabrielle Brooks, and Nick Latimer for working tirelessly to deliver Zach's story into the hands of readers.

I must also thank Mary Pope Osborne for writing the most wonderful, magical series of children's books—the Magic Tree House series. You've made it easy for my children to fall in love with books, too.

The Voracious Reader and Anderson's Book Shop—my favorite indie bookstores and places to bring my kids: your love and passion for books is contagious and reverberates throughout our community.

A NOTE ON THE TYPE

The type used in this book designed by Pierre Simon Fournier *le jeune*. In 1764 and 1766 he published his *Manuel typographique*, a treatise on the history of French types and printing, and on what many consider his most important contribution to typography—the measurement of type by the point system.

Composed by North Market Street Graphics,
Lancaster, Pennsylvania

Printed and bound by Berryville Graphics,
Berryville, Virginia

Designed by M. Kristen Bearse